Can We Still Be Friends

ALEXANDRA SHULMAN

FIG TREE
an imprint of
PENGUIN BOOKS

FIG TREE

Published by the Penguin Group
Penguin Books Ltd, 80 Strand, London WC2R 0RL, England
Penguin Group (USA) Inc., 375 Hudson Street, New York, New York 10014, USA
Penguin Group (Canada), 90 Eglinton Avenue East, Suite 700, Toronto, Ontario, Canada M4P 2Y3
(a division of Pearson Penguin Canada Inc.)
Penguin Ireland, 25 St Stephen's Green, Dublin 2, Ireland (a division of Penguin Books Ltd)
Penguin Group (Australia), 250 Camberwell Road, Camberwell, Victoria 3124, Australia
(a division of Pearson Australia Group Pty Ltd)
Penguin Books India Pvt Ltd, 11 Community Centre, Panchsheel Park, New Delhi – 110 017, India
Penguin Group (NZ), 67 Apollo Drive, Rosedale, Auckland 0632, New Zealand
(a division of Pearson New Zealand Ltd)
Penguin Books (South Africa) (Pty) Ltd, Block D, Rosebank Office Park, 181 Jan Smuts Avenue,
Parktown North, Gauteng 2193, South Africa

Penguin Books Ltd, Registered Offices: 80 Strand, London WC2R 0RL, England

www.penguin.com

First published 2012
001

Copyright © Alexandra Shulman, 2012

Set in Dante MT Std 12/14.75 pt
Typeset by Palimpsest Book Production Limited, Falkirk, Stirlingshire
Printed in Great Britain by Clays Ltd, St Ives plc

A CIP catalogue record for this book is available from the British Library

HARDBACK ISBN: 978–1–905–49111–7
TRADE PAPERBACK ISBN: 978–1–905–49078–3

www.greenpenguin.co.uk

ALWAYS LEARNING   **PEARSON**

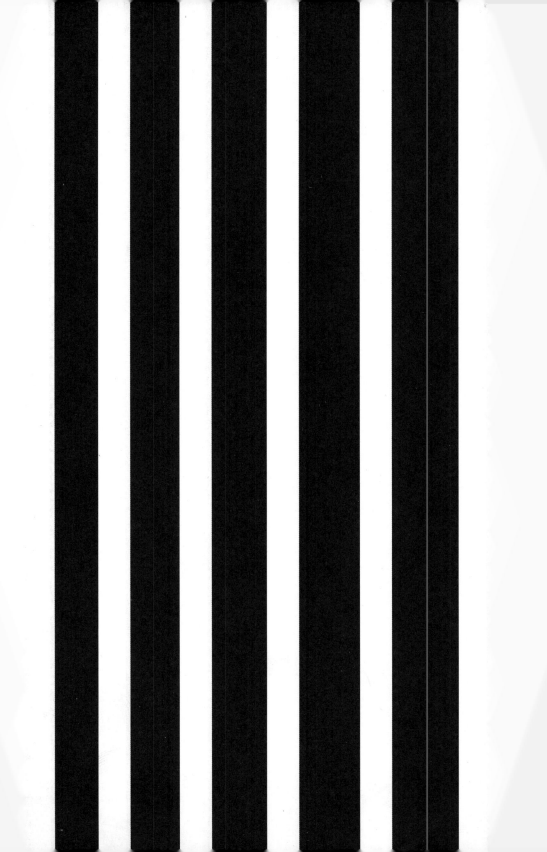

Can We Still Be Friends

For my mother
Drusilla

Acknowledgements

Thank you to all my friends, family and colleagues who have put up with me while I wrote this book. My thanks also go to my agent Eugenie Furniss for helping me so much and to Juliet Annan for being such an enthusiastic publisher.

A special mention to Sam and David for living with me throughout and making me happy.

1983

I

The terrace – if you could call the concrete slab with its two white plastic chairs a terrace – looked down on the small Kanariki beach. Kendra leant over the black iron rails and rubbed her leg, vaguely exploring whether her newly acquired suntan might flake off into dried skin, as she watched the families below, laden with the cumbersome paraphernalia of small children, pick their way slowly down the path on to the rocks and stones. The sun was already high, sparking light off the calm Ionian sea that lapped gently where the stones met the water.

'What happened to the long university holidays?' she asked herself, entering the room she was sharing with Sal. The floor was strewn with clothes and, with the shutters closed, the room was dark, pierced only by one bright shaft of sun from the terrace door. She heard the rustle of Sal's sleeping form turning under her thin sheet. Rummaging around for a dry bikini, Kendra was torn between making an exaggerated amount of noise to wake her friend to share the precious hours of this last day and the alternative of acknowledging that it was Sal's last opportunity to lie in.

'What time is it?' Sal's slow voice emerged, and Kendra heard the near-simultaneous click of a lighter and an inhalation. Sal's smoking had been driving her crazy all holiday so there was no point in making a fuss about it at this late stage; nonetheless, irritation infused her voice, clipping her words.

'About 10.30, I guess. I'm going down to the beach.'

'See you there,' answered Sal, now propped up against the whitewashed wall, her small bare breasts white against the tan of her arms and torso. 'Last day and all. Musn't waste it, must we?' She smiled, her eyes still closed against the light as she blew a thin stream of smoke into the air above the bed.

The holiday had been Sal's idea. Her eye had been drawn to a small ad in the newspaper: 'Big Discount. Traditional Greek village studio on beautiful beach – two weeks only.' 'Come on, Kendra,' she had urged, telephoning immediately. 'It's a bargain, and you haven't moved from London since we left university. Girls only. Catch the rays. I've found the flights. Annie can do one week, but she can't get any more time off work.'

Annie and Sal were Kendra's closest friends, yet her reaction to Sal's enthusiastic proposal, as ever, was a certainty that she didn't really want to participate in whatever activity was being suggested, rivalled by a niggling suspicion that this reaction showed her in a negative light. Sal would, of course, be suggesting something that would make life more interesting, more vivid. Over the four years since they had first met on their shared university corridor Kendra had become well acquainted with this feeling of inadequacy rippled with apprehension. Crashing a party hundreds of miles away, hitching to the sea at midnight, experimenting with a new drug – for Sal, it was all in her sights, up for grabs; for Kendra, it was all a potential source of anxiety and trepidation. Annie was often able to straddle the extremes of the two friends with her gentle determination, but experience had taught them both that, although it was, in Sal's words, 'narrow-minded', 'so unadventurous', to say no to some of Sal's wild plans, to say yes would often end in a medley of chaos, and the ramifications would stretch far and take a lot of undoing.

Corfu, though. Only a short charter flight away. And Sal was right, Kendra had been precisely nowhere in the last year.

Having been deposited at Corfu airport at three o'clock in the morning, the girls lay on the hard floor of Arrivals until daybreak, when a taxi took them out along the winding roads towards the north-eastern end of the island. Tiredness had reduced them to companionable silence for most of the journey.

'Hey! Look, down there. Fantastic!' Sal spotted the beach at the bottom of the slope as the taxi bumped towards the water.

A woman in a pair of unbecoming white shorts stood outside the small taverna on the beach. The black folder she held and her bored demeanour gave her away as the holiday rep.

'Sal Turner?' she queried as the three disembarked with their bags.

Sal stepped forward, smiling.

'You're in Villa Ariadne. Follow me.' The rep led the way back up the road; the girls stared after the dingy white bra straps sliding down her shoulders, and followed her stolid figure, lugging their suitcases like mules. Soon they turned on to a narrow path, on which stood a square whitewashed building, its dark-green shutters closed. Outside climbed a staircase, to a room with four narrow beds, and a kitchenette in one corner.

'The plumbing's a bit temperamental in this one, so go easy on the toilet paper and, on no account, put *anything else* down there, or I can't be held responsible,' the rep recited.

Annie opened the shutters to the balcony, taking in the bright sun and the crystalline sea. Why were the first moments of her holiday being tarnished with a conversation about lavatories? She only had a week.

'Of course. Thanks.' She took the room key from the rep as Sal signed for it.

'I'm Amanda. You can find me at Villa Serafina, outside Kassiopi, if you need me in an emergency. All breakages will come off the deposit.' And, with that, she left.

Annie opened the low cupboards under the sink at the dark end of the room.

'I don't think we'll be doing much cooking here,' she muttered. Sal and Kendra glanced at each other. 'I know you two can't cook, or won't, but Mum lent me her Elizabeth David and I thought I might do something. Like mayonnaise. Real mayonnaise is so delicious. You know, with local olive oil –'

Sal was already flinging the contents of her case around in a hunt for her bikini. 'Come on,' she said. 'Let's leave the mayo for a bit. I'm on for a beer. What's the Greek for beer? I'm baking already.'

From then, their days followed the same pattern: hours lying on the large stone slabs that rose from the pebbles of the beach, interspersed with forays to the taverna. Occasionally they would trek up the hill and over to another hamlet, but an unspoken agreement had determined that this was a no-action holiday, a time when they could indulge in each other's company day and night. 'No pulling, I guess' was how Sal had wrapped it up.

They had never shared a house while at university, although they had become the best of friends, plaited in an intricate weave of shared experiences. After the first year on campus they had found separate lodgings. Annie rented a room in a mouse-infested house in the local town with a couple of her fellow history of art students, Kendra shared with an itinerant population of students and Australians on working visas, and Sal – well, Sal floated from place to place, finding a bed with friends and a constant stream of extremely short-term lovers. She liked to say that she 'surfed the wave of spontaneity' and, on the occasions when the wave crashed and she was left stranded, she had always been able to find space with one of the others.

Each of the girls realized that their friendship was preserved by this distance. The intensity of their engagement with every aspect of each other's lives was given some respite by their not living together. Of course when they did discuss the prospect of sharing a home they all vowed that it would be a wonderful thing to do.

There had been an afternoon just after finals when a large pack of that year's students had headed up on to the downs to party into the night. In the clear, brilliant light that came straight off the south coast some distance away, they set up an encampment, lying on blankets, listening to a medley of music on a bulky cassette player. Sal, wearing denim cut-off shorts and a vest, sat on the long grass rolling a joint on her lap while Kendra paced, a bulky Nikon camera slung across her neck, taking photographs of the group. Annie unpacked French loaves, bags of cherries and crisps, packets of tomatoes and triangles of Dairylea.

As the sun faded slowly into the rose-tinged light of the evening, the group lay in a tangle of denim and bare legs. The three girls wove daisy chains around each other's wrists, slicing the thin stalks with their fingernails and pledging that, one day, they would all live together.

'As soon as I've got some cash, I'm going to look out for somewhere for us. It'll be brilliant,' enthused Sal, drawing on the heady smoke and passing the joint to Annie.

'We'll be the Three Graces,' Annie offered, and lay back looking at a vapour trail in the clear sky. Kendra handed over her precious Nikon to a bespectacled boy in a Sandinista-sloganed T-shirt.

'Tony – take a picture of us. Here. The aperture needs to be open in this light. Are you sober enough to focus? We should capture this moment. Remember it when we're old and grey.'

Kendra and Annie sat on the grass, smiling gently, blearily, into the lens, Sal leaning behind and into them, her arms around their shoulders. From the cassette player the sound of John Lennon's 'Woman' wafted into the air. They heard the click of the pictures being taken, one after another. Sal stood up, swaying a little. 'We should make a toast – to us. Together for ever. Sisters under the skin. All that stuff. Shall we make a blood bond?' She picked up the large knife that had been used to cut the bread.

'Don't be crazy, Sal,' said Annie. 'The daisy chains will do. We don't need to carve ourselves up to know we love each other.'

Pulling her sarong tightly around the lower half of her body, Sal walked over the stones to where Kendra was lying in sphinx pose on a scarlet towel reading a thick paperback.

'Watch the back of your legs – just this bit here, you're starting to burn,' said Sal, gently touching the skin on the top of Kendra's thighs. 'Do you want a coffee? I'm going to order one.'

Kendra jumped up awkwardly, pulling her untied bikini top over her full breasts and narrow back. With her tangle of tawny hair, her height and her generous figure, she was a golden Amazon, in contrast to the small, lean proportions of Sal.

'I think we should go into town for our last night. We've been loyal to Vassily and his kalamari and moussaka, but we've got to hit the big city lights tonight – or at least go to Kassiopi,' mooted Sal as they strolled over to the taverna.

Kendra realized that, although she had no desire to leave the hamlet, where the fishing boats came in at night to deliver their haul of mullet, squid and octopus to Vassily and his son, especially the night before the inevitably tiresome experience of a charter flight home, there was absolutely no point voicing this.

'Let's go in early, watch the sun go down from there and get something to eat. That way we won't be back too late,' she offered, hoping that this would satisfy Sal's appetite for action.

They sat at the table they had now come to regard as *their* table, and ordered gritty coffees, spooning thick honey into bowls of creamy yoghurt.

'You know, when we get back I really need to get a real job,' mused Sal. 'I'm getting cash for shifts working on that diary page in the newspaper, but I can't even guarantee the rent for a room somewhere. Funny, isn't it, how it's Annie who's got the good job?' replied Kendra, narrowing her eyes and looking out over the bay to the cypress- and gorse-clad hills opposite, which were veiled in a blue, gauzy light from the heat of the sun. 'Well, she's always been the practical one. I couldn't face Terrible Tania and her tribe, but Annie doesn't really care, does she? She's not looking for a career. She's just passing time, waiting for her dream man.' She rolled the paper packets of sugar in a bowl on the table around in her fingers, enjoying the crunching sound of the grains. The thought of Annie's last boyfriend, a rugby player with thighs instead of brains, asserted itself: 'And we've certainly been through enough Mr Wrongs on the way . . . Anyway, I might investigate this Chapel place I've heard about,' Kendra continued. 'It sounds like it could be interesting, it's a kind of community centre. I just . . . I don't know . . . I feel I want to do something useful. Sounds wanky, I know.'

Hanging in the air was the shared knowledge that it was Kendra who was the more financially secure of the three, allowing her, Sal thought in her more uncharitable moments, to get involved in a load of goody-goody stuff. She remembered her first visit to Kendra's home in west London. It was a huge house, with white walls dominated by large abstract canvases, parquet floors and tubular steel and leather furniture. Kendra's mother, Marisa, was the least motherly person Sal had ever encountered. Extraordinarily tall, with the long pale face of a Modigliani, she wore her black hair scraped back, her full mouth outlined in a dark beige and dressed entirely in black.

'Ah, Sal, we meet, finally,' she had said. 'I can't stay and talk . . . But, darling, you know we are giving a dinner for Philip Roth tonight. You both might like to join us.' Her voice was slow, a languid New England drawl. 'I gather from Kendra that you are reading English and American literature – you would be interested in meeting him, I am sure. Any time after nine. And, Kendra: *tenue de ville.*' She drew out the word '*ville*' so that it sounded like 'veal', and with it left the room, and the two girls, standing in what Sal felt to be the emptiest space she had ever been in. She looked at her friend. 'She means look smart,' shrugged Kendra in explanation.

That had been early on in their university days and, as the terms passed, it emerged that Sal was one of the few people Kendra had allowed a glimpse of her family. It was not clear whether Kendra was embarrassed by the cool, moneyed chic of her circumstances or despised it, but her background was determinedly disguised. She lived on pulses blended into soups and curries, walked or cycled everywhere and adopted a simple uniform of loose shirts, jeans, combat pants or the occasional long skirt, ensuring her legs were never bare. Her hair was often tied up in a turban of raggedly dyed scarves. Sal, who liked to show off her lithe frame in body-hugging shapes – boob tubes, leggings, clinging jersey dresses – would tease Kendra fondly about her dress sense but, despite the differences, their loyalties ran deep, each discovering in the other missing aspects of their own personality.

University represented different freedoms for them. Sal's yearning to escape the gentility of the quiet Cheltenham townhouse of her childhood had propelled her into achieving first-class exam results as an escape route. When the day of departure finally arrived, she left the bedroom where she had slept all her life torn apart like empty packaging. In her urgency to be off, she didn't notice her mother glance at the wooden-framed photograph she left behind on the chest of drawers, of her parents with her and her brother as small children huddled beside a cotton windbreak on a beach. She felt no sadness as she closed the door and hauled her large suitcase down the narrow staircase, just the energy of anticipation.

Her mother had gathered cardboard boxes packed with an electric kettle, two mugs, a box of Duralex tumblers and a stack of Tupperware containers on the Formica-topped kitchen table.

'Joy, we should be leaving shortly,' her father, Maurice, shouted as he walked into the room, stooping through the door, glasses balanced on the balding dome of his head. 'Salome, are you ready? I don't want to be too late back, as I have a lecture to prepare for the morning.'

Her mother sat in the front seat of the ancient Vauxhall, and Sal was wedged in the back between her suitcase and bundles of bedding. It had been a golden early-autumn day, and the Cotswold stone villages they drove through on their journey were at their picture-postcard best. As her parents listened to Radio 4, exchanging the odd comment, Sal felt the coil of impatience tighten in her; she was eager to colonize a new world.

By mid-afternoon, Sal was alone in her small campus bedroom. 'Call us soon' were her mother's last words before she and her husband departed along the dingy green internal corridor. Sal sensed the loss her mother was feeling at her daughter leaving home, her clipped tones bright but her eyes somewhat dimmer. She hid her guilt at not feeling one jot of sadness by brusquely urging them to leave. 'You should go now. Dad, you won't get that lecture done if you hang around here. I'm fine.' She stood on her toes to kiss him briefly on the cheek before giving her mother a forced hug.

Unpacking was far too dull an option for the first afternoon at university, and she wandered out of her room, looking into the shared kitchen at the end of the corridor. A boy was seated at the table, his mother handing him a mug, 'Now you will remember to fill the kettle before you switch it on, won't you, Dave? Dave, are you listening?' Sal turned away and walked straight into a tall girl dragging a soft bag that had split open.

'Sorry,' she murmured, moving away, but then turned back to look at the stranger, who was now bending to stuff back in the clothes that were escaping.

'Here you are,' said Sal, handing her a T-shirt that was lying on the speckled linoleum.

'Thanks. This bag split as soon as I got off the train. I'm Kendra.'

'Sal . . . I'll help. My parents drove me. I couldn't stop them. Did yours come with you?'

'No. They're abroad.' Sal heard a trace of an American accent in Kendra's slow tones as they walked past the identical doors that lined the corridor. 'I think this is my room.' Together they lifted the broken bag and dumped it heavily on a narrow, single bed only fractionally larger than it.

'Let's go and explore. Leave the unpacking till later,' suggested Sal. That had been four years ago, but that first meeting had set the tone for their relationship, Sal urging exploration and activity, Kendra a compliant, supportive companion.

For the rest of their last afternoon on the island the girls basked on the rocks like contented seals, watching their tans deepen, feeling the salt dry on their skins. By six o'clock, the small hamlet on the opposite side of the bay had come into clear view as the light changed and the sun moved behind the hill. The beach was emptying of noisy families.

It was Kendra's favourite time of day there, when she was able to lie still and hear the noise of the water, spared the continuous chatter and shrieks of the beach's other inhabitants. She stood up and waded in, slowly feeling her way on the large flat stones underneath. Once the water was waist deep, she flung herself in, swimming with deep, strong strokes, out past the two anchored fishing boats beyond sight of the bay, her long hair glued to her back in rat's tails. Then she stopped to tread water and look back, to Sal in her emerald bikini, now an almost indecipherable dot. Ahead of her stretched the darkening sea, to the horizon.

'It's lovely up here in the late afternoon,' Joanna Mitchell announced as she and Annie clambered up the stepladder in the small hallway and through a trapdoor on to the decked roof terrace. From the steps below, Annie watched Joanna's sheer nude tights and tight red skirt fill the space between the ceiling and the sky. 'All I ask is that you don't let the plants die – you can run a hose from the bathroom tap. See. Here is the end you shove through the window,' said Joanna, leaning precariously over the small parapet.

One for Sal, thought Annie, then instantly corrected her assumption – or Kendra. Not her, at any rate.

Finding the flat, on the top floor of one of London's terraced streets, was undoubtedly a piece of luck. Joanna had mentioned that she was looking for a flat-sitter when she had last had a coffee with Annie's mother.

'I know I could make good money renting it on the open market, but what would I do about darling Flick, who would hate the apartment in Spain?' she had said to Letty. 'I can't bear to leave her, but it would still be better for her to be able to pad around her own home rather than having to think *dónde* the cat flap? Can Annie be trusted? She's a sweetheart, I know, Letty, but I'm not keen on wild parties or such things. Now she's working for that PR company, she's probably got a taste for the good life.'

Once she'd been offered 23d Cranbourne Terrace, Annie swore there would be no such thing as parties, wild or not, and that she would nurture everything, including the miniature orange tree on the kitchen shelf above the sink. And of course Flick. A place of her own would rescue her from the childlike state enforced by remaining in her mother's comfortable yet stifling Hampshire farmhouse. How liberating to come home at night without having to tiptoe around the creaking boards on the stairs and in the upstairs hall (she knew the culprits intimately) and see the light in her mother's room switch off as she walked past in acknowledgement of her safe return. When her father had died, nine years ago, Annie and her sister Beth had been left to look after their mother. But enough time had passed now, surely, for her to move on.

'Now, I'll lock all my linens and valuables in this cupboard here in the spare room – although I don't imagine you will keep it spare. You're welcome to use my bedroom for yourself so you can get a pal in to help with the rent. But only one. I only want two living here. And a girl, of course,' said Joanna, giving her blonde perm a comforting pat as she and Annie continued their tour of the flat.

The rooms were wallpapered, the sitting room a cheerful stippled green, the bedrooms in smart stripes, while the floors were covered in smooth matting. It was orderly and attractive – like its owner, thought Annie. She imagined the boxy sofa covered in her faded Indian throw and could see the perfect spot for the rag rug she had in her room at home. It would be so easy to make the flat more her own. Joanna plumped up the small square silk cushions lined up on the sofa and walked over to tweak the yellow curtains that hung to the floor.

'I love this place. It's a wrench to leave it, but I'm sure you'll be a great caretaker, Annie. Now, I warn you, the soundproofing is *non-existent*. The bedrooms might as well not have walls – which is no problem for me, all on my lonesome.' She offered a small, neat smile. 'You can hear Bob and Gina upstairs as if they were *literally* in the same room as you. They love to pop on their old records: *Oklahoma!* and *South Pacific* are particular favourites. Most odd. At times, they seem to be up all night.'

As Annie left the building, she was immediately immersed in the relentless stuff of city life: the piles of rubbish outside the small local stores, the dusty display of the charity shop, the rich sickly smell from the kebab stand. Looking through the filthy window of Major Mini Cabs at the huddle of silent men waiting for a job that would allow them to move their illegally parked cars, she thought of Sal and Kendra. Weren't they returning tomorrow from Corfu? It was a real shame that they all couldn't live there, all three of them.

Yanni's bar was situated just outside the busiest part of Kassiopi's harbour. The smells of grilled meat and fish, oregano and rosemary, mixed with a tang from the sea, hung over the main drag, where couples strolled arm in arm, dodging the multitude of juddering, badly driven mopeds.

'A couple of drinks, Ken, and then we'll head back,' promised Sal, threading her way through the tangle of tables to one near the darkened bar that had a good view of the harbour. 'Metaxa for me,' she said to the small, black-haired waitress scurrying between the tables so fast she barely stopped. She turned to Kendra. 'And you?'

'A retsina and a glass of water, please,' she replied, looking at Sal in her red slashed-neck T-shirt, her thin brown arms protruding from its boxy shape, hair slicked back in a smooth cap. Kendra envied Sal her streamlined quality; she was always primed for action, lithe as a Siamese cat. She watched her light a cigarette, blowing the smoke in rings into the night.

'It drives my dad mad when I do this,' said Sal. 'He always says, "Cigarettes are not a circus trick, Salome. But if you want to dig your own grave" dot dot dot ... Always that "dot dot dot ..." Funny, how nobody else calls me Salome. I think it was my mum's one flamboyant gesture, calling me that, and now I'm always Sal.'

'Well, since you never tell anyone you're called Salome, how are they meant to know?' responded Kendra, mildly irritated by Sal's predictable show of self-obsession.

The irritation was lost on Sal, who continued, 'She might as well have called me Sally. Well, thank God she didn't. Living in Cheltenham was dull enough without being called Sally. I'll get these,' she volunteered as the waitress appeared with drinks on a metal tray.

'Can you see my bag?' Kendra rummaged on the floor for the two identical woven-cloth bags they had bought from a small stall earlier in the week, blue, with the traditional white key pattern edging them. She peered into each and handed Sal hers. Sal dug around for some notes. 'There goes my last drachma. I'll have to borrow off you tomorrow.' Three boys were approaching. They stopped just before reaching the girls, their voices carrying in Greek, the shortest pushing the others in a bantering move. Two sat at an adjacent table while the third penetrated the dark hole of Yanni's and returned with a backgammon set. Sal smiled at Kendra, raising an eyebrow and her glass. 'To Greek nights,' she toasted.

As the dusk was replaced with darkness, the town began to light up, candles twinkling on the hundreds of bar and restaurant tables that lined the quayside. Sal felt the familiar embracing warmth induced by ouzo, wine and rough brandy. The world was grand.

'Lover's leap?' she asked, leaning over towards the backgammon players, questioning the red player on his brazen manoeuvres.

'He's brave,' replied his friend, the fine gold chain and cross around his neck lying on his white T-shirt. His voice came as a surprise; it was heavily accented with American.

'Oh, you're a Yank, are you?' Sal twisted her chair towards the table. 'I had you down for Greeks.'

'We're all Greek guys,' answered the boy playing black, looking up at Sal as he slid the counters crisply across the board. 'We go to college in the States and we're home for the holidays. Gotcha,' he concluded triumphantly, lifting off the final counters. 'Alexei –' He gestured, introducing his opponent and finishing off his bottle of beer. Alexei waved at Sal and Kendra. 'Marcus,' he continued, 'and I'm Kosti.' He emphasized the first syllable. The clock in the bell tower chimed midnight as the music from the bars grew louder, drawing in the groups of people parading along the front. Sal was in her element. She toyed with the three boys like a skilled puppeteer. The two weeks' holiday had given her a dark tan, making her unexpectedly pale-blue eyes more vivid.

As Sal chatted vivaciously, Kendra could see Alexei, the loser of the game, being drawn into Sal's compelling orbit. Kendra had witnessed Sal on form before. She could laugh one minute in an utterly dismissive way that would bruise the *amour propre* of her would-be suitors and then instantly, in a glance, or a small movement, bathe them in warm, sexy appreciation. The ashtrays filled up and Kosti bought another round of drinks. Sal draped her arm around him, turning her gaze away from Alexei, fiddling with the piles of backgammon counters. Alexei, suddenly unsure of whether he had pulled or not, looked confused. As she downed another glass of lethal rough brandy, Sal became ever more garrulous and all-embracing.

'Come to London. Yeah – come and stay with us.'

Kendra looked at Sal, who she knew had no permanent bed in the capital, let alone somewhere for three boys to stay. 'We'll take you around – there are fantastic clubs now. Great music.'

'"Ninety-nine luftballons."' Sal sang along cheerfully to the summer's Euro hit.

'It's sad, but we're going back tomorrow,' Kendra told them.

'Yeah, it's our last night, so it has to be fun.' Sal smiled warmly at Kendra. 'One to remember.' Kendra rubbed her arms, a little cold now, as she watched Sal disappear on to the small dance floor behind the bar with Alexei, his dark-blond curls a contrast to her neat, dark head.

Without Sal, the table felt empty, and the remaining three shifted uncomfortably, unsure what move to make next. Kosti stood up and stretched. 'I'm going to check out Athene's, just along the street,' he said. As an afterthought, he offered, 'Coming?' to Kendra, who accepted the invitation, glad of an opportunity to move from where she had sat for far too long. She scooped up her bag, weighty with the book she was reading.

'You can leave it here, I'm staying. Or I'll give it to your friend,' suggested Marcus.

'Great, thanks. I'll be back soon,' replied Kendra, walking quickly to catch up with Kosti, who had exited the crowded bar area and was striding away. It was a relief to be outside, and walking, and when she returned she could pick up Sal and leave for home.

Kosti was a friendly enough companion, explaining that the three of them came from Athens and were taking business courses in the States. 'We love Corfu – it's party time.' He gestured at the bustling harbour. 'We head here every summer before we're into lockdown with our families. Greek mums want their boys with them, especially ones like us who've managed to escape across the Atlantic for half the year.'

'It's a beautiful island,' said Kendra. Even with the lights of the noisy town, she could see the stars above clearly. 'These are the last stars I'll be seeing for some time,' she continued. 'West London's not exactly renowned for its clear skies. Is that the Plough or the Sickle?' She was still struggling to keep up with Kosti. It was obvious that he had little interest in her, or in stargazing.

After a quick look at Athene's, where Kosti found nothing to keep him, they walked in near-silence back to Yanni's. The tables they had occupied were now empty, the ashtrays clean, the glasses removed. There was no sign of Marcus.

'My bag,' gasped Kendra, with a rush of relief when she saw the white key pattern in the tangle of cane chair legs. 'Thank God.' She pulled it up, immediately sensing its unfamiliar weightlessness. There was nothing inside apart from a tube of lipsalve and some cigarettes. 'Shit, it's Sal's. Where's mine? Where's Sal?' Kendra remembered that she had offered to carry the room key in hers and, of course, Sal had spent the last of her cash.

She looked towards the bar and ran into the dark room where the cheap fluorescent light picked up the figures on the dance floor shifting to the synthesized beat. Even as she scanned for the bright red of Sal's T-shirt, she knew she wouldn't be there. How could she? Idiot. And how could she, Kendra, have left her bag with some Greek college boy and trusted Sal to stick around? She had seen the third metaxa downed, witnessed the transition from friendly sobriety to taunting recklessness that Sal displayed when drunk. She might have guessed she would disappear. She would simply have forgotten about Kendra. The bell tower chimed two.

'She'll turn up later. Don't worry. She's with Alexei,' said Kosti as they stood in the still-busy harbour. 'I can give you this for a taxi home.' It would be worth the drachma to get rid of this tall, serious girl. He saw her into a battered white Nissan and watched it move off creakily on to the coastal road. Kendra leant back on the plastic seats clutching Sal's useless bag. The road was dark and unfamiliar, lined with pines and gorse and lit only by the occasional headlight speeding in their direction. The air was still warm, but she was chilly.

After ten minutes, the taxi drew to a halt by a white sign with the Greek lettering for 'Kanariki' above the English version. The driver gestured down the dusty, winding road.

'Please, can you drive me?' asked Kendra, pointing in the direction of the road. 'It's so dark.' She mimicked blindness, putting her hands across her eyes.

'*Ochi*.' The driver shrugged and delivered a stream of words which Kendra understood to mean that he wasn't going to risk his tyres. Pointing at the meter, which was at 3,000 drachma, he put out his hands to show five fingers then jabbed at his watch to indicate late-night rates. Kendra climbed out, shoved the 3,000 drachma Kosti had given her into the driver's hands and started to run down the hill, the noise of her shoes on the pebbles and dried pine cones amplified by the silence of the night. As she rounded a corner a shaft of moonlight appeared and she could see to the end of the road and the shimmer of water. Something ran across her path – a fox, a wild dog? Jesus, what kind of things lived in these woods? She increased her speed.

The hamlet lay in darkness as she climbed up the outside stairs to their room. She would have to sleep on the terrace. During the day, the wash of the sea sounded so delightful, but now, in the night, it felt threatening. This was it, finally. Sal had pushed it too far this time. She was selfish. No – more than selfish. Kendra thought back to the last incident with Sal, where Kendra had been left stranded at a party in a suburban mansion off the A1 to which she had agreed, against her wishes, to go as Sal's 'date'. Each time, though, her fury

with Sal was tempered by a greater feeling of annoyance for allowing herself to become the victim. Why did she do it? She wasn't a
helpless person with no control over events. Why on earth had she
left Sal on the dance floor? What had she been thinking to leave her
bag? She lay on the floor, Sal's thin cotton bag under her head and
the red towel, hung out to dry in the early evening on the railings,
as her blanket and closed her eyes, hoping in a childish way that, if
she could not see anything, it would not see her. No fox, no rapist,
no fucking coyotes . . . did they have coyotes in Greece? Or was it
wolves?

2

'Hmm, well, the flight back was bad,' Sal explained to Annie as they sat in the window of a wine bar around the corner from Cranbourne Terrace. 'She was furious. I felt terrible when I came back and found her there curled up outside our room. I didn't know I'd taken her bag. Not even then. I hadn't even thought about who had the keys. Bit too much to drink, I guess.'

'Oh, surely not, Sal?' mocked Annie, who had already had a version of the evening related to her at length by Kendra. 'Well, you're both back now. She'll forgive you. We always do. I suppose it would be easier for Ken if she had a boyfriend. It seems like ages since that last one, Misha. Not that he lasted very long. She was twice his height and, anyway, he must have been gay. Or maybe . . .' Annie stretched her arms to reposition her long blonde hair in the pile on her head, held firm with an engraved chopstick. She leant back on the thin bentwood chair to look at the bustling street outside. 'So what do you think of the flat? Do you want to share? Twenty pounds a week and bills on top is what I've worked out I need to pay Joanna.'

'Annie, of course I want to. But I'm jobless right now. Tell you what. I've got enough to pay a month's rent, and I'm sure I can get something sorted out soon. Give me a chance at it. We'll have such a great time. I'm already planning barbies on that terrace.'

'Oh, sure. Which one of us is the barbie queen? I've never seen the point of barbecues. They were invented to make boys feel good.' Annie continued, 'Joanna wants me there next week. I'd love to have you to help with the move.'

Sal knew what would be involved. Annie was the homemaker of the three and, wherever she travelled, so too came a startling quantity of clutter. At university, her rooms, no matter how small, were havens of colour and prettiness. There would be embroidered shawls to throw over grubby chairs, scarves to dim lampshades, vases of all shapes and sizes collected from market stalls, an array of plants in painted cachepots and stacks of bowls to be filled with fruits, pens, flower petals . . . Where Sal's bedside table, if she had one, would house old batteries, loose change, a dirty ashtray and bus tickets, Annie's would have a neat pile of books, a pretty glass and some kind of decorative box to conceal anything unattractive. Sal admired Annie's taste and homebody skills, while not envying them. Annie enjoyed Sal's insouciance and careless approach, content herself to play mother.

'I'll move when you do. I can't wait.' Sal looked happily at her friend. 'I don't expect I'll be bringing that much, but you can rely on me as a Sherpa. Have you told Kendra about this?'

'About what?'

'About us living together.'

'I didn't know that we were, until now. Not for certain,' said Annie flatly, upset that Sal should have raised this tricky point. 'It's difficult. I wish we could all live there, but Joanna has insisted that I can only have one "pal", as she put it, and I thought you probably needed the room more than Ken. She can always stay in that huge house of hers.'

'With Morticia Addams?' queried Sal, referring to Kendra's mother. 'You forget with Ken – that she's rolling in it. Well, not her, but her mum and dad. In fact – you know what? – maybe she could buy somewhere for us all to live?'

'I'm not sure I'd suggest that to her just now, Sal. She's still feeling bruised by Corfu. Living with you is not ambition number one. "I could have been savaged, Annie, while I slept, while Sal was doing God knows what with Adonis."' Annie mimicked Kendra's soft, measured voice.

'Wish I could remember exactly what I *was* doing – but the bits I do remember were pretty good!' Sal emptied her glass. 'He looked just like a Greek statue, a beautiful boy, but not so *piccolo*, if you get me – not one of those weird small acorns they always have.'

'Well, Kendra has a different memory of that night,' laughed

Annie, gesturing for the bill, aware that she had to catch the train back home. But not for much longer. Soon she'd be able to spend the nights in her own flat.

The marble counter that ran the length of one wall of the kitchen was empty, except for the white mug Kendra had just put down. From a nearby room she could hear the jangle of jazz, dissonant sounds that filled the high ceilings and conjured the same comforting recognition in her that others might feel on hearing the theme tune to *The Archers* or *Coronation Street*. Wandering across the parquet floor towards the source of the sound, Kendra entered the study at the back of the house. Her father, Art Rootstein, was seated in his black leather recliner, immersed in a thick folder of papers. There always seemed to be another deal on the table, thought Kendra, of her father's music publishing career.

'Hi, doll,' he said, without looking up. 'What's new?'

Not for the first time, Kendra wondered how many black turtlenecks her father possessed. She stood beside him and ruffled the greying waves of his hair, the scent of his skin sweet and familiar.

'I'm going to go for an interview, at this place called the Chapel.'

'Jesus, what is it? You taking religious orders?'

'Dad, I told you and Mum about it at dinner last week. Don't you remember anything I tell you?'

'OK, so tell me again. I'm all ears now.' Art put his papers down on the floor and cupped both his ears, giving Kendra a big smile. She moved away from him to stand against the white wall and look out into the paved garden.

'It's this community centre in Kentish Town where they work with young people who have problems at home. They give them a place to be, a kind of retreat. They get them involved with art, music, dance, that kind of thing.'

'Ah. They pay?'

'I s'pose so.' Kendra's voice adopted the sullen quality induced by explaining anything to her parents.

'Darling, are you sure this is right for you?' Art leant back in his chair. 'Jim McKenzie over at Britannia has said he can fit you into one of his departments. You know he and Jill go way back with me and Marisa, and I helped their eldest boy – God knows what he was called; now what was it? Ryan, or something. Anyways, I got him started, and now I gather *he's* doing great.'

'Dad, you *know* I don't want to work in the music business. I'd rather *die* than do that. I've told you and Mum I don't want your help. Christ. The music biz – with all those creeps.'

Art surveyed his only daughter and wondered how it was, with him and Marisa as parents, she had turned out the way she had. Neither nature nor nurture appeared to have exerted much influence. Physically, she was expansive – her hair was a riot of curls, her body possessed a rangy physicality, in contrast to her mother's tautly controlled frame and his own wiry build. Emotionally, she had always, even as a small child, identified with the underdog.

It had frustrated them, the way in which, at school, she would make friends with the kids whom, obviously – to them – nobody else *wanted* as friends. They had sent her to places that were bursting with the children of clever, interesting people, children who would go some place, achieve something. But Kendra would bring home the runts of the class, silent little things often literally dwarfed by their tall daughter. They would be unmoving, petrified, whenever he or Marisa appeared in her room, where Kendra would be presiding over one of these pathetic chicks like a mother hen. Art had a strong feeling that his wife was not going to like the sound of this Chapel fandango.

'Well. Time will tell, I guess.' Art returned to the comparative safety of his paperwork. 'Let's wait till we know a bit more before we tell your mother your plans, shall we?'

Kendra left her father to fetch her bicycle from the basement. The tussle to negotiate its frame out of the small side door and up on to the street was familiar but nonetheless aggravating and resulted in a dark smear of oil scarring her jeans. As she cycled through the streets, the cloudless blue sky formed a backdrop to large white houses with their tidy window-box displays of geraniums and violas. Glimpsed through the large windows were empty rooms, dark against the sun. Kendra's loose shirt billowed as she pushed the pedals with increasing speed. Leaving the plush streets of Notting Hill behind, she wound north, following the canal towpath up into the dirtier, denser roads of Camden and on to Kentish Town, each push of the pedals increasing the welcome separation from her parents' house.

She was infuriated by her conversation with her father. How could he understand her so little? How could he suggest that she might work at Britannia? She remembered the last time she had seen Jim McKenzie, only a month or so ago. It was in a small Italian restaurant near their house and he was seated at a table against the back wall with a girl who was certainly neither his wife nor his daughter. She could see his fat legs rubbing up against hers under the table. Kendra had tried to avoid catching his eye, but he'd waved at her. She hated the way men like him played it cool.

He could at least have had the grace to be embarrassed.

'Hi, Kendra. Do you know Natasha?' Of course not. 'Now, how *are* Art and Marisa – two of my very favourite people in the world? Send them my regards – I owe them a call.'

'Sure.' Kendra wished herself as far away as possible. She certainly didn't want to have to work with a slimeball like him every day of her life.

Stopping outside a bookmaker's on Kentish Town Road, she propped her bike up to consult her *A–Z* street map: Albert Crescent, Albert Grove, Albert Terrace, Albert Way – 58d. Albert Way fell into the stitch of the book, a small cul-de-sac which, it appeared from what she could see, should be a few streets to the right of her.

She wiped the sweat from her forehead and upper lip and retied her thick curls into their elastic band. Now that she had stopped moving she could feel a trickle of sweat from beneath her heavy, braless breasts slide towards her waist. Perhaps she should walk the next few streets. It would probably do her good to cool down a bit before she arrived for her interview, rather than turning up at the door like a soaking rag. Was she looking for a church or a big hall?

When Kendra walked into the Chapel she was at first disorientated by the contrast between the brilliant light of outside and the darker cool of the large deconsecrated church. Wedged between low-rise industrial blocks, the Chapel sat incongruously in one of the many London streets sculpted by wartime bomb damage. Originally St Saviour and St John, locally rechristened the Chapel, the building had survived where its neighbours had not, a pale stone spire reaching above the utilitarian fifties builds. Outside the wide green doors was a clutch of teenage boys who silently watched as Kendra tethered her bicycle to a parking meter. Its shining metal and ladylike wicker basket discomfited her as she sensed their gaze, and she wondered what the chances were of her bike still being there when she returned.

The large room that confronted her was empty. 'Hello,' she offered, surprised by how small her voice sounded. 'Hellooo,' she repeated, more loudly this time. From somewhere in the room came a reply.

'Coming – hang on.' A woman with a deep voice, she thought, although she supposed it could be a bloke. As she stepped further into the room and her eyes acclimatized to the light, Kendra took in guitars and a keyboard placed against one wall, a basketball net hooked up in a far corner, paintings on paper pinned up on the walls, a number of deflated beanbags piled up alongside a big trestle table and dirty-looking plastic chairs.

'Come next door and we'll have something to drink,' suggested the voice. It belonged to a figure silhouetted against the light of a doorway at the far end of the room. Gioia Cavallieri was quite unlike anybody Kendra had seen before. Her olive-skinned face was framed by a head of dark Medusa-like locks of hair bound tightly with flashes of coloured thread. Bracelets climbed up her bare arm from wrist to elbow, an articulation of metals and colours as she offered her hand.

'Welcome to the Chapel. It's Kendra, isn't it?'

Kendra felt an immediate sense of relief. For once, she didn't need to stoop, to diminish herself, as she so often did on meeting people. Gioia, unusually for a woman, was taller than her. They looked straight into each other's eyes, Gioia's lined heavily with kohl. As the tea bags stewed, she explained that the Chapel was maintained through a mixture of local support, some private philanthropy and a dogged dedication to understanding the labyrinthine grant system.

'The money's there, love, it's just a question of who gets it. *She*'s doing her best to make our lives difficult, but we're not going to be beaten by her and that lot. Can't believe she's still with us. What a country. We could have got her out this year. The bloody Falklands kept her in. What a fuck-up.'

Kendra empathized with Gioia's condemnation of Margaret Thatcher. She couldn't believe she'd held on to it, that last election. At university, none of her friends had had any time for Tories, but now, in the real world, it seemed there were thousands somewhere out there posting a blue vote. Her parents were two of them, although she knew they wouldn't have dreamt of voting Republican if they had still been living on the East Coast. People like them didn't do Republican, but it seemed supporting milk-snatcher Thatcher was fine this side of the pond.

'We've had some mind-blowing results here. Kids who spent all their spare time sniffing . . . down the tracks' – she gestured broadly – 'now they've got into a band, or acting, or at any rate something that means they're likely to live long enough to see their twenty-first birthday.' Gioia walked towards the sink under the window and ran some water into a blue china jug. 'Robbie made this for me. He's one of my long-termers here. We funnelled him into art, now he's doing ceramics evening classes. Incredible.' She pulled down her white cotton vest, which had ridden up to expose her stomach, and its fine dusting of dark hair. Plaits of coloured leather and metal hung from her neck.

'So, tell me a bit about yourself, love.' Gioia's London vowels were cut with some different accent. Kendra wasn't sure what to say. What could she say that could possibly be relevant to this strange creature? She found herself transfixed by Gioia's elaborate eyeliner, her oiled curls. Generally, she was unaffected by styles of dress and immune to the immediate impact of appearance, but Gioia she found . . . extraordinary.

'I've never done anything like this before,' she began. Her voice sounded tinny in the space and, for a moment, hearing its weakness confused her. 'I graduated in sociology, and I've been hunting for something to do since. I'd like to feel I was spending my time doing something, y'know, kind of worthwhile. Lots of my year went into banking, property, that kind of thing – even ones you didn't think would – but that's not really me.'

'Have you worked with kids before? Holiday jobs?'

'Well, no, not exactly. But now I've spent some time thinking about what I want, and I know I really want to get into this type of work.' Kendra decided to leave out the fact that she had never felt the need of a holiday job. Her allowance covered everything.

Gioia stood up briskly and walked over to the kitchen counter. She pulled out a packet of tobacco then some Rizlas from her pocket. 'Smoke? No?' She rolled a cigarette and lit it, inhaling deeply before embarking on further questioning. Eventually, the interrogation ceased. 'This isn't bleeding heart stuff, you know. It can be a bloody nightmare, and I don't know if you'll have the stomach for it. Banking, property or the Chapel? What makes you think you'll stick it?'

Kendra felt her face turning red with embarrassment. She'd blown it. 'I just want a chance to show you that I can do this. If you don't like me then you can get rid of me any time.'

'Let's have a look at the paperwork there. Aha . . . Notting Hill, huh. Not local then. A levels: Art, English, French. Well, we don't really care about that kind of thing here. References – your tutor?' she mocked, before narrowing her eyes and considering the girl in front of her. 'If I give you the chance, you'll have to learn quickly. The kids are tough. They make up their mind whether they're going to deal with people pretty damn pronto. We don't have any of that growing-into-the-job stuff here. And the money's £200 a month.' Hearing the salary, Kendra immediately realized that the pay was going to make it hard for her to move out of home. 'Take it or leave it.'

Kendra was trying to decide what to answer when the telephone rang.

'Si, si da mi. Non ti preoccupare. Chi vidiamo piu tardi. Ciao, Dad.' Gioia's face, which had the bluntness of a Mayan figurine, lightened as she spoke briefly before replacing the receiver. 'He's down from Glasgow – for a few days.' She shared the information casually with the job applicant.

Kendra was surprised. Gioia, in her extremely limited acquaint-ance, didn't seem like the kind of person who would have a dad of any kind, let alone a dad who would provoke that warm smile or that fluent Italian. She tried to focus on the decision she had to make, a decision that, as she looked down at the linoleum floor through the dust motes that floated in front of her eyes, she felt incapable of making. She knew that she was looking for something, but what? Was this it? Sal would tell her to 'Come on, Ken. Go for it. What's to lose?' Her mother would most likely say, 'Are you los-ing your mind, darling? For this nonsense we educated you?' Hearing that voice so clearly decided her.

'I'd love the job,' she said.

'Start Monday – sooner the better. Rest up this weekend. You'll need it. I'm a grand taskmaster.'

After giving Kendra a brief tour of the Chapel, Gioia walked her out to the street. The boys had gone and the road was empty. Ken-dra felt embarrassed by the relief she felt on seeing that her bicycle was still where she had left it. She was going to have to change her attitude if she was going to work here. Poor kids, condemned auto-matically by her knee-jerk middle-class suspicions.

'Lucky that bike's still there. They vanish in seconds. Bring it inside next time,' Gioia said. 'Nice one.' She put a hand on Kendra's shoulder and watched as she rode off towards Camden Town.

'So that's a dozen gingham table napkins, two French linen table-cloths, five broderie anglaise cloths, the three blown-glass jugs, a maple standard lamp, and six blue and white cotton cushion covers. White Horse Studio is sending a car for them.' Annie repeated the order down the phone for the samples from La Vie Loire.

Tania Torrington Public Relations operated out of a terraced house in Chelsea. Behind the glossy black-painted door was a bustling office handling fashion, beauty and lifestyle clients. Tania had been a successful glamour model in her youth, a stalwart of the *Daily Express* William Hickey column, her energetic love life guaranteed to fill a bottom-left column. When the inevitable happened, and her breasts were no longer of a shape and pertness to feature in newspapers, Tania swapped her transparent cheesecloth blouses and hotpants for the more forgiving camouflage of Issey Miyake pleats. Presciently noting the growth of interest in homes and lifestyle, she started her business, shrewdly calculating that it would be more able to deal with the passage of time than her own body.

Tania staffed her office with attractive young people, harnessing their good looks, enthusiasm and energy into the business of promoting product. Although it was weekly luncheon vouchers that provided food and drink and pay packets were pitiful, if you were part of Tania Torrington you could be working on an exciting new nightclub account, a themed launch of a designer perfume or even shepherding a celebrity through a party or launch as if you were their friend. Tania Torrington, she would often pronounce, shows you how things *happen*.

Annie looked at Lee, who was seated across from her. If he hummed that song once more, she thought she might go mad. The operatic pronouncement of Spandau Ballet's 'True' was being tattooed on her brain.

'Lee, please, anything else. How about "Every Breath You Take" instead? Just a break from "I know . . . this . . . much . . . is *true*."' Annie drummed her fingers on her dress to highlight the song's drama.

Lee looked up from the pile of press releases he was stapling together about the opening of a new restaurant nearby called Chelsea Bridge.

'Don't know how you can put Spandau and that tosser Sting in the same sentence, Annie. Thing is, you know nothing – no – *less* than zero about this kind of stuff.' As he talked, the heavy peroxide fringe of his wedge cut fell limply into his eyes, which were framed by lashes tinted with a vivid blue mascara. He had been told more than once that this made him look more like the Princess of Wales than his sartorial hero, the Thin White Duke.

He left the room with the press releases, climbing the staircase lined with framed newspaper cuttings and photographs of Tania in her heyday alongside product coverage organized by the company. A double-page spread in the *Sunday Times* colour supplement of a range of Lycra exercise wear hung next to a black and white photograph of Tania, the white arch of a trattoria behind her and the arm of a grinning, darkly tanned Italian actor around her shoulders. In another she stood in a plunging halter-neck gown chatting to a youthful Prince Charles, and next to it hung the spread of an interview, a decade later, that Tania had orchestrated with one of the British evening-wear designers favoured by his wife, the young Princess of Wales.

The telephone rang again, and Annie heard Tania pick it up in the next room: 'Oh, love. Yup – yes, OK. Annie can drop them round. Not a problem. Cheers, darling.' The light on Annie's phone flashed orange. She picked up, pressing the lit button to connect to an extension.

'Annie, that order for White Horse. There's some problem with the car firm – can you just get it all together and drive it over? Take the VW.'

Annie was delighted to have an opportunity to escape the office on a day like this. Through the small windows she could see the midday sun creating sharp shadows through the leaves of the plane trees that lined the street. She hauled the bags of props into the boot of the company VW Golf.

As the car began to move, the croaky sounds of Stevie Nicks's voice on Fleetwood Mac's *Rumours* filtered tinnily through the speakers. The music prompted a memory from an old family holiday, of her father singing along, his arm lying on the open window of the car, a No. 6 between his fingers, as they drove through the Scottish Highlands. She remembered the back of his neck, where his hair was neatly shy of his summer shirt, and the printed cotton skirt of her mother's dress flared over her legs, and what she called 'my summer flop-abouts', striped canvas shoes that she would bring out every holiday. They were playing Hangman, and she and her sister were taking it in turns to draw the sinister, dangling figure. Her father, as always, won. He was a competitive man – proud of his pretty wife and always pushing his daughters forward. That must have been a couple of years before he died. Unwanted, another image replaced that of her healthy father on holiday. It was of a waxy figure lying under a thin hospital blanket, devoid of all her father's warmth.

The parking lot of White Horse Studios was full, and the nearest slot where Annie could leave the Golf was some distance from the steps to Studio 3. There was too much to carry in one trip, but she loaded herself up and staggered slowly into the studios and approached the oak refectory table that served as a reception desk.

'Message for Jackson. Annie from TT is here. She wants help with the order,' relayed the receptionist into an intercom. 'Someone's coming,' she said to Annie, continuing to study her *Cosmopolitan*. Reading upside down, Annie noticed the name of the feature she was engrossed in: '50 Unforgettable Things You Can Do to Your Man (And 10 He Can Do to You)'.

The doors at the end of the room opened and a figure appeared and started walking towards her.

'Hi. Jackson.' His offered hand was firm. 'I'm the producer on this job. Good of you to come. We've had a melt-down here – there's not even a gofer I could send out to help you.'

Annie followed his quick, loose-limbed stride out to the car park. Together they unloaded the remaining contents of Tania's car, heaving bags into the studio space, where a room set was in play. A deep linen-covered sofa sat to one side, waiting, she imagined, for the mounds of cushion covers she had delivered, while at the front was a big trestle table piled with cameras, boxes of Fuji photographic film and the general paraphernalia of a photo shoot.

'Someone let us down on all the table dressings, hence the panic phone call this morning,' explained Jackson. 'OK, everyone, clear the table and get it laid up, we need to get a move on here.' Figures scurried out from the shadows of the studio at his command. Annie watched as the heavy lights were pushed around and the stylist and her team began dressing the set, arranging the cushions to a perfect degree of plumpness, placing a vase of wildflowers in the centre of the table.

'Sandy, go easy. Let's see what it looks like a bit sparse and homespun – we can load it on later if we need to,' Jackson directed. 'Annie here – it is Annie, isn't it? – has brought us enough kit to furnish a whole house.' Annie felt flattered to have Jackson refer to her by her name. A girl came over to him and took him by the arm to a corner of the set, her yellow dress a bright spot in the dark room.

As the table was transformed from a basic trestle into the French farmhouse of an advertising agency's imagination – the gingham napkins folded flat on heavy white plates, chunky tumblers and slabs of wooden boards laden with bread, grapes and cheese – Annie could see that Jackson's attention had been diverted. She felt uncomfortable and unnecessary. Was it rude just to leave?

'I'll be off then,' she said, to no one in particular. Jackson stopped talking, held her gaze for long enough for her to wonder what he was looking at, and then waved, before turning back to the girl in the yellow dress, whose whispering and waving hands appeared to be gaining in urgency.

By the time Annie arrived back at the office the day had become unbearably hot.

The shade of the office was now welcome, and she walked through into the back, where a small patio-garden was filled with potted plants and palms. Tania was seated at a green ironwork table with her habitual cigarette and a glass of white wine.

'Everything all right? Jackson grateful? I hope so. I've known him since he was a runner on *Constantinople Dreaming*. He was still at school. I was an odalisque – black wig and rouge on the nipples. All I had to do was lie around on a pile of tapestry cushions and he, bless him, was so wet behind the ears he was embarrassed by us naked girls. *That* didn't last. He's carved his way through half the city, so I hear.'

Annie walked into the small kitchen, where the sink, as usual, was filled with a pile of stained tea cups and the rubbish bin stank. She ran herself a glass of water and opened the freezer compartment door to discover the rubber ice trays all filled with the disappointing wobble of water. As she climbed the stairs back to her office she allowed herself the luxury of a quick daydream of a date with Jackson. It beat calling the thirty fashion assistants she needed to contact about the Swatch watches that were Tania's new client: 'Annie, we're talking style bibles, fashion bibles, even The Big Fat Blinkin' Bible here. I want to see Swatches everywhere, and quick.' Annie still wore a Timex on a thin brown leather strap which her father had given her when she was thirteen. She supposed she should put in a call to *The Face*. On her desk was a When You Were Out slip: 'Call your mum, and can you cover for me till I get back? Lee.'

She knew her mother would be trying to discover what time she was arriving for the weekend. Pleased as she was to have moved to London, weekends could be claustrophobic in the small flat. Only three hours now till she could leave work.

By five o'clock, Annie had dispatched ten of the Swatches to various publications, carefully matching the title to an appropriate colour and size and asking the fashion editors and assistants to get back to her with info on how they could feature them. For a Friday afternoon in August, the office was surprisingly active – intercom lines buzzing throughout, deliveries coming and going. As she began to stuff her Swatch press releases back into the box file where they were housed Lee walked back into the room and thumped a huge wicker basket of peaches covered in cellophane and tied with a bright-pink ribbon on to her desk.

'*Ta da.* Somebody's lucky day then.' He stood over her as she opened the small envelope addressed to ANNIE which dangled from the ribbon. 'Can I buy you dinner? Jackson.'

'*Very* impressive.' Lee drew out the words in camp exaggeration. Annie was silent, just looking at the gift, before seeing Tania's bulky presence in the doorway, arms folded across her indigo smock.

'Here we go,' she boomed, looking at Annie's delighted face. 'Don't say you weren't warned.' Annie rewound her memory of Jackson in the studio orchestrating the proceedings, his undeniable good looks, his cool aura. An injection of excitement and happiness surged through her, changing the ordinariness of a hot working day into something filled with thrilling potential.

3

Sal stood in the small changing room of Joseph on South Molton Street. The floor was piled with black and white clothes – fine-knit sweaters, fitted short skirts, jackets with broad shoulders and large buttons. The summer sale had lured her in. It wasn't the kind of place she normally shopped, or would even browse in. Way too expensive. She wasn't keen on shopping but occasionally she'd dip into Miss Selfridge if she needed a dress for a party, or buy a cheap pair of earrings or belt if she just wanted something new. Come to think of it, where was that metallic cummerbund she'd bought a few weeks ago? At Joseph, the precise monochrome world and thin, black-clad assistants were daunting. One wearing a pair of tight black trousers and a knitted white vest approached her, thick silver hoop earrings glinting through glossy black hair.

'Looking for anything special?' she asked, with an expression that indicated she thought this extremely unlikely.

'Not really, thanks,' Sal muttered, trying not to look too obviously at the price tags when she riffled through the rails of sale items. She put her heavy handbag down, and pulled a cotton Katharine Hamnett suit from the rail and started weighing up its possibilities. On the positive side, it wasn't too structured or formal, but did it have the authoritative quality she might need? It was worth a try anyway.

Eventually, she had scurried into an empty changing room with a huge pile of clothes in her arms, regretting that she didn't have Annie there to guide her. Annie was brilliant at putting things together. She could make anything special, everything looking better for the way she mixed things. It was the kind of thing Sal was hopeless at. She was best when she stuck to plain fabrics and tight shapes. Her shopping past was littered with mistakes, clothes bought in a flash of enthusiasm which overrode common sense.

It was ridiculous to feel in awe of a shop, she told herself. She was meant to be a reporter. What kind of a reporter broke out in hives on South Molton Street because a sales assistant came near her? She told herself to grow up. Not everyone got a contract to work on the features desk of the *Sunday Herald*, and she had just banked her first pay cheque. She deserved to buy something special. And it deserved to come from Joseph.

On Sal's first day at the *Herald*, she had been immediately subdued by the prevailing atmosphere of masculinity. The offices were a sea of grey suits and white shirtsleeves, although Jackie, the features desk secretary seated outside the senior management offices, was wearing what seemed to be the women's uniform: a floral shirt and a calf-length skirt. Jackie had shown her the Ladies, the kettle and where the stationery was stored before bustling off, gesturing to the fax machine on her way.

Nobody spoke to Sal for what appeared to be hours and, for the first time in her life, she felt unable to deploy her naturally flirtatious exuberance. Her white shirt was fine, and she had taken trouble to check it was a thick enough cotton that her bra wouldn't show through, but the red skirt made her feel conspicuous. She couldn't see anyone else wearing a bright colour. As the lunch hour approached she saw a posse of men pass and glance over to where she sat. She ate an apple at her desk. As they returned hours later, they looked again at her, more brazenly this time, before heading off in pairs to the Gents, hoisting the waistbands of their trousers.

Her presence was a reminder that the newspaper industry was changing. New printing presses were on the way, there would be fewer jobs and, to many of the old guard, the hiring of young people like her, who had found short-cuts through the traditional provincial route, was a provocative move. Towards the end of her first afternoon a man, his collar unbuttoned and tie askew, approached her.

'Give this number a ring and check out what the story is on Paula Yates at the Embassy last night.' He handed her a scrap of paper scrawled with a phone number. 'I'm Stuart.' She guessed he must be from somewhere up north, with his flat vowels. 'There may be something there.' He looked over her head as he spoke.

She had not known who she was ringing, or what kind of story Stuart had in mind, but her diary shifts had taught her the knack of following a trail, asking questions that would lead to fuller answers than the interviewee expected. Within an hour she was back to Stuart with three hundred words written not about Paula but about one of her girlfriends who was discovered in the small bathroom with another girl that night, screaming as they mistakenly flushed a wrap of coke down the loo. The information was greeted with a marked lack of interest by Stuart: 'Just another day in Shangri-la, then.'

Now, weeks into the job and with a few small stories to her name, the office had begun to lose the impenetrability of the new and, from what initially had appeared as a collective personality, the journalists and editors were starting to emerge as individuals. One lunchtime, she had been delighted to be asked by Stuart to join an outing to a dark Fleet Street wine bar where bottle after bottle of red wine had been drained. As the afternoon merged into evening, they all moved on to the famous El Vino's bar, unbothered by a return to the office. Seated at a table in the corner with Doug, one of the home desk stalwarts, she learnt of his difficult custody battle with his wife.

'I'm dossing on friends' sofas at the moment. She's in the house and she'll only let me come round when her mum's there.'

'That must be awful for you.'

'Yeah. I'm living out of my desk drawer.' He tipped the dregs of the bottle into her glass and stood up to walk over to the bar for a replacement. When he returned, Stuart had moved into his seat and he had to perch on a low stool, shouting across the table.

'Stu, how about William knocking off Noreen? He got her out of there double quick once our venerable editor got wind of the situation.' The affair between the foreign editor and the managing editor's PA had become common knowledge. 'It's normally the women who get the sack with this kind of thing,' he informed Sal. 'Happens all the time.'

From her reflection in the full-length mirror in the Joseph changing room, it was clear that the Greek suntan had nearly gone and that Sal was overwhelmed by the black jackets. A scratch below her eye had swollen. Perhaps black was a mistake, but it would tick the cost-per-wear box surely, and it would be useful camouflage, adding the veneer of professionalism. She eased a Lycra-saturated skirt over her bottom – great: you couldn't see the line of her knickers – and buttoned up the matching jacket. It was obvious that she had nothing save a bra on underneath, which gave the outfit a casual sexiness, she thought. She didn't want to appear too buttoned up, too sexless. The older women on the paper all looked like that. They had a faded appearance, as if they had been punctured and all the pleasure had run out. The price on the tag had been crossed out three times, each one lower than the previous. A black Joseph suit at a bargain price – she had to have it, even though it cost more than her month's rent to Annie. She wished she didn't feel so awful.

Last night, she had been in the flat alone. Sunday had passed slowly, and she had spent it lying on the terrace, hearing the squeals and bickering in the gardens below. Flick had made occasional appearances, padding along the parapet wall with feline ease and then scampering down the stepladder on seemingly irrational whims. At around four o'clock, Sal had climbed down from the terrace to consult the contents of the fridge. A tub of hummus crusting along the edge and a small chunk of dry Cheddar was all that was on offer. There was a basket of rotting peaches sitting on the kitchen table. It wasn't that Sal expected Annie to organize the food, it was simply that Sal always forgot about it. The effort of walking down to the local shop was more than it was worth. It was too hot to be hungry anyway. She carried a glass of water back up to the roof. It was August, and the city was in the usual disarray of that month. Kendra had told her that London was a crazy place in August, that anything could happen, because all the shrinks took the month off.

'Mum can't deal with it because Laila always goes back to Lisbon for the whole month too. No cleaners, no sanity. A bad scene,' she concluded.

Sal didn't think she knew anyone that visited a shrink, and they certainly didn't employ a cleaner, but it was true, there was something different about the city. With families away on holiday, the streets were emptier, windows open, everywhere music and shouting. At night the air was thick with the smells of the city, the heat that had bounced back off the dirty pavements.

The sound of the telephone beside the sofa pierced the long silence of the day. It was Stuart Jeffries, immediately obvious from the strident tones she had heard the previous day, as he gave the West Berlin stringer a rocket for filing late.

'I'm just round the corner from you. Fancy a drink?' Sal envisaged Stuart's lanky frame and unremarkable face. She certainly didn't fancy him, but a drink and some company she could do with.

'Sure, that'd be great. When? OK. See you in fifteen.'

Fifteen minutes to the second, and the doorbell buzzed. Sal ran down the three flights of stairs to the front door, where Stuart stood, looking up at the top-floor windows.

'I thought it would be quicker if I just came down,' Sal said, giving him the slightest peck on the cheek she could manage without being rude. He smelt of popcorn.

'So where shall we go? Do you have a favourite place?' he asked, opening the passenger door of his car.

Sal immediately regretted her decision to meet him. She didn't mind having a drink with him if she didn't have to think about it, but she didn't want to invest any thought in the proceedings. That would look like she was keen, which she most certainly wasn't.

'Oh, anywhere will be fine. There's a pub at the end of the road.'

'I think we can do better than that. Trader Vic's sound good?'

The famous bar at the Hilton Hotel in the centre of London was a more exciting choice than Sal had anticipated from Stuart. She had never been there but she knew its reputation: it was an impersonal rendezvous, convenient, and particularly appealing to transient Middle Easterners who would abandon their abstinence from alcohol in favour of a substantial supply of bourbon and the company of compliant women towards the latter end of the evening. It would certainly be more interesting than the Builder's Arms.

The car travelled quickly through the empty Sunday streets, and Stuart chatted away. 'I'm not normally in London at this time. I'm usually with Jenny and the kids in Walberswick. They spend August there with her mum and I generally jump on the last train on Saturday. But I've got an early meeting tomorrow so it didn't seem worth it. Anyway, it means I get to do something like this.'

'Doesn't Jenny mind being stuck out there without you?' Sal couldn't think of anything worse than a bucket and spade holiday with children and her mother.

'She's happy as Larry.' Stuart shrugged, as if it were nothing to do with him. 'Bloody hot, isn't it? I went to see *Heat and Dust* this afternoon, just to be somewhere cool. It might have been better to see *Ice Station Zebra*. That Greta Scacchi, she's gorgeous. Come to think of it, she looks a bit like you.'

'Oh, thanks. That's very flattering, but you must be blind – she's blonde, for a start.'

'No.' Stuart turned to look at her, smiling. 'There's something about the mouth.'

Sal lit a cigarette, winding down the car window to throw out the dead match, and to allow her to turn her face away from him. She supposed he was on autopilot – he probably flirted with all the young female journalists.

By ten o'clock there was a pile of coloured paper cocktail umbrellas on the round table. Sal had surprised herself by her interest in Stuart's conversation. In his late thirties, he was a passionate newspaperman, concerned about the direction his industry was taking, the likely confrontation with the unions.

'It's all changing now. It's going to be a bloodbath. With Murdoch in the frame – you don't know what he's capable of. I've not got much time for the NUJ, but you know us scribblers are thought of as dispensable if we don't fight our own front. Now it's the printers who are manning the front line.'

Like many journalists, he was enthralled by the sound of his own anecdotes, and as the evening went on told them with practised, theatrical gusto, accessorized with endless Silk Cuts. Sal's initial lack of enthusiasm for her date had been replaced by something approaching admiration, and she was flattered to be thought of as a worthy recipient of his indiscreet gossip about what went on in the office.

The bar's famous Mai Tais, which had kicked off the evening, had been replaced by Tequila Sunrises for her and weighty glasses of bourbon on the rocks for him. He asked about her family as she stirred in the grenadine, turning the orange drink crimson.

'I've got a brother, Jonathan. He's ten years older. My mum and dad are ancient and I think I was a bit of an accident,' Sal replied. 'I love them, but I don't see them that much now. I should go home more often, I know. Dad teaches, and my mum does research. They're not that pleased that I've gone into journalism. They would have preferred me to be like my brother. He's a solicitor. At least they got one of us where they wanted.'

'Ah, well, there's a lot that have that opinion of journalism, you'll discover. We of the fourth estate have our detractors.'

'I suppose so.' Sal was flattered again at being included in the journalistic tribe. 'Well, at home, they only take the *Observer* on weekends, though Mum will buy the *Herald* if I've told her I've got something in.' She paused momentarily. 'Not that I do that often – tell her, I mean.'

Checking his watch, Stuart asked for the bill and paid with a £50 note from a folded pile of banknotes. 'Collected my expenses yesterday,' he explained as he picked up the receipt and stuffed the notes back into his wallet. 'Let's have a breather.'

Outside the air-conditioned cocoon of the hotel, the city enveloped them. Sal felt a rush as the alcohol which had lain dormant in her system kicked in, triggered by the heat and the sounds of the city. It was much too early to go home, what with Monday being a day off, so Sunday night, well, that was their Saturday, really. Stuart was OK. And he was obviously enjoying being with her, even if he was old. Too old to want anything more. Anyway, he'd been married for years. She was enjoying the chat, and surely it was a good idea to hang out with one of your bosses?

'Let's walk to the Serpentine – the park is still open.' Sal clung on to Stuart's arm as they laughingly dodged the lanes of traffic outside the hotel. Horns honked as they ran. Breathless, they entered the park, where the sounds of the traffic soon faded. The lampposts were lit at intervals, picking out the odd passing couple – shadowy, indistinct figures. In front, a small woman in a fur coat, despite the heat, walked slowly, holding on to a chihuahua by its lead. The grass was scorched by the sun and the broad paths were vivid white scars, even in the dimness. Stuart's jacket was now slung over his shoulder, his arm bumping against hers as they headed towards the still lake. Sal's trilling laugh punctuated their conversation; her body was next to his, relaxed into familiarity. At a boathouse, they paused.

'It's a bit different from the beach in Suffolk, isn't it?' Sal said, gabbling. 'Now, let's think. What would you be doing now? A nice bit of telly? No, you'd probably be all tucked up in bed.'

Her voice, since she had entered the park, had taken on an increasingly raucous tinge, words slurred over several syllables. She smiled at Stuart, her eyes catlike as he stood in front of her. The path was empty and the only sound the slap of water against the boathouse.

'Would I now? And what would that be like?' he questioned, his vowels overlaid with the sickly husk of desire, and turned to her, firmly grasping her bare arms. He pulled her up towards him and bent his face down to hers. As his mouth landed sloppily on her lips, one hand moved behind to grab her bottom, pulling up the thin dress, clamping her to him, his belt buckle cutting into her hips. His tongue slid into her, large and unwelcome. Sal felt a rush of nausea . . . the smell of the bourbon, the cocktails, the ghastly proximity of the man. Her unresponsive mouth didn't seem to deter him. Instead, her lack of movement appeared to encourage him to let go of her arm and move on to her breasts. She pulled away, thinking she might be sick.

'God. No. I didn't mean this,' she muttered, looking down at her feet.

'Yes, you did, my lovely lass.' He lunged at her again, his large hand pressing her chin upwards to receive another kiss. She could see the slack skin around his throat, lizard-like. The water splashed against the tethered boats, but there was no other movement. His hand was stroking the inside of her thigh and moving up. In a fury, she freed herself and kicked him, again and again, wildly. His hand lashed out at her face, his ring clipping the ridge of her cheekbone.

'Salome, huh? What kind of a scalp hunter are you? Cock-teaser more like.' His voice had changed, the momentum of desire now replaced with that of humiliation. Sal looked briefly at his disappointed face, the slump in his gait, and she ran, too tired, too embarrassed, too confused to try to make things all right. She could hear his shouts, but she didn't look back or halt, heading for the lights of the bridge over the Serpentine where the cars sliced through the park. She couldn't think about what had happened. She focused on moving away from Stuart, the park, the mess of the evening. Seeing the welcome yellow light of a free taxi, she raised her arm to hail it and slumped into its dark cabin as the streets slid by.

Annie's drive back to Cranbourne Terrace had been unpleasantly long – slowed by the interminable stream of cars returning from the weekend exodus. As the traffic halted outside Richmond she looked across into the next lane, where a couple sat in an open-topped MG, snatching kisses as the jam stopped and started. Had Jackson called? After all, she'd been away since Friday. But then he couldn't call, *obviously*, as she hadn't given him her home number. Although, come to think of it, he could have got it from Tania. Maybe. Honestly, telephones could be hell. If only they had one of those answering services. Maybe Sal had been there? She hoped she was in when she got back so she could find out. If you ask someone to dinner like that, send them an amazing present, how long would you wait to call? Maybe he'd changed his mind.

Annie knew the flat was empty as soon as she walked in the front door. She dumped her bags in her bedroom and ran a bath to rid herself of the fumes and stickiness of the drive. In the bath, with her hair piled up, she squeezed water from the natural sponge Sal had brought back from Corfu. The door to the tiny bathroom was open to let in light from the hallway and avoid the necessity of using the light cord attached to the ugly rumble of an extractor fan. She couldn't be bothered to light the stub of a candle on the narrow bath surround and watched Flick pad in, clawing the floral embroidery of the silk dressing gown lying on the floor.

'Poor old thing. Have you been lonely? Bet she forgot to feed you.'

The countryside had been a relief from the dusty heat of town. Her mother had cheerfully taken care of the huge bag of laundry she had deposited on the kitchen table and plied her with delicious salads.

'I hope you're eating properly, Annie. Not just Pot Noodles. I'm sending you back with supplies – though I don't suppose Joanna has a freezer in that flat.' Letty was obviously enjoying slipping on the mantle of motherhood.

'You look very cheerful,' Letty remarked, unwilling to risk a more direct probe as they had supper in the garden, assuming Annie had met a man. Letty Brenham firmly believed that a suitable marriage was the wisest course of action for her two daughters. Annie and Beth knew that it was their father who had always intended that his girls go to university; he would have insisted on it had he lived. Left to their mum, things would have been different. She made it clear that she didn't really see the point.

'It's not as if you two are going to be doctors or scientists or anything like that' was her position, 'in which case, why not do something more useful? I've always regretted I never got a foreign language.' She made it sound as if you could buy one, like a new handbag. 'Why not go to live in Paris for a year? Or I gather there's a very respectable art course in Florence. You'll make some nice friends. Get a bit of culture, and then there are all kinds of places where you could get a job.'

One day during university holidays Annie had heard her mother standing in the hall talking on the phone to a friend as she fiddled with a flower arrangement:

'Thank God she doesn't want to be one of those banker types, not like Freddie and Julia's youngest, who's gone on this milk train – or is it the gravy train? Anyway, something like that, where the banks pick out their favourites . . . Mmm. Yes, terrible hours they have to work.' Annie knew that implicit in Letty's critique of banking as a career was her belief that you couldn't expect a man to want a banker for a wife. He'd surely prefer a girl who worked in something more feminine. Annie didn't want to be a banker, or have 'a career' anyway. It was a different kind of a life she was after, but that didn't mean Letty was right.

The front door of the flat banged and Flick bolted out of the bathroom, where she had been investigating the toilet bowl. 'Sal?' called Annie, hauling herself out of the water and wrapping herself in a towel. She walked into the hall, where Sal stood, pale and tearful, with what looked like a nasty bruise under her eye. Her thin white dress was crumpled and she was bereft of her usual bounce. 'What's happened?'

Annie let her towel fall to put an arm round the shaking frame of her friend and guide her to the sofa, where she stood beside her, naked. 'Let me put something on,' she said.

'It's OK. I'm OK. Just thick,' said Sal, fumbling in her bag for a cigarette.

'I think I'd better have one too,' said Annie, now wrapped in her gown. 'So tell me. What's happened?'

Sal recounted her evening; the boredom of the quiet day, her excitement at being taken somewhere glamorous.

'I just thought it would be fun to go for a walk. Stuart and I seemed to be having a great time. I guess I should have known right from the start. I mean, what was he doing round here anyway? I suppose I could have got away from him less violently. But Annie, I was frightened. I promise you, he was holding me so tight. It could have been rape. What a wanker.'

Annie knew that attack was always Sal's chosen form of defence. Tempered negotiation had no part in her make-up. It never had been, whether she was dealing with people or with inanimate objects. Another person would no doubt have been able to extricate themselves in a less combative manner. But then another person might not have found themselves walking drunk through Hyde Park with a married boss late at night. Sal's usual bravura had disappeared, and tears had begun to streak her face, her nose now red with crying. 'I don't know why they do it. I mean, can't they tell we're not interested. I'm so pleased you're here.' She paced around, walking over to where Annie sat. 'I just feel terrible. How could I be so *stupid*? And what am I going to do about work? I don't want anyone to know.'

Annie gave her a hug, wrapping her small bony frame. Sal could smell her friend's bath essence. 'You'll be OK. You know what? I don't think he's going to want anyone to know about this either. He was just drunk. Keep your head down. It'll pass.'

'But only the other day Doug was telling me about how it's always the girls who get fired. This kind of thing happens all the time,' Sal wailed.

'You won't get fired. Trust me. Come on. Let me tuck you up. Make you a cup of tea.'

Annie spoke from a position of total ignorance but, if she or Sal were to get any sleep tonight, Sal had to feel secure about her job. Sal Turner, *Sunday Herald*. That was who she was. It was not, she decided, the right time to ask Sal if Jackson had called. Nor even to mention that she'd met him. She would have to wait till the morning, when Sal would hopefully be feeling better. Annie's good news would not gain the response she felt it deserved from her friend in her current state of mind. She wanted to present it in all its glory, uncontaminated by one of Sal's messes. Even if she learnt that Jackson *had* called, she wouldn't be able to bask in the knowledge when she was having to deal with Sal's misfortune.

As Annie surveyed her options, she could hear her mother's voice, with its faintly nasal cadence, as if the surface had been ever so slightly scratched: 'Darling, I always think that *blue*'s your colour. I regard myself as a pink person, but you're definitely a blue girl. Pink does you no favours.'

Hanging on the open door of the built-in wardrobe was a bright-blue dress threaded with silver strands, the deep V of the neck leading to a high waist. It was Annie's lucky dress. She had found it on a crowded rail in a Christian Aid shop a year ago when she had seen the silver glinting and pulled it out to discover a dress that fitted perfectly. She always felt the better for wearing it. She couldn't remember a time when it had not exerted its lucky charm, but perhaps putting herself in the hands of such superstition would be tempting fate tonight.

The untidy heap of clothes on the floor was evidence of Annie's excitement. She started to pick them up, looking anew at their possibilities. Her collection of belts and necklaces was tied to the white ironwork bedpost and on the corner of a pine dressing table stood the cache of antique perfume bottles which had travelled with her since before university. She'd started collecting them at school, loving the way that even their names invoked sophistication – Je Reviens, Mitsouko, L'Heure Attendue – luxurious with their bevelled edges and cut-glass stoppers. She sprayed her wrists and neck with Cinnabar, noticing that there were still several inches left in the oriental-looking bottle that Sal had bought her, as asked, in Duty Free.

By the time Jackson contacted Annie, she was convinced he would never call. The morning after the Stuart debacle, Sal had woken early and, quickly restored by the night's sleep and several mugs of coffee, had shared Annie's news about meeting Jackson with exactly the right amount of enthusiasm – even attempting to eat one of the over-ripe peaches that still sat in their basket on the table in front of them as she questioned Annie on the details.

'How old is he, do you think?'

'I don't know. Working it out from what Tania told me, I guess maybe thirty – something like that. Much older than us. He's amazing-looking. You'd probably say he was too good-looking.'

At university, the girls had spent many an hour debating the appearance of each other's admirers or fancies, concluding that there was something suspicious about textbook good looks, particularly after Annie had suffered an unfortunate one-night stand with a chisel-jawed boy blessed with the looks of a plastic Mattel doll.

'You know how I love men's forearms?' Annie continued, conjuring up her memory of Jackson at the studios. 'He had the best – long and tanned. I noticed them when he was unloading the car.'

Sal received this information with an amused grin. 'I thought it was the hands that counted. Did you check them out?'

'Don't be gross.' Annie got up and walked over to the telephone, lifting the receiver to hear the dial tone then replacing it in its cradle.

'It's working.' Sal tilted her chair back against the wall, tapping ash into one of Annie's large shell ashtrays. 'Otherwise, how would Stuart have rung? Jackson didn't call while I was there yesterday, Annie. He will. I promise you. He's obviously obsessed.'

It was one of Sal's winning qualities as a friend that she could be relied upon to look at any situation optimistically, always convinced that anything any of them would or could do was right. If plans were thwarted, it was always because of the actions of someone else. The fault was never theirs. Her loyalty was unquestioning.

And she was right: he did call. That morning at work, everybody was seated at their desks and the phones were permanently ringing. There was a bit of a crisis on, Lee informed Annie as soon as she got

sounding daft. 'Lovely . . . thanks,' she managed to get out. Annie replaced the receiver, glad that everybody else was too busy to have overheard her conversation. She went about the rest of the day hugging every word of the short call to herself.

Now the evening had arrived and the pleasure of anticipation was cut with nerves. She pulled a scoop-neck purple top out from the chaos of the bed and tried it on with a straight white skirt cinched in with a brown leather belt. It emphasized her figure, which managed to be simultaneously curvaceous and slim. Her pale long face was in contrast to the pneumatic quality of her body, her narrow back emphasizing her round breasts, a small waist broadening out to hips carried high on rounded legs. She was pretty, she knew, and could enter a room certain in the knowledge that she would be noticed, but her prettiness was not accompanied by confidence. Almost the reverse: it was as if she felt the decorative carapace of her looks disguised something lacking deeper.

Viewing the outfit in the long mirror inside the wardrobe door, she could see it looked acceptable, but she felt uncomfortable about the way it fitted. The skirt maybe, or was it the way the belt drew the eye to her curves? It was getting late. Quickly undressing again, she pulled the blue dress from the hanger, reaching behind her for the zip so that the fabric pulled tight across the bodice that flowed out from the high waist. She took a string of jade-coloured beads from where they dangled on the bedpost and clasped it around her throat, the beads hanging down to the start of the shadowy cleft of her bosom.

Annie saw Jackson standing by the famous curved bar as soon as she entered the deep room with its seductively dim lighting and noisy chatter above soft music. Halfway down its length there was his dark head, bent towards a girl with a spiky blonde crop who Annie remembered from the shoot, his red shirt standing out and clearly indicating his arm around her shoulder.

She pushed her way through the room, suddenly wishing that she were anywhere else but there. As she approached, Jackson looked up, his warm smile defusing her nerves.

'What a great dress. Meet Patsy. She's my everything on the shoots.' And in one proficient manoeuvre he disengaged his arm from Patsy and kissed Annie in greeting. He pulled out a tall bar stool, helping her on to it. 'Frank, let's get some champagne for me and my friend,' he commanded one of the bartenders.

There seemed, to Annie, to be mirrors everywhere. She couldn't help seeing the reflection of herself and Jackson in front of her, and reflected again from behind, the effect intensifying the already crowded space. After a few glasses, they moved away from the bar, to a banquette on the other side of the narrow room. Jackson suggested they order some food and, although Annie was really far too excited to eat, she was aware that after several glasses of champagne she should get something inside her. She didn't want to do a Sal.

Their conversation was endlessly interrupted by Jackson's waves to passing friends, their table constantly being greeted by the social traffic.

'Mungo, my man. Congrats on the Brillo account. Snatched, I hear, at the eleventh hour from under the nose of BBH.' Jackson gave a stout, bearded man a squeeze on the elbow. 'Good job too. John Hegarty's getting far too big a slice of the action.' Mungo wedged himself on to the edge of the banquette, pouring a generous slug of Jackson's champagne into his wine glass.

'*Vorsprung durch Technik*,' he said, giving a mocking military salute in reference to BBH's Audi campaign.

'This is Annie. She's one of Tania's team.' Annie felt Jackson moving closer to her.

'Aha. Tania. Do you remember her covered in gold paint at that party at Morton's. She was a real goddess then,' Mungo recalled, smiling amiably at Annie, who was surprised to feel, at that moment, the touch of Jackson's left hand on her leg, while his right refuelled her glass. She wondered whether Mungo would notice.

The juxtaposition of the intensity of Jackson's attention on her and the obvious entitlement he felt to being a central figure in this world gave Annie an immediate sense of inclusion. Jackson was adept at making her feel as if she had a rightful place there, rather than being the neophyte she was. As the hours passed, her nervousness was replaced by ease. The bar which had appeared so threatening when she first arrived had become a luxurious cocoon.

'Tania, good to see you. Thank you for sending me this gorgeous Annie,' said Jackson. Annie looked up to see Tania in a huge white ruffled shirt and flowing trousers.

'Not at all, Jacko. Not at all. Just part of the service. I'm meeting Chris for a nightcap.'

'Chris, now where's he been? I haven't seen him in ages. Good guy. Is he still with whatshername, Calliope? Nope, that's not right. Names aren't my thing . . .'

Tania exerted unusual restraint in resisting pointing out that girls' names weren't Jackson's thing because so many of them passed his way, but she was fond of Annie. Let her enjoy tonight; it probably wouldn't go further than his mattress. Gosh, she looked a real beauty sitting there. Luminous even in the low light, her only make-up, maybe mascara? It had been years since she'd been able to get away with that. She wouldn't walk out for a pint of milk without her slap nowadays.

'See you tomorrow, Annie.' Annie watched Tania sway back down the bar, a white tanker parting the waves of drinkers.

Zanzibar was becoming yet more crowded when at midnight Jackson suggested that it was time to move, rising from the table as he spoke. Although it was September, the night was still warm enough for them to be coatless and, as they walked down the street, Jackson's arm was around Annie's waist, the fabric of the blue dress sliding under his hand. The kiss, when it happened, was impeccable.

'You are so beautiful, my lovely Annie,' Jackson whispered, his hand caressing the nape of her neck as he unlocked his car.

They drove along the London roads. Looking down at herself, she saw stripes reflected from streetlights moving along her flesh with their shadows. She was aware that they were heading towards Regent's Park rather than in the direction that would take her home to Cranbourne Terrace. At each red traffic light Jackson kissed her again, seamlessly combining gear shifts with caresses. As she returned his kisses, there was a part of her watching, in thrall to what was happening to her.

They drew up at a large red-brick building and Jackson led her up the steps to the front door and then inside his ground-floor flat. An enormous dog bounded up against her.

'Buster, she's mine – out you go. Catch you later.' Jackson opened the double doors at one end of the large room they had entered, pushing a recalcitrant Golden Retriever through them. Annie could see the shape of trees in the garden. She walked towards them, horribly unsure how to behave. The confidence that had grown throughout the past hours had evaporated in an instant. She could feel the magic of the evening seeping away as unwelcome self-consciousness took hold. What on earth was she doing there? Was this going to be a one-night stand? But as Jackson turned to her, sweetly kissing her face, then her neck, then her eyelids, as he lifted her dress off and bent to kiss the side of her hips, moving back to just look at her in obvious admiration and then returning to her lips, her worries faded. He took her hand to lead her to the bedroom, laying her on the large bed as if she were the most precious object, never taking his eyes off her.

4

Marisa Rootstein was adjusting the display of books on the enormous glass coffee table that sat before the fireplace in her drawing room. Kendra watched her mother place the thick catalogue raisonné of Andy Warhol's silk screens on top of the slim pamphlet from the Francesco Clemente show at the Mary Boone Gallery. Then, deciding against it, she left the Clemente catalogue visible and positioned alongside it instead Salman Rushdie's just published *Shame*. The Rootsteins' coffee table was a carefully edited display of contemporary culture, and its obvious artifice and ostentation made Kendra want to vomit.

The huge room, with its elaborate cornicing and tall windows looking out on to several acres of communal garden, was rarely used by day, functioning mostly at night, when the Rootsteins would regularly fill it with crowds of what Art liked to call 'folk', a term which deliberately downplayed the professional and social networking their soirées were renowned for.

It was in preparation for one of these regular Thursday-night open houses that Marisa was styling the table. The word 'open' was misleading. Naturally, these gatherings were not remotely open, but Marisa and Art preferred the casual notion that *folk* would *swing by*, ideally accompanied by suitably interesting new blood. They aimed to achieve a sense of spontaneity for these carefully orchestrated evenings. A successful Thursday night would find a group of artists, writers and socialites, with a spattering of celebrities who were in town from New York, Los Angeles, Paris, Rome, drinking Art's favourite white, Gavi di Gavi.

'Darling, I know that it's your life's ambition to cause your father and I maximum anxiety but, surely, this idea of yours, of being a kind of *childminder* in a poor kids unit, is taking self-destruction just a step too far.' Marisa continued to tinker with the placement of the things on the table as she spoke, avoiding eye contact with her daughter. She adjusted the arrangement of white hydrangea.

For several weeks, Kendra had avoided telling her parents that she had taken on the job at the Chapel. Their house was large enough, and the Rootsteins immersed enough in the whole business of being the Rootsteins, for the fact that Kendra was working to have escaped them. The hours Gioia needed her were irregular, and the family structure loose enough, for Kendra's absence during the day not to be noticed.

However, that morning, Marisa and Kendra had coincided in the kitchen, a rare occurrence, since Marisa's early mornings were usually spent in the company of Stephen, her analyst on Fitzjames Avenue, immediately and unrelentingly followed by a Pilates session. The combination, Marisa maintained, set her up perfectly for the trials of the day ahead. 'An early start,' Kendra heard her say, frequently, 'is crucial if you want to get things done.'

'We must find you some better clothes, Kendra. You haven't been a student for over a year now, and those old T-shirts look terrible. You've got great legs but, God knows, you do your best to disguise them. There's a Jasper Conran private sale next week where we could find you some nice pieces. His grosgrain jackets would look terrific on you. The cut would suit.' Two decades of her daughter's rejection of Marisa's offers of stylish clothing had not deterred her from continuing to try to wean Kendra from her chosen look, which, in its hippie drabness, never failed to frustrate her mother.

'Thanks, Mum, but I don't think I'll have much use for them at the Chapel. You know those kind of clothes aren't really my thing.' Kendra waited for her words to impact, visualizing them like weapons lobbed from a PacMan game.

'The Chapel? *Qu'est-ce que c'est*, the Chapel?'

'It's where I'm working now. I joined a few weeks back, helping underprivileged kids. It's run by a really inspiring woman called Gioia Cavallieri. It's a proper job, Mum.'

Marisa drained her canarino, leaving the twist of lemon peel in the china cup, and moved towards the door.

'I'm running late, and have no time for this. I have to do Laila's list for tonight. The Schnabels are in town.' Kendra could see her mother's shoulders, prominent from the back in her slim-fitting black cashmere sweater, tighten with restraint and the effort of not engaging in an argument with her completely incomprehensible daughter.

During the school week, the Chapel still had a few of the regular kids hanging around. Although they were meant to be in class, Gioia took the view that if they were going to play truant it was better they were with her than causing mischief on the streets. She would talk the talk, try to get them back to their desks, but she considered that task number one was to provide a refuge rather than add to the rejection colouring most of their lives. Andy, a lanky, near-albino teenager, was shooting a ball into a hoop on the wall, the endless drumming of the bounce almost soothing in its repetition. At the far end of the room, a large table was backed up by a range of metal filing cabinets.

'Gioia, what time is the concert starting?' Kendra haltingly typed words into the battered Olympus typewriter. 'Christ, it's impossible to get the "r"s into alignment; they keep jumping.'

'Just get the words down – don't fuss about how it looks,' Gioia replied from where she was kneeling on the floor, the filing cabinets rattling as she opened them.

The Chapel was regularly hired for performances by local musicians, mime artists, performance poets. But Kendra was typing a flyer for an evening that Gioia was organizing in a few weeks' time. She had lined up a Rastafarian band, a bongo drum trio and a guitarist friend of hers on the up. There was talk that Billy Bragg might do a number.

'Don't ask, won't get,' Gioia had informed her. 'You know, I came down here from home and didn't know anyone, anything. But I have a voice. I use it.'

It occurred to Kendra that her mother would like some of the performers, which was an unwelcome thought, allowing Marisa, who she wanted to keep as far away from her new job as possible, to infiltrate. She couldn't bear the idea of her turning up here. Given half a chance, she'd get the bongo trio to come round one Thursday night. But, as for Sal and Annie, she wanted them to be there, even though she was apprehensive about the judgements they and Gioia might make of each other. The knowledge of how disloyal it was even to imagine such thoughts made her stop typing. She wondered vaguely why she cared so much what Gioia thought anyway.

She watched as the older woman went over to talk to Andy. In the few weeks that she had been working alongside her, Kendra felt different. Maybe this was what people meant when they said they were fulfilled.

'No, you *don't* – no, you don't *ever* – do you hear me, Andy? – speak to me like that.' Gioia's tone was loud but measured. Andy sprinted to the door, slamming it behind him as his critic watched, shaking her head, the heavy coils waving. 'He'll be back, poor kid. He's not got anywhere much to go. His dad knocks around Camden in the pubs and his mum's got a smack habit.' She walked over to Kendra and smiled. 'Hey, girl, let's get out for a bit.' She put her arm around Kendra's shoulders for a moment and then quickly walked on, out to the street.

'Coffee?'

Annie opened her eyes to see Jackson standing by the bed with a mug in his hand, a towel around his waist. He knelt beside her and kissed her lightly on the lips. 'Good morning, my beauty.'

'What time is it?' As Annie woke, she felt the judder of a nearly sleepless night and the seep of a hangover. Jackson pulled back the sheet to look at her, stroking her breasts and stomach.

'Shame,' he said with regret; 'but I'm due on set in half an hour. It's eight. I'm going to take a shower. Stay as long as you want.'

'No, I must go too.' Annie pulled herself and the sheet up. She knew it was ridiculous, but she didn't want to stand naked before him.

'Sweetheart, I've spent all night looking at your wonderful body – come in the shower with me.' Annie felt the unfamiliar thump of a powerful jet of water cover her, drenching her hair, streaming down her face. At Cranbourne Terrace she and Sal had to squeeze a pink rubber hose over the taps to wash their hair and, invariably, the water spurted everywhere. Jackson vigorously rubbed soap into the palm of his hands, covering both himself and her in the lather. She could taste the night and wanted to keep it with her for as long as possible. As Jackson briskly soaped her body, she worried that he was washing the previous hours away. He was charming, affectionate, but she could tell he was moving on from their lovemaking to the day ahead.

She was going to be late for work, but she could hardly go to the office in the same dress Tania had seen her in last night. It would be like announcing that she'd slept with Jackson over a Tannoy. When she arrived back at the flat, Sal had already left for the day. The kitchen table showed evidence of her breakfast – two cigarettes and the dregs of a mug of Nescafé. A plastic clothes dryer was in the middle of the sitting room, with white cotton knickers and a tangle of tights draped over it, a dark mark on the matting where they dripped as they dried. Sal was infuriating. Why hadn't she put the wretched thing over the bath?

Tearing her blue dress off, she contemplated herself in the mirror wearing just the bra and pants she had worn the night before. Did she look different? She felt like she had after the first time she had had sex, when she had been convinced that her body would surely show, in some way, that she had changed. She held her breasts, reliving the way Jackson had traced lines around her nipples. 'I'll call you later,' he had said as he kissed her goodbye. What *exactly* did he mean by 'later'? When was later?

Sal watched the wet streets on her bus ride home. In the morning, if she left late enough, the bus might be empty and she would be able to grab her favourite spot on the top deck at the front, but that also meant she was late for work. Not that it mattered much during the early part of the week. From Thursday onwards, though, lateness was out of the question. Once morning conference was over, it was as if somebody had pressed a button, and the desks became tightly controlled operating units in search of stories.

Marsha was always there before her, scouring the other newspapers, coffee mug in hand, her precise blonde bob swinging heavily when she moved. Sal had been at the *Herald* for over two months, yet Marsha and she had still not had a conversation, despite their being of a similar age. Sal had made attempts, but her conversational starts had been met by a cool stare and only the briefest of words in return, and, sometimes, not even that. At every opportunity, Marsha would remind anyone within hearing of her training at a local newspaper, thereby, Sal felt, emphasizing her own lack of this experience.

The men were more welcoming to her than the other women, which made it hard to figure out where she fitted in. While the men operated as a bantering collective, the women seemed more insular, less integrated. The female journalists, sober in dress and general appearance, were more intent, more focused, their need to prove themselves often obvious and strained. At the end of the day they would grab their handbags and move quickly to the stairs, lugging home a supermarket bag of food, packs of ready-made meals poking out of the top. In contrast, most of the men appeared to have conspicuous amounts of time for chat and camaraderie, both inside and outside the office. Certainly, their family life, if they had one, was well disguised. When a group departed for some local watering hole at the end of the day, it would more often than not be predominately male. Sal thought she would rather be one of the guys. They looked like they were having more fun.

The wet weather had been persistent all afternoon, raindrops chasing each other down the window of the bus. In a brief telephone call earlier, she had realized that Annie was besotted by her new admirer, although their shared offices didn't encourage a long private conversation. Sal wanted *details*.

She knew that Annie had set her long-term sights on what they called 'the marriage option' and exhibited none of Sal's professional ambition or desire for independence from her background. Instead, she had always made it clear that, unless she was with a man, she felt in some way diminished, less than half of herself.

'It's just the way I am, you know. I feel better when I'm with somebody. Everything's easier.' Her conspicuous beauty made it easy for her to attract men, but the relationships were short-lived and often Annie would come away the loser, the one who had been left and hurt.

'You should feel more confident about yourself, you know. You don't need a boyfriend *all* the time,' Sal told her.

'You're clever, everybody loves you. You never find it hard to fit into places. Why do you have to be tied down to one bloke? There's millions of them out there,' Kendra added. Annie had stopped trying to explain to them how she felt.

They had agreed on a supper of spaghetti with tomato sauce. Annie liked to make the sauce properly: she fried garlic in olive oil and added tomatoes and what, she informed Sal, was the all-important dash of sugar. So, although Sal would have happily made do with sloshing on something out of a bottle, she stopped off at the local shop to buy the ingredients Annie had requested. She hoped that Annie had managed to get Kendra over as well.

A bottle of red wine was open on the kitchen table where Sal deposited the carrier bag, her packet of Silk Cut rolling out on to the blue-checked plastic cloth. Sal tore it open and lit up. As she turned from the hob, where water was already on the boil, Annie's face was flushed with the heat of the room.

'She can't stop grinning,' said Kendra, leaning against the sink.

'Let me get rid of this wet jacket, and then I want to hear *all* about it.' Sal shook her wet hair. 'I'm already *sick* with jealousy. *I* haven't had sex in weeks. No – you can make that *months*.' She went into the sitting room and threw her damp jacket on the sofa.

The low-ceilinged room now showed proof of Annie's tenancy. A round table by the window was covered in a faded linen cloth and the floral print of the sofa was disguised by a patchwork Indian bedspread. Joanna's framed botanical prints still hung on the walls but, on the mantelpiece above the fireplace, Annie had placed hand-tinted vintage postcards and a pair of Clarice Cliff-style pottery candlesticks, the candle wax now dried in permanent drips down their sides.

As the water boiled, Annie related most, but not quite all, of the previous evening: her terror on entering Zanzibar, the awesome cavalcade of people Jackson knew, the quantities of champagne drunk. 'And then, somehow, I don't quite know how, I was just there in his flat. It seemed like the right thing to do, but then I panicked. Sex-on-first-date nerves.'

'I think it's good to get it over and done with as soon as possible, that way you know if it's going to go anywhere. After all, if the shagging's hopeless, what's the point?' offered Sal.

'But it can be awful, can't it?' added Kendra. 'First sex. You can make a terrible mistake, and then you're stuck.'

'Well, it wasn't like that,' said Annie firmly, wishing Sal wouldn't use the word 'shag' in association with her romantic night. She drained the pasta over the sink, the steam from the water completely fogging up the window, and tossed the contents of the frying pan into it.

'Do you think you'll always be veggie, Ken?' asked Sal, twirling the spaghetti around her fork. 'It must be a shame never to eat something like spag bol, especially since it's about the only thing I can cook.'

'I don't know. Probably. I was talking to Gioia about it. She's vegetarian too. She says it was all the slicing of salami and ham at her dad's deli that did it for her. One day, she cut her finger on the slicer, it bled all over the Parma ham and the sight was *so* disgusting that she couldn't take meat after that. And she had to have a tetanus injection because she was cut by a knife that had been in contact with meat. It would have been OK if it had just been cheese.'

'Sounds like you've found your perfect boss,' Annie replied. 'Can't say I've done the same. It's a nightmare at the moment, with Tania stomping around every day in a terrible mood because her big opening is clashing with something else. Poor Lee's getting the worst of it. He's like a puppy, jumping up all the time trying to help, which is just making her worse. Anyway . . . You must both come. I can get you invitations. Ken, I saw your mum and dad's names on the guest list.'

'When is it?' Kendra asked, walking over to the sink to fill her glass with tap water.'

'October 20th – 6.30 to 8.30. I've got that tattooed on my brain. It's in a few weeks.'

'I know,' said Kendra. 'It's the night of Gioia's concert. Remember? I told you both about it. You said you'd come.'

'Can't we do both?' Sal suggested. It was unusual of Kendra to request anything of them. She was always the one who fitted in with *their* plans. 'If we can't, I'll definitely come to yours. But I bet it's possible.' As she spoke, Sal knew that, professionally, it would be a coup to be invited to the Chelsea Bridge party. She'd like the guys who worked on the diary to see that she could get to an event like that with a proper invitation, not just a name on the press list. But friends come first. If she had to miss it, she would.

'Maybe,' Kendra offered cautiously. 'I don't think we're starting till eight, and Gioia says these kinds of gigs always run late. We're still finalizing who's performing, but it's a big deal for the Chapel.' Sal was opening another bottle of wine. 'Not for me.' She gestured at the bottle. 'I'm on my bike.'

'Sleep here. You can have my duvet and the sofa. It's still early.'

'You can share with me,' offered Annie. 'There's masses of room in my bed. I'm surprised Joanna bought such a huge one. I don't think she ever has boyfriends.' It was a big stretch to imagine Joanna, almost her mother's age, having sex. 'She probably just likes to stretch out, with Flick.'

'It's a deal. The house will be packed with people I don't want to talk to, and Mum's still upset about the Chapel. She doesn't want to tell her friends what I'm doing, so she makes a big perform-ance about how "time will tell" . . . "early days yet". . . that kind of stuff, when people ask. I just don't know how to make it all right for her. I never know. You think my parents are so liberal and broad-minded but, really, they're so conventional. They probably want me settled down soon with a nice Jewish boy, but they'd never say it.' She leant for the bottle and poured a couple of inches into her glass.

'I don't think it's as bad as that,' said Annie. 'Your mum loves you, and your dad is crazy about you, but they don't really get what you're about. I don't think my mum does me either. I knew she was desperate for me to tell her about my love life last time I went home – as if I'd ever want to discuss it with *her*. I can't bear it when she stands there looking at me with her I-used-to-be-your-age smile.' Annie stopped, as if she had just thought of something. 'I'd never be able to discuss Jackson with her. The thought makes me feel ill.'

'But at least she doesn't want you to be someone you're not. She just wants to see you happy and with a nice man. And so do you, really.' Sal entered the conversation. She didn't know what she felt about her own parents. Sometimes she thought she should feel more. Occasionally, she wondered whether it could be right to be so disengaged from them. Although Cheltenham was hardly far away, she hadn't been back for months.

'You can get the last train down on Saturday night if you need, and be back early Sunday evening,' Joy would suggest, her voice always making it clear that she knew Sal would not accept the sug-gestion. Her acknowledgement that Sal would wish to be there for such a short time only increased her daughter's guilt at not wanting to be there at all. She knew her parents would not want her to visit them because she felt she ought to, but that didn't really help. Her father inhabited his self-sufficient world, sitting in his study, looking out over the small garden with books piled up high enough to cre-ate not only a psychological but physical wall between him and the world outside. But her mother would be missing her, even as she would be saying to herself that Sal should be free, that she must make her own life.

Sal could convincingly argue to herself that, with a job on a Sunday paper, it was just one of those things: she didn't have weekends, like most people – but there was another voice, one that she tried to ignore, which would counter that thought. She should go home soon. Some of the women in her office must be about her mother's age. Now she thought of it, they probably had children of their own, but they didn't ever mention them. Not to her, anyway.

5

The boardroom was more of a concept than a reality, the reality being that it was the only room large enough to contain the whole team. It was also the only room in the building kept pristine, offering the public face of Tania Torrington Public Relations, and intended to combine a knowing fashionability with an upmarket Chelsea vibe. The rest of the building was fading, the once-smart rooms littered with office detritus and paintwork that was long overdue a touch-up. The royal-blue carpet that led visitors up the stairs to the boardroom was new and plush, but if they had explored further they would see it turn into tatty old rush stuff from Habitat.

In the room, a large walnut veneered table was offset by steel armchairs with leather sling seats and two huge sofas upholstered in a shadowy animal-print brushed velvet which added a racy touch while also, due to the nap of the fabric, doing an excellent job disguising stains.

It was the morning of the Chelsea Bridge opening.

'Here you are – something to keep your blood-sugar levels up. You're going to need it.' Tania flung a couple of large boxes of the classic dark-green Bendicks Bittermints on the table. 'Now, let's run through this once more, for luck. Though luck will be having nothing to do with it. Nina and Robin, you're on the door. If somebody isn't on the guest list, they *don't get in*. I don't want to hear "They're a friend of so and so," or "They're a plus one," or any of that stuff. No name: no entry. Any problems and we've got the boys from Make You Secure to see them on their way. Annie and Lee, you're shadowing me. If I need something, *jump* to it. You have to be near enough to hear what I want without it seeming obvious that you're hovering. I don't want you buzzing like a pair of wasps.'

The list continued. Outside the room, the telephone rang continuously. 'Tania Torrington PR,' intoned Felicity, who manned the switchboard as well as reception. 'Can I put you on hoooooold' was a constant refrain.

Annie kept her head down, looking at the typed itinerary they had in front of them and trying to work out how on earth to manage the evening. She had promised Kendra that she would get to the Chapel, even if it meant arriving in the middle of the concert. But last night Jackson had called just after she'd gone to sleep. Woken by the phone's ring, she had heard Sal telling him she was asleep and had rushed out of bed to grab the receiver from her hand.

'Didn't realize it was so late,' he said. She could hear music and chatter in the background. 'Just wanted to let you know I'm going to Tania's Chelsea Bridge thing tomorrow. I thought I might run into you? We could go on after it.' She felt too sleepy to know how to tell him that she had to go to the Chapel, and she wanted him to come too. She wasn't sure that was going to be his kind of evening.

It had been over a month since their first date. She didn't feel that she could quite call Jackson her boyfriend but, even so, she had fallen in love. She knew she was in love because everything looked different – brighter, more vivid. Life was filled with possibility. The possibility of seeing Jackson.

There was a pattern to her days. She would wake in the morning, her stomach churning with excitement about his potential phone call and the thought that they might meet. By the middle of the day, she would begin to feel anxious if she hadn't heard from him. It drove Lee mad to watch, the way she'd pretend she wasn't listening out for every call to the office, the way she'd deliberately not answer her own extension for the first two rings. On the days that he didn't call, and there were many, the anticipation would finally be extinguished by early evening and there would be a lull. But a few hours later Annie would relegate the day to the past and look forward to the next when, once again, the hope of seeing Jackson would bubble up, undaunted. She had to admit, though, he was hopeless at making plans. She had taken to writing the words 'Dinner with

Jackson' in her diary after the event, because she rarely had the opportunity to place it there in advance. But she liked seeing the words written, as proof. It never occurred to her to take the initiative in making a date.

When they were together, Jackson was utter in his adoration. He would do loving things like remember a song they had heard when it cropped up again. Whenever Heaven 17's 'Temptation' was played she would look at him and see him smile at her. It had been playing when they had left the dance floor at the Embassy one night and rushed out to the alleyway behind and had sex, quickly, pressed against the brick wall, so that afterwards her back had a sore patch. He had introduced her to the habit of putting a twist of lemon rind in her white-wine kir – 'It cuts the sweetness' – and bought her a bottle of Chanel's Cristalle on the flight home after a day's shoot in Paris. He had also taught her precisely how he liked her mouth to wrap around his cock, moving up and down as he held the back of her head.

Jackson had taken her to a party at the ICA where she had struck up a conversation with a performance artist who painted himself and members of the audience with blood. He was a startling redhead, with a generous mouth and extraordinarily dark lashes and brows. As he was intensely describing to Annie his concept for the show he was performing at the start of December, Jackson had come up and put his arm around her proprietorially, joining the conversation in a desultory way for a few minutes, obviously keen to remove her.

'We're great fans of the ICA, aren't we, babe?' he had concluded. 'Count us in for the show.' He steered Annie away to a corner of the room and kissed her passionately, his hands moving through her hair, uncaring who might see. Annie was thrilled. Was he jealous? And December? That was months away. Maybe he really was serious about her.

The water in the plastic bucket kept splashing over the sides as Kendra pulled it across the floor of the Chapel. She had found a mop in the cupboard, but it was inefficient and, although Gioia had told her to give the lino a clean before the concert that night, she was finding it hard to keep the water from pooling.

Kendra had never been any good at housework. At home, Laila would arrive by eight and would keep the large house in order with her arsenal of cleaning products. Until she went to university, Kendra had rarely made her own bed. On the weekends when Laila wasn't working, the sheets would remain crumpled, the bedspread lying in a heap on the floor, where it would stay until Laila next appeared.

'Kendra – what you going to do when you get the husband? Who is going to make his bed?' Laila would fondly say, gathering up a pile of dirty clothes.

Following behind Kendra and her mopping was a phalanx of teenagers putting out plastic-seated chairs in rows, deliberately banging the legs into each other with a noisy crash.

'Gerass, I owe you,' Gioia shouted across the room at a stocky, dark-haired young man carrying the chairs in from a van outside. Gioia's younger brother Gerassimos could be relied upon to obtain almost anything that was needed. It never did to enquire the source of the alcohol, tinned foods, vans, bicycles, car radios he produced, but Gioia relied upon him – often. She calculated that the good she was doing probably outweighed the dodgy deals he was involved with and that, at the end of the day, the scales of justice balanced out evenly.

At the far end of the large hall a couple of teenagers were fixing the bulky black PA system, every few minutes letting loose a burst of noisy feedback. Despite the fact that it was a chilly October afternoon and the Chapel was heated only by ranks of Dimplex heaters, everyone was working up a sweat. Kendra was aware of Gioia's escalating tension. The evening had taken weeks of preparation and string-pulling. Despite the seemingly haphazard aura of the Chapel and Gioia's unconventional appearance, Kendra had learnt that the world she had constructed was tightly controlled. Nothing was left to chance. Her darkly leonine appearance belied an ordered intensity that never let up. Or not that Kendra had ever seen.

'Come on, you guys – we've only got a couple of hours, and we haven't even started on the bar yet.' The Chapel didn't have an alcohol permit, but Gerassimos had figured out a way that you could skirt around this inconvenience by selling drink from a temporary bar outside at the back. Due to his contacts in catering, they could make a nice profit on the bottles of Italian beer and plastic glasses of cheap Italian wine. He had a friend who gave him a good deal on Frascati.

As Kendra placed the bright-yellow paper programme she had photocopied on each chair, she was surprised by how apprehensive she felt about the evening. She knew it was important for Gioia.

'This whole place is like a house of cards,' her boss had explained. 'You build one thing on the next and, if you fuck it up, the whole thing comes tumbling down. The reason I've got these guys performing tonight is because Chrissie Hynde did a number here last year. Bless. Long story. But it meant that word went out this was an OK gig for them. That's how I got Ricky tonight.' Ricky was on the verge of signing a deal with Island Records – they'd loved his demo tape. He'd been at school with Gioia in Glasgow, she said, and it had been ten years, but now she was calling in an old favour.

Kendra leant on the mop and looked at the hall. The part usually taken up by the office area had been transformed into a makeshift backstage area, the part where the kids would play volleyball turned into the auditorium, and a clumsy, irregular lighting rig established to override the fluorescent strips that normally lit the room with their ugly glow. For a moment, she saw it through the eyes of Annie and Sal. She had thought she wanted them there, to be a part of this new world of hers, but now she was not so sure.

As the eastern docks of London were colonized by the new corporate city being built, their old warehouses and inlets replaced with architecturally unremarkable office blocks and wine bars, the western end of the Thames remained comparatively unchanged. Large houseboats with their ramshackle decks and bohemian aura remained moored just off the King's Road, and the storage spaces of Lots Road had kept their original facades even if, inside, they were filled with fabric wholesalers and television production companies.

It was a major achievement, as the Tania Torrington PR press release stressed, for Chelsea Bridge to be the first restaurant in this part of central London with a waterside terrace: *'With this unique location, Chelsea Bridge is the perfect place to unwind with an after-work cocktail as you sit on the terrace looking out westwards towards the sunset. Alternatively, it is the ideal dining venue as you feast on Martin Black's inspired new eating concept. This sensational bar and restaurant is destined to become a leading London landmark.'*

By seven o'clock, the cavernous room had begun to fill. The terrace was illuminated, but unfortunately it was too cold at this time of year to do justice to the Lloyd Loom furniture the restaurant's designer had considered would lend a raffish colonial air to the space, in neat contrast to the harder edged main room. There, exposed steel girders had been installed in the roof and giant industrial metal lampshades hung from them, swinging their pools of light on to wooden tables. Precarious steel stools lined the leather bar, which was decorated by perforations, as if somebody had taken a hole-punch at random to it.

'Don't ask, just do,' Tania hissed at Lee, who scurried off to provide whiskey for one of the town's leading restaurant reviewers, despite Tania having announced earlier that there was to be *absolutely no* ordering off menu. What they saw was what they were getting – champagne cocktails, Slow Comfortable Screws and Gin Slings – or Perrier. The owners had talked about bringing in another brand of bottled water but Tania had told them that *nobody* would offer anything other than Perrier nowadays if they wanted to be taken seriously. That was, after all, the point of hiring her. She knew what was what. It was those little extras that made all the difference.

Sal pushed into the crowded room, flanked by Ollie and Robert from the *Herald*'s diary pages. Among the expensive tailored jackets of the social crowd and the jazzy ties of the restaurant fraternity, the boys' cheap grey suits and pasty faces made them stand out as hacks. It was a mark of respect among journalists not to care how you dressed, the insignificance of appearance a badge of honour.

'Let's get something to drink.' Sal headed to the bar at the far side of the room, where she leapt on to a vacant stool and grabbed a cocktail. She drank most of it in one gulp. Ollie and Robert positioned themselves either side of her, leaning on the bar as they would in a pub, looking out at the crowd.

'So, who's here?' Ollie took a deep drag on his cigarette.

'They said Jennifer Beals was tipping up. She's over here for *Flash-dance*,' Robert replied, narrowing his eyes to scour the room for the sight of a recognizable face that might offer them a paragraph for the page. 'Let's have a couple of drinks then head over to Kremlin. It's just down the road. They've got Bryan Ferry coming by. Fitz called himself to tell me.'

Sal was watching Annie, now standing near the front door, some feet behind Tania, like a lady-in-waiting. She wasn't carrying Tania's handbag, was she? Her friend looked different, dressed in a pair of high-waisted black trousers and a white shirt with a lace collar, her hair scraped back in a ponytail which emphasized her straight nose and full lips. She looked much more professional than usual. Maybe it was the trousers. Sal knew Annie didn't like to wear black, but it had been Tania's orders that black and white should be the uniform of the night, in keeping with the industrial feel of the building. Tania's long black Yohji Yamamoto coat had cost her a small fortune, but she had learnt it was well worth shelling out to look the part and, for an evening like this, that meant either Yohji or Comme.

The room was so full it seemed impossible that any more people could fit into it. Along the walls, single figures stood, some nursing a glass and staring with interest at the crowd, others disguising their solitary state by reading a menu or jotting something in a notebook. They clung to the sides of the room, unwilling to leave the protection of the exposed brickwork and fling themselves into the centre, the jungle of the real party.

There, Jackson sat at a table with three girls. From the bar, Sal could see him engrossed in their company, his hands drawing pictures to accompany an anecdote, the girls smiling and involved. She thought they looked foreign – Italian, Spanish, something like that – with their thick dark hair and tanned faces. Sal could also see Annie watching the scene unhappily and then being summoned by Tania, who deftly passed on a very thin blonde woman and man in a jacket with huge shoulders – was it Simon Le Bon? – for Annie to escort.

One of Tania's strengths was her address book, which spanned film and music, minor royalty and socialites. She could beat Fitz on home numbers any day. Although there was no demarcated VIP area, the back right-hand corner of the restaurant had been designated an inner sanctum and, under Tania's experienced handling, the more celebrated of the guests were ushered in that direction, where they would find other well-known faces and be sheltered from the general mass.

Rob had just seen Trevor Eve make his way there and was about to leave the security of the bar in an attempt to crash the privileged nexus. 'Do you think your friend Annie could give me an intro to Trev over there?' he asked Sal.

'Don't know. I'll ask her.' Sal was pleased to have an excuse to interrupt Annie and walked over to where her friend had deposited her last consignment of celebrity.

'You look great. Is it hell?'

'It's a bit full-on right now,' Annie replied.

'What time do you think you can get away?'

'God knows. Not before 8.30. But Jackson's here, and he wants me to do something with him afterwards.'

'Well, you've got to go to the Chapel with me.' Sal's voice clearly indicated there was to be no discussion. 'Jackson can come with you. Come on. You're always doing what he wants. We owe it to Kendra.'

'Yes . . . I know . . . But it's difficult . . . look at those girls he's

with.' Sal started to walk quickly over to Jackson's table. 'Sal. Don't'
– but Annie's words were lost, and she knew that, even if Sal had
heard, she would most likely have continued undaunted. Jackson
looked up as she approached. In their brief acquaintance, Sal had
already decided that he was far too pleased with himself and, personally, she didn't get his looks. The way he swaggered into a room
as if he owned the place drove her nuts. And she wasn't wild about
the way he always called Annie at the last minute either. But she
knew it was pointless to make her feelings known. It wouldn't make
any difference.

'Sal. Good to see you.' Jackson stood up and kissed her hello.
'Cruz, Gaby, Simone – meet Sal.' There was something about their
languor and ease that made her feel gauche.

'I just thought I'd tell you, because Annie's so tied up here now,
that we're all going together, at about 8.30.' She spoke quickly.

'All going where?'

'You know, to Kendra's gig.'

'News to me.' Jackson smiled at the girls around him.

'Well, it's not news to Annie, and it's important to her. She must
have forgotten to tell you, and she's sort of busy so I thought I'd
organize it.' Sal was determined not to let him off the hook, and to
make it clear to Cruz (stupid name) and whoever the others were,
sitting there with their silver jewellery and eye make-up, that Jackson was already spoken for.

Annie could witness the conversation and was close enough to
see that Jackson was annoyed. He was scratching his head the way
he did when he was irritated by something. She would have to go
over.

'Hi.' She smiled brightly at the group.

'Sal here was telling me about some plans of yours . . .'

'Yes. I know. It's this gig, at that place of Kendra's. We don't have
to go there for long but . . . I'd really like to show up. If you don't
mind?' The words tumbled out, lamely. It would be so much easier
to say to Jackson that it was fine, they wouldn't go, they'd do whatever he wanted – anything to stop him going off with those girls

tonight. After all, the gig was miles away and it wasn't as if he even knew Kendra. But Sal was standing there watching her, her eyes narrowed as they were in moments of conflict, her mouth tense, a pocket-sized dragon empress.

'Sure.' Jackson shrugged, sitting back down and turning emphatically back to Cruz, Simone and Gaby, who had continued to chatter while the conversation took place. 'So, will I see you girls tomorrow night at Robbie's thirtieth?' He leant forward to Gaby, offering the flame of his Zippo to her cigarette, deftly excluding Annie and Sal from the table. Sal had completely forgotten to ask Annie about Trevor Eve.

As Jackson drove the two of them across London in silence, Annie didn't have to look at him to know that he was angry. Worse, he was bored too, which is what she most dreaded him being when he was with her. He always made it clear that he had so many options. She wished that Sal had not interfered and that she could rerun the past hour and be somewhere that he wanted to be: a friend's party, another bar, in bed. Instead, they were trying to find a parking space for his large car in this drab neighbourhood with its shadows and back alleys, and had spent at least five long minutes driving up and down small, dark sidestreets in an unsuccessful search.

The heavy door of the Chapel was firmly closed. Sal struggled with it, and when it finally opened it did so with a crash. Annie could see that she had passed the tipping point. After her confrontation with Jackson, she had probably necked down several more drinks. With Sal, it was straight from red to green, with no amber that she ever recognized.

'Ssh,' Annie whispered as Sal noisily pushed past the back row of seats, failing to notice as she knocked the backs of heads with a leather shoulder bag.

The room was almost full. That's great for Kendra, thought Annie, peering around to see her friend. The band playing was picked out in a pink light that warped the traditional Rasta colours of their T-shirts into murky shades and, in the corner by the side of the stage, she could see a tall figure wearing what could be an elaborate turban and, beside her, the equally tall but in comparison scaled-down Kendra. That must be Gioia. Annie was curious. As her eyes adjusted to the lighting, it became clear that it was no turban but an intricate style of plaits that was piled on Gioia's head. Even from where she sat at the opposite end of the room, there was something in Gioia's stance that radiated confidence. She could see her whisper something in Kendra's ear, Kendra replying with a grin. Annie nudged Sal to look too.

The reggae band was replaced by a balladeer in a Hawaiian shirt slowly tuning his acoustic guitar. Kendra had told them that Chris Blackwell had personally signed him to Island. The opening chords spun into the room.

'Sounds a bit like Jackson Browne,' Jackson whispered to Annie. She could feel, with relief, his hand slipping into the waistband of her trousers and stroking her lower back.

Sal was tone deaf, and made no pretence of being interested in music of any kind. She was tapping her leg, slightly out of time, and was nodding her head a bit too often, like a furry dog dangling in the car window. Looking at the room, Annie wondered what it was that Kendra was so attracted by. It was a bleak place, with its small, high windows, linoleum floor and walls painted a dull grey. She flashed back to a concert during their last year at university. It was in the union building on campus and, while Sal and Annie had been there because they were interested in a couple of boys, Kendra had been part of the activist group outside who were handing out leaflets in support of Solidarity.

There was a crash, loud enough to make some nearby listeners turn their heads, as Sal's bag fell to the floor, loose change, lighters, keys rolling out. Annie could see Kendra looking right at them, to where Sal was bent over, trying to stuff everything back.

'Just leave it,' Annie mouthed at her, and when this failed to stop Sal, gave her a kick. 'Leave it till the end.'

There were three encores, ending in a reggae rendition of the old hit 'Can We Still Be Friends', the audience joining in enthusiastically, swaying as they sang. As the pink light faded and the room brightened, the crowd broke up, some leaving, others milling around the emptying space. Uncertain of what to do next, Annie looked at Jackson for guidance.

'Let's go and see your mate. Now we've come all the way here, we might as well congratulate her.' He strode towards Kendra, but Sal was already ahead of them, unsteadily but determinedly weaving her way to where the performers were standing around.

'Kendra,' she shouted across to where her friend stood talking to the Scottish guitarist, hands in the pockets of her wide khaki trousers, the sleeves of a plain navy sweater rolled up to her elbows. 'That was fantastic, amazing.' She put her hand on the singer's arm. 'You were fantastic, amazing.'

Annie wished that Sal would talk a bit more quietly and stop repeating herself, but she envied her her confidence. Kendra's face was flushed, small beads of sweat on her hair line where the tawny curls were tied back in a cotton bandana.

She looked at her friends and then across the room to where Gioia was rolling a cigarette, talking to the Rastafarian contingent. Annie could see her trying to decide whether to make the introduction.

'Come on,' she said. 'Come and meet Gioia.' Kendra led the way, offering up her two friends to her employer. Gioia looked up, her face at first ungiving, with bright dark eyes hard like shiny pebbles. She drew slowly on the roll-up.

Kendra persevered. 'Here's Sal and Annie – they thought it was ace.'

Jackson intervened. 'You guys – didn't I hear you at the Tabernacle a few months back?' Annie felt proud. That was one of the things she loved about Jackson, the way he always knew the right thing to say.

'Welcome, Sal. Annie . . .' Gioia took a deep drag.

'And this is Jackson, Annie's boyfriend,' Kendra added.

Annie felt her face go crimson. Of all nights not to mention the boyfriend word, this was it.

'Yeah, we had to drag him out of the Chelsea Bridge party to get here. We were worried we might miss everything,' Sal chipped in, still tunelessly humming 'Can We Still Be Friends'.

Gioia surveyed the group, her unreadable face breaking into a big smile. 'Well, it's great you did. It's been a mega gig. Good for the Chapel. Kendra here, well, she's been a fine girl. Couldn't have managed without her.'

Jackson looked at his watch. 'OK, girls. Time to split. Sal, I can drop you somewhere.' Annie could see that Sal was considering staying on, hunkering down into the aftermath of the gig, but she knew that the last thing Kendra needed was to inherit her for the rest of the evening, since by now Sal was demonstrating the too familiar signs of clumsy, drunken exuberance. She took the unwilling departee by the arm, waving goodbye and moving her firmly towards the door.

'Let's stay for a bit. I like the look of that band. There's a bar at the back –'

'We're going, and we're taking you with us.' Annie's natural gentleness was replaced by an unusual determination. She wasn't sure how much longer Jackson's good humour was going to hold out and she didn't want to push her luck any further.

It was well after one o'clock by the time the last chairs had been loaded back into Gerassimos's van. Gioia and Kendra stood outside in the street and waved him off.

'Nightcap?' Gioia asked Kendra. 'I'm just round the corner and I've got a bottle of Amaro. Good stuff – just what we need after tonight. You don't want to be pedalling that bike of yours all over London at this hour. You could stay over.'

In spite of the late hour, Kendra was wide awake. They walked through the small streets, Kendra wheeling the bicycle between them, and stopped at a tall house. The roads were silent save for the odd screech of a distant siren. By the time they had carried the bike up the four flights of stairs, trying to manoeuvre it around the narrow landings, they were both breathless.

'Next time we leave it downstairs.' Gioia unlocked the door.

Ahead was a square room with wooden floorboards covered in rough woven rugs, a kitchen counter across one wall and a large bed in a corner underneath a skylight, the ceiling sloping at the side.

Kendra perched on the sagging sofa piled with soft cushions in the middle of the room as Gioia rustled around in a cupboard for the Amaro.

'You'll love this,' she said as she unscrewed the top off the tall, dark bottle, poured then held out two tumblers.

'Cheers.' Kendra took a sip of the bitter drink, which burnt as she swallowed. 'How long have you lived here?' She looked over to Gioia, who was riffling through an untidy pile of LPs on the floor.

'Two years next month.' The arm of the turntable clicked as the needle landed on the record. 'Satie. He's one of my favourites.'

Kendra closed her eyes briefly, listening to the music: eerie, almost mystical. Gioia asked her about her family, but she just shrugged.

'It's complicated. I don't want to think about them now. They're fine. I guess I'm lucky. But it doesn't feel that way.'

'Yeah, can't live with them, can't live without them. I know. I had to get my arse out of Glasgow. There were thousands of us there. All jumbled in together. Everybody knowing everything about everybody else. They call it community, but it can be as suffocating as a coffin. Killing you with love. Still, I do love them. It's just better from a distance. A big distance.'

Kendra stood up and walked over to the books that were housed on a row of rickety bamboo shelves. The spines of old paperbacks were jammed together. She recognized a collection of old James Bond novels, some Raymond Chandler. Further along, Truman Capote's *In Cold Blood*. They had the same book at home in Art's study. She took reading seriously. One of Art's friends had told her, when she was still a child, that he only had the time left to read good books. There weren't enough years to waste on junk. At the time, he had seemed ancient, but he could only have been about forty, she realized. Old, but not about to die.

As she stood at the shelf Kendra could hear – or was it feel? – Gioia's presence behind her. Instinctively, she moved to the side. A hand stroked her hair, pulling the cotton bandana back and running fingers through, firmly massaging her scalp. She turned.

Gioia leant forward and kissed her forehead, dotting kisses deliberately along the line of her hair before moving down towards her mouth. 'Do you want to try this?' she murmured, taking Kendra's glass from her hand. Kendra watched as Gioia unbuttoned her own shirt, revealing olive-skinned breasts, the large nipples prominent, one pierced by a ring. Her stomach was flat and muscular where the waistband of her trousers lay. She unpinned the coils of her hair.

Kendra felt unable to move and let Gioia guide her to the bare wall near the bed and place her against it, removing her sweater, unzipping her jeans and slowly placing her hand between her legs. Kendra could feel the metal and silk of her bracelets against her thigh. Then Gioia knelt, as Kendra looked out through the skylights opposite, where the clouds were scudding across the man's face on the moon.

6

It was debatable whether the heels on Sal's pixie boots were the right height. If they were too low, she knew the cone shape could make her appear squat. She extended her leg out from under her desk to examine them. But if they were higher, surely they would look strange? She had already run the gauntlet of good-humoured teasing around the office.

'Well, well, well, here comes the garden gnome,' taunted Doug, a much happier man now he had started an affair with the best friend of his estranged wife and his shaving kit had graduated from his desk drawer into her bathroom.

'I forget. Are you Dopey today, or would Grumpy be closer to the mark?' mocked Ollie as he flicked through the day's papers. 'Dwarves and pixies. 'Course they're all the same to me.' But, despite the teasing, Sal was delighted with the black suede ankle boots she had treated herself to a few weeks earlier. She had been planning to get ahead with some Christmas shopping but instead had found herself looking covetously in the windows of Dolcis.

It didn't seem to be a slow morning for anyone else, but Sal was struggling to make her story stand up. Andrea, who organized features, had tossed her the job about a new chain of pizza restaurants to rival Pizza, Pizza, Pizza, announcing in strident Roedean vowels, 'I gather everybody's interested in *pitsa* nowadays.' She made it clear that she was *not* everybody. 'The *Pitsa* wars – we could do worse. It'll make a nice filler.' But, so far, Sal had only managed to dig up an unacceptably anodyne quote from one of the managers of Pizza, Pizza, Pizza in Wimbledon: 'We have a loyal clientele here and an unbeatable menu.' Where was the drama in that?

On the far side of the huge room, Sal could hear an unusual amount of noise. Chairs were being pushed back, the usual buzz of conversation ramped up to shouts. She could see the news desk struggling into their jackets, pens between teeth as they stuffed belongings into their pockets, half running, half walking through the room to the ancient lifts.

'Big news coming in,' Sal heard someone shout. 'Something's going on at Harrods.' Outside the editor's office in the corner she could see Stuart, his long arms waving like a conductor's. Since their disastrous evening, they had only exchanged cursory sentences, but she had heard that he had moved on.

'Stu's knocking off one of the girls on the *Times* diary,' Ollie had told her, unaware of her own unfortunate encounter. 'Can't understand how she'd go for him, but I've sussed that girls like a married man. Can't be any other explanation.' Ollie's own love life was a series of unrequited passions. On the rare occasions Sal did see him with a female, it was almost always his doughy flatmate, who he had trained to evacuate their small flat on the nights he had an inkling he might get lucky.

'Come on, come on.' Andrea pushed past her as Sal followed Marsha along with a crowd of others to cram into the editor's office. Despite having been at the *Herald* for several months, Sal had never been directly addressed by 'The Editor', as Patrick Lewis was always referred to. The paper was almost military in its hierarchy, and the formality of this term was intended to induce the same unquestioning obedience as on the battlefield.

This reverence was not genuinely echoed in the minds of most who worked there. Gossip about Lewis's frequent extramarital affairs was a favourite conversational ball to toss around in spare moments.

''Course, he signs his own expenses, doesn't he? That helps.'

'A permanent table at the Savoy. Not like he has to make a pass in the taxi home. He's probably tamed the concierge to keep a room on tap.' His senior editors were torn between jealous admiration for Lewis's undeniable powers of seduction and the need to poke fun at his goings-on in order to keep the loyalty of the lower orders.

Currently, Lewis enjoyed the absolute trust of his proprietors and was regularly chauffeured down in his Jaguar on Saturday afternoons to join their Wiltshire shoot, leaving his deputy to sign off the final pages. Recently, he had improved his stock considerably by being asked to play the harp at Highgrove, the Waleses' new country home.

'HRH tells me he finds it refreshing that a newspaper editor understands the symphonic capabilities of the harp' was one of the lines that regularly did the rounds as his lieutenants shared several pints after work. 'He's a tosser, but a clever one' was the general consensus.

From his desk, Patrick Lewis could see across Fleet Street to the curves of the shiny black *Express* building but, today, any view was blotted out by the crowd of *Herald* staff lining the windows, the most senior seated as a panel on chairs near the boss's desk. Even through the wall of men's suiting Sal could see that the editor was wearing one of his trademark white-collared, pink shirts.

'There's been a bomb at Harrods. The first news guys are nearly there.' Stuart, seated to the left of Patrick, addressed the room. 'Ten to one it's the Provos, but no one's claimed responsibility yet. This is *our* story. We've got ten hours till we hit the presses. We're going to blow the others out of the water. I want you all *on it*. We're tearing up the features section for more space. Andrea, get your lot out there too. Colour. Anecdotes. The personal stuff. We don't know casualties yet but get on to the families as soon as we do.'

Sal could see Patrick's leg swinging like a metronome under his desk as he swept the dark curls that were the subject of both envy and speculation from his face then examined his fingernails as he listened to Stuart. The editor cleared his throat.

'It's important that we are intellectually rigorous in our coverage. I've got General Sir Richard Potterton filing for the op-ed. Anthony, I assume you've contacted Leon Brittan. Tomorrow the country is going to want to know who, what and most importantly *why*. Context is vital. That's the *Herald*'s strength.'

The editor's lack of interest in the bare facts of the news agenda was a frustration in the office, as was, at times, his sense of reality. Even Anthony, his deputy, who bowed to no one in his admiration for Patrick, thought it unlikely that Brittan, the Home Secretary, would have time to file a piece for the *Herald*.

'Absolutely,' mouthed Stuart to his superior, making a note on a yellow legal pad. The room emptied.

'Sal, you cover the local stores, get the story from their angle. After all, this is one of the biggest shopping days of the year. Marsha, you take the man on the street.' Andrea looked up at the television on the far wall. No news. All she could see was horses strolling around some paddock in preparation for the afternoon's racing.

'Call the desk in a couple of hours. The copytakers can take the initial stuff, and we'll see what we've got. I'll be here knocking it into shape.'

Sal and Marsha shared the cab from Fleet Street. Sal suspected that if Marsha had managed to close the door quickly enough she would have happily left her on the pavement, but she flung herself on to the seat too, scuffing her new boots in the process. Marsha ignored her companion, busying herself with a notebook. What on earth is she writing, thought Sal. We haven't talked to anyone yet. It was unnerving watching Marsha concentrate, as if she had discovered an exam question that Sal had somehow managed to miss.

'So, shall we pool our findings?' she said, rummaging in her bag for a cigarette.

Marsha turned, tucking her bob neatly behind her ears. 'I think you'll find it works best on big stories if we keep to our own patch. That way we can cover the ground. Andrea wants you in the shops – perhaps you should go down Sloane Street. Talk to some of those boutique places. I'll handle the close-up picture.' She yanked down the window in a showy objection to Sal's smoking. This was Sal's first major news story, the first time she had rushed out of the office as part of the whole speeding newspaper machine. Even so, she knew that it was important to be at the heart of the action; certainly in. Kremlin, a new vodka bar off Sloane Square, was holding its opening party the same night as the Torrington event for Chelsea Bridge.

'Keep your distance from the Führer this morning, she's in a right pickle,' Lee had hissed over the desk at Annie.

'Crazy idiot. We've had the date down on the Restaurant Register for at least two months. What does he want to go head to head for?' Tania announced to the room, her palazzo pants flapping as she stomped around. She picked up the phone on Lee's desk to call Mark Fitzherbert, the restaurant PR and near-certifiable alcoholic who handled many of London's big launches and was masterminding the Kremlin bash.

'Fitz, you and I go way back. We've got to work together on this, darling,' Tania began. 'It's just not an option for both to open that evening.' Her eyes rolled wildly, in a performance for her listening staff, silenced in anticipation of the outcome of the call.

'Yes. Well. So have we lined up a great guest list. Of course we have, Fitz. What do you think I am? I didn't fall off the back of the turnip truck yesterday. I've had the whole shebang in place for months now. We listed the date in the Restaurant Register. Don't your people tell you anything?' Cradling the phone in her neck, she pulled a cigarette from a packet on the desk, lit it and took a deep drag.

'You don't sound good, Fitz. Bit early for a drink, love, isn't it? Maybe that's what's clouding your judgement?' But Tania knew she had lost this round. She slammed the phone down.

'He was always a rotten lay,' she informed the room. 'Who's his special guest, then? Any of you lot know? I pay you to be eyes and ears, so I hope you're not deaf, blind and dumb.'

'Bryan Ferry? Maybe?' Lee offered cautiously, aware that by handing over this titbit he was putting his head above the parapet.

'Bryan Ferry? Christ. Where did you hear that?'

'Someone mentioned it at Slum It In Style last night. But I didn't know it was going to clash with Chelsea Bridge.' Lee could feel the sympathetic eyes of the others on him. When Tania was like this, they had learnt it was wise to keep quiet. Even so, if Fitzherbert really had got Ferry, they were going to be under pressure to trump that. And it was only weeks away.

'Lord help me. Now I'm getting my feedback from Slum It In Style. Maybe that's why you've had a bit of a style bypass today,' Tania tossed back, leaning over Lee. He could see the line of foundation that had gathered around the joint of her nose, the small clots of mascara at the end of her lashes. She could be a right bitch sometimes. Yet despite knowing that her last comment was a missile she could have hurled anywhere, Lee suddenly worried that, possibly, it was true: his T-shirt might be ripped in some of the wrong places.

It was war.

'Get on the phone and track down Jennifer Beals and that guy who's with her in *Flashdance*: they're over here at the moment. Her agent owes me one big-time,' Tania commanded.

Annie had just put the phone down when Jackson's call came through. Expecting another celebrity's PA explaining that their boss would be out of town, she had answered half-heartedly.

'Annie? Hello, it's Jackson. Can I persuade you to come and have a bite with me on Thursday?'

Annie felt her stomach lurch. It was always that way, the call coming just when you weren't prepared. Should she pretend she was busy? Was Thursday, only three days away, too soon for her to be free?

'The peaches . . . they were amazing . . . thanks.'

'My pleasure. You had to cart all that stuff around for us. It was the least I could do. But, from my end, the meeting was certainly lucky.' His voice was deep, inflected with the drawl of a public-school education.

'Thursday . . . was it?'

'Yes, Thursday. I thought we could meet at Zanzibar about eight thirty?'

'Ah . . .' What should she say? Something, though. She was

not wandering down a posh shopping street. Marsha must think she was really naïve.

'I'm going to try to get a bit closer than that,' she said. If Marsha hadn't been such a cold bitch, she would have added that she was scared, that her stomach was turning watery and that she didn't begin to know how to achieve what she knew she was meant to.

'Well, good luck to you. The police will have the whole place secured by now. You'd have to be a real pro to get through.' Marsha looked away, as London landmarks passed outside the window – Nelson's Column, the crenellations of Westminster, Apsley House – their route to the bomb mimicking that of a tour bus.

The traffic into Knightsbridge was unmoving and the taxi became grounded at Hyde Park Corner. Sal jumped out and ran into the streets, dodging around bewildered shoppers taken aback at the commotion surrounding their Saturday trip into town and unclear what had happened. It was many people's last opportunity to shop before Christmas and, at midday, the crowds were already laden with carrier bags. All around, there was the wail of sirens. In the distance, Sal saw the dome of the huge rust-coloured department store. There were police everywhere, standing beside barriers of white tape blowing in the cold wind. From her position among the wandering crowds, it was clear that the area around the shop was empty – of cars, buses, shoppers. There was an unusual smell. She walked into a small jewellery store near the Tube station.

'Sal Turner, *Sunday Herald*,' she announced. Did that sound convincing? 'Do you mind if I ask you a few questions about what's just happened?' Sal offered her NUJ card as ID to the small bespectacled man who was arranging a tray of rings, their cheap gold exposed by their brightness against the black velvet.

'What has happened? Nobody's telling us anything.' He didn't look up.

'A bomb . . . in Harrods. We don't know right now if it was inside or outside. They suspect the IRA. Could I ask you what you saw? What did you hear?'

'A bang – that's it, my love. I heard a bang. There were no

customers in here and I was just about to change the window display. I've got some lovely gold chains in. Perfect, they are, for Christmas. I went to look outside and people were running everywhere, so I thought it wise to stay in. Saturday is one of my best days and I didn't want to be evacuated or anything. Kept myself to myself.'

Sal scribbled away. Her half-cocked shorthand worked well enough to speed her up, but she had never been properly fluent and a blunt pencil didn't help. As the afternoon passed, Sal kept hearing the same from everyone – a bang, the sirens, the smell. Everyone mentioned the smell. The minutes to her deadline were ticking past and the darkness of the December afternoon was starting to close in, the Christmas decorations in many windows a strange contrast to the destruction around Harrods and the sinister emptiness behind the cordons. Marsha was right. She wasn't getting anywhere.

The cold, the growing possibility of failure and the prospect of Marsha's patronizing mocking made her desperate for a pee. She found a small sandwich bar, where a young woman dressed in a white apron smeared with dirt was sitting on a stool staring down at a mug of tea. Across the road, in the distance, Sal could see a yellow curtain flapping, ripped outside the window, the glass blown out, even at that distance from the blast.

'She's been there a couple of hours now. One cup of tea. Don't know how she thinks we're meant to make a living. And that's without bleeding bombs going off round the corner.' Behind the cabinet of sweaty sandwich fillings a man poured boiling water into the pot of tea Sal had bought mainly in order to grant her access to the toilet. She carried it to where the girl was sitting, next to the wall, preparing to read back her notes in the hope that she might find more than she knew was there. She prayed Marsha was finding it equally difficult to dig anything up.

'Are you all right?' she asked her neighbour. It was a few moments until the girl turned to look at Sal. Her hands were shaking as she picked up her cup. After two hours, that tea must be stone cold. 'Can I buy you a hot one?' she asked.

The girl shrugged, staring out into the dank street ahead. 'Thanks. That's very kind of you.' Her voice was unreconstructed Sloane.

Sal offered her new acquaintance a cigarette, but it was waved away. 'I've been sent to cover the bombing by my paper but, to be honest, I've got nothing and I'm on deadline. I can't find out anything. It's a nightmare. The first time they send me out to cover something proper, and I'm cocking it up.' Sal's view of the world was entirely subjective and did not allow her to think that this sad creature might not be interested in her problem. She was younger than Sal had realized initially.

'I was there,' she said simply, looking away. 'Yeah, I was right there. Wish I hadn't been.'

Sal sat up. She needed to talk to this girl. She would have to take notes, but if the girl saw her doing it, would she stop talking? If she formally asked for an interview, wouldn't that sound a like a police caution? The image of Marsha preparing her story in the cab flashed across her mind. She had nothing to lose, and took out her own.

'You are the only – and I mean *the only* – person I've come across that can tell me anything. I mean, I imagine it was pretty . . . traumatic.' It wasn't as if Sal was trying to say anything very complicated, but it seemed difficult to get anything out.

'Sure. I'll tell you. There's not a lot to say. I was there in Harrods. I was working there. It's my holiday job. I'm Ali Charter, by the way. They take on lots of us just for Christmas, and I was in the food hall. I'd been stacking Christmas puddings most of the morning, and the place was packed.' She sipped her hot tea. 'I was on a break and went downstairs to the loo. That's where they are, the staff loos, and I wanted to catch up with my friend, who was working there too. He was in menswear. Ground floor. I know they were putting him on ties today. I think the bomb is in menswear . . . or was. I can't find him. I'm worried sick. We were going to go to this party tonight, but now I don't even know if he's alive. Well, he probably is, don't you think? He probably is?' Sal assured her that he probably was, then urged Ali to continue.

'I was in the Ladies. There was one woman in there. She said she was in perfumery. She was putting on mascara when we heard the noise, and she jumped so hard she stuck the wand in her eye, and I was saying, "God, what was that?", and she was saying, "Christ, I've got mascara all over my eye."

'I've never heard a noise like it. Not surprising really, I'm not used to bombs. It was like the end of the world, and there we were, underground. We didn't know what to do. I don't remember what we did . . . I don't think we moved for a bit. And then there was this smell and some smoke – not much, but some – and we knew we had to get out. So we ran. And upstairs it was bedlam and everyone was shouting, "Get out!" and the glass was all blown in, and there was this car – what *was* a car, anyway – and I saw a man lying on the ground. Some of a man . . .' Ali took another sip of tea and rubbed her eyes as if to clear the image away. 'When the air hit me I thought I was going to faint. I don't do chaos well. My mum always tells me I catastrophize. I think that's the word. You know, when you think the worst is going to happen? But then, a bomb on a holiday job – well, that is the worst, when you come to think of it, isn't it?' Ali spoke quickly. Sal asked her a few more questions. Andrea was going to love this. She was always banging on about how they needed more human interest. Marsha couldn't possibly have found someone who was actually in the building at the time. Ten minutes till deadline though. She would have to find a phone.

'That sounds terrible. Poor you.' Sal dug around in her bag to find her purse so that she could pay.

'Yeah, I've just been sitting here. Can't really move. Don't know why. What paper do you write for, anyway?'

Telling the man behind the counter to bring Ali another tea – 'Put tons of sugar in it. I think she's kind of in shock' – Sal paid and ran out of the door, making a guess at where she'd find the nearest phone box. A couple of minutes, and she saw a block of red at the end of a street. It was only then that she realized she didn't have any change. How often had she been told she should always keep some coins in her purse for exactly this?

She dialled 100 and asked to make a reverse-charge call to the paper.

'Will you accept the call?' Sal heard the emotionless voice ask the girl at the *Herald*'s switchboard.

'We don't accept reverse charge' was the reply.

'Caller, they won't accept the call. Will you pay?'

'Tell her that it's Sal Turner. Features. I need to be put through to the copytakers *now*. It's about the bomb. You know, the bomb at Harrods. You're putting me through to a newspaper, for heaven's sake.' For what seemed hours she was in limbo – connected to nobody, maybe even cut off – until, finally, she heard the familiar clattering noise of typists.

'For one young woman, yesterday was a shocking departure from her normal Saturday job (*full stop*). Ali (*capital A for alpha, L for Lima, I for India*) had just been on her break at her holiday job in Harrods food hall . . .'

It was only after she had finished that she realized she had dictated a report straight from her head. She asked to be put through to Andrea. To her surprise, she heard Marsha's voice.

'So you went back to the office?' Sal asked, surprised.

'Yes. I finished up and got back to help the desk out. We were beginning to wonder if you were going to file.' Telephones rang constantly in the background as Marsha spoke. 'Andrea says there's no need to come in now – she thinks it better you stay on the ground in case something else happens. I'll tell her to look at your copy. We don't know how much space we've got yet but I'm sure she'll try and squeeze you in.'

'The flag above Chelsea police station is flying at half mast this evening in recognition of the loss of life sustained by members of its force.' The BBC reporter's nose, red with cold, was emphasized by the thick grey of the scarf around his neck. Kendra leant over to turn up the volume on the television sitting on a nineteenth-century Chinese tea chest.

'What's going on, Ken?' Art stood in the doorway, a hefty tumbler in his hand. Kendra heard the clink of ice. 'Terrible stuff. Those poor guys. Jesus, what times we live in. It's not even safe to go to Harrods nowadays. I'm always telling Maris to stay local for the shopping nowadays. The West End's going down.' Art eased on to the sofa beside his daughter. 'Good to see you, babe. We don't see so much of you these days.'

Kendra shifted to accommodate her father. He was right, she hadn't spent much time with him in weeks, maybe months, and it was nice to be sitting there, just him and her, in this room, which was her favourite. Maybe because it was 'the snug', colour had been allowed and it was accentuated by furnishings which, anywhere else, Marisa would deem frumpy: a floral on the sofa, dark-green velvet curtains, a small side table with a lamp. Marisa liked scale: 'I'm not into the knick-knacks you find in these London houses, cluttering up the space when there isn't enough in the first place.'

Kendra couldn't bear to think what her mother's opinion would be of Gioia's flat, with its books and LPs piled on the floor and clothes hanging off hooks all over the walls, or of Gioia as a person, or, God knows, Kendra's relationship with her, which had invaded her with a force quite unlike anything she had ever experienced.

Kendra was used to emotion. She knew that she cared about things – events, people, causes. She couldn't even pass a cat on the street without worrying whether it had a home to go to. She was an enthusiastic and compassionate listener to problems, her open face, with its clear grey eyes and thick brows, always ready to register the necessary degree of astonishment or sympathy. But she had never cared very much about herself.

She had placed Art and Marisa into a box labelled 'My parents, and I know they are weird', and she left them there, largely unscrutinized. At university, Kendra had often been found in the kitchen brewing up a variety of dried herbs as a stress remedy while she nodded sympathetically as a friend recounted their problems. She was always an early port of call in any emotional drama. She was particularly good at keeping quiet. She had learnt that it was almost always pointless to offer anything other than support. Friends didn't really want your opinions, just your sympathy.

And of course she had had boyfriends. Not many, but a few. She hadn't ever felt very much about them, she now realized, and certainly, they had not made her feel anything at all about herself.

She had always wondered why Sal and Annie spent so much time and energy on the whole business of whether they had a boyfriend or not. Why Annie would mould herself to each new crush, prepared to change her hairstyle and eating habits in a trice, spending hours in the bathroom shaving her legs, washing her hair, putting on gooey face masks before a date and becoming hysterical about a small spot on her face. And Sal – well, Sal could just go simple. She'd see a boy she fancied at a party and she'd target him like a nuclear missile. He didn't normally stand a chance. Invariably, after spending the night with him, she'd go off him the next day. Kendra had never felt even slightly compelled to behave either way.

She enjoyed the companionship of the boys she went out with, and even liked the sensation of another body close to hers in bed, but the actual sex had left her unaffected. The best thing about it was the knowledge that, as far as she could tell, *he* was having a good time. At least, that was what she supposed his moans and energetic movements were indicating, as well as the fact that, almost as soon as he had stopped, the whole thing would all start again.

With Gioia, it was different. Everything was different. After the first night spent in Gioia's flat it was as if Kendra had been melted and recast in a different shape. Her perception of what she was and had always been had dissolved but had immediately been replaced with an alternative. There was nothing unsure or strange about the new her – it was utterly familiar. The sensations that Gioia had induced were delicious and intriguing, and her lover's command of the lovemaking, the fact that she expected nothing of Kendra and only appeared to want to seduce and satisfy, felt oddly acceptable. Normally, Kendra would have been uncomfortable about being such a passive recipient of pleasure, but with Gioia it really was as if she, Kendra, was some amazing treasure to be touched and held and cherished.

It was different at work. Gioia would bark commands at Kendra the same way she did to the kids who hung out there. She delegated the administrative task to her: the bill paying, the endless dealing with utility companies over the continual problems with hot water, or the lights. Sometimes she would ask Kendra to send out an invoice from G. Cavallieri, keeping a carbon copy in a book. Gioia would say, 'If you take care of the bloody bureaucracy, I can get on with what I'm good at. After all, you're the one with the degree. That makes you chief form filler-in. I can't be doing with all the forms. You're the brains and beauty, which makes me the beast.'

The Chapel was an old and rickety structure and in need of a complete overhaul, which Gioia could never find a way to finance. They knew that the roof was dangerously unstable, the pointing more like crumble than concrete, but it was one of those things that would just have to wait. One morning, Kendra had been waylaid at the door by an elderly woman.

'Do you work in this place?' she asked as Kendra unlocked the big door, shaking rain off her donkey jacket and dripping hair. 'I've been trying to tell that woman she has to do something about that roof. I live on the top floor. Over there.' She gestured with a wrist slung with string shopping bags to the small terraces of houses around the corner. 'When I look out my bathroom window, I can see it will only take one strong gust of wind, and somebody's going to get hurt when the whole thing comes crashing down.'

'Gioia knows that we have to get something done. She's working on it,' Kendra muttered as the lighting flickered into life.

'It's just not safe for us round here. I've been down Citizens Advice on Kentish Town Road. They say somebody could take action. Not that it isn't bad enough having those scoundrels hanging around the street. And we've got our eyes on those vans arriving all hours of the night. It's criminal, the goings-on. Criminal.' She tightened the knot of her headscarf under her chin with the satisfaction of a hanging judge. 'You tell that woman she'll be facing the law. They'll have this place closed down.'

Gioia's response when Kendra brought the subject up later in the day was that she would get the old bat closed down first and that it was just a question of skimming up a ladder to fix the roof. It was a free country, wasn't it? Or had she missed the news? Gerass was allowed to drive around whenever he wanted to. She supposed she'd better get him to take a look at the roof.

'You lunching with us tomorrow?' Art asked his daughter, interrupting the companionable silence as they watched the news. 'Alfie's joining us, and I think your mother has corralled a few others.' Alfie was one of Art and Marisa's oldest friends, and Kendra was fond of him. It was a tradition for them to spend Christmas Day with Alfie and his boyfriend, John. The Rootsteins' home was largely a Christmas-free zone, although there was an illuminated aluminium Ettore Sottsass tree that was installed for exactly a week in the corner of the drawing room.

But Alfie and John did the whole thing properly. When Kendra was younger she had been thrilled by their huge, real tree, which dominated the crowded sitting room and was hung with multi-coloured lights and balls and candles they would light in the middle of the meal, which was never served before late afternoon. They had crackers and wore paper hats and, every year, the group would have the same conversation about how extraordinary it was that the Americans didn't have crackers.

'Kendra. *There's* a way to make your fortune,' Alfie would invariably say as he refilled his glass with the vintage port Art would have supplied, his face a florid contrast to his unnaturally blond wavy hair.

'Oh, Dad. Sorry, I can't make lunch. I made a date to see Sal and Annie – it's maybe the last time we can all get together before Christmas. They have to go back home to their folks. I wonder if Sal got to work on this bomb? She's been aching to be given a proper story.'

Marisa came up behind Art, placing her hands on his shoulders. 'Alfie will be sad to miss you. You know John isn't well at the moment. He's lost a lot of weight. Not that he couldn't do with dropping a few pounds around the middle.'

She crossed the room to align the joins of the curtains.

'Art, we need to leave around eight. I said we'd pick up Jim and Jill McKenzie. Jill's been telling me she had a little chat with Jim about his new squeeze. I can't believe how predictable you boys can be. She discovered he took her to Ireland with him last week when they were having some corporate pow-wow. And, surprise, surprise, the maid found her Janet Reger in his suitcase. There might be a touch of *froideur* in the car tonight.' She turned to Kendra, smiling. 'Talking of lovers, darling, are your father and I ever to be introduced to your new *amour*? We assume there is one, seeing as you're out like a cat most nights. You know we couldn't be more delighted. I do hope he's a great fuck.'

When Kendra arrived at the Builder's Arms the next morning she found Annie and Sal at their favourite table near the window, a pile of newspapers on the floor. The relentlessly jolly beat of 'Uptown Girl' could be heard over the noise of the bar. Annie's grimace was obvious from the other side of the room. She held her fingers like a pistol to her head then pointed at Sal, who was hunched into a huge grey coat even though the pub was steamy.

'Hi. What's up?'

Sal picked up a newspaper section from the floor. 'This is what's up. Bitch.'

Kendra slid on to the bench beside Annie. 'Let's see.' There were several pieces covering different aspects of the bomb attack, some larger than others.

'Look. There. That was meant to be my story, but can you see whose name is above it? MARSHA SWEETING, that's who, with . . . "additional reporting" by a cast of thousands, including yours truly.'

Kendra was unclear about the detail of what was wrong, but it was obvious that, to her friend, this was serious.

'Sal's been stuffed by Marsha,' Annie explained. Marsha was

already known to them as public enemy number one. The impenetrable neatness of her bob was used by Sal to illustrate the utter impossibility of her being human. 'Wine?'

'No. I'm going to have a lager.'

Annie grabbed the opportunity to go to the bar, eager to escape Sal's lowering gloom and fury as she regaled Kendra with her tale.

'I was sent off to cover the bomb. Well, me and Marsha were. It took me for ever, but I did – in the end, I *did* find a story. My story. I found this girl, a real eyewitness, who gave me some great stuff, and I couldn't write the story because it had got so late, so I phoned it in. On the hoof. Marsha told me I should stay out "on the ground". . . Fuck her – "on the ground" – and that she'd pass it on. But she used it all in her story. Look, that's what I wrote, what I phoned: "For one young woman . . ." And, of course, I don't have a copy of the story typed out to prove that it's mine. What a cow.'

There was no consoling Sal, who, fuelled by several glasses of the pub's sour red wine, was hard to distract from the injustice. Annie and Kendra tried their best to lighten the atmosphere.

'OK. Let's get Marsha. How about sending her off on a date with Stuart? We could kidnap her and pour henna all over her hair,' Kendra suggested. 'Or even better, I know Mum's got some Clairol black stuff in the bathroom – how about that? A kind of modern-day tar and feather? It's rotten. Really it is. You'll get your own back though.'

They ordered Sal a Ploughman's, along with theirs, even though they knew she was unlikely to eat anything. Annie nibbled at the edge of her bread. She always did that, observed Kendra, as if it were going to stop her eating the whole thing – which it didn't. Not that Annie had any problem with her weight. She could probably eat anything she wanted and it wouldn't make a difference.

Eventually, Sal's fury lifted. The call for last orders, when it came, seemed early.

'Let's get another bottle from next door and go back to Cranbourne,' she suggested. The others, relieved at having managed to distract Sal, agreed, and they headed back to the flat.

Annie had put a string of coloured fairy lights around the empty fireplace, and there was a faint smell of curry.

'Joanna warned me about the people on the first floor playing music, but she didn't tell us about their vindaloo habit. You can always smell the stuff.' She squeezed a few drops from a small bottle on to a ring and placed it on the light bulb. A tiny thread of scented smoke wafted into the air as the bulb warmed. 'Tania's just got the Floris account, so we all got a bottle of this burning essence to take home.' She looked at the dark-blue packaging. 'Stephanotis. Lee's using his as perfume.' Annie sat at the table overlooking the street and fiddled with the array of bottles of coloured inks she had placed there.

'So. *I'm* going home the night before Christmas Eve. Mum's giving her usual Christmas Eve lunch do and says she wants me there the night before to help.' She sighed. She had been trying to pin Jackson down to get him to make a date. 'It's so unfair that I've got to leave London so early. I really wanted to be with Jackson then, but he seems to be incredibly busy with all these work things he has to go to. I suppose it isn't surprising he can't take me with him to them.' She sounded lame, even to herself, but she was very aware of the horrible possibility that she might only get to spend one night with him before Christmas and that then she was going to be stuck at home for days. The whole 'familiness' of Christmas was out of place in their relationship. She knew Jackson was planning to be with his lot in Wiltshire on the day, but he was reckoning on leaving as late as possible on Christmas Eve with the excuse that the roads would be empty. She wished he had asked her if she'd like to be there with him, even though of course she wouldn't have been able to go. But just him asking would have counted for something.

Annie knew that Christmas was important to her mother. Letty had decided as soon as she was widowed that nothing about the family's Christmas was going to change. Their traditions were the mast she could hold on to in her changed world. She carried on organizing their pre-lunch drinks on Christmas Eve, serving the same cocktail sausages and spreading homemade chicken liver pâté on to Ritz crackers, washed down with a 'more than reasonable' sparkling white that she'd discovered in Marks. Annie had noticed the determination in her mother's face that first time she had had to struggle with the cork.

On Christmas Day, after stockings (Letty still produced them for Annie and Beth and stuffed them with bubble bath and bottled sauces, and they now jointly produced one for her, which they left outside her bedroom door), they all walked down the lane, through Beechams Common, to Freddie and Julia's for a huge meal. Annie loved Christmas, and was looking forward to it despite not being able to spend it with Jackson. When she woke on Christmas morning, the day always felt special and, though she knew it was childish, she still got excited when she investigated the content of her lumpy woollen stocking. The one bit she didn't like was walking home through the dimly lit lanes once it was dark and the presents had been opened and then seeing the tatty armchair where her father used to sit to watch ludicrous Christmas telly late into the night. It was the only time she still really got upset about his absence.

'When are you heading back to Cheltenham, Sal?' she asked.

Sal was on the sofa, her red V-neck sweater pulled over her bent knees, striped socks poking out from her jeans.

'I haven't really thought about it. Maybe I'll do the shopping Saturday morning and then catch the train.'

'I bet you've got all yours done, haven't you, Annie?' Kendra teased. 'Probably all wrapped too.' She was near the mark. This year, for her wrapping, Annie had decided to stick silver stars on brown paper.

'I don't know what to get Jackson, though. Men are a nightmare. I can't just get him socks or a tape.' Sal brightened at the opportunity to suggest unsuitable presents for Jackson, for whom she was developing a passionate dislike. She couldn't explain, even to herself, what it was, but there was something about him she didn't trust. The three of them had often joked about how Annie had Bad Taste in Men and Annie, for her part, took the jokes with a pinch of salt.

'The thing about Annie,' Sal said to Kendra when Annie was out of the room, 'is that she's always been a lookist, and she can't see past that. Jackson's a classic. I mean, where is he half the time? It would be fine if she wasn't so serious about him, but she sits gazing at that phone like some pathetic puppy.'

'How about one of those new phones I've read about that you carry around with you, so that she could keep tabs on him? Great invention. It might mean he'd stop calling her in the middle of the night too. Or, if he did, I wouldn't know about it,' Sal suggested on her return.

'Pot calling the kettle,' interjected Annie. 'At least he doesn't come round throwing pebbles at the window, like that poor boy you tortured the other day. The one you met at that party, *obviously* promised your body to, and who drove you home, and sat out there all night. I kept thinking Joanna's windows were going to get smashed.'

Sal laughed. 'Oh, Tom. I told him he couldn't come in, but he was having none of it – anyway, at least he drove me back from Brighton. How about you, Ken? Christmas at Alfie's again?'

'Mmm. We're worried about his boyfriend, John. Mum says he's lost weight, and everyone's kind of ducking around the subject. I guess I'll see what he's like next week.'

'Poor guy. It sounds so frightening. There was a story on it in the paper a couple of weeks back. I heard the foreign desk discussing it. Something about the disease . . . about how you get it. Everyone says it's got really bad in New York. It's shit being gay, isn't it? Everything's against you. I'm so pleased I'm not.'

'Yes, and never having . . . well, a normal family, and kids and things,' said Annie. 'That's hard. I mean, I know it isn't really . . . Well, I probably shouldn't say *normal* family, but let's face it – they can't have the same kind of life we have, can they?' Annie's face showed concern as she held a lock of her hair up to the light, scrutinizing it for split ends. 'Lee's got a friend who he thinks is ill. He told me that they've worked out for sure that you can't catch it sleeping in someone else's sheets.'

'No, Annie. It's not like bed bugs.' Annie and Sal were taken aback by the sharpness in Kendra's voice. 'And, as for being gay . . . well . . . well, you might as well know. I think I am. No, I don't think. I am. I definitely am.'

'You are . . . what?' Annie looked at her. There was a silence. 'Are you saying you're . . . *gay*? What's happened? I mean, how do you know?'

'I'm . . . Oh, Christ. I'm sleeping with Gioia. OK. Now you know.' Kendra's broad face was flushed.

'You *what*?' Sal uncoiled herself from the sofa. Kendra watched them looking at her as if they expected her to transform into something else before their eyes. 'How long's this been going on?'

'You sound like my mother.'

'Oh . . . Sorry. But I don't understand. Do you, Annie?'

Annie didn't know what to say. What was the right thing to say? Is it the kind of thing you say 'Congratulations' to? Or 'Well done'? Or 'Thank you for telling us'? How was it that one of her best friends was a lesbian and she hadn't known? It wasn't as if she was a man. Annie knew gay men. Obviously, there was Lee. And there'd been gay boys at university. But gay women? Even that word . . . 'lesbian'. That was a different world.

'I know it must be a bit of a shock for you. It was sort of a shock for me. I really, really didn't know I was gay until Gioia. Maybe I wasn't. But . . . no that's not true. I didn't *catch* it from her. I just discovered something really important about me. Something that makes it all make more sense. But it doesn't matter, you know. It doesn't change anything. It doesn't matter to us. We can still be friends.' This last point was an attempt at humour.

'What do you mean it doesn't change anything?' Sal spluttered. 'Of course we're still your friends, but the point is we thought we were your best friends, and it's really strange that something important like this, important like, who you want to fuck, who you want to *be* with . . . well, you don't even *tell* us. It's like we don't know you.'

'Sal. I don't feel I have to explain this to you. I don't have to excuse myself. I still feel the same about you. It's just . . . it's just Gioia is my girlfriend. I don't make a fuss about who you are with.'

'Ken, have you told your parents?' Annie got up and began to pace in front of the windows. How long had they known each other? Five years, four years?

'Are you crazy? No, of course I haven't. Look. I haven't caught a contagious disease. You are making me feel so bad. I thought you were my friends, and now you're behaving as if I've done something terrible. And you should be happy for me. I've never felt like this before. You two often have. But I haven't. I understand everything more now. You know how I used to ask why you cared so much when you were talking about boys? Well, I asked because *I* didn't. I didn't know why I didn't. But I didn't.'

'Didn't what?'

'Oh, shush, Sal!' shouted Annie. 'She's trying to explain to us.'

'I wasn't *not* telling you before. Not until a few weeks ago, anyway. I've only been *not telling you* for a couple of months. And now I have. So there we are.'

'Golly, Ken. This is major.' Sal walked over to Kendra and put her arm around her. Her face suddenly crinkled in amusement 'What's it like then? Doing it with a girl?'

It was early evening when Kendra left. The bottle they had bought from the off-licence was finished and there was no more alcohol in the flat to stave off the come-down.

'I still don't understand it.' Sal was half watching the news on the small TV. 'Oh, that's awful.' Her voice sharpened. 'There was a boy from the *Express*, from their Hickey column, killed in the bomb. You know, that could have been me. Oh, that's terrible. Ollie and Rob must know him.' She concentrated on the screen as details emerged of the deaths and injuries.

Then she turned back to Annie. 'I don't understand how we can have spent all that time with Ken and not known she was gay. I just thought she'd never met the right bloke. I know this is awful, and don't say it to her, but do you think she ever fancied *us*?'

'I don't know. I doubt it. I don't even know that she really is gay. It could be just that Gioia's kind of taken her over. It's odd. It's as if so many of the things we've done seem different now. Things we've said, things we talked about.' The well-trodden paths of their friendship, on that Sunday evening, suddenly appeared strange. 'I've had it with today. I'm going to go to bed to read,' said Annie. The combination of Kendra's news and the lack of any word from Jackson all weekend now made Annie consider the day past rescue. She put the kettle on and fetched her hot-water bottle. Even the rubber as it heated up felt horrible rather than comforting. She wrapped a T-shirt around it and carried it into bed. She should probably drink some water, but she couldn't be bothered.

1984

7

The pile of potted cabbage roses in Lee's arms was threatening to collapse as he carried them up the narrow stairs to the boardroom. Following, Annie was loaded with Perrier bottles, which Tania had decreed would stand sentry on each side of small terracotta pots for the meeting. Tania was always going on about how important first impressions were, and how you only got one chance.

'Stop fussing around. What's this about anyway?' Lee asked Annie, attempting to wipe off the small spots of earth which had spattered out of the miniature pots on to the sleeve of his crisp white shirt. Lee had recently embarked upon a radical style revamp as a result of meeting Ray Petri, the famous Buffalo stylist. From that moment on, his previous wardrobe was history.

Annie was not entirely sure that the dark foundation Lee was using really suited him, but she knew that he was aiming for a touch of the swarthy colouring of Petri's Buffalo models, the young princes feted as multicultural urban warriors in *The Face*. It was funny the way he cared so much more about the labels, the precise way his ankle sock was turned down – the whole *look* – than she did.

'Clothes make the man,' he said to her, only partially aware of the obviousness of that idea. Still, this new wardrobe, with its boxy shapes, looked good on him. Lee had struggled with the billowing blouses of his New Romantic era as he was on the short side. 'Five foot eight and three quarters, if you must know,' he would say when challenged. For him, the ace thing about Doc Martens was that the thick sole gave him a bit of a lift.

'It's about some charity opening. I heard Tania say we're down to the last two companies pitching. It's something to do with the NSPCC. That's who's coming in. But I don't understand why they're paying Tania to give a party . . .'

Lee shrugged. 'Hers to know and ours to take what we can get. Can you grab the ashtrays? They're in the kitchen.'

Just then, the doorbell chimed and the two heard Tania's voice in greeting, the one she used when she wanted to impress – all oozy and warm and chuckly. Tania's hair, more often a halo of expensively maintained blonde curls, had been slicked back in a small bun, and she had replaced the intricate gold jewellery that frequently dangled from her neck and wrists with a single silver bean from Tiffany's Elsa Peretti range. As she moved, it bounced against the substantial shelf of her breasts, contained by the dove-grey tunic she wore.

'It's bitter out there, isn't it?' she was saying. 'Come in, sit down and we'll make ourselves comfortable.' Tania rubbed her hands and gestured to Annie and Lee to help get everyone seated. A small woman with a briefcase sat first, the back of her nylons spotted from the rain. She glanced as if for permission in the direction of her colleague, whose long face was almost entirely covered by a pair of startling red-framed spectacles, his tieless shirt buttoned at the collar. He reminded Annie of the men her father used to make for her out of bendy pipe-cleaners.

'Tania, I think you know Marisa Rootstein. Marisa is chairing the committee for selling tickets and has kindly agreed to sit in on this morning's meeting. We are very grateful for the Rootsteins' involvement in the event. Their generosity and commitment has been invaluable.' He removed his spectacles briefly, as a gesture, then immediate replaced them.

'Of course I know Marisa.' Tania beamed broadly across the table to where Marisa sat, her pale face expressionless as she rolled a thick fountain pen between her fingers. It was, Annie noticed, one of those expensive ones with the white star on the tip. Jackson had one of those too. He kept it on his bedside table at night, always stuffing it into a jacket pocket the next day.

'Can I firstly say how excited we all are at Torrington by the possibility of being involved with this event. As you know, design is my *personal* passion, and I feel that we are well placed to ensure that this event will be a great success. Annie, can you distribute the papers?'

Annie had only met Marisa once, when she had collected Kendra before a film. Marisa had opened the door wearing a silver sheath that reached the floor, shouted for her daughter and then turned, wordlessly, to Art, who was standing behind her, to adjust his bow tie. She had not invited Annie into the house but had simply left the door open, making it unclear whether Annie should step in or stand out on the doorstep and let the cold air fill the hall.

Seeing her in the room close up, Annie couldn't stop looking at her skin. Kendra had beautiful skin, but completely different – olive, impervious. She never got spots, or blackheads even, though, as far as Annie could remember, she had never used a cleanser or toner in her life. Marisa's skin was more like marble, with small violet veins under her eyes. She had only a few creases along her upper lip, where her lipliner met the flesh.

'Perhaps you could elucidate what contribution you feel your team could make. As you know, *Design for the Eighties* will be a collection of the very finest work from the contemporary design scene. Charles' – she nodded at pipe-cleaner man – 'has told us that we should consider you for the role of public relations team for this event. I'm sure you also know there is a large amount of competition for this project. Tania, I hope you don't mind my asking, but are you acquainted with this period of design – Starck, Sottsass, Patrick Shaw?' Marisa glanced over at the decidedly animal-print sofas.

'Oh gosh yes. I'm an old mate of Patrick's – he and I used to have a right old time together at parties. In fact, and you can ask him about this' – Tania leant forward conspiratorially – 'I remember him having a scene with my flatmate Jackie – we were in a lovely place just up the street from here – back in the early seventies when I was doing my modelling, as young girls did.' The smile Annie and Lee knew she considered to be winning was not working as she directed it at Marisa. Her flushed face showed that she was feeling nervous, and being nervous didn't suit Tania. Luckily, Annie thought, it wasn't a lunchtime meeting and she couldn't bring out the wine. That could sometimes make things worse.

Charles stepped in. 'We feel this is a uniquely appropriate time to demonstrate how key contemporary design is to the way we live now. It's no longer the preserve of the few but has a validity in everybody's life. It's an exciting shift of the moment and as such this is an ideal exhibition to encourage support of something equally as central to everybody's life as . . .' There was a pause as he surveyed his audience. 'Children.' Despite producing the word as a revelation, it was obvious that this aspect of the event was not something he was entirely at home with.

Tania talked through the papers that had been distributed. Under the dark-green intertwined double 'T' that headed the thick paper was a proposal under the headings:

Guest list
Campaign strategy
Charity message
Sponsors

As Tania shared her thoughts on the structure of the evening her voice calmed, and her hands, which during the initial moments of the meeting had flailed, were confidently still. The room had become her stage and she the leading actress in command of her audience.

She's good at this stuff, thought Annie. She's even got Marisa paying attention. Only the previous evening, Tania had sat at the table after another presentation and given Annie a lesson in what she called 'Tania's finishing school for life'.

'You've got to make them feel they can rely on you and *only* you. It's like you're telling them to take a nice hot bath with a long glass of pop. Tell them to relax. When they get out, you've made sure they've got a warm towel at the ready and *then*, and only *then*, mind you, you whack it to them . . . all the troubleshooting you've done, how you've headed off heaven knows what at the pass – because you were there. They didn't have an inkling.' The lecture had ended with a heavy sigh. Occasionally, Annie wondered whether Tania was happy.

An hour later, the glasses of Perrier hardly touched, the group raised themselves from the table.

'Thank you, Tania, for your time and your extremely interesting proposal,' Charles said as he picked up the papers in front of him and then prodded the glasses which threatened to slide completely off the sharp slope of his nose to a safer place. 'We'll get back to you within the month.'

'I look forward to it, and do let me know if there is any other information we can provide. Lee, be a dear and get the TTPR press pack for everyone, and we'll meet you downstairs.'

Left alone in the boardroom, Annie started to gather the glasses.

'It is *Aarna*, isn't it? Kendra's friend?' Marisa stood in the doorway, her voice a flat drawl. Her stillness was more potent than any gesture. 'You're her good friend, aren't you?'

Annie nodded. Should she correct Marisa's strange pronunciation of her name?

'How you girls have gone your different ways.' It was unclear whether Marisa expected any kind of response, as her gaze focused past Annie and over to the large windows where the dirty light of the winter afternoon had now been replaced by darkness.

'I wouldn't have expected Kendra to be involved in public relations, but she has, as I'm sure you know, taken a somewhat strange – some might say deliberately obtuse – route at this point in her life. I take it you've met . . . her friend, that ridiculous creature?'

'You mean Gioia? Um, yes. Well, not often. She seems . . . nice.'

'Nice. What part of her do you consider is nice, I wonder. Hmm. Nice? Do you really think so?'

Marisa turned to leave the room. 'You need to get her out of this mess,' she said as she walked away.

After Christmas Day with Alfie and John, and after Gioia's return to London from Glasgow, when they spent a wonderful two days in her flat watching cheesy movies on the TV and making love so often that time turned on its head, Kendra lay wedged between

Gioia's legs in the bath and decided that she had to tell her parents about her girlfriend.

She had begun to leave things in the flat, and she loved the way in which Gioia appeared to accept any part of Kendra in her life. Kendra had never previously left so much as a toothbrush in anybody's home. As far as possessions were concerned, she had relatively few that she really cared for. Art was always offering to buy her stuff, but she couldn't think of anything she really wanted, and she hated the way that some people took anything they could get their hands on, just so they could own it. She had to admit her mum wasn't at all grabby. Everything she possessed fitted perfectly in its place, and there was nothing superfluous. But of course that was because she was always trying so hard. She couldn't ever relax about anything.

Even so, when Kendra saw a pile of her knickers and T-shirts sitting on the open shelves under the window, the leather case of her camera slung on a hook near the door and a few of her compilation tapes lying on the stereo at Gioia's place, she was pleased. She had used her father's state-of-the-art sound system to compile the tapes for Gioia and was particularly proud of one that led Talking Heads into a track from Black Uhuru and then changed pace entirely, with Nino Rota's jangling music for Fellini. Gioia played it all the time, raising her arms in support and singing loudly to the Heads' 'Burning Down the House'.

'Kendra, your mum and dad can't be that bad. Just tell them. You know. It's your life. They can't live it for you.' Gioia had told her that only the other day. But Gioia didn't understand. It wasn't like that. Kendra couldn't *just tell them*. She knew that they would be frustrated, disappointed, angry, confused. It would be awful.

It had been a last-minute idea of Art's to go out for dinner at L'Angolo.

'The last time I went in there I saw that friend of yours, Jim McKenzie, with some girl, probably younger than me. It was *revolting*,' Kendra volunteered.

'Kendra, I don't know where you get that puritan streak. Truly I don't,' Marisa had replied, looking intently at her daughter as if she could find the answer. 'Jill knows about his little rendezvous. I believe that one is now in the past.'

They had walked the five minutes to the lively trattoria. The previous day, London had been covered by a snowfall and transformed into an entirely different place, the sounds of the city deadened by the white blanket that sparkled and crunched. But now the snow had melted into a filthy slush and their steps squelched along the street. The walk took them past large gardens where the snow still balanced on the branches of trees, occasionally tumbling hopelessly to the ground. Kendra was grateful for the noise and activity of L'Angolo when they arrived, Art giving the manager Riccardo a clap on his shoulder in greeting. They were guided, with ceremony, to their table.

'I think I'll order the *fegato di vitello*,' said Art, examining the room.

'You should tell them to go easy on the butter, honey. Maybe have it simple . . . *alla griglia*.' Marisa folded her steel-rimmed reading glasses. 'I'll just have a plate of my usual *verdura al olio*.' Kendra knew it was unfair of her to be irritated by their use of Italian, since after all they were *in* an Italian restaurant, but somehow, after hearing Gioia chattering colloquially in that language, they sounded . . . kind of wrong.

'So tell us. What's new around your place, doll.' Art poured them all a glass of wine, swirling his in the glass.

'Oh, not much. You know. The kids are back at school, so it's all after-school stuff now, and we are trying to put together an arts programme for spring – taking them to see some exhibitions, maybe seeing if we could do a theatre trip. Gioia believes that it's important to get them out of the space and into other worlds sometimes. Kind of inspire them.'

'Aha!' Art's concentration was temporarily diverted by the arrival of the calf's liver, which, despite ordering plainly grilled had arrived with an accompanying plate of sautéed potatoes. He refused to acknowledge Marisa's disapproving look.

'I don't know how you can eat that stuff, Dad. Calves. It's not even as if it was a fully grown cow that maybe, just maybe, was old enough to die. And calf's *liver.*'

'To each his own, darling. Your mother and I, after all, do not have the same feeling for this project of yours. We would be much happier if we could get you involved in something more suitable for somebody like you.'

'It's not a project, it's a job. And you should be pleased that I'm doing something worthwhile with my life. And, as for "something more suitable for somebody like me", what *is* somebody like me?'

Marisa cut up her vegetables with the precision of a surgeon. 'You have had the benefits of a great education. You have had an upbringing surrounded by cultural activity and intellectual debate. You have lacked for nothing in the material sense. Surely even you would admit that, in spite of your best efforts to cause us consternation, you have been brought up in an atmosphere of enormous nurture and, as a result, "somebody like you" is somebody who should be applying themselves to greater things. Things that count in the real world.'

'Now, we are meant to be having an enjoyable family meal here. I'm not asking for the Waltons, but I have no interest in paying these prices to hear you two argue,' Art intervened. 'Kendra, why don't you bring Gioia over next Thursday? If she's interested in all these things, your mother and I would surely have something in common with her. We would like to meet her.' His tone did not encourage debate.

On her own turf, Marisa considered herself insuperable, armoured by her impressive house, her huge acquaintance, her solid marriage, her social grace. It would not be any kind of a fair contest, which was the way in which Kendra viewed the potential meeting.

'I'll ask her. She probably won't be able to make it.' Kendra wiped the plate with bread, concentratedly soaking up every trace of her tomato sauce. 'It's not her bag at all . . . but . . .' She shrugged. The occasions were few, but when her father spoke in that particular tone it was best to go along with him.

'Delicious *verdura*.' Marisa turned around to look across the room, her thin hand rhythmically massaging the back of her neck. 'Art, isn't that Lucian Freud over there? Look, in the far corner?'

Kendra was surprised by Gioia's enthusiasm at the prospect of visiting the Rootsteins. She seized on the occasion as an opportunity to display her style at its most dramatic.

'Hey, girl, no holding me back' had been her reaction when Kendra brought up the idea as they were tidying the Chapel the next night.

Gioia's hair for the past few weeks had been piled into plaits on the top of her head with an increasing number of thick strands escaping but for her presentation at the Rootsteins' she unwrapped it, letting it lie in glistening snakes over her shoulders. As she padded across the room to fetch an intricate collar of silver chains hung with metal and wooden charms, her leather trousers accentuated a muscularity that had nothing to do with athleticism.

In contrast, Kendra stubbornly decided not to change, leaving her hair scraped back with an elastic band and her UCLA sweatshirt coffee-stained.

'They know what I look like, you know. I don't see what the fuss is about,' said Kendra, countering Gioia's attempts to up her style level a notch. 'It's you that are going to be exhibit number one.'

Kendra was working on the basis of safety in numbers and, since her parents prided themselves on the mixed-age constituency of their soirées, she had also enrolled Sal into the enterprise, knowing that Sal would be excited by the opportunity. Marisa had spoken about rustling up some people from LA, leaving Kendra with an image of her mother with a lasso, herself running in the opposite direction.

'I said we'd meet Sal at the Tube. I can't believe I'm doing this,' Kendra mumbled. 'She's dead pleased, as she thinks she might get some kind of a story out of it, and she says it's important to network. That's what she calls it. I call it torture.'

Sal was already there waiting, her legs stork-like beneath an electric-blue ra-ra skirt, its width accentuating their thinness. She had sculpted her dark crop into chunky spikes and her head emerged from a bright scarf wrapped around her neck and mouth.

'Have you been waiting ages? Hey. Nice mousse job.' Kendra gave her a kiss.

'No, just got here.' Sal touched her hair. 'I think I overdid it. It feels like concrete, but I don't suppose anyone's going to be wanting to run their fingers through it tonight. I don't imagine your mum and dad's is going to be the best place to find a boyfriend. Into battle we go?' She looked at Gioia, hoping for a gesture that might indicate they were in this together.

Gioia laughed. 'I've been telling Kendra that she's got herself into a right old state about nothing.'

By the time they arrived, the white sofas in the Rootsteins' drawing room were entirely covered with figures, a many-headed Hydra of chatter. The level of the music was perfectly calibrated to allow the gravel voice of Nina Simone to penetrate the noise while never rising to a pitch that could interfere with conversation.

As they walked into the largest of the rooms, expertly lit with a mixture of enormous table lamps, their light filtered through creamy silk shades, and large pillar candles which contributed to the flattering glow, Kendra could see her mother standing by the window with a bald man who seemed to be recounting something that he obviously found tremendously amusing. Alternately nodding and stroking the stem of her wine glass, Marisa was the model of concerned interest. It was, everyone said, amazing how Marisa could get people to tell her things. It was something to do with her knowing how to use silence.

'Let's get a drink.' They pushed their way to a long table covered in a white linen cloth. Around it, people stood chattering, picking at the bowls of olives and pistachios.

'Miss Kendra.' Laila's son, Alessandro, who always helped out on Thursdays, appeared by her side. 'You like white wine?' Kendra looked agonized at the way he addressed her.

'Yes, please,' jumped in Sal. Gioia nodded. Kendra led the group back through the throng towards one of the smaller rooms, where Alfie's startling head of blond curls was apparent. As the trio approached the wide-open double doors between the rooms, Art appeared, his trim frame made somehow smaller by the expansive Gioia next to him.

'Hi, doll. And you are . . . Joy?' Gioia took his hand in greeting. Art then gave Sal a kiss on the assumption – one he often made – that she was somebody he knew even though he had forgotten her name.

'It's *Gioia*.' Kendra spoke crossly.

'Quite a crowd. Quite a crowd tonight. We have some very, very close friends in town from the West Coast and we thought we'd rustle up a little party for them. We've mixed it up with the design gang Marisa's gotten in with, now she's doing some whacky charity exhibition. I say to her, "Maris. Make it easy on yourself. Why do these things? You know how it takes it out of you." But she never hears it.' He beamed at the notion. 'You interested in contemporary design?' he asked Gioia.

'I'm more of a performance person. Music, dance, theatre – that kind of stuff.'

Sal moved away and stood by one of the long windows, the colour of her skirt a flash of cobalt against the white wall and heavy white curtains. She watched the clusters of guests shift around, gathering and dispersing to re-form a few feet away. Although she didn't recognize anybody, she didn't feel threatened. Instead, the evening housed possibility. For a few moments she happily stood alone. It was so different to her own parents' sitting room, where the dark walls were covered in bookshelves, the few small watercolours invariably awry. She could only remember her parents giving a party once. What could it have been for? She had been impressed by the unfamiliar sound of the doorbell ringing again and again and the bang of the door with arrivals and departures as she sat in her bedroom. She must have been about fifteen.

'Allow me.' Sal looked up to see the flame of a lighter held by a man, his pronounced girth covered in a pink sleeveless pullover. 'I guess you're with Art's girl? Jim.' He bowed slightly in introduction and lit her cigarette along with one of his own.

Sal knew who he was. Jim McKenzie. A Richard Branson type. It was one of those names that floated around the pages of the papers. He was exactly who she expected she would meet that evening. Was he in film? Publishing? Something like that.

'Yes – Kendra's one of my best friends.'

'You been to one of these before?'

'No. I don't think Ken often comes. You know. She's doing her own thing.'

'Yeah, and she's not so keen on her mum's social vibe, I hear. Anyway. Tell me. Who's the leather queen with her? She's quite a piece of work.'

'Oh, that's Kendra's boss. Gioia.' Sal was certain that this was as far as Kendra would like her to go in explanation.

'She is? Interesting.' Jim drew the word out. 'Come and meet my boy, Ryan. He's somewhere around the place. More your age than I am, though, you know . . . I try, I try.' It was coming to her. She could hear Ollie's words.

'Christ. Can you believe it? Katy . . . you know, the girl I told you about from university. She's shagging Jim McKenzie. I saw them together at the Virgin bash. She showed me the necklace he's given her. Tiffany's, she said. Didn't look much to me.' It had been further ammunition for his theory about girls and married men.

Sal was grateful for the attention, particularly from somebody as well known as Jim McKenzie, but was relieved that she wasn't going to end up having to extricate herself from an embarrassing situation. With his jowels and receding hairline, she couldn't im-agine how anybody of her age could bear to have sex with him. He had to be nearly *fifty*. She followed him across the room to where a young man was seated on the arm of a deep chair talking to a woman with a heavy fringe and the angry face of a Pekinese. He certainly didn't resemble his father. She took in long legs and a suede bomber jacket.

Jim slapped him on the shoulder. 'Ryan. I found you some lovely company. Jill, let's leave the youth to get acquainted. Chaim's over there. We should have a word.'

Kendra had left Gioia discussing Coltrane with her father. She was thrown by Gioia's willingness to engage with him and her own annoyance about it, and walked through the deep architrave over to Alfie and John, who sat squashed on a small straight-backed sofa. At their feet crouched a woman Kendra recognized as one of Marisa's friends from Pilates, her legs encased in black stirrup pants finished off with the double 'C' of Chanel pumps.

'Kendra. Our favourite girl.' John stood to embrace her. He looked even more gaunt than he had at Christmas. In contrast, Alfie was rotund, a superannuated choir boy, the effect highlighted by his penchant for bright reds. Tonight it was a turtleneck which gave him the appearance of a supermarket tomato.

'So, we assume *that* is the mysterious Gioia whom we have heard so little about?' Alfie raised one well-maintained eyebrow. Kendra had noticed the look Alfie had given John as they saw her arrive; it had been knowing and arch.

'Hello, Jacquetta,' she said, appealing to Marisa's friend as a shield against any awkward questions. 'Are you still doing Pilates with Mum?'

'Oh yes. Me and Marisa. Dreas calls us his early birds. We simply swear by him to keep us in one piece. Did she tell you we had Christopher Lambert in the other day on the reformer next to us?'

'What?' Alfie shrieked, opening his eyes in exaggerated interest. 'Tarzan. Ooh . . . some *girls* get all the luck. Do dish. What's the body like?'

'Alfie! Don't be so trashy. Jacquetta, I am sure, had her mind on higher things.' John smiled fondly at his partner. Kendra was only partially listening. She could see Marisa had joined Art and Gioia and appeared to be attempting to claim her husband, gesturing towards the other end of the room.

'Bring her over here.' Alfie followed Kendra's gaze. She beckoned to Gioia, who walked through the throng, head held high.

'Gioia – meet Alfie and John. You know, I told you about them. And this is Mum's friend Jacquetta.'

'So, you must be some woman to have captivated our Kendra.' John smiled kindly. Kendra felt a blush climb up her neck. 'She tells us that your outfit, the place you run, is quite, quite wonderful. Alfie. Do you remember that unit Patsy had down near Christopher Street when we were in New York? We had a friend who did something a little similar. I don't know if she's still there. The neighbourhood's changing so much.'

Thank God. He had only been referring to the Chapel, and not their relationship. Still, Kendra had had quite enough, but Gioia had removed her jacket and accepted another drink. The crowd was starting to thin out and, in the distance, Kendra saw a glimpse of Sal's blue skirt as she left the room with Jim McKenzie's son.

It seemed like ages, but it was no more than twenty minutes later when John said he and Alfie should be going. Alfie had made a date to come and look at the Chapel. He gave Kendra a warm hug good-bye.

'Now you look after yourself. Call me for a chat sometime. We could have a nice dim sum and you could fill me in on things.' She watched them leave, John's jacket hanging loose, even to her inexpert eyes.

'Some place your family have, Ken,' Gioia said as they moved towards the stairs. 'I guess I understand why you didn't want me to come here. But, you know. We all have to play the game, and they're not so bad. Well, your dad was fine.'

'I can't tell them tonight, Gioia.'

'Sure. No sweat. Let's go.'

As they walked down the stone staircase, its broad steps with the indentations she knew from childhood, Kendra was confused by a momentary desire to stay in the house, tucked up in her bed in her room with its familiar view high above the gardens. A door opened, and Sal and Ryan emerged together from the downstairs loo.

'Hi, Ken. Are you off?' Sal appeared unembarrassed, unlike Ryan, who hovered lankily next to her.

Kendra turned to see Marisa and Art at the top of the stairs.

'Where you going, doll? We can get Gioia a cab on the account. No need to see her into a taxi, it's cold out there.' They made a stately procession down the stairs towards the foursome.

'No. It's OK, Dad. Thanks. Um . . .' Kendra grabbed Gioia's hand. 'I'm . . . I'm going home with her. You know, don't you?' she said quickly, furiously. 'You know what's happening.' She yanked Gioia out through the front door, which slammed, the sound bouncing harshly off the stone.

'What the hell – ' Art stared at the door.

'*Quién sabe?*'

'Oh, for Christ's sake, Marisa. Is Kendra some kind of dyke? What's going on here?'

They looked at Sal, who, although fizzing with the two lines of coke she had just shared with Ryan, was unsure now which way to move or what to say. She shrugged off any knowledge of her friend's behaviour, heartily wishing that they had stayed in the loo rather than becoming involved in Kendra's coming-out scene. The ensuing silence demanded some comment, but for once she was lost for words. And Ryan obviously had no idea what was happening.

Marisa glided back up the stairs to the sanctuary of the tail-end of the party, while Art shuffled down the corridor.

Sal made a bid for the front door. 'It's all getting a bit Tennessee Williams. Let's get out of here before we have to start doing group therapy. I don't think we need to say our goodbyes.'

8

The countryside was bursting with the promise of spring when Annie and Kendra pulled up at Letty Brenham's house for the weekend. Since Jackson was filming in America, Annie had taken the opportunity to suggest to Kendra that she come home with her for the weekend. 'It's been ages since we've been just us. We can go for some walks and catch up. Mum'll love looking after us and Sal can come after she knocks off on Saturday.'

The entrance hall of the farmhouse smelt of furniture polish overlaid with drifts of scent from small vases of freesia and narcissi placed as companions to the unchanging tablescapes – silver photo frames, china ashtrays and small ceramic animals, regularly dusted and replaced, just so.

'I know it's April but, really, there's still such a chill, isn't there?' Letty showed them into the sitting room, where the fireplace housed a welcoming blaze. 'How nice to have you girls with me. Kendra, I've put you and Sal in the blue room. The bathroom is just down the hall. There are towels on the bed.'

It occurred to Annie that her mother would have been thoroughly thrown if she had realized that Kendra was now having sex with a girl. Certainly she wouldn't have known *what* to do about 'the sleeping arrangements', as she called them.

'That's great, Mrs Brenham.'

'Oh Kendra, I think we know each other well enough by now for you to call me Letty.'

As Letty brushed the wave of her fair hair back from her face, Kendra could see her friend in the older woman. They shared the same light colouring and slim figure, but whereas Annie's pallor was luscious, her almost clear eyes captivating in the way they took on reflected colour, Letty was like a tracing, a faint outline that sometimes threatened to fade entirely.

'I do hope the traffic wasn't too terrible. I always say to Annie that it would be so much better if she could get on the road by four, and that way she'd miss the worst of it. But you girls with your jobs. She tells me nobody leaves the office until at least six, by which time that bit all around Twickenham is a complete nightmare.' Letty plumped the square cotton-covered cushions that lined the sofa back. 'And then poor Sal, she has to work Saturdays, doesn't she? What time is she arriving tomorrow?'

'She's going to call. What's for dinner?' Through the window, Annie saw that her mother's purple hyacinths were still in place. There had been a discussion last spring about whether it would be better to swap them for white.

'I've got a coq au vin in the Aga. There's only the salad to toss. You two must be starving.'

Kendra sensed that Annie was about to remind her mother, a little late in the day, that she was vegetarian. She shook her head to prevent her. She'd had years of practice hiding pieces of meat under her knife and fork or scooping vegetables out from casseroles. The warmth and undemanding comfort of the house was lovely and she didn't want anything to spoil it.

The next morning when she came downstairs she found Annie in her dressing gown sitting at the table with her mother, digging into a boxed honeycomb.

'It's so nice for me to have you girls here. I'm hoping I might be allowed to meet Annie's boyfriend one day.' Both Kendra and Annie knew she had deliberately brought Jackson up between offers of toast, tea and eggs, hoping Annie might be more open on the subject in front of her friend. But the truth was that Annie didn't really know what to tell her mother, and she certainly couldn't imagine bringing him home to meet Letty.

The more she was with Jackson, the more she wanted to be with him. She never felt she had had enough of him, and there was always this horrible empty feeling immediately after they parted. It was ridiculous, she told herself, to be so needy. Not that she told him. Once, as they lay as spoons in his bed, she had made an attempt, speaking into his back.

'Jackson, I was just thinking . . . Maybe we could decide to see each other in a bit more of an organized way. Just, kind of . . . maybe we could try and plan a bit so that then, when I'm not seeing you, I can organize other things?' He had just turned over and rolled on to her, gently nudging her legs apart and stroking her and telling her how very, very gorgeous she was and, as they made love, he called her baby and darling and gasped, 'I love you.' She knew that it didn't really count when a man said 'I love you' like that but, even so, that didn't stop it sounding wonderful.

Although it was spring and the garden was filled with daffodils and trees that were starting to fill out, losing their skeletal winter shape and hinting of the summer to come, it was still cold. Wrapped in the collection of old coats and scarves that Letty kept in the downstairs cupboard, the two friends set off for a walk.

'Get some fresh air while you can,' Letty had said as she waved them off. 'Lunch will be at one. Just cold cuts, so nothing to fuss about.'

The fields were still hard, and their feet crunched over the muddy verges as they walked around their edges.

'Do you think Sal's OK?' Kendra asked after they had walked for a while in silence.

'How do you mean?'

'She just seems so out of it so much of the time. I know she's always been keen on a drink, but in the last year it seems to have got worse. It's not like she's falling-over drunk – well, not always – but you know that look she gets, kind of wild, glassy? Don't you think it's happening more often? You live with her.'

'Sometimes she's fine.' Annie stopped on the brow of the hill and looked over the patchwork of fields stretching ahead. 'But I was worried the other day when I found out that she'd been going to the Builder's Arms on her own. I don't think that's normal. You wouldn't do that, and I wouldn't. It seems a bit sad.' She could hear her heart-beat from the uphill walk. 'And then there are the nights she doesn't come back and I don't know where she's spent the night. Obviously, I'm not her mum or anything, but I kind of like knowing if she's coming home or not. When she does return she's normally com-pletely felled by a hangover. Sometimes she'll tell me about who she's been with and she'll make it all sound like a big joke, even when it's clear it was all a bit of a disaster.'

'I don't know why she has to drink so much. The way she talks, it sounds like work's going well – she's getting more stories now. But one day she's going to blow it if she carries on like this.' Kendra's face was screwed up in concern for Sal's future and the immediate question of how to negotiate a substantial barbed-wire fence. 'Maybe she'll calm down. Or do you think we should say some-thing? But I don't know how to do that.' But, by the time they had managed to find a way out of the field, the issue of Sal and alcohol had been forgotten.

When they walked back into the kitchen at the house, Letty switched off the radio, wiping her hands first on her blue and white striped apron.

'I really don't know how Arthur Scargill can behave this way.' She took the cellophane off a plate of cold ham, unpeeling it slowly from the bottom. 'At least we've got a strong government. Annie knows I don't have a great deal of time for Margaret Thatcher – there's something that I don't like about the woman. But you can't fault her for sticking to her beliefs.'

'I don't want to be rude, Letty, but she's awful.' Kendra paced around the table. 'I mean, it's like living in a dictator state. You know they're letting the police carry guns now. And it was really *brutal* the way they cleared the women's camp at Greenham last week. Tony Benn said it was an erosion of our civil liberties.'

'Well, civil liberties or not, I know they've made a terrible mess of that place. My friend Serena lives only a few miles away. She's says it's a tip.' Letty was giving each piece of cutlery a wipe with a dishcloth before putting it on the table.

'The news team thinks that the miners' strike is going to be the big story for months,' Sal told Kendra and Annie when they had collected her that evening from the local station and were on their way to the pub. 'They're working out the numbers they need to cover it, and Brenda – she's the news desk secretary – is having to line up places to stay near the big picket lines. It's all guns blazing on this huge story, and most of the time I'm stuck telling you the odds on the new royal baby's name. George. At 4–7, if you're interested. If it's a boy. I don't think Diana looks very happy. Even though she's pregnant, her face has gone all sharp.'

'She didn't look like that with William.' Annie swerved into the forecourt, wedging her small car between a mud-spattered saloon and a rusty camper van. 'She's made the royal family much more interesting, though, hasn't she? I think she's absolutely lovely. There's something really special about her. Tania's always trying to work out a way we can get her to one of our events. She's hoping we might be able to link her into this thing we're doing for the NSPCC. After all, she's meant to be crazy about children.'

'Mum's doing that NSPCC thing, isn't she?' Kendra pushed the seats forward to curl her long legs out of the side door of the car. 'She's the opposite. Not the slightest bit interested in children, but give her a contemporary designer and she's in overdrive. "Nappies were never my thing," she says. Like they are anybody's *thing*.'

Annie thought of Marisa's face in the doorway, the cold fury of her tone: 'You need to get her out of this mess.' Was Kendra in a mess? It didn't seem like it.

The evening in the pub was like the best of old times. They monopolized the jukebox with songs they used to listen to on the one at university. 'Do you think jukebox people have a central pool of singles? Look. "Nights in White Satin" – irresistible, and coming on next – and yes, there it is, the inimitable "All Riiiiiiight Now",' commented Sal as Annie collected the drinks and they stood reading out the song titles, their faces lit by the flashing of the slot machine next to them. Kendra had reduced them to tears

'Broadhurst's agent has made it clear that he'll only do the interview if it's with a *young female* interviewer. He won't meet with Crispin. But the editor thinks you're right about the story and that we should get on it this week. We're booking you out tomorrow. It's the quickest but the riskiest option, if you ask me, but I wasn't consulted. You can fly in and straight back.'

It was a relief to be out of the airport. She'd been filled with all kinds of worries about getting through immigration. 'No wisecracks or they'll turn you around and send you back. They've done it before,' Marsha counselled, as if she was in New York every other week. 'The guys at JFK regard it as their duty to make you feel like an alien.'

And it was true that, standing in the synthetic-cherry-scented line at passport control, she could see the officials scrutinizing each traveller with unforgiving sternness, custodians of entry to the land of the free yet obviously regarding each person as a potential criminal. There was a terrifying moment when she couldn't find her passport, its dark-blue cover invisible in the darkness of her handbag, but after a frantic scrabble and having to empty her shoulder bag on to the floor, where her grubby packaged Lil-lets and broken Maybelline eye pencil could be observed by the queue, she found it, wedged between the pages of *I Know Why the Caged Bird Sings*. Kendra had told her the book was brilliant, but she hadn't yet managed to get into it. Every morning, she meant to read it on the bus, but by the time she'd read a newspaper there wasn't long left. It was always a mystery to her how Marsha managed to read all the papers. Of course, she didn't have any proper life.

The blue-uniformed questioner slowly turned the pages of her passport.

'You're in New York City for the week? Welcome, Ma'am.' A noisy stamp, and she was through.

On the wall behind the curved desk of the reception hall of 1501 Madison Avenue was such a long list of businesses that Sal was having trouble finding Waters, Schwartz and Leipkin PR. The uniformed man at the desk stared straight through her as he intoned:

'Eighteenth floor, second elevator.' The original meeting had been shifted, leaving her a whole day in the city to herself.

It took only a few hours for Sal to decide that New York was definitely where she wanted to work. Even walking down the streets, with their funnelled horizons and giant buildings, exciting; the speed, the noise, the largeness of everything immediately intoxicating. After checking into her midtown hotel, she had wandered straight out, buying a warm pretzel from the stand at the corner, the salt sticking to her lips.

Ollie had informed her with authority that the trick of beating jet lag was to stay up as late as possible the first day, but after several hours of walking up and down Madison and Fifth and discovering Gap, where the T-shirts, the fashion desk had advised, were cheaper and better than anything you could find in England, she was wondering how she was going to keep herself awake for long enough. It was nearly midnight in London when, lying on the hard hotel bed, she dialled the number she had for Crispin.

Within the hour, she was in a leatherette booth in an Upper West Side steakhouse. Men of all ages stood two deep along the wooden bar, their ranks occasionally broken up by colour, the vivid green or red of a woman's suit, her pale legs standing out among the dark trousers.

'Martini. The only drink, my dear girl,' Crispin pronounced with conviction as he ordered. 'Stan, make it one of your best for my young friend from London. We want to show her what this town is all about. Now,' he said, turning to Sal, 'fill me in on Patrick's empire back at home. Sometimes I feel as if I'm in the colonies over here. But, if you live in New York, you know, they regard England as the colony. They like our accents and the pretty girls, of course, like you, who all sound like the Princess of Wales to them. They have a fondness for Jermyn Street too. Turnbull & Asser.' Crispin pulled at the cuffs of his shirt. 'Far more effective, my dear, than our ambassador for transatlantic relations.'

Sal wasn't sure how to respond to Crispin, who was not as she had imagined. His reputation in the office was as a useless freeloader only hanging on to his job because he had been at Cambridge with Patrick. The fact that he was one of Nancy Reagan's favourites, so often given a tip-off and consistently filing enjoyable scoops, was conveniently ignored by the foreign desk. She had expected somebody shabbier. The spotted bow tie suited him. Even his eyebrows, so fine they could have been penciled in, gave him the air of an aesthete rather than a hack.

'Everyone's talking about the miners' strike. They think it's going to run and run. Probably good for us to have a big story like this going on. Of course, I only get to write about the royal babies and that kind of thing. I never get proper news.'

'I think you'll find that improper news is a great deal more enjoyable in the long run.' Crispin gestured for another round of martinis. 'A fraction dryer this time, if you would, Stan. If I were you, I would leave the Libyans and the IRA and that dreary Scargill alone and concentrate on making more intriguing contacts around the place. An attractive young woman like you shouldn't find it any problem at all nosing out all kinds of delicious information. Now, we should eat. I recommend the steak and a side of fried onion rings. Or are you the kind of young woman who frets about her figure?'

When she woke the following morning, Sal could dimly recall Crispin walking her into the hotel lobby and insisting that somebody see her up to her room. She had no idea what time it was, but she had woken fully dressed, the sleeves of her jacket pulled tight and her skirt bunched underneath her. The blinds in the window were open and a dirty light was filling the space. She could make out the Z of the fire escape climbing a building opposite. She looked at the clock – 5.15. Obviously, the staying up hadn't really worked. Perhaps a shower was the thing. She pulled off her clothes, walking in her pants around the room. Here she was, in New York, on assignment.

Several hours later, as Michael Broadhurst's publicity agent walked Sal along the internal corridors of Waters, Schwartz and Leipkin, past the water coolers with their plastic cups and a coffee station that gurgled as the coffee filtered into a jug, she made it clear she would not be wasting much time with Sal Turner. Her American accent came across as more of a machine than a voice, thought Sal.

'Michael has half an hour. He will *only* be talking about the new play and *The Wings of the Dove*. He will *not* answer any questions about his personal life. I have his bio here with all the details. Your photographer has just left. We have photo approval.' She knocked on a wooden door at the end of the corridor, her demeanour changing as she walked into the room ahead of Sal, the rapid fire of her voice, softened to allow the odd inflection, encouraging the idea that she might even be human.

'Michael, honey . . . here's the *Herald*'s lady. Sally Turner.'

'Um, Sal, actually – well, Salome, but everyone calls me Sal.'

'Hello, Salome.' Michael Broadhurst stood up from the leather sofa where he had been sitting hunched over a coffee table piled with thick reams of paper. 'This is my set – actor with scripts.' He walked over to shake hands. 'I think we'll be fine, Mimi. I'll press the panic button if not.'

Sal had expected a film star to be daunting, but this interview was more of a conversation than an interrogation. Broadhurst didn't appear to mind being asked questions but, even so, she started with the easy stuff, the work he had just finished, a bit of background bio chat. By halfway through her interview slot, she had begun to relax, but she needed a good line from him. She hadn't got it yet.

'Are you apprehensive about the transition to the stage?' she asked. That sounded suitably respectable.

'Scared? Of course. But then you need that adrenalin surge, don't you, to perform? I'd have more to worry about if I wasn't nervous. And, of course, Joshua's a terrific part for me. He has this complex relationship with his father, who is a bully, completely furious about Joshua's undetermined sexuality, and it's a real challenge for me having to delve into a really different mentality.'

Sal knew this was the cue to ask the question that readers of the paper would really want her to ask. Was he homosexual? There were hardly any famous actors who admitted to being gay, even though everybody knew they were. She couldn't just ask him straight out though and, anyway, she could tell he wasn't. She even thought he might fancy her, the way he kept shifting forward on the edge of the sofa, leaning his elbows on his knees and looking right at her. But of course that might just be that he was really getting into the conversation.

'Hmm. Sexuality's such a difficult thing, isn't it? I mean, when you're acting?' she suggested.

Broadhurst smiled. 'Is it? What do you mean by that?'

Sal hadn't meant anything much. It just seemed a way to carry on the conversation while she worked out a better question. She could feel herself blushing.

'Oh, just . . . you know. It's such a big deal as an actor. Like, nobody wants to say they're homosexual, do they? Take an example. Everyone thinks that Clark Gable was, but you can't really look at *Gone with the Wind* the same way if you think that.'

Broadhurst looked at his watch. 'Tell you what. My terrifying PR is going to come back in a minute, but why don't we meet up later and I can give you a bit more. It's kind of nice to catch up with someone from home.'

'Of course. That would be fantastic. I would love that.' Sal stood up, pulling her white shirt down into the waistband of her skirt, unintentionally pulling it tight across her braless nipples.

'The Odeon at nine?'

'Sure.' She didn't want to ruin this perfect moment by asking what the Odeon was, or where. At that moment, the doors opened.

'Sally, you're into overtime. Michael doesn't have all day for your paper.' Mimi came and stood proprietorially beside her client. Sal decided not to say that she was seeing him later.

After she had left the offices, Sal immediately realized that she hadn't packed anything appropriate for a date with a famous actor. Annie had told her that American department stores had wonderful towels and sheets, and at the time she hadn't been able to imagine how this information could be of interest. But it had come back to her now. Would that be the same for clothes? Was it Bloomingdale's or Saks that was meant to be the place to go?

As she waited for the ornate lift to take her up to the womenswear department in Saks, she thought back to the day of the Harrods bombing and the girl in the café with her white face and uniform smeared with dust. Stepping out into an enormous space, where the rails of clothes stretched far into the distance, Sal was reminded why she never shopped in department stores. There was too much choice, and how could you ever find your way around?

Wherever she looked, she saw suits that were the kind of thing Krystle would wear on *Dynasty*. She riffled through a rail of silk blouses. They felt nice – smooth and expensive – but she didn't think they were really her. And she'd never seen so much beige. Sal hated beige. It was the ultimate dull colour. Her mother wore beige when she wanted to look smart.

She walked around pulling things off the rails until a sales assistant, who was very friendly and called her Ma'am, approached. Her long nails were startlingly pale on the tips of her black fingers as she folded the clothes across her arm.

'Your first time in New York? Oh Lord. You are going to love it here.' She glanced at the clothes Sal had gathered. 'Do you have the correct sizes?' Looking at Sal, she frowned, her pale-blue eyeshadow forming creases on her lids. 'These are going to be too large. I've never been to your country, but the ladies who come in say that in England you have different sizes.' She held up a pink and white striped top Sal had picked out. It was nearly twice Sal's width.

'Let's get you into the fitting room and I'll find you what you need. You look to me to be a petite.'

Three quarters of an hour later, Sal emerged with a shiny Saks carrier bag banging against her legs. The dress, wrapped in tissue, had slithered beautifully on to her, and she had felt as if she was wearing nothing. She loved the bluey-green colour and the cutaways on the shoulder. And, most importantly, it didn't make her look as if she was trying too hard.

'You should take the elevator down to hosiery and get yourself a pair of blue pantyhose. They would be the berries with that dress,' the assistant had advised. She had screamed when Sal told her she was buying the dress because she was going on a date with Michael Broadhurst.

'I just love that guy. He's such a Brit. Our guys never look like that. I guess they don't go to the same kind of schools or something. Is it true that the guards at Buckingham Palace make tea for the Queen?'

Even the exterior of the Odeon looked special, its name picked out in illuminated Art Deco typeface. The journey took Sal from the shopfronts and offices of midtown Manhattan, where it appeared that every inch of the city, including the sky, was being used for something, to a grimier part of the city where the buildings were lower, the brick warehouses dark and forbidding. Crispin had told her downtown had become the trendy area of the city, with huge lofts being bought up by artists and socialites, but to her it was bleak and threatening.

Queueing at the reception desk, she looked around the packed restaurant trying to spot Michael Broadhurst. From the ceiling, opaque white glass globes hung above white tablecloths. It was more like a party than a restaurant, people moving from table to table air-kissing, slapping each other on the shoulder, high-fiving in greeting. She saw him seated, jacketless, on a bar stool, his white shirt loose, with a narrow black tie.

He was deep in conversation with a dark-haired man and failed to notice her approach, or even when she was standing right next to him. His companion looked at her as if to ask, 'Who are you?' and, when her date turned, for a disconcerting instant, it was clear he didn't remember her.

'Ah, yes. Sal, isn't it?' He was a little smaller than she had thought earlier in the day, and a lot smaller than he appeared on screen. 'Do you know Keith? This is his gaff. He and his brother Brian own this city. Just the way two London boys should.' They walked over to a table by the wall, Keith moving away from Broadhurst with a 'Catch you later' and joining the buzzy hive in the centre, where nobody ever sat for long. Broadhurst raised his glass in a toast to a table there – 'Jay McInerney. He's got this place on the cover of his book. He's always in here.' The jade of Sal's dress stood out, her shoulders appearing smooth and ivory from the cutouts.

'I know you were given a raw deal with the interview time this morning, but can we agree tonight is off the record?'

'That's fine. 'Course.' Sal was flattered that he wanted to see her, and not for the interview. For the first hour, Sal rode the wave of his attention. Guiding her through the menu, he explained that the French salad was popular with most girls and the steak frites the best in New York. Did people always eat steak in New York, Sal wondered, thinking back to her dinner with Crispin. It was so exciting to be there with him that she didn't mind for a moment that, like many actors, Broadhurst was endlessly fascinated by himself. He could recite lines from his reviews even as he denigrated the writers of them.

'Of course the only review that's going to count on Broadway is the *Times*'s John Simon. But you have to remember they're only critics – they can't act, they can't direct, they can't write a play. They've just ended up knocking what other people *can* do.'

Sal wished she could remember more of the work of the *Herald*'s theatre critic. He was called Brian something or other, but he hardly ever came into the office.

'Brian, our critic, is very well respected. Do you think the play will come to London?'

'Yeah, Brian Feinstein. He's a bit of an old codger. I doubt we'll take it over there. Anyway, I've got another TV series lined up. TV is where the money is, and I'm looking at a couple of scripts my agent's sent me. I don't want to be typecast as the posh Brit. I've got more potential than that.' Sal was intoxicated by being in one of the most fashionable restaurants in the city in the company of one of that year's most successful television stars. It was perfect just to be there, as if somebody had pressed Lift-off and she had gone smoothly into orbit. By the second bottle of champagne, she had stopped wondering whether he was going to make a pass and, if he did, what would be the right thing to do.

Eventually, Sal stood up and squeezed out from the table to go to the bathroom.

'They're over there,' said Broadhurst, waving over to a corner. Sal walked slowly in that direction, vaguely taking in a table to the left where a couple were locked in a very public snog. As she neared, they broke apart and, even in the busyness of the room, she recognized Mimi, her earlier suit swapped for a bronze lamé top that sparked in the soft light, her dense curls a cape across her shoulders.

Sal hoped Mimi hadn't seen her with Michael. She was sure that she would do something to mess up the evening. But, then again, maybe she wouldn't mind. She was off duty now, wasn't she? It wasn't as if she was his nanny. And, anyway, it was starting to look like he wasn't going to make a move, which was a pity, since it would have been interesting. Unlike Mimi's man. From behind, she could see that his hand was tracing the line of Mimi's cheek, then he turned towards the room and gestured confidently to a waiter. Surely it wasn't. But, clearly, it was . . . She could see Jackson smiling at Mimi in that same goofy, adoring way she had seen him look at Annie. His arm was draped over her shoulder, gently stroking the curve of her collarbone. He leant in again to kiss her.

She moved quickly down to the toilets, grateful for the cool of their tiled walls to lean her forehead against while she took it in. Fucking jerk. Her mind went back to the previous weekend, when Annie had spoken about wanting to go to Venice with Jackson and how he would know all the best places to go. Of course, Sal had been right all along: he was a two-timing git. Well, he was going to get a fright when he saw her here. He probably thought she only ate at McDonald's. Suddenly she felt the slithering of ripped nylon. Damn, her tights must have laddered somewhere around the back. She stretched to examine her thigh – she was just able to reach around to daub some wet soap to stop the run.

The door slammed behind her as she walked out into the corridor, just as Jackson and Mimi reached the bottom of the stairs.

135

Jackson's hand was clearly fondling Mimi's bum. It took only a second, almost less, when he saw her, for him to adjust his face into a generous smile, moving away from Mimi and grasping Sal lightly by the shoulders in an embrace.

'Sal. You're looking great. That colour really suits you.' He leant in to kiss her cheek.

Sal jumped back, words and thoughts circling her mind, but she was silenced by confusion as she debated which *bon mot* should emerge first – 'You complete prick'? 'I've always thought you were crap'? 'Don't pretend you aren't getting off with that cold bitch I met today'? 'How can you be such a shit?'

Jackson smoothly introduced Mimi. 'Mimi, this is Sal, a pal of mine from London. Great place, isn't it? I always try and drop by when I'm in New York. Keith's a terrific guy.'

'We met earlier today, at the office,' Mimi said, with clear distaste. 'She was on the press junket we persuaded Michael to do.'

'Jackson's my best friend's boyfriend, you might be interested to know, and he's a total shit,' Sal heard herself say, her voice surprisingly calm when she finally spoke. She was oblivious to Mimi's pointed downgrading of her precious interview. 'He's been a shit from day one,' she restated icily, 'but, unfortunately, Annie is too sweet and kind and beautiful to realize it. *You* are much better suited.' She shoved past the couple, back up the stairs as quickly as she could, both to get away and to prevent them seeing the widening gash of the ladder in her tights, now highlighted by the white soap.

'I've got to have another drink. It's an emergency,' she gasped when she got back to the table. As another bottle was produced and she told Broadhurst the story, painting Jackson as a professional cad, she failed to notice that his interest was quite obviously on the wane. He'd taken a pen from the jacket beside him and was doodling on a scrap of paper. 'He thinks he's irresistible, one of those men whose dick is always halfway outside their pants. And the thing about Annie is she's just so *nice*. There isn't anybody who wouldn't love her. She only wants to meet the perfect guy and have babies, really. That makes her sound boring, but she isn't. It's just the way she is.' Sal paused only to gulp at the champagne. Her date was now looking around the large room, clearly for an escape route. 'Kendra, she's our other friend, thinks it's probably to do with her dad dying when she was still quite young. That seems a bit obvious to me, but Kendra's done quite a lot of psycho-stuff. Anyway, it's awful, it's really awful. If it were me – not that I would have had anything to do with him in the first place – I could deal with it. I know how to survive all that crap. Annie doesn't.'

At this point, Michael Broadhurst nodded sympathetically and placed his napkin on his plate deliberately.

'You should be going, don't you think?' he asked as he gestured for the bill, whatever oblique interest he might initially have had in Sal now utterly dispersed, as her compact, feline attraction was replaced by a less appealing slurring floppiness. 'You have a flight tomorrow, don't you? Is it the daytime or the red eye?' He handed her the white slip of paper but she couldn't take in the long list of items.

'I imagine the *Herald*'s standing us this dinner.' It was not a question. There seemed to be all kinds of things at the bottom of the bill – taxes, and God knows what else. Was she meant to tip? She couldn't. The bill left her only fifteen dollars of the float she had taken out with her to the States. When Andrea had handed her the envelope of cash, she had made it clear that she expected Sal to come back with some. The senior staff like Stuart and Patrick had American Express cards, but a junior wasn't eligible for a company credit card and she certainly didn't have one herself. Her cheque limit was £50 – not that she could use cheques in New York – and, anyway, she didn't have £50 in her account.

As Broadhurst mouthed 'Catch you in a minute' to a table where Debbie Harry-lookalike twins were holding court, he manoeuvred her outside, to where a few cabs were waiting. One minute they were on the pavement, and the next, without quite knowing how, she found herself in the back of one, the door slammed behind her. He blew a kiss off his hand and headed back into the restaurant. 'Good luck with the piece.'

She'd blown that, hadn't she, thought Sal, opening the window to help relieve the sickness she was feeling as the cab drove back uptown, weaving through the potholed streets. The whole thing had been strange. He was odd. What had he wanted in the first place? When she'd met him in the morning, she thought he might fancy her, but it hadn't turned out like that. Maybe he *was* gay. Though why had he asked for a girl to interview him then? Was it a double bluff? Anyway, it wasn't her fault, although God knows how she was going to deal with Andrea over the money.

Switching on the television back in the hotel, she flicked through the channels. It was incredible when you thought they only had four back home. She didn't feel at all tired. On the contrary, she was wound up and angry: her date had been confusing, since he didn't fancy her and didn't want her to write it up. But that didn't matter really, not like running into Jackson. That meeting, combined with the large amount of alcohol she had drunk, convinced her that she had a duty to sort this thing out. She picked up the receiver, asked for the hotel switchboard and gave them the number of Cranbourne Terrace, waiting to hear the English ring tone.

'Hello?' Annie's voice was soft, sleepy.

'Annie, it's me, Sal.'

'Are you OK? What's the matter? Where are you? Are you still in New York? What time is it?'

'Yeah. Oh, I don't know, about midnight, I guess. I just saw Jackson.'

'What do you mean? Why are you calling me in the middle of the night?'

'Annie. You've got to dump him. He was in this restaurant. The Odeon. I was there with Michael, and I saw him with his tongue down Mimi's throat. Mimi is the ultimate horrible PR for the penultimately horrible Michael. He was all over her. I promise you. You've got to get out of this.'

'You're drunk. You're crazy and drunk like you always are. I can't believe you're doing this – calling me out of the blue and waking me up to tell me this.'

'Well, yes, I've had a few drinks – guilty as charged – but that doesn't mean I didn't see him. I told him what a bastard he was, Annie. How he didn't deserve you. You know, I always thought something like this was going to happen. How many other girls is he getting off with? Annie, you've got to think about yourself. You deserve better.'

'I don't want to hear. You don't think, do you? You just do what comes into your head and you never, ever think. Maybe, just maybe, I didn't want to know.' Annie's voice had a catch to it as she slammed the receiver down.

Sal lay back on the bed, staring at the ceiling. The room was starting to move around her. She fixed her eyes on the smoke alarm wedged into the corner of the room and waited for the spinning to stop.

9

The effort required for Annie to move from her bed, with the commitment to the day that action would imply, was too great. It had been a month since she had broken up with Jackson, and she wasn't even beginning to feel any better. If anything, the pain was getting worse. She could feel it sometimes, stabbing in her chest. This must be what heartache felt like. She'd never known it really existed.

'I really loved him, otherwise it couldn't hurt like this,' she had told Kendra the previous evening on the phone as she sat, like she had every other evening that week, staring out of the windows. The fact that London had exploded with the lushness of early summer, the evenings light, the garden squares filled with flowers, made her unhappiness even more acute. This was one of her favourite times of year and she was absolutely miserable.

To make it worse, she was furious with Sal. Surely your friends were meant to make you feel better, not worse. If Sal hadn't told her then Annie wouldn't have known. If she hadn't known, then she would have still been with Jackson and, maybe, she wouldn't have had to feel the way she did this morning – every morning. She would still be able to sit in the cinema with him, holding his hand through the whole film, his thumb stroking her palm. She would be able to watch him watch her undress, an intensity in his gaze and an admiration for her body that never seemed to dim. And, most of all, she would be able to look forward to seeing him, to hearing his voice on the phone, to waiting for the doorbell to ring so she could rush down the stairs and find him sitting in that big black Jeep, outside in the street. And now all that had gone.

It had seemed like for ever between Sal's early-morning call from New York and Jackson's return to London, even though it was only a few days. She was in the office typing out a press release when he rang.

'Annie. Hi. I'm back. When can we meet?'

She had been dreading the call. It meant she had to finally decide to break up.

'How about tonight?'

'Hmmm. Could be a little difficult. Are you free Friday?' Friday? She couldn't wait that long. If enough time passed she knew she would find excuses for his behaviour. After all, she had up until now.

'Can you have a drink after work tonight? It's important.'

'Okaaay? Anything you want to tell me over the phone?'

'No.' Annie wished she wasn't aware of Lee pretending not to look at her from across the office. She could practically see his ears moving.

'OK. Seven at the King's Head.'

Annie left her desk and ran down the stairs. She'd been crying so often over the past few days that she was thinking of moving her desk around so that she faced the wall and not into the room, where everyone could see her. She looked at her watch. Only four more hours till the end of everything.

'It's Jackson, isn't it?' Lee had come out to stand in the street with her. 'What's going on? You look a right mess.'

Annie held on to the building's painted railing, staring into the basement well housing the rubbish bins.

'Yes. I'm dumping him. Tonight. But I don't want to. I don't know if I'll see it through.'

'So why are you then? Sorry to sound thick . . . Shit. Do you think this is a moth hole?' He held out the skirt of his kilt to Annie. It was his current favourite, and he prided himself on the particularly fetching combination of the tartan and his treasured aviator jacket.

Annie told him the story, including a conversation with Kendra, who she had hoped might say that there was no reason to dump Jackson and that things might work out. But although Kendra had rushed out to have a cup of tea with Annie as soon as she had rung, she hadn't let her off the hook and offered a reprieve.

Kendra could see her friend's misery in her swollen eyes and puffy face, as if unhappiness was crawling around under her skin.

'Thing is, Annie, I know it was crazy of Sal to call you like that – completely mad. Waking up to hear Sal drunk on the phone on the other side of the Atlantic telling you about Jackson and some American girl, it's unbearable. I can imagine it all too well. But it's not like everything's been really straightforward, is it? He doesn't seem to be that committed to you, and you're always worrying about when you're going to see him next. It's like, well, it's not a very equal relationship.'

'You mean like you and Gioia?' Annie said dully, stirring a spoon round and round in her cooling cup of tea.

'No, I don't mean that. We're not talking about me and Gioia. But I don't see how you can just ignore this. Don't you think you'd feel better if you were with somebody who you could really trust?'

Annie didn't think she'd feel better, ever, with anybody other than Jackson, but she knew that would sound ridiculous.

'Come on.' Lee linked arms with her as he listened. 'Tania's out, and we can skive off for half an hour.' He marched her down to the local park a couple of blocks away, where they strolled along the paths of crimson and pink rhododendrons and azaleas, the plop of tennis balls mixed with the shrieks of small children. Annie was grateful for the cotton handkerchief he had given her from his pocket, even if it wasn't completely clean.

'You know, you don't have to listen to Sal and Kendra. They can't live your life for you. Friends always want to interfere. It's like when I knew Jayjay was screwing his nuts off somewhere every night I wasn't with him. Everyone told me he was nicknamed the Corkscrew, and I just didn't want to know, because when we were together it was great. But I have to admit, in the end, I'm better off without him. At the time you break up it looks like there's nothing out there, but after you get over the first bit, it changes and it's exciting. Any day, any time, you might meet someone else.'

'That's a very optimistic way to look at it. The worst bit is that I know everybody is right.'

'Now. Let's get our priorities straight. What are you going to wear?'

'This, I suppose. I can't go home and change.'

Lee looked disparagingly at Annie's outfit – a white shirt with a Peter Pan collar and a droopy navy skirt.

'No, you are not. You are going to look your best. Make him ache with longing for you. Tell you what. Give me your keys and I'll dash over to the flat and get you kitted out. I've got to collect something for Tania in Kensington anyway, so if I leg it, she won't notice.'

'But you won't know where anything is.'

'Can't be that difficult to find stuff. Anything would be better than that sad look you've got on today – third-rate Princess Di stuff. Trust me. I'm a bloke, but I've got unusually good taste.'

By the time Annie was walking to the King's Head, Lee had achieved his aim and, even in her distress, she knew she was looking good. He'd returned from the flat brandishing a black and pink polka-dot dress that she'd found in Portobello Market with a tight bodice that fitted her perfectly, accentuating her narrow back before flaring into a wide skirt.

'It's not totally sappy fifties revival. It's got a nice dash of punk to it' was Lee's verdict. In the top drawer of his desk, he had a complete make-up kit.

'I think we'll do a marvellous sweep on the eyelid,' he suggested, wielding a thick eye crayon.

'No. What if I cry? And I'm bound to cry. I don't want black all down my face.'

'Think Elizabeth Taylor. She was always crying, and that didn't stop her wearing her eye make-up.'

Annie didn't know what Lee was going on about. She put her foot down about the eye pencil though.

She found Jackson sitting at a table in the garden at the back of the pub. He jumped from the chair to embrace her.

'Gosh, I've missed you. You look even prettier than I remember. I've got you one of your gimlets, babe.'

It was unfair. He was wearing the bright-blue shirt that she always thought suited him so well, the sleeves rolled up to his elbow, his veins, which she liked to run her fingers along, prominent under the skin. The garden was full of after-work drinkers, a bantering huddle of young men, pint mugs in hand, ties loosened, cigarettes waving between thumb and forefingers. At the neighbouring table a grey-haired couple looked quietly at the *Evening Standard*. Annie envied them their placid togetherness.

'So how've you been? What's new at Tania's?' Jackson rattled on. It wasn't clear whether he was ignoring the fact that she hadn't spoken, or hadn't noticed. 'It was amazing in the States. Very exciting. Everybody's talking about pop videos. MTV. It's a whole new area I could get into.' He reached across the table to take her hand.

He hadn't even asked her why she wanted to meet. What was so important to her? He was going to avoid the subject if he could. She took a sip of the sweet vodka drink.

'Don't you want to know why I wanted to meet?'

'Of course. I imagined you were going to tell me.' He spoke softly, smiling at her. 'I'm so pleased we have. I would have loved to have dinner tonight, but I fixed something up weeks back that was hard to change. But Friday – we can spend Friday together, can't we?'

Annie could hear the rumble of chatter in the garden. Everybody was having a normal drink at the end of their normal day. They were going to finish their beers, or wines, or gin and tonics and go off with friends, or home to their children, or to see a film. At any rate, they would probably be doing the same thing as they always did and they weren't about to have to ruin their life. She could feel the tears pricking at the back of her eyes.

'No. No, we can't.' Annie couldn't look at him. She stared at her glass.

'Oh. Are you busy? How about Saturday then? I think I'm free.'

'Not Saturday either.' She sat up straight, bracing herself, as if by stiffening her spine she was stiffening her resolve to get the words out. 'Sal told me about New York. That she'd seen you getting off with someone there.'

'Ah.' There was a pause. 'She did, did she? Yes. I thought she probably would. And that has upset you, has it?'

'Of course it has. What do you think?' Please, Annie pleaded with herself, don't start crying now. 'It wasn't my favourite news.'

'Well, it didn't mean anything to me. She's just a girl I know. Nice girl, but nothing important. Come on, cheer up.' He moved his chair nearer to put his arm around her. 'Annie, you're gorgeous. Captivating. Don't bother about it.'

'I *am* bothered about it. We've been together for nearly a year, and I don't think this is going anywhere. I never know where you are. You won't make plans. I don't know if you're sleeping with other people, but you probably are. I don't really even know if I am your girlfriend. And I hate it. It makes me miserable. It's not what I want.' Annie felt the tears rolling down her cheeks and was sure that her nose was about to run too.

Jackson held her against him.

'Sorry,' she said, wiping her face.

'Don't worry. Tears don't stain.'

For a moment Annie contemplated whether this was true. After all, weren't tears salty and didn't salt stain?

'So what do you want to do?' Jackson asked, rocking back in his chair, and running his hands through his hair.

'I think we have to break up.' Annie spoke so quietly she wasn't sure he had heard. She hadn't said 'I want to break up', which would make it harder for him to say something like 'I really love you. You're the most important person in the world to me.' There were millions of things he could say which would stop what was happening from happening. If she kept talking, would it make it more likely he might say one of them? Or would it be better to keep silent?

'Darling Annie, I don't want to make you unhappy. You're lovely. I know I'm a shit. I disappoint myself sometimes.' Annie noticed that he was trying to look at his watch without her seeing.

She didn't want to look at him again in case she wouldn't be able to leave. So she pushed the chair back and stood up quickly, forcing her way through the clumps of drinkers, through the dark pub and out into the street. She thought she might run for ever because, if she stopped, then she would really feel the pain.

It was high summer, but neither Kendra nor Sal nor Annie had holiday plans. In central London the streets were filled with tourists wearing over-sized white T-shirts and ill-advised shorts stopping in the middle of the pavement to take photographs. Sometimes the wait for a snake of Italian teenagers to cross the road was so long that the traffic lights had turned red again before it was possible to move. It was a place of foreigners and workers whose usual smart clothes were more crumpled than usual, as if there was nobody left they needed to impress.

The large doors to the Chapel were propped open by a stack of bricks and Kendra could hear Gioia's deep voice talking in Italian to her brother. She had taken advantage of the sun to sort out some plastic boxes of painting materials outside on the pavement, piling up pots of paint with the colour encrusted around them, reorganizing stubby pastel sticks, their tips now of an indefinable tint. It was so different from the art room at her school, with wooden easels folded at the back, smocks hung on pegs on the walls. Gioia was proud of some of the paintings her brood had produced.

'That's good stuff. You have to express yourself, not just copy what you see,' she had told John yesterday as he worked the paint with his fingers on to a piece of cardboard. A mixture of colourful abstract shapes, interspersed by some figurative paintings, were taped up on the walls. There was one that showed fields, a red church and, standing by a stream, a white cow – or was it a horse? It was hard to tell. Several were of the nearby railway tracks and the tower blocks of the urban landscape. One showed a large black woman with fangs at the side of her mouth holding a bottle and a cross.

Kendra carried a box back inside and went to where Gioia was seated at the plywood trestle that served as a desk looking at the telephone, having just replaced the receiver.

'You know, we've got to get something done about the roof. The weather's better now. You remember I told you about that woman who said she was going to complain? I saw her looking up at it the other day.'

'Heavens, girl. We've got enough on our plate here just keeping things going. We don't need to worry about the roof. Nobody's dead yet.'

'No. But by the time they are, it's going to be too late. You've got to face it, Gioia, there are people around who don't want us here. You know that. We know the kids love it, and that's what counts, but some of the locals seem to have a problem, and it's not going away. It might be good to at least look as if we're listening.' Kendra heard an unattractive bleat in her voice.

Gioia got up and walked into the quiet street, Kendra following in the wake of her exasperation. Standing with her arms akimbo, with her loose crimson trousers tied in some elaborate bow in the front, she resembled a genie, just landed in the north London street.

'It's changing round here. Skips everywhere. Yuppie types taking over the asylum. Look at the estate agents on Kentish Town Road – they've sprung out of nowhere. The old Christian Aid place, that's gone.' She bent to scratch her bare foot. Kendra watched the silver ankle bracelet hanging on its curve. It reminded her of the line in that Eagles song, about sparkling earrings lying on a girl's brown skin. She would like to be lying in Gioia's arms, surrounded by the rich, sweet scent of her, rather than having this discussion about crappy roofs.

Sal had only taken a few days' holiday all year, even though Andrea had warned her that she wouldn't be able to carry it over. But holidays were complicated. You needed to have somebody to go with. It was one of the best bits about having a boyfriend – knowing that they solved the holiday problem.

She had tried to persuade Annie to think about going away with her, but although they were still sharing the flat, a keen part of Annie's distress was her resentment at Sal. It wouldn't have been so awful if Sal had been sober and had told her in a considered way, the way Kendra would have done. If she'd taken the time to ease her into it in some way – if it was possible to ease her into it. It was the fact that she had been drunk and confronted her with all the consideration of a blunderbuss. When Sal was drunk, she didn't care about repercussions. She had no comprehension of cause and effect. Even when she was sober she often couldn't see how an action of hers had caused the subsequent chain of activity.

Annie spent most of the summer weekends in Hampshire with her mother. It was peaceful just lying on the grass in the garden watching clouds move above her, but the very fact of her being there was an illustration of her failure. As soon as there was a problem, there she was, back home, grounded in the cosy kitchen, where she had always been. Even so, it was easier than staying in the flat hoping for a telephone call that wasn't going to come and that she knew she shouldn't want anyway.

As every month passed, Kendra's separation from her parents became more entrenched. She had been surprised by how easy it had been to break away and, after moving in with Gioia, it seemed best not to look back or forward. Better just to be. Gioia's world was so different to everything she found familiar, but it was new rather than strange, something that, piece by piece, was becoming hers too.

The arrival in her bank account of a monthly allowance from Art made her feel guilty. It didn't seem fair that he should still be paying for her when she was running away. But there was always something that prevented her from asking him to stop, such as when her bicycle was stolen. She could have bought a dead cheap one from a second-hand place nearby, but the old bike had been really good and, after all, she did travel everywhere on it. Even as she wrote the cheque out for the shiny new acquisition she fretted, but Gioia had told her she was crazy.

'Don't be daft, Ken. Listen, if my folk had the cash, they'd probably be giving me an allowance. Let them love you the way they can and, in the meantime, you've got a cool new set of wheels.'

In early August Gioia borrowed a car from a friend and they drove out to the coast, the skies becoming larger as they headed east past the straggling city. Kendra could smell the sea before they reached it and was excited to catch the first glimpse, which arrived suddenly. The long beach was hedged by dunes and dotted with coloured windbreakers and the plastic toys of children as they carried the sleeping bags from the makeshift car park set back from the sands. When they arrived at a dent in the dunes, far from the families, Kendra sat and watched as Gioia ran into the water and then stood waist deep before collapsing at the edge and letting the water wash over her.

Untying her long wrap-around skirt, Kendra could still smell the Hawaiian Tropic oil she had been using on that holiday in Corfu. She walked over to Gioia.

'Aren't you coming in for a proper swim?'

'No. I'll just stay here.' Gioia's long black hair already had silver slivers of seaweed tangled in it.

'You're like a seal lying there. Come in with me. I want to swim with you.'

'I can't.'

'Why can't you?'

'Jesus, Ken, do I have to spell it out? I *can't swim.*'

It was the first time Kendra could remember Gioa admitting to not being able to do something. She was always so capable and, even if she couldn't do something herself, she knew how to find somebody who could. It was unimaginable not to be able to swim. Everybody could. When Kendra was a child she had been taught in the local pool. She'd won a badge to sew on her costume for a lifesaving course that involved pyjamas, although she couldn't remember what she did with them. She could see them now, inflated red blobs with elephants on them.

She sat in the shallows next to Gioia, who stared out across the sea, her ankles kicking in the water. There were too many people around for Kendra to do what she wanted to do, which was to take Gioia's head in her hands and lick the indentation at her neck and stroke the base of her spine where there was a covering of soft, dark hair. She would have to wait until dark.

Further down the beach were houses with gardens that led directly on to the sands, but where they had set up their camp it was deserted. As the daylight faded, the houses began to light up and the odd sound carried along to where they were gathering driftwood and grasses and piling them up into a bonfire. The evening was warm but, even so, Kendra liked the idea of a fire.

A crimson streak was all that was left of the sun by the time they sat on the scratchy blanket. Gioia produced a bottle of grappa from her knapsack, an unlikely accompaniment to the sandwiches Kendra had made, now littered with gritty grains of sand.

'It's lovely here. I never had a seaside kind of holiday when I was a kid. Dad always closed the shop in August and sometimes we went to his family back near Bologna. Not much sea there. Funny how big the sea is when you look at it. Like it goes on for ever.'

'I think Russia is the nearest land in that direction.' Kendra gestured across the water. 'You get massive winds because there're no hills between us and the steppes. It's why there's all the nuclear stuff on this coast. It's meant to be our first line of defence . . . kind of creepy. All that danger just out there, and this is so beautiful. As if we're being deceived. It makes you worry about what could be in the sea. Uranium, plutonium – God knows what.'

'Maybe we should go and live by the sea. Not here. Somewhere hot and away from everything. Give it all up. Move on.' Gioia shifted on the blanket so that she was lying looking up at the sky. A few stars were now visible.

'What are you talking about? You love the Chapel – it's your life.'

'Yeah. That's the problem.'

'What do you mean?'

'They're trying to close me down. I should have told you, but I hoped it would just get lost. I got this letter from some bloke about wanting to develop the land that the Chapel is on, with that scrap-yard behind. Not sure if he means any of the houses.' The information emerged in staccato points, distancing Gioia from what she was saying. 'It came last week. The second one. I got one a few months back. Chucked it in the bin.'

'They can't do that . . . Can they?'

'We can make it bloody tough for them. And we can make it long and hard, and that's probably what I'm going to do. I've just got to get my head into it. But lying here, listening to the sea and looking out there, I think, fuck it all. There's another world somewhere. We can go if we want.'

'I can't believe you're even talking about giving the Chapel up. We've got to do something. When we get back, show me the letter. I could get Dad's lawyers on to it.'

'Did I hear correct? Daddy's lawyers?'

'OK. Maybe not. Forget that. But Gioia, we're not giving up the Chapel. That would be insane. I can't believe you're even thinking about it.'

'I'm not. Not really. Just testing.' Gioia leant over to kiss her on the forehead. 'You're my girl, aren't you? We're going to be all right. It's all going to be all right.'

'Why did they want you to bring a friend?' Sal was peering at her reflection through the steam of Annie's bath. She was hoping the humidity might help with a stubborn blackhead on the side of her nose. The other day, she had taken a pair of scissors and cut herself a very short fringe, the kind she'd seen in pictures of the young Iris Murdoch. She imagined it gave her a kind of Bloomsbury look. On a good day, she reckoned that on the whole the new style had been a success, but when she got worked up about something she could see it managed to accentuate her mood. She practised looking furious in the mirror for a moment, trying to work out if there was a way to do it that was a little more flattering.

Annie laughed as she watched her. She had made a decision, suddenly, one morning as she was getting dressed, to stop being angry with Sal. It was easy to continue to feel resentful but, as the weeks went by, she realized that, if they were going to stay in the flat together, something had to change.

'I like the short fringe. It's unusual. I wonder if I should cut one into mine?'

'Nope. Big mistake. You're so pretty you don't need to do anything. I know I'm OK, but I have to try harder. Don't mess with your hair. I'd kill for it.' Sal leant against the wall, looking at Annie, who accepted the compliment as she lay in the bath, white foam popping in pools above her body, her knees, poking up, almost as white. 'What do you think it's going to be like?'

The invitation was from the owners of Elephants, an expensive gift shop in Chelsea and one of Tania's smaller clients.

'We're having some people over for supper tomorrow. Come and join us, and bring any fun friend you like.' Tony Potterton had paced around his small office at the back of the store as he offered the invitation. Annie had been sent to collect the Elephants version of Russian dolls: Chelsea dolls with Penelope Tree-style fringes and heavy eyelashes, five of them, fitted one inside the other, the last the size of a thimble.

He kept an eye on the small television showing the afternoon's racing, jumping up suddenly and banging the desk. 'Goddamn . . . came in third. Should have put it on each way . . . I generally come out on top, you know.' Annie imagined this was probably untrue. The loss claimed his attention. 'Nothing dressy, just a get-together, and we could do with some young faces around. Eightish. You know the kind of thing.'

Annie didn't know the kind of thing, but she didn't feel she could turn the invitation down. They were clients, and she'd learnt that, in her business, you needed to show them they were valued. Tania was always saying 'We're in the people business. Nurture them, water them, feed them – they're like babies.'

When they arrived, a white-jacketed butler opened the front door then handed their coats silently to a woman in a striped dress and apron. 'They're in the drawing room,' she said. It was very warm inside, a contrast to outdoors, where the sharp temperature drop of November was enough for even their short spell on the doorstep to cause them to shiver.

'Ugh. I hate that vomit-coloured paint thing everyone's doing,' said Sal, referring to the stippled apricot walls.

'It costs thousands,' Annie whispered. 'It's done by a specialist painter – we've just signed up to represent one. He takes a month just to mix the paint, and Tania's already got the *Sunday Times* interested in doing a big story on him. It probably helps that he's the son of an earl. And that he's got a massive coke habit. Not that we're encouraging that as part of the story.'

'Sounds mad to me.'

At the far corner of the L-shaped room Annie could see Tony Potterton. He had said it was going to be nothing dressy but, to her, all the women looked extremely smart. There was a certain style – their hair in blow-dries held in place by sticky-looking lacquer, large jewellery (pearl earrings the size of golf balls) and big coloured-glass necklaces. Annie recognized one from the window of Butler & Wilson, from when Jackson had taken her there. Seated on a kelim-covered ottoman in front of the fireplace was a woman wearing a flame silk dress displaying a massive cleavage with the dimpled consistency of a scone.

'That's Trish, she's the wife. And Christ . . . there's Lee. How come he never said he was coming here tonight?' Trish appeared to be completely engrossed in some story of Lee's. 'That's the thing about him. He's good when it comes to doing all the chat stuff,' Annie observed of her co-worker.

'He's waving at us.' Sal negotiated a path through the many armchairs and small tables, her fitted tartan shift merging with the cacophony of printed fabrics contained in the room – kelims, paisley prints, the swirls of Art Nouveau.

Lee stood up, looking past Sal to Annie, who was wearing a bias-cut skirt in a pale grey which stood out against the garish colours of the older women. He introduced the two to Trish, just in case she couldn't remember who Annie was.

'I see Tony has recruited some bright young things too,' Trish commented. 'I rely upon Lee to keep me cheerful. Sometimes I think I'll tell Tania that she's keeping that retainer only because he's such a nice boy to an old bag like me.'

'Oh, please don't do that,' Lee squealed. 'It could go down so badly you couldn't even imagine. Anyway,' he added diplomatically, 'Elephants is one of her favourite accounts. She's always coming in to us all excited by something new you've got. I thought she was going to go up in smoke when she saw those distressed copper wall sconces.'

Trish stood to look at her sitting room, mentally ticking off who had arrived, who was missing, who was talking to who.

'I think it's time to eat. Help me round everyone up – it's serve yourself. Just shepherd's pie.'

Shepherd's pie was a mystery to Annie. It was such ordinary food, the kind of thing she would have for tea at home. Letty wouldn't dream of serving it at a dinner, but since she had been working in London she'd been amazed by how many times it seemed to be on the menu at places which she thought were meant to be grand. Maybe she was missing the point.

The huge central table in the basement kitchen soon filled with guests and Annie carried her plate back upstairs to find a seat where she could manage the task of balancing a plate of pie and bright-green peas at the same time as holding a wine glass. She poked at the peas with her fork as they disobligingly rolled all over the plate.

'You look like you're having a spot of trouble with those peas.' Annie looked up to see a pair of dark-blue trousers in front of her. 'Can I sit here?' their owner asked.

'Yes, of course.' Annie felt the sink of the sofa as he lowered himself, his legs extending into the room like planks.

'Charlie. Charlie Sethrington. I won't try and shake hands, as it looks like you've got enough going on as it is.'

'Hi. I'm Annie. I work for Tania Torrington. Elephants is one of our clients.'

'Tony told me. I do some business with him from time to time. I asked him who you were earlier – got your whole CV.'

'Well, it must have been very short, because he doesn't know much about me. And, anyway, it is pretty short. I was just in the shop yesterday and he asked me to come. Me and my friend, Sal.'

'Well, that's good news for me. Tony and Trish like to have some pretty girls around, it makes them feel they're not past it.' Annie wasn't sure how she felt about being described in this way, even though she knew it was intended as flattery. Sal would no doubt have pulled him up on it, but she didn't feel inclined to be awkward and, anyway, there wasn't anyone else to talk to.

Tony approached the couple, his face flushed with the warmth of the room and the good red wine he was serving. 'Ah, Charlie,' he boomed. 'I wouldn't have expected anything less from you but, even by your standards, pretty quick off the mark. You have to watch this one, Annie. He's a wily sod.'

Annie was wedged between the two, content to listen to their easy banter and happy to be the subject of their appreciation, even if it was just a way of passing the time. As the evening wore on, she began to feel a tinge of attraction for Charlie, with his hawkish nose and the high colour of his sharp cheekbones. He had an intensity about him that made you want to listen to what he said. She was amused by the way that, when he stood up and became animated, he swayed slightly, as if there was a wind blowing at his height that didn't affect lesser beings. From up there, it was clear that he was watching her and, for the first time in months, she felt intrigued by a man's interest in her.

'You should consider Docklands for another Elephants, you know, Tony. It's moving fast, and there are some real bargains. We're getting stuck into all kinds of new areas in one way and another, but you need the right kind of footfall. The property market's wide open right now.'

Annie could see Sal moving across the room in their direction. When she arrived it was like a rush of air. 'Hi,' she said, as she crouched on the floor, her tartan dress riding up her thighs.

'This is Sal. She's a journalist on the *Herald*.'

'Ah. Do we have to watch what we say now, with a hack among us?' Tony joshed, his eyes glinting with pleasure at the sight of Sal.

'I've just been talking to some bloke down there about the bomb at the conference. He was saying it was the best thing that could happen to the Conservatives, because now they've got this huge sympathy vote. It'd take more than that to get me to feel sympathetic to them. Every time I think of them I have this vision of that creep Cecil Parkinson. They're all like him.'

'I'm surprised you're working at the *Herald*, with those views,' Charlie intervened.

'They don't mind. It's not like they ask me to do anything political. I'm their bit of fluff. Until a couple of months ago I felt like I was spending my life on baby watch for Prince Harry. What a relief now he's popped out. It raises the chances of me being given something more interesting to work on.' She shifted, knocking over the glass of red wine that Charlie had placed at the foot of the sofa. 'Oh shit. Sorry.' She watched the wine spread, darkening the blues and reds of the Persian rug. She pulled at the hem of her dress to use as a cloth. 'Lucky it's tartan. You won't see the difference.'

Annie was aware that, as always, the conversation was instantly all about Sal. Some people slowly infiltrate a group, but Sal immediately inserted herself. Her confidence in her own opinions, along with her quicksilver movements and easy laugh, often at her own expense, somehow made it work.

At the end of the evening, as Annie drove Sal and Lee home, they were in good spirits.

'I'm dossing at a friend's in Soho, so if you can drop me off somewhere a bit nearer than here, I'll walk,' said Lee. 'What about that tall bloke? He looked keen to me.' He leant forward from the back of the car, poking his head between the two girls.

'He's got my number, but he's not really my type. Everyone's telling me I've got to keep my options open though.' Annie fixed her eyes on the road ahead, still full of cars although the Chelsea pavements were empty save for the odd dog-walker.

Sal leapt in. 'Well, Tony asked me for my number. What do you think he has in mind? Afternoon assignations at Blakes? Isn't that where guys like him hole up? Wouldn't mind a bit of an affair, but not with Tony Potterton. Can you imagine?'

'Oh, I don't know. Think of the gifts. You could have a whole line of Chelsea dolls to put on your mantelpiece. Surely that would swing it. I'll hop out here.' The white sailor cap atop Lee's retreating figure could be seen for a long while in Annie's rear-view mirror.

1985

flight that morning from Heathrow. Only three days ago she had been in the pub in Hampshire, and now here she was, a whole world away.

Outside, the sky was a startling blue. She hadn't expected that, nor the number of trees by the road – thick, wooded sections interspersed with the toy-town housing of suburbia. And then, suddenly, without any indication of its arrival, the dramatic sight of the island of Manhattan, as extraordinary as she had imagined. Even from the back seat, with its dirty glass screen separating her from the driver, the strange Lego-like shapes of the city ahead struck Sal with wonder and anticipation, their thousands of windows sparkling in the sun. She could see the unmistakable shape of the Empire State Building and, bordering the water as they drove over a bridge, the double pillars of the World Trade Center. Everyone had told her she must go to the top and see the view.

It was a miracle that she was sitting in the cab and not at her desk in Fleet Street. She knew she was one of the most junior reporters on the *Herald*, and junior reporters didn't usually fly across the Atlantic to interview TV stars. To be here, writing a piece on Michael Broadhurst, was definitely a triumph. His clean-cut good looks attracted everybody – male and female. Even her mother had put aside time to watch the Trollope series on Sunday nights, pronouncing him 'excellent for the period'. It had come as little surprise when he was signed up for an expensive PBS dramatization of *The Wings of the Dove* and recruited for a Hollywood series. He was the kind of Brit Americans wanted Brits to be.

His move to Broadway had only added to his appeal as a seriously nice chap. Sal had thrown out the suggestion of an interview to the arts editor with no thought that she might herself be given the job. Crispin, the *Herald's* long-time man in New York, with a cast-iron reputation for ligging and of unclear sexuality, was the obvious choice. She was still trying to get a new angle on the Princess of Wales's second pregnancy when Andrea had strode up to her. Why was it that even when a woman had good news to tell, her manner was confrontational?

of laughter as she mimed, with accompanying hand movements, Madonna's 'Holiday'. They teased her that she was a dead ringer for the singer on the cover of the latest issue of ID: the dirty-blonde hair, the tied cotton hairbands, even the thick brows.

'So how long is Jackson in the States?' asked Sal.

'He's coming back next weekend. He called me once and said he's flming back to back.' Annie scraped around the bottom of her crisp packet, to discover only small crumbs. 'I'd love to go away with him somewhere. I keep telling him I've never been to Venice.'

'Neither have I. Maybe we should all go. Have you, Ken?'

'I went with Mum and Dad and some of their friends when I was about fifteen. We saw paintings all day and I had my first pizza. I still remember how delicious it was.'

'No. Much as I love you, I want to go to Venice with a boyfriend.' Annie imagined Jackson lying in a sea of a bed with white white sheets and the view of a church across the water.' I might bring it up when he gets back.' Her friends both thought this unlikely since, as far as they could tell, she was unable even to suggest meeting him for glass of wine.

'Well, I guess that's one good thing about having an older boy-friend,' Sal suggested. 'He's got the dosh to take you places.'

'Yeah. He always pays when we go out. Do you think that means I'm not an emancipated woman?' Annie was only partially joking.

'Definitely,' Sal and Kendra said in unison. There was a short silence. It struck them all that it was awkward to ask Kendra her position on being paid for. She saved them from the embarrass-ment, jumping up, banging her knee into the low table.' My round. I'm getting another bag of crisps.'

The yellow cab stuttered, in thick traffic, down the Long Island Express Way on its journey from Kennedy airport into Manhattan. Sal looked out of the window, watching the small clapboard houses at the side of the road, the enormous billboards dwarfing them. She could not believe that it was really her that had boarded the Pan Am

She recognized the sound of his car as it turned the corner into her street, the cranky gear box catching when it reached second gear then halting. The recognition was comforting, an audible endorsement of their relationship, which had been unusually simple in its evolution. Charlie had conferred the status of girlfriend on Annie almost without her noticing. He wanted her to spend not only the nights with him but the days too, he included her in all his plans and he had slid her into the fabric of his life with an ease that was unlike any boyfriend she had ever had. Some might say that his predictability, the way that he was never early, never late, the fact that he always made a cup of Earl Grey tea in the morning to drink with his brown toast spread with apricot jam was dull, but she liked the way she knew where she was.

It had taken her ages to decide what to pack for this first weekend with his old friends, and just as she was tugging the zip on the squashy Mulberry leather bag Letty had given her for her last birthday, she had had a crisis of confidence about its contents. He'd told her they would be changing for dinner, but into what? Did that mean a long dress, or just something tidy? At least it was only for one night. Charlie had been keen to leave the previous day, but Tania had wanted her at a dinner to pitch for the account of an evening-wear designer.

It had been a month ago, just before Christmas, when Tania had called her into her office, where she was sunk in an armchair, a bottle of Soave open on the small table beside her. The sound of the Salvation Army playing 'O Little Town of Bethlehem' outside the nearby shops drifted in.

'Good news, love. I'm promoting you. Happy Christmas.' She leant forward and poured Annie a glass of the wine. From her flushed face, Annie realized that Tania had been drinking since lunchtime. It had been the same all that week, but then everybody was doing it in the run-up to the holiday. Even Stella in Accounts had broken her two-glasses-on-a-Saturday-night routine at the office lunch at Foxtrot Oscar.

Tania continued, 'You can manage some of the smaller accounts on your own now. It'll free me up to get new business if I don't have to be thinking about people like Tony and Trish and that Elephants of theirs, which, truth to tell, I only do for old times' sake.' She smiled boozily at Annie. 'You're probably thinking about the cash. I can scrape together another grand. Stella tells me that'll bring you up to £12,000 a year. And you'll be Junior Account Executive. How does that sound?'

And so January 1985 had arrived for Annie Brenham with a new boyfriend and a bigger job, both of which had appeared unexpectedly and yet seemed completely natural. Somewhere inside she wondered, at times, whether both shouldn't have been a little bit harder to achieve, just so that she could feel that it was them she wanted.

Pulling her over-sized cream sweater over her head, the one she liked because it was so wide it made her legs look skinny in comparison, she grabbed her bag at the hoot of the car horn, noticing as she did that Sal had dumped her damp towels in the hall that morning. As she picked them up to fling on to Sal's bed, something fell on the floor. An empty vodka bottle. Not good, thought Annie, pushing it out of her mind. Now was not the time to worry about it.

Charlie's tall frame was folded into the interior of his old car, of which he was particularly proud, even though it made a terrible noise and could be freezing cold, with its ill-fitting canvas roof.

'You'll see. It's magical when the weather warms up and we can put the top down. You'll love it,' he promised Annie. She couldn't help noticing that he obviously thought they would still be together in the summer. There he was, joyful as Mr Toad, when normally he was so efficient and driven that you'd expect he'd far prefer something modern, like a BMW or an Audi. It was sweet really.

★

On Saturdays, Fleet Street was empty of its normal traffic. The buildings towered over quiet pavements as Sal left the office, her coat wrapped around her, and walked in the direction of the river. She felt terrible – so bad that she couldn't focus on her story about the Dorchester's takeover by the Sultan of Brunei. Not that she had the foggiest idea where Brunei was. Fresh air might help. She hoped so, anyway.

She stood on the bridge looking down at the fast-moving water, the current obvious from the crazy swirling below. The stubborn London grey of the sky overhead suited the Dickensian quality of that part of the city, with its many churches, old clocks and narrow, winding streets.

It had been a big mistake to go out last night, but Annie wasn't going to be at home and she hadn't been in the mood to stay there alone.

'Charlie's taking me to stay with these old friends of his. He says they're people he's known for ever – well, the husband, anyway – and he wants me to meet them. I hope I do OK,' Annie had informed her before she ran out of the door that morning. Sal had thought that it was Charlie who had to prove himself, not Annie, but she didn't say so. At least Annie had a boyfriend. It wasn't the kind of thing she liked to spend much time considering but, if she looked back, she hadn't had one in ages. Not someone she saw regularly, made plans with. And sometimes, like this weekend, it would have been nice to curl up with someone and watch TV, an Indian take-away on their laps. Someone she knew well enough that they could laugh about their curry breath the next morning.

That might have been a reason not to go out and get plastered at some lager-sponsored party with Ollie on a Friday night when everybody, even the most alcohol hardened of hacks, knew they had to keep it together for work on Saturday. It hadn't even been fun. When she got home, it was still early, not much after midnight, and Annie's door was shut, no light coming from it. She remembered that she had a bottle of vodka in her chest of drawers. She wasn't sure why she kept it there instead of in the kitchen, where they kept the wine (when they had any). She supposed she didn't particularly want Annie keeping an eye on the level of the bottle. Anyway, there it was. The wooden drawer stuck, as it always did, when she tried to open it, making a loud noise. The bottle was under a pile of knickers, and there was only a small amount of clear liquid left in it. Just enough for a nightcap, and it would help her sleep. The bass from the speakers at the party was still crashing in her ears.

Even the memory made her feel sick. Maybe fresh air hadn't been such a good idea after all. Gripping the wall of the bridge and looking out at the city on either side, she thought she really ought to make more use of it, before turning to walk back to the office. Go to the museums, go to the theatre. Her mum had told her the last time she'd gone home how much she envied her.

'When I was your age I would try to get up to London occasionally, just to walk around and visit the museums. Free museum entry is one of the most civilized things about this country. You are a lucky girl, you know, having it all on your doorstep.'

'It's not at all certain that we will remain civilized under this government if free museums are the measure,' her father had proclaimed. 'I'm not sure we have ever had such a philistine prime minister. I question whether she has read anyone other than Jeffrey Archer.'

When she arrived back at the desk, the newsroom was at full throttle. Andrea was there, one hand holding the receiver, the other guarding her mouth. Even though the room was noisy – the clatter of typewriters, the rattle of the telex, the telephones that rang ceaselessly – it was possible to hear each other's conversations. Words drifted over – 'drink lots of liquid . . . yes, every four hours . . . no, no – they're downstairs . . . your father . . . call me if it gets worse.' Sal realized that Andrea must be talking to a child. How old were her kids? Andrea never struck her as a mother but, now she thought of it, she didn't know anything about Andrea's life. And Andrea knew nothing about hers. The office was its own world, a place where you went to be the person you were at work. For the first time, Sal wondered whether Andrea might actually be a different person somewhere else.

'Have you finished yet?' Andrea yelled across at Sal as she put the phone down, reassuming her professional persona.

'No, not quite. I'm having a bit of trouble finding someone who stays at the Dorchester. I need a quote. You know, something about how the bathrooms need updating, or that the room service is poor. Five hundred quid a night to stay there, that's if you want a suite. He's paid 43 million for it. S'pose he thinks it's worth it.'

'There's a rumour that that Egyptian bloke Al Fayed, the one who is in the deal with him, is going to bid for Harrods. You should wrap that into the story – how central London is soon going to be owned by foreigners. Patrick likes a slant. One example is an incident, two is a story. But get your skates on.'

Sal tipped back in her chair, fiddling with the mood ring Annie had given her at Christmas. She couldn't decide whether it was now brown or green. At any rate, it was wrong, since her mood was definitely black.

'Maybe there's something in all the new building going on. All the developments over in the East End. I've got a contact in the property business I can talk to.' Charlie could make himself useful, thought Sal.

'Well, get this one done pronto and we can talk about that afterwards.'

'So, how many children do you have, Andrea?'

'Three. And the middle one's come down with some virus. But talking about that won't get the story done.'

'Here's my copy.' Across the desk, Marsha ripped the paper out of her typewriter. Sal was pleased to see that there was a dark line around the roots of her central parting. Any dent in her relentless perfection was worth noting. 'I've got time to work on that story you mentioned earlier, if it's needed. Incidentally, Sal, your father called while you weren't here just now. He said could you call him. I didn't know when you'd be back.'

'I only stepped out for a few minutes. I hadn't gone to Outer

Mongolia. Anyway, thanks.' Sal started banging on the typewriter keys in a conspicuous and noisy display of activity.

Charlie dominated any room he entered, Annie thought, looking at him positioned near the fireplace, his height reducing much of the furniture to dolls' house proportions. It was one of the things she found attractive, the way he assumed ownership of any situation. It made her, by association, feel safe. Although it was only five o'clock, it seemed as if it had been dark for hours. They had arrived at Sophie and Mark's Cotswold manor house just in time to sit down to a lunch of stodgy fish pie, and had been confined indoors ever since by the continual rain.

'As I was saying, it was a pity you couldn't have been here earlier and got in a walk. Mark and Simon made it up to Chalkers Stump this morning. It gave me and Fizz an opportunity for a good old catch-up.' Sophie poured tea from a polka-dotted pot.

'I'm taking myself off to check out the footie. Leave you to natter.' Charlie gave Annie a hug as he passed, allowing the room to return to a more normal size. Sophie tucked her hair behind her ears. It was what Sal called plastic hair, impossibly smooth, and a deep brown, falling past her shoulders.

'We're so pleased Charlie has got a nice new girlfriend. You know, Mark and he have been pals since God was a boy. Mark has always said that Charlie's just waiting for the right one and he'll be walking down the aisle in weeks. It's been hard for him, with most of his friends hitched by now.'

Annie wasn't sure of an appropriate response. They'd only been together for a couple of months. Surely it was too early to be talking about weddings. With other boyfriends, she had always felt the need for them to continually demonstrate that they wanted to become more deeply involved, but she didn't feel that about Charlie. Which was wonderful. He was always there, so she never had to want him in that needy way.

'We haven't been together long. We're having fun, though. He's planning to take me to Venice for Easter.'

'Yes. He knows Venice well. We all went together for a weekend a few years ago, when he was dating Charlotte Stuttaford. Not that they saw much of the city. We had to keep dragging them out of bed.'

Annie forced a smile, even though she didn't want to think of Charlie in bed with someone else. He was certainly keen on sex; she'd discovered that soon enough. He'd bought her a whole new wardrobe of expensive underwear – teddies, suspenders, tiny lacy pants – which he loved to see her wear. It was curious, she thought, the power of these scraps of fabric.

'I hate tights. Most men do. Stockings are so much more exciting. It turns me on to think of you wearing them,' he had said only weeks after meeting her. She was trying to wear them for him, but she found them uncomfortable and, on the days she wasn't with him, reverted to tights. Embarrassed by the idea of Sal spotting the stockings, she would rinse these new additions by hand, hanging them in secret on the radiator in her room rather than on their shared plastic clothes horse where everything else would dry when they hadn't gone to the launderette.

'Hi, Fizz. I was just telling Annie how pleased we all are that, this time, Charlie's got a nice girl.'

Fizz was carrying a grubby-faced toddler. She looked over at Annie, as if she were confused about whether she were the girl in question. 'He's certainly had a few horrors. Do you think we could get some tea for them? This one's starving.' She jigged the child around.

'Of course. Let's see what Mrs B. can produce.' They all followed Sophie out of the room, down a chilly flagstone corridor to the kitchen, where a woman in a floral apron was peeling carrots at the sink.

'Mrs B., this is Annie Brenham, who's here with Charlie. You know how he wolfs down your steak and kidney.' Sophie gestured at Annie. 'I think the children can have fish fingers – there's tons in the freezer. Then, can you lay up for tonight? We've got Lord Cavening and his guests joining us for dinner – it may be a bit of a squeeze, but we've managed before.' The figure at the sink demonstrated no sign of having heard any of this, and continued her scraping.

'Mrs B., you are a gem.' Sophie turned back to the other two with a raised eyebrow. 'Let's rescue the boys. They've got the kids with them in front of the TV.' She put a hand on Annie's shoulder. 'It must be fearfully dull for you, being stuck with us and the children.'

'Not at all. I love children. I've always wanted them,' Annie replied as they left the kitchen.

'You might find Mrs B. a bit frosty,' Sophie whispered. 'She doesn't really approve of unmarrieds sharing a room.'

Out of the immediate vicinity of the fireplaces, the house was cold, as if the stone had soaked up the chill from the gusting wind bending the large trees in the garden. Lying on a quilted counterpane, Charlie leant over to the bedside table to check the small alarm clock, his other hand caressing the soft flesh where the black suspenders dented Annie's pale thigh. She had been changing for dinner when he had interrupted her and positioned her in front of the tilted cheval glass mirror and bent her over. She liked to watch herself and him, the way his face screwed into a frown of totally engrossed lust and concentration.

'Pity we've got to get up for dinner. I could just lie here all evening with you. Ferdie Cavening is a drone, but he's harmless. Sophie said it was champagne in the drawing room at eight. What are you wearing, darling?'

Annie showed him the silk velvet jacket she had thought would be a safe bet for the evening. She was going to wear it with a full dark-red wool skirt she had bought from Edina and Lena. Edina was an old friend of Tania's and always gave the office a sale preview so they could grab some of the best pieces early.

'Very nice. But I can't wait to get you some proper clothes in Venice. The Italians have the best fashion now. There are all these new guys working there, and the tailoring is brilliant. Still' – he looked at her body appreciatively – 'it's what lies beneath that counts. All this loveliness – and just for me. I'm a lucky man.'

Annie was seated between Mark and Ferdie Cavening at one end of the mahogany table. It was obvious that the room temperature was calculated on the basis of the men's uniform of thick evening jackets. She wished she had put on a vest under her thin velvet. This whole cold business was crazy. Her hosts were obviously wealthy, so why didn't they bother to heat the place properly?

She listened to Mark as she battled to carve flesh from the partridge lying in a pool of tepid gravy on her plate.

'Charlie tells me you're in the fashion business,' said Mark, peering into his wine glass as if he had found a problem at the bottom of it. 'I'm frightfully sorry. I don't know much about that world.' As he smiled, Annie noticed his small, pointed teeth.

'I'm not really. We do some fashion, but the company handles public relations for all kinds of thing – lifestyle brands, restaurants, events.'

'Soph used to do a bit of work in that area before we married. She helped a friend who did party planning. Don't tell her, but I always used to think it was a laugh that she was paid to plan anything. It's not her greatest strength.'

'She seems incredibly organized to me. Our bedroom even has biscuits in a tin by the bed. And look at the table. Perfect.' Mark glanced at the gleaming candelabra, the silver salt and pepper cruets and the bright-yellow mustard in little blue glass bowls.

'Well, my mother gave her a talking to when we got engaged. Told her how to run the place. She's always been a stickler for everything being just so. Sophie got the hang of it pretty damn quick. I suppose, when you find the right chap, you'll give up that public relations stuff.'

'What makes you think that?' The flush that had started to creep up over her neck and face had appeared since she was a child. 'It's my career, and I'm very interested in it.' She was surprised by her indignation. After all, she was the first person to scoff at the notion that she was in a career. But she minded, greatly, Mark's supercilious supposition that what she was doing didn't count for anything. 'I have my own clients now who I am responsible for. I'm not going to just chuck it in because I'm married.' She thought, but didn't add, that she didn't much like the idea of turning into somebody like Sophie or Fizz.

'Oh, you women all say that, but when the bubbas come along it's different.' Mark reached over to grab a heavy crystal decanter of red wine, offering it to her before splashing it carelessly into his glass. 'Ferdie, tell us, what do you think about women and their careers?'

'Can't say I think much about it.' Ferdie looked at Annie with a leer derived more from habit than desire, enabling Mark to turn to the girl who was seated on his other side. Annie noticed that the cold hadn't prevented her from wearing a dress with a deep plunge neck, the bareness of her skin emphasized by a five-strand pearl choker.

'Looks like you've got me now.' Ferdie had an incongruously youthful face, topped by a startling blond thatch. 'So where did you meet old Charlie? Lucky devil. I don't know him well, but I've bought into a couple of his property deals. He's got a good eye for the up-and-coming area.' He leant across the table to where Charlie was talking to Fizz. 'Charlie, my man, are you coming over tomorrow to follow the hounds? The meet's at eleven. Are you a rider?' he asked Annie. She thought of the gymkhana rosettes on the wall of her bedroom in Hampshire and how she had adored everything about horses: the tack, the stables, their glossy bulk, the tight fit of the black hat on her head.

'I used to be. But it's been a long time.' Even on a subject which she should have found easy, Annie couldn't muster any enthusiasm for the conversation. The evening was proving to be excruciating, and she was dreading the moment Charlie had warned her of, which surely must be approaching, when the women would get up and leave the men. On her own with them and out of Charlie's orbit she knew she was going to feel out of place, an interloper in their world with her working life, unmarried status and no babies. What was she going to talk about with them? Maybe she could claim a headache and go to bed, but that wouldn't be fair on Charlie. He'd brought her here to be a part of his life and introduce her to his old friends. Hadn't she always wanted to be with a man who would do just that?

The clock in the hall was striking the hour when Charlie closed their bedroom door and pulled a bolt across it, before walking across the room and starting to unbutton her jacket as if peeling a fruit.

'I'm sorry. I just don't feel like it now. It's been a nightmare, tonight. I was so out of place. The girls obviously found me odd because I couldn't join in their conversation about kids and, as for the men . . . they treated me as if I came from another planet. You're not like that. Why on earth is Mark your friend?'

'Well, I've known him since we were kids, when we used to spend all our time together. We don't hang out much now but, when you've known someone for ages, they're part of your history, aren't they?' He loosened his bow tie to hang around his neck. 'You're being too judgemental. And Sophie's fine, really. She's just different to you and your friends. She means well. Come on.' He tried to pick her up and carry her to the bed.

'No, Charlie, I mean it. I'm just not in the mood.'

'Fine.' He dumped her on the floor and walked to the sink in the corner to wash his face. 'Be like that. But you're ridiculous.'

Annie pulled her dressing gown out of the bag and unbolted the door. The bathroom was at the other end of the corridor, but it seemed a better idea to take her clothes off there rather than remove them in front of Charlie. She pulled the flex of the bar heater on the wall, which instantly glowed red without offering any immediate heat, and pulled off her jacket, skirt and the suspenders, everything cutting into her uncomfortably after the roast potatoes and chocolate mousse.

Wrapping the robe around her tightly, she picked her clothes up from the floor and ran back along the icy route to the room. She knew she was being unfair. After all, it wasn't Charlie that had been making asinine comments. But, even so, she didn't want to have sex. She wasn't just a doll, up for it no matter what.

II

It had been a scramble to catch the seven o'clock from Paddington, and Sal had made it with less than a minute to spare. It wasn't her fault. Patrick had only given her the go-ahead that morning for her story on the launch of *EastEnders*, which, as she pointed out to Andrea, was absolutely ridiculous. Everybody knew this was going to be a huge investment for the BBC. There'd been talk about it for weeks, and now she was expected to pull something together at the last minute. It was typical of Patrick to be so out of touch.

When she had finally remembered to ring her father back earlier in the week, nagged by Annie, who had answered two calls from him, he had made it clear she should come home for a visit.

'Your mother wouldn't want to bother you, Salome, but she isn't at all well. I wouldn't be calling if I didn't think it would be a good idea for you to come and see her.' Now that the agreed visit had come around, it was frustrating. Nobody who really counted on the paper liked to leave early (apart from Patrick). It was like the hard core at a party – the best times were often at the end, when the lightweights had gone home, leaving the real players behind.

The days were starting to lengthen, bringing with them hints that, contrary to appearance, spring would someday arrive. Yet it was pitch black and wet when she emerged on to the platform at Cheltenham and hard to see which car was which in the squally dark where they all sat, headlamps shining. Eventually, she recognized the shape of her parents' car at the end of the lot. She walked towards it, stamping out her cigarette on the ground before she reached it.

As she greeted her father, she noticed he was anxious. His default mode was an imperturbable expression, and he was usually able to process events without the impediment of spontaneous feeling. She expected him to make his usual observation that she smelt like an ashtray but, to her surprise, he didn't, and on the short drive to the house she was grateful for the noisy car heater, emanating more sound than it did warmth, for helping to disguise the pauses in the conversation.

'Was it difficult for you to get away this weekend?'

'No. Not really. I was a bit worried because I got given a story to do last minute about a new telly programme and I wasn't sure I was going to be able to knock it off in time. But I managed something.'

'Ah. I take it that a new television programme is now regarded as substantial news by our national papers.'

'Obviously it's not the lead story. That's a follow-up on the whole Clive Ponting thing. His acquittal was great, wasn't it? Of course, he didn't break the Official Secrets Act. It's the normal cover-up stuff.'

'Yes. I must admit it confirms one's belief in the jury system. I suspect that we won't have heard the last word from Margaret Thatcher, though.' Maurice drove slowly through the town, the genteel terraces with their ironwork balconies drab in the bleak weather.

'She and Kinnock have been going hammer and tongs about it this week. Her and her precious *Belgrano*. Of course, although our front-page story is pretty even-handed, the comments page is anti-Ponting.'

'Of course.' Those two words registered his disapproval of the fact that not only was she a journalist but his daughter was working on a right-of-centre paper. She'd only been with him for a few minutes and already she felt as if she was in the wrong.

'Tell me more. About Mum.'

'I think she should discuss it with you herself, it's more of a woman's thing. You'll see she has lost a great deal of weight.'

'But is she . . . is she seriously ill?'

'We don't know yet. She might be.'

This admission silenced both Sal and her father. They had no established mechanism for this kind of conversation. Objective discussion had always been encouraged, but talking about the messy business of what they might feel rather than think had not. Feelings were too insubstantial and subjective to be worth analysis. That was the message.

Sal's mother was never ill. One night, she had given in to terrible toothache and taken to her bed, but it was such a rare occurrence that it had lodged in Sal's memory. As they walked into the dimly lit hallway, Sal had an urge to turn round and run back into the night and the distance of London.

'Is she in bed?'

'Probably.' Maurice was already making his way back into the sanctuary of his study. 'Do go and see her.'

The bulb had gone in the light on the half-landing, and her mother's bedroom door was closed. For several minutes Sal stood outside, nervous of entering and confronting what she might find. 'Who is to bring me that doodle-doo?' She heard the words of Captain Hook in her head, urging his band of pirates to climb down to the hold and battle with the unknown demon. What a time to think of Captain Hook. Grow up, she told herself, first knocking and then opening the door.

The room looked reassuringly the same. Her mother shifted in the bed, the dim bedside light illuminating pill packets on the table.

'Mum,' she whispered, sitting on the bed.

Joy drowsily reached out, her hand touching Sal's face. 'What are you doing here, love?'

'I've come to see you. Do you want to sleep? It's OK. I'll be here later . . . and tomorrow.'

'Of course not.' Joy moved herself into a sitting position. Sal could see the grey of her dark curls at the temples now, dried saliva at the corner of her mouth.

'Can I get you something?'

'No. Thank you. Tell me about work. We must get the paper tomorrow. Tomorrow is Sunday, isn't it? I'm a little vague just now. It's to do with the pills Dr Harris has given me.'

'Work's going pretty well.' Sal was relieved that Joy hadn't brought up the subject of her illness immediately. The office was more comfortable as a topic than her mother's health. 'I'm being given more to write. Sometimes, I suggest an idea, and they get someone else to do it, but that gets me good marks anyway. I'm learning a lot. This weekend I've done something on *EastEnders*. You know. The new BBC soap.'

'I think I heard about it. Maybe on the radio.' Joy's voice began to fade a little. 'Sal, can you see my spectacles anywhere? Perhaps you could look for them downstairs. They could be on the kitchen table.'

When Sal returned, she heard the flush of the lavatory in the bathroom down the corridor from her parents' room. She could see the spectacles on the table under the window. Wrapped in her woollen dressing gown, it was noticeable that her mother had lost weight, her wrists emerging thin and pale from the dark wool. As she climbed back into bed, Sal took the two pillows, trying to shake them out of their dismal flatness.

'Dad . . . he wasn't clear what the problem is . . . I mean . . . what's wrong with you?'

Joy looked towards the thick curtains. 'We don't quite know. I've been having tests. I get the results next week.'

'OK. But what made you need tests?' As she asked, Sal was torn between an urgent desire to remain ignorant of the whole matter and the awareness that this wasn't an option. She wished she hadn't introduced the topic, since her mother appeared unlikely to have done so.

'I've got to that time when women's bodies can go wrong. It's possible that I have some trouble with my womb. I've been getting pains, yes, and other little problems. And they've laid me low. I'm sure it's just one of those things and in the end it'll probably right itself of its own accord. You know, dear, how I don't want you to worry. It's not necessary to make a fuss about this. We'll find out what's what soon enough.'

'What does Dr Harris say?' Dr Harris had been their doctor all of Sal's life. She used to hate his cold hands as they felt her stomach and the way he always looked at her over his glasses as if she was pretending to be ill. However, now that her mother appeared so vulnerable, the mention of his name was reassuring.

'He thinks I might need an operation. But we'll cross that bridge if we come to it.' Joy smiled at her daughter. 'I'm so pleased to see you here. Your father needs someone.'

'Mum. Don't be ridiculous. Surely he can fend for himself. I'm not here to look after him. I've come for you.' Sal didn't feel much the wiser about her mother's condition, but Joy's closing eyes brought a halt to the conversation. Women's bodies, she thought, became such a murky business as they aged. She remembered a man on the paper remaining in the pub one night till last orders. Normally, he was just a quick-one-for-the-road man but that evening he had stayed with them because he said his wife 'was getting her undercarriage done'. If you thought about it, which she rarely did, one minute you were worrying about not getting pregnant and spending hours in the birth control clinics and then, after all that, once you did have children, your reproductive system turned against you and you had to have it removed.

'Have you spoken to Jonathan?'

Joy's eyes instantly opened again, and she smiled at the thought of her son. 'He dropped by the other day. He's in good spirits. Awfully busy, of course, these days, with his cases, and Fiona and the boys.'

'Yeah, but did you talk to him about the operation and things?' Sal pictured Jonathan there, briskly arriving and filling the thin house with his aura of capability while not actually doing anything.

'Why don't you see if you can get your father something to eat? That would be such a help for me. I did ask him to get the basics in. You could rustle up scrambled eggs, or something. As you know, he can't even make toast for himself, and it would be a relief to think of you having a nice supper together.'

The kitchen had become a gloomy place, the fridge bare apart from milk bottles in which she could see the cream congealed under the silver foil cap. But she managed scrambled eggs and some baked beans and toast and, much to her relief and surprise, her father had suggested a whiskey. She didn't remember them ever sitting down to eat, just the two of them, before. They were both silent on the matter of her mother's gynaecological problems, neither prepared to take steps into the potential embarrassment of the conversation. As Maurice cleared the few items from the table Sal stood at the sink squeezing on the rubber gloves, discovering the unappealing squelch of cold water in their tips.

'So I thought I'd get the afternoon train back tomorrow.' Sal spoke above the running water. 'That would be all right, wouldn't it? Or should I stay another night?'

'The latter would be nice for your mother. I'm sure it will cheer her up to have a new presence in the house. You'll take her mind off things. And next week we should know more from Dr Harris.'

It was only ten o'clock when Sal was left pacing around her old bedroom. She was plugged into her Sony Walkman listening to Frankie Goes to Hollywood, the raucous urgency of 'Relax' acting as an antidote to the oppressive quiet of the house. It was strange being in the room, preserved just the way she had left it when she started university six years ago. She could see where the paint had chipped when she tried to peel off the poster of John Travolta in his white trouser suit and the cigarette burn mark on her desk which she had tried to disguise with paint. Saturday night, and here she was, stuck in the permanent Sundayness of Cheltenham.

She flicked through her teenage diary and address book which sat in the top drawer of her desk. Doodles almost obliterated the floral cover and the only dates entered were of people's birthdays and school terms. At the back there were addresses, rarely more than one assigned to each letter. She looked at a name, Pete, scribbled in dark-purple ink. Painswick Pete. She hadn't seen him for ages. He was a laugh. She'd call him tomorrow and see if they could meet for a drink. She had his new number somewhere, she was sure.

The previous night's rain had cleared by morning and the old town sparkled in the bright light of spring. Sal had woken in a good mood, even attempting hospital corners as she made her mother's bed. Seated in the small button-backed armchair, Joy was holding a copy of the *Herald* in her lap. Her daughter's article on *EastEnders* occupied nearly half a page in the middle of the paper and was accompanied by a large picture of the cast in the market square.

'I do feel proud of having a daughter with her name in print.'

Sal looked over her mother's shoulder. 'But they cut some of my best bits. Dad's already let me know what he thinks of the paper carrying pieces about TV. I suppose one day I'll write something he rates.'

'Don't be silly. He's proud of you too. It's just not his way to show it. Now go off and enjoy yourself and I'll see you back here later.' Joy's eyes were clearer this morning. Perhaps it was true, thought Sal as she ran down the stairs. Maybe it would all right itself, like she had said.

She saw Pete immediately through the crowd in the pub where they used to meet when he took the bus into town from nearby Painswick. A greyhound was curled like a fossil at his feet.

'My lady Salome, a pleasure.' Pete leant forward to kiss her. He had never quite recovered from his stint as a roadie, adopting the faux formality of the concert stage, with its grandiose gestures and introductions. 'Do you want a pint? Or have you got London habits now? Is a G and T more your bag?'

'Don't be daft. A pint, please.' Sal looked around the bar, several tables filled with faces she recognized from years back.

Pete carried the beer mugs to a table in the corner. In his worn jeans and scuffed brown boots, his lank black hair framing a pale face lent an unexpected exoticism by slanting almond eyes, he had lost none of his teenage appeal. He still had the dark-red stud in his ear, the one that he always swore was an Indian ruby but most of her gang were sure was just glass. Sal suddenly felt uncomfortable that she was wearing her office shoes, plain black courts, as if their presence semaphored 'ambitious career girl', a condition she thought Pete would probably despise. She'd known him since she was fifteen and, although they'd once attempted sex, in a damp dawn garden, they had both agreed to give up mid-session and just lie looking at the stars instead.

'Are you going to introduce me to your dog?'

'That's Gina. She found me a few months back. We've become soul mates.'

'Hmm, I can imagine. She kind of looks like you. Not exactly a cuddly animal, is she?'

'"Cuddly"? Where's that at?' Pete reached across to run a finger across her fringe. 'Like the hair. Very Iris Murdoch, isn't it? What was that book you used to go on about?'

'That's amazing, you remembering. Yeah. *The Sea, The Sea*. But I remember you quoting Baudelaire at me, and I was ever so impressed by your French. What was it? Something about a serpent?'

'"*Le serpent qui danse*" is the ode you're referring to. Always a hit with the girls. No idea why.'

Sal drained her glass. The beer had made her feel bloated, but she didn't want to fulfil Pete's expectations of her going poncey on him by ordering a vodka.

'Another round?' She went to the bar, ordered two pints and downed a quick vodka and tonic before returning to the table. By the time the bell rang for last orders Sal was in full throttle, wallowing in old jokes and memories, made all the more enjoyable by being in the lofty position of the one who'd got away. She couldn't have stuck living there like Pete, hanging out in the same old place, but it was good to be there right now.

Sal could hear Pete explaining about his occasional work with a posh painter and decorator, but it was background to the thought that had struck her, out of the blue, that what she wanted, quite desperately, was to go to bed with him. She contemplated just coming out and saying it: 'Can we go back to your place now and make love?' But that wasn't really possible – even with all the talk about feminism and glass ceilings, girls didn't say that kind of thing. Of course, boys didn't either, not when you came down to it. You had to go through the process, didn't you? He looked gorgeous, though. And she hadn't had a shag in so long she might be in danger of closing up.

After the smoky room of the pub, when they left, the bright sun outside made her dizzy.

'Why don't you show me where you live now? I don't want to go back home so early. It's a lovely day and . . . you know . . . it's good seeing you again.' She shrugged. Pete considered her, silent for long enough for her to worry that he wanted her to leave. 'OK. Let's take Gina for a run.'

They set off across the town, Sal finding it hard to keep up, the way she always had, his loping stride leaving her trotting alongside. With one hand holding Gina's lead, he reached for hers with the other. After what appeared to be an unnecessarily long walk, they found a patch in the park that satisfied Pete and, letting Gina off her leash, he collapsed on to his back, fumbling in his jeans pocket for a small brown lump of dope.

'Brilliant,' said Sal. 'Just what we need.' She lay on her stomach, feeling the sun through the thick denim of her jacket. When she took the joint, the smoke at first caught in her throat, before she exhaled and watched it float away like a streamer. When she sat up to remove her jacket, she saw him looking at her. He took her hand and circled a finger around her palm, gradually adding more pressure to the movement before pulling her slowly towards him. His kiss tasted sweet, and made her want to kiss him for ever.

The lights of the cars flashed through the window, making a pattern on the mattress below. Wearing Pete's T-shirt, Sal stood circling a scrap of silk scarf in the air as she undulated to the fuzzy sounds of the Jesus and Mary Chain. Against the dark sheets, Pete's was the whitest man's body she had ever seen, his chest hairless save for a thin black line leading from his stomach to the darkness of his groin. She didn't ever want to leave the room. The music mixed with the dope and the drink into a perfect nowhere land. She felt deliciously sore between her legs – she'd lost count of the amount of times they'd had sex. Pete stood up and walked across the small room to open a can of dog food for Gina.

'It's nearly midnight. You should be getting back, Sal. Come on. I'll walk you.'

'No – it's fine,' Sal drawled, following him and running her fingers down his spine. 'I can stay here. It's not a problem.'

'But it's not fine. Is it? Your mum is ill and they'll be in a right state about where you are. I don't want to be the one causing trouble. Get your kit on.'

He helped her into her skirt and shoes, leaving off her knickers and tights, which required too complicated a manoeuvre, and wrapped her in his ratty old fur coat. The sun of the afternoon had been exchanged for a bitter night, and he propelled her quickly through the empty streets, his arm around her shoulders, supporting her when she occasionally stumbled. Turning off the main road and into the row of houses where the Turners lived, they saw the blue flashing at the other end of the road.

'Isn't that outside your place? Shit. It's the fuzz.' Pete plunged his hands into his back pockets and was relieved to discover that the dope he usually housed there was absent. As they got closer, they could see it was not a police car but an ambulance, which was moving away. They ran the last few yards, but it had left the road behind by the time they reached the front door.

'Go on, babe. Better find out what's happening. Call me tomorrow.' He gave her a kiss on her forehead. She didn't move. 'Have you got your keys? Come on, Sal. Don't be a wuss.'

Sal nodded, finally unlocking the front door. There were no lights in the house, and every move she made was amplified by the silence as she walked towards the stairs, past the dark of her father's study.

'Where on earth have you been, Salome?' His tone was curt. He never shouted – anger made his enunciation crisper, more measured. 'I suppose you don't know what time it is. Lost track, presumably.' Sal stood at the entrance to the room, wearing the fur, her legs bare beneath it, and even in her condition she was aware that she was probably demonstrating the day's heavy substance intake.

'Dad, I'm sorry. The ambulance. Was that Mum?'

'Yes, your mother has just left for the hospital. It's precautionary, they say.'

'What happened?'

'It's too late. I don't wish to talk about it now. But I will say that the evening has not been helped by her having to worry about where you had got to, on top of everything else. But, of course, Salome, that is not something you would have thought about.'

'But is she all right?' There was no answer and, knowing that her father at this stage of the evening considered her to be a tiresome irrelevance, Sal climbed the stairs, passing a pile of sheets outside her parents' room. Blood stained the white cotton. She ran up the next flight, to her bedroom, and shut the door quietly. She should have gone into his study to see him, she knew. Tried to make it better instead of walking away from him. It was typical that, when they should have been able to prop each other up, act as mutual support, the distance between them had never been greater. It was always like this, the pair of them isolated in their own worlds, neither making the effort to try to engage with the other. Lying on her old bed, she could see the streetlight outside, noticing the way it made a pear-shaped patch on the door opposite the window, as it always had. Then, she was asleep.

When she woke in the morning the house was empty. On the kitchen table Maurice had written a note in his small italic script. 'Your mother is under observation but is stable. She is in the Leonard Ward at St George's but will be returning home today.' Sal filled the kettle and plugged it in. When she went back to her bedroom, she noticed that the pile of sheets had gone from the staircase.

She was angry with her father. After all, it wasn't her fault her mother was ill, and she'd come to see her, hadn't she, as soon as she was asked? He always made her feel as if she was failing him. When had he ever congratulated her on anything? He was a master of finding and focusing on the lapse in any situation, and that was if he focused on anything to do with her at all. At school she had managed to consistently achieve straight 'A's while appearing to do a minimum amount of work, and it was always the 'lack of application' that he would mention rather than the good results. On one occasion, Joy, listening to his dry criticism of their daughter after a weekend of heavy partying shortly after her excellent A level results had been received, had stood up for their daughter, suggesting that 'We should really applaud her for what even you, Maurice, must acknowledge are particularly good results. She deserves that.' But this small speech had resulted in days of tension within the house and had never been repeated.

It had been a big mistake to get back so late, but even if she'd been there all day, that wouldn't have changed anything. She ran down the stairs and out of the house, leaving the kettle boiling.

The route to the hospital took her along one of the town's busiest streets, its windows full of tweeds and waxed jackets, the needlework shop where the same needlepoint cushion had sat for as long as she could remember, and the coffee shop where her mother would order scones as a treat. Maybe it would be better not to bother her at the hospital. Let her get her strength back without having to waste it on chatting to her, since she knew how hard her mother would try to make Sal believe that she was OK. Also, her mother would be aware how furious Maurice was with his daughter and that would be a whole other thing for her to worry about. Her mum was always trying to make everything all right for him, which Sal thought was a thankless task. Nothing could ever be good enough.

She changed direction and headed towards the station.

12

The taramasalata was too pink. Annie knew the pinkness was in inverse proportion to its authenticity, but the Germolene-coloured tub had been the only one in the corner shop. The colour was more convincing once it was decanted into a china bowl and surrounded with a pile of pitta bread, chunks of cucumber, and placed by another plate bearing a round box of ungiving Camembert and one of salami. Sal's arm appeared through the skylight waving a bottle as she emerged on to the roof terrace.

'Ken. Don't forget the glasses . . . and an ashtray,' she shouted back down.

It was impossible to ignore the enormous diamond on Annie's left hand which flared in the sun as she fiddled with the food, ensuring that, even though the ingredients were basic, they had an elegant appearance. Sal was always amazed how long it could take for Annie to adjust a plate of salami to her satisfaction.

'The sparks off that rock could light a fire,' she remarked, as she saw Annie looking proudly at the weighty evidence of her new status. 'I'm surprised he didn't get charged for excess, carrying that to Venice.'

Annie laughed. 'I can't believe I'm getting married. It's not like us at all. It seems so – well, so . . . grown up.'

'No,' agreed Kendra, who had now joined them on the terrace and was examining a blister on her big toe. 'It's not like us. But I suppose "us" is changing. Letty must be thrilled, isn't she?'

Letty had only met Charlie once previous to the engagement. She had taken in the tailoring of his Paul Smith suit, his polished black shoes, the authority of his deep voice and concluded that her daughter was in safe hands. She knew, of course, that appearances could be unreliable but, even so, everything she could see about Charlie induced confidence, and his absolute certainty, even in the smallest of matters, came as such a relief. She had always liked a man who could take charge. His conviction that the only thing to order for tea at the French brasserie where they met was the croque monsieur rather than the more predictable tarts invited no debate not because he was a bully but simply because he was so obviously correct.

Annie had called her from Venice with her news. The line was faint and Letty's response, although enthusiastic, was hampered by the slight time delay of an international call, which meant that they both kept speaking simultaneously, especially with Annie's excitement at the turn of events.

'You must come down as soon as you're back. You and Charlie. I do want to get to know my prospective son-in-law.'

'Charlie's asking if we can come down next weekend? We can tell you all about it,' Annie had said as she lay on the bed looking out over the Grand Canal, Charlie fondling her bare legs, moving up from her feet and approaching her knee. When she put the phone down to her mother, Annie looked out of the window opposite. It was exactly like she had always hoped it would be. She batted away the thought that it had been Jackson she had imagined would be in the bed making his way up her body rather than Charlie, but not before she explained to herself how much better it was, the way things had turned out. Charlie was the kind of man it was going to be wonderful to be married to. They would be able to plan everything together, and he was so good at making sure that those plans would work. Already he had suggested some changes to his flat which would make it feel more like it was hers as well, which was a small point, but it showed that he understood her. The only thing she really wanted to resolve was his relationship with her friends. Or lack of it. He didn't really get the point of them, she could tell. But there was tons of time. That's what was so lovely. They had all the time in the world to sort things out.

That afternoon sitting on the roof with Sal and Kendra was different, overlaid with an understanding between them that things had changed. Annie knew that her friends were pleased for her that she was marrying, but also that neither of them understood why she was doing it – even though they hadn't said so. Their silence was a Chinese wall. She supposed it was hardly surprising. After all, she'd been so madly in love with Jackson only a year ago, and then she had found Charlie (although it was rather more that he had found her) and, when it came down to it, Sal and Kendra hadn't had much time to properly get to know him.

There hadn't even been a real opportunity to share the complaining stage with them, the bit when the unquestioning joy of having a new bloke was over and he'd done enough annoying things you could tell the others about to reaffirm that boyfriends were always a potential problem and girlfriends, naturally, were the ones you always returned to. There hadn't been any of that. None of the commiserating nor any of the jokes. And now Annie worried she was going to be excluded by dint of the ring on her finger, a thin line of separation.

'What's happening about the wedding?' Kendra asked as she folded a chunk of cucumber into some pitta bread. 'I'm only asking one thing. Don't you dare ask me to be a bridesmaid.' The thought of Kendra trussed up in the girly costume of the traditional bridesmaid made them all laugh.

'Oh, you surprise me. I thought you would be so disappointed if I didn't ask. And there was I, wondering how to get out of it.'

'You joke, but actually I'd quite like to be a bridesmaid. It would be a laugh,' said Sal, peering at her bare legs, with their scattering of short black hairs like scratches on the white skin. 'Oh, what a pain it is to be dark. Do husbands love you even if you don't shave your legs? That might be good enough reason to get hitched.'

'I don't expect Annie knows the answer,' Kendra answered. 'She's never not shaved her legs.'

'Well, Charlie's not a great one for jungles of underarm hair. I don't know how keen he is on *au naturel*.'

Uncharacteristically, Sal could see this conversational turn might easily provoke Kendra into a sulky unease about Gioia, who was definitely on the *au naturel* side. It was extraordinary how her two best friends had ended up with people who couldn't be more opposite, but then they had always, all three of them, been so different, right from the start.

'How're things at the Chapel now?' She moved the topic on to safer territory.

'Not so good. I wish I knew the details, but there're big problems with the building, and Gioia's being hassled to move out by some developers. She won't really talk about it. It bugs me that she treats me like one of the kids and thinks I don't need to know.'

'What would she do if she had to move? Could you go somewhere else?'

'It would be difficult. The Chapel has been her life for ages, and it's not like we could easily find somewhere else where she could do the same thing. I think she'd go Tonto if we had to go.'

'At least she's got you now. That must mean something.'

Kendra realized that Sal was simply being loyal but, all the same, she found that last comment insensitive, in its implication that Sal had no understanding of Gioia's deep commitment to her work.

'How are things with your folks, anyway?' Sal continued, completely unaware of how Kendra was feeling.

'Oh, you know. I'm not exactly living their dream – the job, the girlfriend, *ya di ya di ya*. But I guess I haven't made it any easier. I've just kept away. It seems simpler. I'm in such a different place now.'

'Come on, you two. This is meant to be a celebration, not a wake. We haven't toasted the bride yet. It calls for another bottle.' Sal slid down the ladder, watched by the others.

'So what's happened with her mother?' Kendra asked Annie.

'I don't know. She won't talk about it, but she came back from Cheltenham with an A-grade hangover.' Annie adjusted her ring slightly to make sure the diamond sat entirely central on her finger. 'And just before she went I found an empty vodka bottle in a pile of towels. The drinking's getting worse. I'm pretty worried about what's going to happen. I'll be moving in with Charlie soon, and she'll have to move out of this place then. It's going to be hard.' She sighed. 'There just never seems to be a right time to have a conversation.'

'I suppose I could try.' Kendra didn't sound convinced as she looked over the parapet towards the house opposite with the hanging garden of plants attached to its wall. 'Yes. I guess we could both try.'

As Kendra cycled home, she was grateful for the breeze. Nearing the flat, she passed the Turkish restaurant where she and Gioia would occasionally treat themselves to filo pastry parcels stuffed with cheese and a spicy aubergine dip. She could hear the whistle from the nearby park signalling closing time.

When she looked up at the roof, the skylight windows were open. Gioia must be home. She hesitated before opening the front door, preparing herself to re-enter their world, a place that as yet was still apart from anything she shared with her friends, and positively alienated from her family home. Reaching the top floor, she opened the door to the flat, the pedal on her bike banging against her ankle as she tried to prop it up against the wall. At first she didn't see the woman sitting next to Gioia.

'Ken. My mum's come by.'

Kendra took in the slight figure on the edge of the sofa, a head of tight grey curls, the milky white of her eyes accentuated by deep-brown skin. It made sense, she supposed, given how dark Gioia was, and the wiry consistency of her hair even when it was oiled and sculpted into its wonderful shapes, but, even so, it came as a shock to see that Mrs Cavallieri was obviously not Italian, as she had assumed.

She shook hands, acutely aware of being sweaty from the ride across the city. Mrs Cavallieri, in contrast, was bandbox neat: her white shirt pristine, a daub of coral lipstick brightening her lips, flat sandals polished to a sheen.

'Mum's come down to help out Gerass with some things.'

'I hadn't seen the boy in months. It was time. There never comes a moment when you don't worry about what your children are doing. It's God's way.' Gioia was, as usual, sprawled, legs slung over the arm of the sofa, while her mother sat straight, her hands placidly on her lap.

'I was saying to Mum how we wanted to take a trip to the seaside with some of the kids these holidays. It's the kind of thing I couldn't do on my own, but now I'm working with you it's easier. Look what she's brought me – over there, by the sink.'

Kendra walked over to the kitchen area of the bedsit, noting the *me* rather than *us*, the *working* rather than *living*. Kilner jars were labelled in pen: salsa pomodoro, spice mix, plantain chutney. A large Italian cheese lay in its web of string. She was waiting for Gioia to say something to explain Kendra's presence to her mother. Surely she wasn't going to pretend that Kendra wasn't living with her. Jesus, should she ask her if it was OK to take a pee?

'You must look after yourself now. We all work, but you must make sure that you take time to enjoy yourself, before you have a family and all those responsibilities.' Mrs Cavallieri had a sing-song lilt to her voice. Despite being half her daughter's height, the woman commanded attention. When Kendra came back from the bathroom, she stood to leave, Gioia jumping up to place a large arm over her mother's narrow shoulders.

'*Non preoccupare, Mama. Sto bene.* Ken. I'll be back in a moment. I'm just going to walk with Mum down the road to meet Dad.' What was it with this family? They were always telling each other not to worry, *non preoccupare*, thought Kendra crossly. As far as she could see, at the moment, there was quite a lot to *preoccupare* about.

Alone in the flat, Kendra wriggled out of her dirty clothes, throwing a black T-shirt over a clean bra and pants. She pulled her hair back tight from her forehead as if it might help restore order to her tumbling thoughts. She certainly felt like a stranger in the flat, returning from the afternoon with Sal and Annie to find that the life she had assumed she was having was not exactly what she had thought. What was all that about, Gioia not letting on that her mum was Jamaican? And, more to the point, Mrs Cavallieri certainly didn't appear to know that Kendra was her daughter's girlfriend. Had Gioia kept Kendra's presence secret from her own parents even as she watched Kendra go through all the difficulty of telling hers that not only was she living and working with Gioia but that they were also lovers?

'I understand your need for experimentation, Kendra. You're at the age.' That was how Marisa had confronted her the last time they'd met at the house. 'But surely you could have investigated your sexual leanings with somebody more . . . somebody more . . . interesting. There are, of course, some very interesting lesbian couples. And in many cases these relationships are wonderfully creative. But this woman, who is also your, well . . . the closest thing you have to an employer . . . it's all so narrow.' She looked up at the ceiling as if searching for a description. 'So . . . limited.'

Gioia's heavy tread on the stair stopped outside the door, followed by the familiar rattle of her keychain. She entered with a big smile, holding out her arms to Kendra, who remained stiffly across the room.

'So do you want to explain?' she asked, her back to Gioia.

'Explain what?'

'Everything. It strikes me there's a lot to explain. You could start with why you, obviously, haven't told your mum about us. You've watched me dealing with my parents and how they feel about this but you haven't even tried to sort it out with yours.' It was rare for Kendra to feel this way. Most of the time she paddled in the shallow waters of acceptance. Confrontation made her feel ill. She watched Gioia decide not to approach after all, instead walking over to the table, where she found her pouch of tobacco in the drawer, and then sitting to roll a joint and saying nothing until she had had several deep tokes.

'Hmm.' She exhaled, waving the spliff in offering to Kendra, who was not about to accept anything that might constitute a peace token at this point.

Kendra tried another line. 'And why didn't you tell me about your mum?'

'What about my mum?'

'Well, that she's Jamaican, or something.'

'Antiguan . . . but that's probably all the same to you.' The way Gioia said that, as if she couldn't really care less, provoked Kendra further.

'What's that meant to mean?'

'What does it matter where my mum was born? Whether she's Jamaican, Antiguan, Dominican or Martian? She's not the same as you, is she? That's what you mean.'

'It's got nothing to do with her being the same as me, you know that. I live here with you. I'm your girlfriend, or that's what I thought I was. What matters is I didn't know. You never told me. That's a big gap in my knowledge of you. My understanding. I thought she was Italian, and it feels strange, as if you kept it from me.'

'It's not my fault that you got it wrong.' Gioia leant back in her chair, reaching her arms out behind her head in a deliberate display of casual stretching. 'Fine. Here's the history lesson. Dad came to England from Italy after the war and met Mum in Liverpool. She'd come from the island with her brother. She and Dad moved to Glasgow a few years later, and he worked in restaurants and the ice cream biz, like they all did. Then he had enough cash to set up the shop, and that's where they stayed. There was trouble with each other's families to start – the Italians don't much fancy the darkies and, so she tells it, Mum's lot didn't go a bundle on her shacking up with an *Itie*, but they stuck it out and everyone got over it. They got over it. Why don't you? Why don't you get over whatever it is that you're all tight-arsed about? I haven't told her about you. No. But I haven't not told her – I just keep my personal stuff private. It's not what she wants to know about. My folks aren't thick. They've got it sussed, I guess. But they've learnt: sometimes it's easier to turn a blind eye. It doesn't always make you feel better to know the truth. It doesn't make you a better person.'

She got up from the table, moving towards Kendra but stopping inches from her, not touching. 'You've got to work out where you're at, Kendra. You have to decide who to trust. If you love me, you have to trust me.'

Kendra knew she had to decide whether she was going to let Gioia get away with this or continue to probe the topic, which, previous experience had taught her, probably wouldn't get her anywhere. It had been such a difficult day. Sitting there with Annie, who she had been so close to but now felt as if she was losing . . . and then coming back to this. She knew that she was making a fuss. That it didn't mean that Gioia didn't love her. But as she looked at her girlfriend, she couldn't help wondering what else she might not know.

'I want to trust you. Of course I do. I always have trusted you. Completely. Why wouldn't I? But imagine if you came back like I did and found out that all this stuff wasn't how you thought it was. How would you feel?'

Gioia shrugged. 'Hard to tell. We can only deal with what's happened, and all I'm saying is that nothing's changed about us, about the way I feel about you. So don't let it mess us up. We've got to stick together. That's all I know.'

13

The church at Little Sponswood was set at the furthest end of the village, just past the row of red-brick new-builds. A pair of cedars of Lebanon swooped over the small graveyard. It was, everybody agreed, the perfect day for a wedding. The dusty heat of August had been ended by a storm that had brought freshness to the air and ensured that September arrived sunny but freed from the stale dog days of summer.

Both Annie and her mother had been preparing for this day for most of Annie's life and, although in almost all matters Annie allowed Charlie to take the lead, on this wedding day her wishes were dominant. It was not in Charlie's nature to collaborate, and on being informed that the wedding was to be a morning service at St Mark's, Little Sponswood, followed by a lunch in the garden, he had stepped aside from the whole proceedings, saying only, 'I'm leaving it up to you. It's your party. There's no point asking me about this and that when I haven't been in on the game plan from the start. But we've got to have something proper to drink. I'll stand us the champagne before lunch so we avoid that stuff from M&S that your mum rates so highly.'

There had been the odd moment when Annie wished that Charlie weren't quite so cut and dried about everything and that they could have a discussion about some of the details: should the top table be long, or round like the others? Was an hour enough time for drinks before they ate? But, mainly, she accepted that with the conviction that she found so attractive came an inability to share deliberation. She got enormous pleasure from spending hours over the decision as to whether the menu should feature an illustration of vine leaves or wheatsheaves or both, but it was immediately clear that this kind of question would have to be resolved between her and Letty, not her and Charlie. She was surprised to find that Sal was unexpectedly helpful too, having firm opinions on matters such as the colour of the tablecloths and even suggesting that, due to the time of year, they could theme the whole day along the lines of the harvest festival.

When the engagement had first been announced there had been a discussion about whether Charlie should take Annie to Rama-tuelle in the South of France, where his parents Josh and Suzie had decamped after finally selling their small estate in Rutland (which had, for many years, been a financial drain). Charlie, with his sense of order, his interest in making money and his unswervable drive, appeared a curious fellow to his parents, who lacked any of these qualities.

'Suze would love to get to know her prospective daughter-in-law,' Josh had suggested when Charlie called with the news. 'We could take in a night in Saint-Trop if you liked. The harvest here's shaping up nicely, and last year's vintage, though I say it myself, is more than drinkable.' But, somehow, a date had never been fixed and the wedding day approached without Annie having met her in-laws. It wasn't how she had expected it would be. She had always thought that she would have a close relationship with a mother-in-law. Annie would completely understand if her mum-in-law wanted to spend time alone with her son, for example, but it seemed that the Sethringtons had a semi-detached attitude when it came to family.

Her own mother was a different matter, treating the wedding as the culmination of a lifetime's ambition. Her hair in rollers, she walked into her daughter's bedroom on the morning of the wed-ding to find Kendra and Sal seated on the small bed watching the bride's hair being backcombed so as to be able to support the gar-land of Michaelmas daisies that would hold the veil in place.

'I must say, I do wish the caterers would get a move on.' Letty's brow creased in concern. 'It's nearly ten o'clock and there's only one dim-looking girl standing around with a clipboard while those chaps in the van just chat. It's beyond me where Penny's going to put her floral arrangements, when they haven't even got the tables up . . .'

'Once they start, they can do this kind of thing really quickly, Letty,' Kendra offered reassuringly. Letty glanced at Kendra, who was wearing a tunic with an enormous scarf pinned over her shoulder in the manner of a Highlander. It was clear that she doubted Kendra had a huge amount of expertise in this particular arena.

'Do you think I should use powder? I've got this red bit, just here.' Annie touched an imperceptible blemish below the corner of her mouth. 'But I don't normally and, when you get powder wrong, it can look awful.'

'I don't think you should.' Sal flicked through the copy of *Brides* on the bed. 'In here they say the important thing is to create, and I quote, "a dewy look of love". They say moisturizer is the key. And who are we to disagree?'

The previous evening, they had all strolled through the garden with Freddie Bishop, who had been chosen to give Annie away, Letty taking the view that, with no father alive, somebody with whom Annie had spent every Christmas Day since she was a small child was an acceptable surrogate. The girls had complimented Letty on her immaculate herbaceous borders, with their array of silvery-green foliage and early autumn colour, which surrounded the marquee pegged out on the lawn.

'Yes,' she had replied. 'I must say I had been worried about them. September can be difficult, you know. Not as bad as August, of course, but June's really the month they're at their best.'

By 11.45, the church was almost full of couples, who had entered two by two, just like they did into the Ark, thought Sal, as she watched Charlie, in his pale-grey morning suit, talking to his best man.

'He's chosen Mark because he says he'll know what's what and won't forget the ring,' Annie had told them the day before. 'He's not really his best friend. But that's Charlie for you. He likes everything to go smoothly. And it makes sense, doesn't it? You don't want your friends mucking things up.'

Sal assumed that the couple beside them were his parents. The dad was shorter than Charlie and deeply tanned, and Charlie's mum must have been very pretty when she was young. She had some kind of cream lacy thing on. Weren't people, especially mothers, meant to steer clear of white at weddings? Maybe cream was OK. And that must be his younger sister beside her. There was a woman behind them with plastic hair with a flying saucer of navy balanced on it. She must be Mark's wife, the one Annie had had such a tough time with that weekend.

At the opening chords of Vivaldi the congregation rustled to its feet, turning collectively to catch its first sight of the bride. Annie really did look beautiful as she walked slowly up the aisle on Freddie's arm. The dress, which she had designed herself, had been made by an old friend of Letty's who used to work with Hardy Amies. It succeeded in making her appear simultaneously ethereal and sexy. They had discussed that last afternoon on the roof how she wouldn't be seen dead in one of those Princess Di meringue numbers. She didn't want Charlie to bolt at the altar.

Sal was finding it hard to believe that she was at Annie's wedding. It just didn't seem real. She'd tried to be enthusiastic from the moment Annie had broken her news, but now that they were all here in the church she allowed herself to acknowledge that it was difficult not to feel that Annie was slipping away. It wasn't the marriage, although there was something about marriage that did mean you were different. It was that neither she nor Kendra could really get the point of Charlie, and it wasn't hard to work out that this was mutual. It wasn't what he said but more that, during the few times they had all been together, he had made his lack of interest in them so obvious. But then she supposed that Annie mightn't much take to Pete if it came to that. She had spent a lot of time with him over the summer. He was certainly different from Charlie and that guy he had as his best man.

The service passed quickly and in what appeared to be no time at all the couple were signing the register. Letty, smiling below her aquamarine feather-trimmed boater, stood beside Josh Sethrington as they served as witnesses. Sal recognized a man desperate to have a fag when she saw him.

'I haven't been to many weddings,' Kendra said, as small groups clustered afterwards outside near the cedars. 'Are they always like this? A bit his and hers?'

'I suppose at some weddings a lot of people know each other, but at this one we're all a little strange to each other. After all, Annie didn't meet Charlie's parents till the other day. Maybe it's because it happened quickly.' Sal waved over at Lee, who she could see talking with Tania and what must be other colleagues.

Lee stood out in a loose cream suit worn over a flamingo-dominated Hawaiian shirt. He knew it was naff, but he had developed a thing for *Miami Vice* and, though this wasn't a look he'd usually be seen dead wearing, a country wedding where nobody much knew him struck him as the perfect opportunity to indulge. The rest of the Torrington flock had chosen en masse to adopt a uniform of Rayban Wayfarers and long coats worn over tapered trousers. Tania's was made by Scott Crolla, although she was beginning to think the damask might be a bit heavy for this mild weather.

'Happy day, happy day,' she flapped enthusiastically, wiping her forehead. 'In my day, we didn't go in for all this white-wedding stuff. It was a see-through Ossie down Chelsea Register Office and then a knees-up at San Lorenzo. But my, how conventional you lot are.' She turned to Gioia, who appeared surprised to be the recipient of the observation. 'I'm always telling my gang that we didn't make such a blinding fuss of everything at their age.' Gioia nodded. 'I know you're not ancient like me,' Tania continued, 'but I bet you've been to your fair share of events. People like us. We've seen it all – or, at any rate, a lot of it. How times change. We're back in a much more conventional period now, that's for sure.' Kendra wasn't certain how Gioia would respond to being bracketed with Tania but, to her surprise, she simply smiled, as if she agreed.

'Tell you what, Gioia,' Tania continued. 'There're those Potter-tons talking to no one, which they won't like one bit. Better do our stuff. They come out in hives if they have to spend too long with just the other for company, but we must remember they *were* the matchmakers.' She waddled over to where Tony and Trish stood in a cloud of Tony's cigar smoke, Gioia following obediently behind.

'Yeah, yeah. I know everyone's talking about the Big Bang. Boring subject of the year. But don't you think it's depressing the way we're all having to move miles out east, where there's literally nothing but a few blocks that look like they've been made out of kids' toys, and a couple of crappy wine bars?'

As she spoke, Sal filleted the vine leaves from the table decoration, leaving them as satisfactory skeletons, the dark green falling in dusty crumbs as it joined with her cigarette ash in small piles.

'I mean, I know you and Charlie are property types and I suppose you make stacks of cash, but it's so sterile what's happening. Fleet Street's going to be a morgue soon, now we're all moving out east.'

Mark wasn't paying too much attention to what Sal was saying, since he was concentrating on the white triangle of her knickers where her skirt had ridden up. He had taken quite a shine to Annie's lively friend with her skinny bare limbs. He looked across the marquee to where Sophie sat talking to Charlie's mum, who, after that move to the South of France, was definitely turning into a bit of an old slapper. Sophie could only be a few years older than Sal but she looked like a member of another generation in her navy suit, the shimmer of large pearl studs appearing through her dark sheet of hair. He imagined what it would feel like to run his hand up the leg in front of him, moving his fingers under the elastic of Sal's pants.

Sal shifted, depriving him of the view he was so enjoying, and leant towards him to pour them both another glass of wine. It was a shame that, any moment now, Sophie would be over here, suggesting they should be on their way.

'I know what you mean about the East End. But give it time,' he responded to Sal's rant. 'Mind you, it's not only the East End that's getting done up. Charlie's got his eye on a development in north London. Grim part of town with nothing to recommend it, if you ask me, but he's convinced it's got potential.'

'Yeah, I know it – Kendra and Gioia's place is up there. They hate the way it's all becoming estate agents and stuff. They work in an old church that Gioia's had for ages.'

'Sounds right up my Charlie's *strasse*.' Mark turned to look behind him, where Sophie had appeared. 'Hello, darling. Have you been having a good chat with Suze? She looks like she's had one too many rosés, but when I was little and would stay with them for weekends, I used to think she was like an angel when she said goodnight to us. All blonde hair and floaty dresses. Have you met Sal? She's Annie's flatmate – or *was*, before the arrival of our Charlie on the scene.'

'Mark, we ought to be thinking about going. We need to get back before seven to relieve Mrs B.' Sophie looked down at Sal, whose legs were once again spread out in front of her. 'It's so hard to get nannies to do weekends now. Charlie's desperate for kids, you know, but heavens, they change your life.' Was Annie going to turn into somebody like her? thought Sal. What a depressing possibility.

The train seemed to be stopping at a station every five minutes as it crawled back into London. Sal could see her reflection in the window as the countryside passed, the day fading to dusk. An empty vodka miniature kept rolling around until Kendra picked it up.

'I can't believe you wanted another drink. We've been at it all day.'

'Maybe that's why,' answered Sal. 'Who knows? Anyway, I've just thought of something. Mark, that best man with the dolly wife, he told me Charlie's involved in some development around your area. He might know about the people who are trying to get Gioia out.'

'Shit. It couldn't be him, could it? Who's doing it? Wouldn't Annie have said?'

'Would she know? But it's probably not. There are millions of property blokes out there now.' Sal drained the last from her plastic cup.

'Maybe not. But you're right. He might be able to tell me something to help.'

'Not much we can do now, as they're on their way to Portofino.

But when they get back I'll ask her. It'll be easier for me. Think of it this way. If it is Charlie, he might not know it's such a problem for you.'

Kendra looked doubtful and turned to glance at Gioia, asleep beside her.

'She's exhausted. I think the worry is getting to her. Anyway, what about you? What's going on with you?'

'Me?' Sal was surprised. 'I'm fine.'

'Have you got somewhere to live?'

'Not yet, but I will. I'm dossing with some guys from the office right now. Don't worry, Kendra.'

There it was again. *Non preoccupare.*

'And your mum? How's she?'

'Oh, that's sorted out. She's better.' Sal stood up. 'See you in a minute.'

Kendra watched her walk down the corridor to the smoking carriage next door, a cigarette between her lips before she even got there. How come they were meant to be friends and yet Sal wouldn't talk about her mother? Should she push her on it? What was her problem?

Sal did not see a problem because, if there ever was a problem, it was Sal's practised position to ignore it. Most of the time, this was an effective ploy and, in the matter of her friends, her optimistic, tunnel-visioned approach was a useful antidote to Kendra's fretting and Annie's compliance. When Joy became ill, it was the first time that this position had not worked. Even Sal's ability to avoid issues she found difficult was challenged.

The drama of her mother's hospitalization had been followed almost immediately by the identification of an internal mass that, after a few tense weeks, was identified as a fibroid rather than the more sinister tumour nobody had wanted to mention. But the resulting operation had left a significant amount of damage and had meant that Joy, for the first time in Sal's life, needed her support. It was not a situation that she felt comfortable with. She was used to her parents providing a distant, stable background to her ambitions. They demanded nothing from her and she little from them, even if from time to time she wished her father might be more admiring. Finding herself required to visit home regularly to help with the recuperative process – 'Six weeks putting your feet up,' the doctors had declared the minimum – Sal was thrown by this unusual demand on her time, if not on her emotion. The only good bit was that she found herself becoming closer to Pete, his room, which smelt of dope and sandalwood, a sanctuary from home. Even in the brightness of midsummer, her parents' Cheltenham house was permanently dim. Sal didn't understand why her parents couldn't just buy a few of the uplighters everybody had begun to use instead of clogging up the place with small lamps which each had to be switched on and off individually.

After a month, Joy began to rally and Sal was pleased to find her, one Sunday, cooking up her notorious paella, a concoction of rice, peas, red peppers and frozen prawns inspired by a visit to Barcelona in the seventies. Even though this dry and tasteless ensemble bore little resemblance to that dish, just the fact of Joy pouring in the water mixed with stock cube indicated that she was on the mend. It was a relief in every way. Being in Cheltenham reminded Sal how essential it was for her to have got away from the place. Whatever happened, she wasn't going back. London and her career were what she wanted, what made her feel like the person she was. As soon as she was at home it was as if she had been expected to drink some potion and turn into a different person that would fit in. She had always felt that way about it, but never so much as now, when she knew what it was like to have escaped.

1986

14

Lee had never seen a walk-in wardrobe before. He could do with one himself but, since he was still a part-time resident of Jojo's squat up near Euston, it remained a very remote possibility. Still, he might not have the space but he'd got the clothes. He was archiving them. It was what designers did, although his, rather than hanging in a storage room, were housed in cardboard boxes divided into months and years. The boxes travelled with him, sometimes built into a wall around the mattress he also transported from place to place. They'd be worth something some day. Particularly if they'd been shot for the cover of *The Face* or had been featured in *Men in Vogue*.

The room was lined with teak cupboards along two sides, and a shoe rack at the end where Charlie's polished shoes were displayed was reflected back by the floor-to-ceiling mirror opposite. It created the effect of shoes travelling like a time machine into infinity. The wardrobe was a tangible illustration of Charlie's delight in order, as well as a display of his success. After all, not many people could afford to have six Paul Smith suits, let alone shelves of laundered shirts, each folded into an individual packet. Lee picked up a pair of black and white Ralph Lauren co-respondents.

'Wild. Does he wear these often?'

'I don't think I've ever seen him in them. He's got a bit of a thing for shoes. He collects them. Come. Look at my space.' Annie had slid open doors to display clothes grouped in blocks of colour: blacks merging into grey and then white, florals gathered at one end next to a large section of quiet creams and browns and toffees. Lee didn't remember Annie going for those shades before she'd taken up with Charlie.

'He says they work well with my colouring. I know what he means. All those bright colours that suit Sal just make me look tragic.' Annie was wearing a pair of jeans belted at her waist and a shirt of palest pink tucked into them. She had a pair of brown leather Johnny Moke loafers on her feet, identical to the navy, green and rust pairs Lee could now see in the wardrobe. 'And look,' she continued, 'look at these drawers. Aren't they incredible?' They moved with a plush mobility indicating true craftsmanship. There was none of the sticking she was used to from years of old chests of drawers.

It was Lee's first visit to Charlie and Annie's flat. To be honest, it was a bit of a relief that Charlie wasn't around. Lee didn't much take to him, but Annie was happy and that's what counted, he supposed. Now he'd seen that walk-in wardrobe it all made a bit more sense. Annie had left the room and was kneeling beside a dark, low cabinet in the sitting room.

'What do you want? There's champagne . . . wine . . . but I could make you a Bloody Mary or a Screwdriver – anything, really.' She listed the contents of the cocktail kit housed there with pride: 'Shakers, strainers, shot glasses . . .' Lee was looking at the huge Keith Haring print hung on the wall above. He was crazy about Haring.

'Is that real, that Haring? A glass of champagne, please, if you're offering.'

'It's a print, one of an edition Charlie picked up recently. He's pretty good on modern art.' They walked down the long dark corridor of the flat that led to the kitchen.

'It's a bit Major Tom in here, isn't it?' Lee looked around at the steel counters, the spike of the Alessi lemon squeezer the only object to disturb their surface. 'This oven's got so many dials it could fly you to the moon.'

'Yeah, I know. I still haven't figured out what most of them do . . . Here you go.' She offered Lee the flute of champagne, serving herself only an inch of liquid.

'Cheers. Are you off the booze?'

Annie fiddled with her hair, 'Cheers. Actually, I've got something to tell you. It's a secret, but I can't bear to keep it much longer. I'm pregnant.' The information was produced hesitantly, as if this fact was open to interpretation. 'It's weird saying it like that. I haven't got used to hearing it.'

'Wow. When? You just got married!' Annie thought that Lee sounded a little squeaky.

'Yes. I know. I've just been lucky. And Charlie's so excited – it's really sweet.' The idea of Charlie being sweet was too great a leap of imagination for Lee.

'What are you going to do about work? Have you told Tania?'

'Of course not. I told you, it's still a secret.' Annie took a sip of champagne as a gesture of celebration, but she didn't want it. She had been feeling sick most of the time and terrible in the mornings for the past few weeks. It had been a nightmare travelling to work on the Tube with everyone crowded around her. She kept reminding herself that the baby was only the size of a bean and they couldn't crush it.

In the last month, she'd been handed some new accounts by Tania, and one was based in Paris, which would involve flying out several times a year. She wanted to be enthusiastic, knowing that the task was a measure of her success in the office, but it was hard when you felt the way she did at the moment. Tania had also given her the account of a new bar in the City, but how could she get worked up over their wine list when she thought she might throw up at any point?

Charlie had told her that she must get a good man to look after her; why didn't she ask Sophie who she used? Her local doctor had confirmed the pregnancy and suggested the nearest hospital for the birth, but it was true that, once she'd had an appointment with Mr Churston at the Portland, who had assured her that everything was 'tickety boo', she felt hugely reassured. Still, that didn't help with the journey to work in the mornings.

The only other person she'd told was Letty.

'Darling! I couldn't be more excited,' she had shrieked down the phone. 'My first grandchild. Now, when we next get together I must tell you about the kind of thing I experienced, because I gather pregnancies have a lot to do with genetics. I'm sorry to say I was sick as a dog with you but absolutely fine with Beth. You know, in my day, they were prescribing Thalidomide for morning sickness and, when I think what happened to those poor mites . . . but I never took it. Anyway, they say ginger is the thing now.' Annie could picture her mother doodling on the message pad by the phone as she rambled on. 'So, darling, what's the plan about work? I hope you're not thinking of staying on for too long.'

'I haven't thought about it yet. It's still so early. You know, people do have babies and work nowadays, Mum. In fact, they've been doing it for years.'

'Don't be ratty, Annie. I just want the best for you, and I worry about all you girls with your big jobs and tiny babies. I'm sure Charlie has a view.'

Charlie indeed had made it clear that he was taking a similar line to her mother, and the subject of maternity leave had become a no-go area of discussion. Annie thought that, once she started feeling better, it would be easier to work everything out. She changed the subject. 'Have you still got all the baby stuff – mine and Beth's? You must have the christening gown? I want to come down and have a rummage.' The thought of the boxes of their childhood clothes all wrapped in layers of tissue in the attic provided a far more enjoyable topic for the rest of their conversation.

Annie recounted the call to Lee now, leaving out the bit about Charlie.

'And what about Sal and Kendra? What have they said?'

'I haven't told them yet. I keep meaning to, but it's difficult. I know I'm married and they aren't, but having a baby is such a big difference. It's going to change everything, and I suppose a bit of me keeps putting off telling them. I'd sort of like them to know without actually having to tell them. I know they'll want to be pleased' – she swirled the small quantity of champagne around in her glass – 'but I'm not sure they really will be.'

Lee looked at her in the spaceship of a kitchen. Annie's softness seemed out of place in its metallic harshness. The old flat where she used to live was far more her. In this new life, it was as if she was orbiting above them and looking down from a distance. He hoped she'd be all right when she landed.

The drinkers started to trickle into the Bank straight from the office. Paddy and Marcus, the bar's owners, were desperate for Annie to fix a write-up in the *Evening Standard*, which, she had pointed out, might take time, since they'd only recently run a City round-up. Before she'd married she would have fancied Paddy, who had a taut ex-Sandhurst physique camouflaged in the mufti of an entrepreneur: loose jackets, jeans, the occasional tie.

In that afternoon's meeting, though, she had told them that the idea of giving the place over for an evening to readers of *Ms London* was terrible – the positioning was all wrong. 'You don't want to get into that bridge and tunnel thing. *Ms London*'s free to every secretary crossing London Bridge, and that's not very cool.'

By 6.30 the bar was three deep. She'd suggested Sal get there earlier so they would have time for a proper chat before she had to meet Charlie, but there was still no sign of her. Thank God that, today, she felt OK. Perhaps she was reaching the good bit she'd read you got to after twelve weeks, although her breasts were uncomfortably swollen. Now she knew what Kendra had been talking about when she complained about hers getting so big and painful before her period. Charlie was enjoying them, though. He had arrived home the other night with some exotic bras that made her look like a Playboy bunny. But she didn't feel at all like sex at the moment. Her body was a tabernacle entrusted with this precious charge, not something for Charlie to tinker around with.

As she sat at the bar she watched the guy opposite pressing buttons on his bulky rectangular phone before holding it to his ear. You saw those new phones around the City more than anywhere else. He must be struggling to hear above the music. Everywhere she went at the moment she heard 'West End Girls'. The Pet Shop Boys weren't her cup of tea, but she knew Lee was a fan. She'd lost count of the times she'd heard him tell the story about meeting Neil Tennant.

Eventually, she saw Sal push through the doors, arriving at the table with a gabbled greeting. 'Sorry, sorry. It got crazy at work and I had to make all these calls. But I'm not that late, am I? It was six thirty, wasn't it?'

'It was six, actually, but it's fine. It's just that I have to meet Charlie at eight. Let's order. Have what you like, it's on expenses.' She handed over the menu, with its complicated graphic on the cover, a mélange of pound and dollar motifs.

'Sure. Like the ashtrays. Clever idea to have them in a pound sign.'

Annie wondered how to bring up the pregnancy topic. It seemed so incongruous in this noisy, brittle place filled with the energy of escape from the office. Instead, she asked Sal whether she had found anywhere to live. 'I'm camping. Ollie says he knows a bloke being sent to Washington for six months and there may be a room in his place coming up. If I could only get a promotion, then I could think about buying. Everybody says I ought to try and buy. But I'd need to find a deposit of at least five thousand pounds, as well as being able to pay the mortgage.'

'That would be great for you, if you could manage it. I think we're going to move soon.'

'Why would you? I thought the flat was pretty amazing.' Sal contrasted the sleek interiors Annie and Charlie inhabited with Pete's room, with its lino on the floor and the broken lava lamp by the bed.

'Because I'm pregnant.' Annie spoke quickly, looking down, rather than at her friend.

'But that's wonderful.' Sal didn't miss a beat. 'You must be so pleased. It's what you've always wanted. It must make you feel like there's someone up there saying, "Go, girl, you did the right thing." I mean about getting hitched. It's happened so quickly.'

'Yes, you're so right.' Annie's eyes welled up in reaction to the warmth of Sal's response, guilty that she could ever have doubted that her friend would be pleased for her. 'That's exactly it. Oh, rats.' She smudged away the tears. 'The whole pregnancy thing does something crazy with your hormones.' How could she have thought Sal would be cross or disapproving? After all, she knew her better than almost anyone.

Sal happily downed two champagne cocktails in celebration, even encouraged by Annie, who told her that it would be a great help if she did, since Paddy kept asking her if she'd taste them and give an opinion, and she really couldn't face it, being pregnant. By the time the second one was finished Sal was confiding in Annie that her relationship with Pete had become something more substantial than the odd night.

'It's weird, because I never wanted to end up with a boyfriend back in the sticks, and when it started it was just for a laugh. But I guess it's kind of nice having someone that you really know to hang out with, especially with work being so full on. When I'm with Pete it's just not complicated. But I know it's not something proper, like you and Charlie.'

'You don't ever know how things are going to turn out. When I first met Charlie it wasn't like I thought I'd met my husband. In fact, I probably thought about it less than I had with most of my boyfriends. I suppose that was because he was so keen so quickly; it made the dynamics different. And look what's happened.' She glanced at her watch. Charlie hated her to be late.

'I was thinking,' Sal said, sticking her finger into the bottom of the glass, where champagne- and brandy-soaked granules of sugar remained, 'that bloke Mark, Charlie's best man. He told me at the wedding that Charlie is involved in some deals in Kentish Town. Do you think he might know anything about the people that are trying to get Kendra and Gioia out of the Chapel?'

'He might. I can ask him tonight. It's just the kind of thing he may know. I'd heard about the problems with the Chapel – isn't the roof falling down too? But I don't remember Charlie ever mentioning Kentish Town. Not that he talks much about work to me.' Annie waved at the barman to bring the bill. 'I wish I could stay all evening, but I've got to go in a minute. The downside of marriage' – she laughed – 'not being able to do what you want all the time. We'll have a proper girls' night soon. We haven't been able to really talk for ages.'

It was true, thought Sal. There was masses to talk about. For a moment she was irritated. Surely Annie could have managed just one evening alone with her friend.

Annie would have much preferred to go home and have a boiled egg, but Charlie hated to go without proper meals. He always wanted dinner, even if they'd both had lunch. As she became more senior at work, lunches had become a greater part of the working day. Clients liked to talk business over at least two courses and a bottle of wine, sometimes more, and sometimes didn't even talk much business. The size of the bill was the measure of the value of the meeting. Most of the time she was charging it back to them anyway. She'd got so used to paying that sometimes she handed over the American Express card without even checking the total.

She found Charlie in the corner of San Fred's making notes in the pocket Filofax she had put in his Christmas stocking.

'I'd been getting a bit worried about you, darling,' he said.

'Terrible traffic.' Annie picked up the menu, even though she knew that Charlie would order the osso bucco and she would have Parma ham and melon. After the meeting with Paddy and Marcus, and then telling Sal about the baby, she felt exhausted. When the meat arrived Charlie immersed himself in the excavation of the bone for the marrow, finally looking up at her to notice the dark under her eyes.

'You look tired. We should start to think about what you're going to do about the job once it gets nearer the time of the birth.' He paused. 'We might want to rethink even earlier than that. After all, you won't want to be trailing out to wine bars on the river, heavily pregnant.'

In her worn-out state Annie didn't want to engage in this particular conversation, knowing that it would lead to Charlie's opinion, frequently aired, that she should stop work once she had become a mother. She knew that he wanted her to be happy, but he didn't seem to understand that she enjoyed her job. She was becoming annoyed by the way he often made it sound as if it were pointless. She wasn't only 'trailing out to wine bars'. She had her own accounts, managed budgets and clients and gave presentations. Although she had always thought that she wanted to be married and have children and that she wasn't interested in a career, Annie knew that she had become very good at her job. She now had a real sense of pride in what she did. She had been surprised at the feeling of achievement small things like negotiating a better rate from a client or ensuring that a product was featured in not just one but all the weekend colour supplements gave her. She wasn't at all sure she wanted to give it up, just when it had started to be fun.

'Babe, let's not talk about it now. We've got months. Can you get me a Coke? That might wake me up.' Annie didn't feel much like talking about anything, but if it would help Kendra to ask Charlie about the Chapel she should do it now. 'By the way, Sal asked whether you might know anything about a consortium that's trying to get Gioia out of the Chapel so they can develop it. She said that Mark had mentioned you might know something about it.' As she spoke, she realized that words like 'develop' and 'consortium' had become part of her vocabulary.

'Chapel?'

'Come on.' He must know what she was talking about. 'The centre Gioia runs with Kendra. I've mentioned it millions of times.'

'Oh yes. That place.' Charlie scraped every scrap of creamy potato from his plate as if it were the last time he would ever taste such a delicacy. 'Yes. As it happens, I do. It's in the Charterhouse scheme. We've got three firms pitching to include some juicy apartment blocks, a shopping mall and some cheap housing.'

The smells of the food, her tiredness and the knowledge that what Charlie had said was a big problem made Annie break out into a sweat. If Charlie was part of a team that was trying to evict Gioia, how could she possibly explain that to Kendra? Heaven knows, London was a huge city. Why did he have to be involved with their place? She should try and talk to him about it, but she was simply too tired right now to say anything that would be effective. All she wanted was to be asleep in bed, she thought, watching Charlie as he pushed around the smears of gravy on his plate.

15

Sal was furious. It wasn't as if there wasn't any proper news. There were all kinds of stories she could get her teeth into, if only the paper would let her. There was the whole Aids awareness thing where it looked like the government was dragging its heels, and she wouldn't have minded working on the debate over women bishops. But what had they given her? A rubbish piece on how the recently engaged Prince Andrew and Sarah Ferguson were managing. She thought she'd left the royal stuff behind. It wasn't like she had ever wanted to be a royal correspondent. Yes, it was better than the story last week about the mad woman in Kent who had left £25,000 to her two pugs. But it was a close thing.

She ran to catch the bus, flinging herself on to the platform before it moved off. For some reason, she hadn't been feeling right recently and, even though she'd never been a morning person, at the moment she was completely wiped out when the alarm went off, even if she'd been to bed early the night before. Maybe Kendra and Annie were right and she should do something about the drink. Go on a health kick and get vitamins and stuff.

Last weekend, she had walked with Kendra around the ponds on Hampstead Heath, where her friend had shown her some of the trees she would play in as a small child, before the Rootsteins had moved to Notting Hill. There was a horse chestnut tree with a deep indentation in the trunk where Kendra remembered hiding.

Sal always felt a foreigner on the Heath, just a moment away from being completely lost. The young families, elderly couples and kite-flying kids all seemed to have been there for ever but it made her feel more a newcomer to the city than any of the shops or restaurants ever did. She picked up a stone from the path, hurling it as far as she could towards the thicket.

'So, what you're saying is that, when it comes down to it, Charlie's trying to chuck me and Gioia out of the Chapel?' Kendra was wrapped in some blanket that even covered her head, which was not a bad idea, since it was freezing.

'No, I'm not saying that. Not exactly. When Annie told me, she said that there are lots of different people involved in this group, this consortium, and they haven't got it all sorted yet. But it's true he's definitely involved in some way.'

'I thought he was dodgy from the first time we met. He looks like a guy who irons his underpants. How could Annie marry him? I know he makes her feel safe, but there are tons out there she could have picked.'

'I don't think she did pick him. He picked her. But what does it matter? You can't fall out with her over this. I know you don't like him, and he's not my favourite biscuit in the tin either, but he's part of her now, and so we've got to deal with it.'

'I like that. You being so Miss Reasonable. If you were in my shoes, you'd be ranting. I don't think you have any idea how miserable Gioia is about this. If you did, you'd understand how much it means to me. If that place goes, I don't know what will happen.' Kendra stopped as they reached the top of a slope where you could look out over the city, the distinctive buildings of the skyscape turning into a blurred mass of greys and blues as they stretched on towards the hills on the far horizon. 'There must be something you can do. Come on. You're a journalist. Aren't you meant to be a campaigner? To have influence? I know the Chapel isn't a huge story, but isn't there something there?'

The cigarette Sal lit was more to create an idea of warmth than because she really wanted one.

'I'm thinking. Look at that city. You can even see the massive new development way out to the east, over there . . . to the left. There's a lot that's being destroyed in all this expansion. Maybe there's a story in that, and the Chapel would fit. Gioia could be part of a piece about the small people in a battle against the forces of commercialism. Patrick might not like it, but Stuart's always trying to get human interest pieces in. Gioia's a character, isn't she? She'd be good copy.'

'What about Annie?'

'Christ, Kendra. I come up with something and now you're going doubtful on me. Bringing up a problem. What about her?'

'That's going to land her in it with Charlie, isn't it?'

'Annie will be fine.' Sal stamped on her cigarette butt, grinding it into the earth. 'She's got her baby. That's what counts.'

By the time Sal reached work, conference had begun in Patrick's office. All the senior staff were gathered there, the rest of the place waiting to be inflated by their return to desks. Marsha was sitting at hers, of course, already on the telephone, scribbling notes about something or other. She had perfected a manner of talking which didn't allow Sal or anyone else to hear what she was saying unless she chose.

It was a funny achey feeling, thought Sal, a bit like she was going to have flu, but different. As she threw her bag on the floor by her desk she realized she was about to be sick. The Ladies was all the way across the office and down a flight of stairs. By the time she was bolting the stall door, she could feel the burn in her throat.

Sitting on the toilet to compose herself, she stared at the linoleum tiles, momentarily feeling the wave recede just before it returned and she had to be sick again. God. You'd think she was pregnant or something. Maybe it was food poisoning – but she hadn't eaten anything last night. Was she pregnant? That was impossible. She'd check her pills, but she was sure she was on target – about halfway through the cycle. She'd missed a couple of days ages ago when she'd spent an unexpected few nights with Pete, but that was right at the start of a cycle. She'd been together enough to clock that. It was safe then. It was about now . . . 14, 15, 16 – those days that were dodgy. She started to feel better.

Stopping at the picture desk as a diversion from writing her piece, Sal leant over the transparencies lined up on the light box. It was a pity that newspapers only published black and white when you saw the foxy red of Sarah Ferguson's hair. It was what gave her that particular look. She could never have been a brunette.

She supposed she'd better start getting something down soon. If she got this story on the engagement finished then she could have a word with Stuart about her property idea. Find some other examples of people being evacuated, swept up in the tide of new commercialism. It might be a goer.

There was a corner of the Rootsteins' paved garden known as Art's corner just near the cuboid water feature where the morning sun flickered in a filtered pattern through the trellis. At first he'd craved the soft lawn and coloured borders of their Hampstead garden but now, Art agreed, Marisa had been right to concentrate on a simple linear scheme. The clean lines cleared the head.

Kendra was pleased to find him seated there, just as she had expected, reading a stack of work papers while Marisa took her Saturday morning Pilates class. The spacious simplicity of the house was heavenly after the cramped chaos of Gioia's flat, with its clothes and books in piles and the pipes that would often whistle, without explanation, in the middle of the night.

She bent to give Art a kiss on the top of his head, and his hand rose to stroke her cheek as he always used to do.

'My, you've got a sweat on you. Get something to drink, doll. Since you've gone we stopped with the Coca Cola, but I'm sure there's something in the fridge.' Kendra's Coke habit was something she battled with. She knew it was practically poison and you had to be completely naïve not to regard the worldwide creep of the company as truly dubious, but she never seemed able to give it up.

The contents of the fridge were as delicious as always. Marisa felt the only fridge worth having was a full one, even though she only ate a narrow repertoire from it. Returning from school, the first thing Kendra would do was open the double doors and delve into the array of cold meats, cheese, dips and ice cream. Her friends had always been impressed by the size of the fridge. Most of their kitchens only had small ones that fitted under the counter. She poured herself a glass of milk and carved a slice of Pecorino.

'It's great to see you.' Art watched her return. 'You've lost some pounds. It suits you. Your mother's at that Pilates. How she has the discipline I'll never know. Still, she's in great shape for her age. I should be doing the same.' He patted his stomach where it protruded in a satisfied bump.

'How's things? How's she? And Laila?'

'Laila's boy's got some apprenticeship, so she's a happy woman. And things are good. You know I didn't feel for Mrs Thatcher at the start, but she's turning this place around. Business is picking up.'

Kendra perched on the low stone wall beside the gurgling water, letting the soothing sound override Art's opinion. She could hear children playing in the large garden that lay just beyond where she was sitting.

'Dad, I want advice . . .'

'Sure.'

'We have this problem with the Chapel. It's being threatened by developers, who want Gioia out. But I remember you talking about things like right of residence, or some deal where they can't get rid of you if you've been there long enough. Would she have any legal leg to stand on?'

'I'd have to see the paperwork, but your friend doesn't strike me as the kind of girl who's got the wherewithal for a battle with the property guys. Do you know who it is?'

'Yeah – Charterhouse, I think it's called. Annie's husband is in with them, which makes it awkward.'

'Husband? Did that pretty girl go get married? Well, well . . .'

'Yeah. But, really, Dad, what do you think?'

'Without knowing more, I couldn't call it, but I doubt she can do much. Maybe she could negotiate some compensation. I take it she doesn't own the place?'

'No, but she's been maintaining it. We were about to try to do the roof, which is threatening to kill someone, so many tiles are loose.'

The front door slammed, followed by Marisa's quick steps. Art recognized Kendra's disappointment at this interruption and looked past her to where Marisa, her black leotard and tights displaying a body that was rigorously slim, stood in the entrance.

'I had no idea you were paying us a visit. I would have changed the class.' She moved towards her daughter. Kendra could feel the knobs of Marisa's spine as they hugged. 'Were you in on this, Art?'

'Don't be paranoid, Mum. I was in the neighbourhood and just called to see if I could drop round.'

'You have the key. You know you're always welcome.' Marisa smoothed back an imagined tendril of hair, placing her fingertips on her shoulders, shrugging them back in a loosening exercise.

'Kendra was telling me that her friend Annie is now married. Can you believe it, Maris? They're all growing up. It'll be babies next.' The words might as well have been grenades, as far as Kendra was concerned. Babies, grandchildren. How had they got on to this already? The previous period of enjoyment, even a slight recognition that she missed some things about home, was replaced by the more usual desire to escape. It never took long for Kendra to feel guilty about something. Truthfully, she had been starting to feel a little guilty about enjoying being there, as if that was in some way disloyal to Gioia.

'Does she still work for that PR outfit?' Marisa was examining a brown leaf that she had snipped from the jasmine that climbed above the water feature. 'I saw her there a couple of times when we did that NSPCC fundraiser a year or so back. I'll never know why they chose to go with that inebriated dame who runs the show. But I'll give it to her, she delivered on the names for the night.'

'Yeah. She's still working there. She's got quite a few of her own accounts now. And, since you mention it, Dad, she's having a baby too.'

'That's nice, isn't it? Well, well.' Art gave his spectacles a wipe on the sleeve of his sweater before replacing them and turning his attention back to the safety of his papers and so concluding this particular strand of conversation.

'She's a little young for all that. This is the age when you explore.

Nobody should tie themselves down. When I think of what I wanted at your age and what has happened to my life . . .' Looking at her mother standing in the splayed feet of a Pilates stance, Kendra found it hard to imagine her ever wanting anything other than what she so purposefully had achieved. 'You have no idea what can happen. People change. Come and look at the Tibetan screen your father and I are considering buying. It adds a different aura to the room.' Kendra followed her mother up the stairs to where the screen was positioned in one corner of the drawing room. It was a beautiful object, that was true, but it didn't help her and Gioia. Why was it that when something really mattered it was so hard to get any help? She'd always assumed her parents could get anything they wanted – at least that was the impression they gave – but now, when she'd hoped Art might be of some use, he had shrugged the problem away. Didn't they understand that this wasn't about a Tibetan screen?

Sal sat on the edge of the bath staring at the pregnancy stick with horror and fascination. It was the third one she'd tried. Just to be sure. But there it was. Nobody could deny there was anything other than blue in the window. She counted the number of tiles around the bath. And then counted them again. If she just sat here and kept counting, maybe this wasn't really happening. Outside the locked door, she could hear the television, a yelled offer of a cup of tea. The laughter probably meant somebody had made a joke, but this large flat full of people made her feel utterly alone. It would have been so much easier if she was still in Cranbourne Terrace with Annie.

There was no question of telling Pete about this disaster. The rules were that they were free; no sweat, no obligation. She wasn't even going out with him really. They just spent time with each other because it was fun. It wasn't like there was any commitment. And the sex was great. She was turned on just by thinking about Pete's fingers caressing her as she lay on his old fur coat on the floor. This could ruin everything.

If she kept calm she could get it sussed. No need to be sentimental about this. Fuck it. She didn't want a baby. There was no part of her, not even the smallest part, that wanted one. And, anyway, it wasn't a baby, it was about the size of a bean. It wasn't like a baby at all.

She'd have to get cash for an abortion at one of those private places. She knew from friends the nightmare of the birth control clinic where they made you feel terrible about it and took ages, asking all kinds of questions. It was awful timing, but maybe she could get Annie to lend her some money. Only the other day she'd been telling her how generous Charlie was and how she'd actually, for the first time ever, got money in a deposit account. Obviously, it wasn't ideal, what with Annie being pregnant, but then in her case she was so happy about it, and she would always want to help. She would see it was different. Sal couldn't possibly have a baby.

That white top was typical of Annie. Sal considered how, if she wore it, she would look like a Jehovah's Witness, but Annie, who she remembered had found it in a local antique shop, had immediately registered its stylish possibilities.

Near where they lay in the park, a six-a-side football match was taking place. Sal watched as a boy in navy shorts wiped the ball with his hand, inspiring noisy jeers. The whole country was still raging about Maradona's handball. She wished she was a bloke. Really, when it came down to it, that was pretty well all they had to care about, being knocked out of the World Cup. They didn't have to have an abortion.

'It's lovely here, isn't it?' Annie said as she plaited blades of grass. 'It's not like being in the city at all. I'm trying to persuade Charlie that we should get somewhere with a garden. I keep thinking of the baby in one of those old-fashioned prams, the ones with the big navy hood.' She looked over at Sal, who was lying on her back.

'You shouldn't get too ahead of yourself. It's still early, really. I mean, they're not even babies yet. It's not safe to get all sentimental so soon. You know, I understand, and everything, that you're thrilled about the baby . . . but . . . all I'm saying is . . . there's lots of time.'

'God, what's up with you?' Annie sat up, pulling down her smock and stroking her stomach as she did so. 'It's as if you're angry with me for being pregnant or something.'

'Of course I'm not. You only think that because your hormones are all over the place.' Sal was surprised by her own aggression – what was that about? She was about to do a massive U-turn when Annie stood.

'I'm just not staying here with you like this.'

Sal pulled at the hem of Annie's skirt like a small child. 'The thing is . . . the thing is – well, I'm, oh shit. I'm pregnant too.' Annie looked down at her. 'No, don't try and say anything, because there's nothing you can say that will make this better. But I have to get an abortion. And quickly. And, Annie, I know it's terrible of me to ask, but can you lend me the cash? I just can't bear to wait. I need to do it. Of course, if you can't, I understand.'

'Whose is it? Is it Pete's?' Annie wasn't sure whether it would be better if it was or it wasn't. She realized she didn't know much about Sal's love life at the moment; she'd been so wrapped up in her own world: Charlie, work and the pregnancy. She sat down again on the grass. 'I'm sorry. It must be terrifying for you. Are you sure that this is what you want?'

'Of course I'm sure. I can hardly have a baby living in some grotty flat in Earls Court and take it into the office like a dog in a basket. I'm just at such a different stage to you. I don't want to analyse it and work out how I feel. I just want it over.'

'How much would it be?'

'It's masses. About four hundred.' The immensity of the figure once it was spoken out loud suddenly made the request sound impossible. 'I've found a place to do it,' she concluded quietly.

Annie wrote the cheque in the italic handwriting Sal knew so well – *Four Hundred Pounds Only, Annie Sethrington* – and folded it as she handed it over.

'I'll get it back to you as soon as I can. Promise.' Sal looked at the piece of paper as if it were a treasured work of art. 'You've saved my life.'

'But Sal, you know we're worried about you? Me and Ken. You just seem to be all over the place and – I know that this is going to make you annoyed – but you're getting so drunk. We didn't want to talk about it, but you must see that you're pretty pissed a lot of the time.'

'So is the loan going to mean that, now, you're in charge of me? If so, forget it.'

'Don't be daft. I only want you to be all right.'

'I am all right. I'm really all right now. Don't worry.' Sal was squinting up at the sky, where a bright shiny pinprick was leaving a vapour trail. 'Hey. I'm really sorry about what I said about the baby. Of course that's a lovely baby you've got there. I can see you and it in the garden with that pram. It's just I couldn't see me doing the same.'

Tania's nose for error was as infallible as a sniffer dog's. There was no room for mistakes when you were dealing with the launch of a big fragrance like Sinistre, snatched from their rivals in public relations. 'Right under their noses it was. But that doesn't mean we haven't got to hit the ground racing like Zola Budd' was how Tania had briefed the team. 'We've got to knock the spots off Dior's Poison.'

Lee had been put in charge of overseeing the catering. Female beauty journalists never ate a single canapé but it was nonetheless regarded as essential that the event be a display of luxury, every detail, from the tablecloths, to the platters, to the angle of the amaryllises in black crystal jars harnessed in the service of establishing the unique qualities of Sinistre. Lee had put together a list of caterers for Tania to consider, but his own favourite, Shooting Up, had failed at the first hurdle, unwisely suggesting a cocktail of chartreuse, rum and lime.

'You lads get a terrific name like Sinistre to play with and you come up with something that stinks of some sleazy Jamaican joint.'

Tania's face had become an unbecoming pink. After they'd been shown the door she turned to Lee. 'What a bunch of plonkers. *Sinistre*. It needs lateral thinking. You've got the whole sinister thing but then you've got the old leftie connotations too – the left-handed oddball, Left bank . . . smack bang in the ball park. That's the way to go.'

Lee didn't let on that he'd been in the adjacent room when a member of the Sinistre team had briefed Tania with this interpretation of the name. As always, it was clear she preferred to present such insights as her own.

He pulled at the collar of his Adidas shirt, looking across the vast room they had turned into Sinistreland in search of Annie, who he spotted making some young kid go through the guest list for the umpteenth time.

'We've just had a bit of a moment in the kitchens. Tans went ballistic over the fact she thought she could smell onions. It turned out they puréed a few shallots for the *jus* to dribble over the mini tartares. Honest. You'd think she'd discovered arsenic.'

'You know she's got her pet hates,' Annie replied, without looking up from the typed pages. 'Didn't you brief the caterers?'

''Course I did.' Lee turned away to fiddle with the bottles lined up on a plinth at the entrance, giant teardrops of dark glass which, when held up to the light, showed a fine cross-hatching. 'You know Calvin's launching his new pong here any day now, Obsession for Men. I've heard they're spending millions. Anybody know what ours smells like?'

'Don't ask me. Luckily, it's not my account. If I smell anything these days I feel nauseous. Tell you what, can you do me a favour and just run your eye down the list for a second?'

Annie walked through the huge door to the pavement outside. She didn't want to be melodramatic – she was past the twelve weeks now and it was probably nothing – but the cramps had been getting worse all day. A taxi stopped outside. That must be Jean-Jacques Gratinard. She jumped back from the low wall where she had been resting. The Frenchman was flanked by three young women, their faces denied any degree of natural skintone by heavy layers of foundation. Tania appeared in the doorway, her new Claude Montana jacket with its dramatic shoulder pads contrasting oddly with those silk trousers she loved. Annie was sure Montana hadn't imagined the jacket looking that way. The effect was of a character in a children's card game where you matched the top halves of people to their bottom halves.

'*Bonsoir*, Jean-Jacques. Welcome to London. Traffic from Heathrow a bugger as always?' Tania shooed the quartet inside, gesturing Annie to join them.

'Annie, would you find Lee? I'm sure Jean-Jacques Gratinard would like to meet him and be talked through the evening.' Tania had developed a reliable antenna for corporate men who surrounded themselves with an entourage of attractive young women but preferred their own sex. It was one of Lee's many uses. He could be relied upon to pitch it perfectly: teasing, admiring and just the right side of flirtatious. Annie watched as Lee claimed his charge, brushing his fringe back from his forehead in a fey manner and guiding the client across the room with the expertise of a ballroom dancer. Her cramps were becoming sharper, as if there were a claw inside her, clenching and releasing, clenching again. The journalists and social celebrities now filling the room were becoming a background to the pain, which was sharply in focus.

She stood talking for as long as she could manage to a tedious raconteur, a veteran beauty editor (Lee had nicknamed her Just Press Go), before she had to escape, walking as quickly as she could without running to the small lavatories down the corridor. It took no more than a second to see the blood: great clots which streaked her legs as she stood up. She sat back down as she heard a couple of girls enter the room and then their chatter from the neighbouring stalls. Would the bleeding stop if she stayed still? She didn't know what to do. Was this a miscarriage she was having, or a bleed? Should she be hurrying somewhere? It felt terrible. She waited for the two girls to leave before she emerged. In the far corner of the room, Lee was still with Jean-Jacques. 'I've got to go. Tell you later,' she hissed at him in passing. In the street, she discovered that she didn't know *where* to go. Hospital or home? She was desperate to find Charlie. He'd know what to do. She got into a taxi, putting her hard square handbag underneath her to stop the blood getting on the seat.

Charlie had been brilliant, of course, ringing Mr Churston at home and making sure he got her into the hospital bed where she now lay, even though both she and Mr Churston had known there wasn't really much point going to hospital.

'Can't do any harm to give her the once-over,' the gynaecologist had suggested, as if the loss of the baby was a defect in a car. 'I'm sorry. But it often happens with the first. You've got plenty of time. It doesn't mean anything's wrong.'

Now she was here in this nowhere land of a hospital room with nothing to do but think about what had happened. She was unable to stop her thoughts going on an endless rewind over which she appeared to have no control. She remembered Sal's words as they lay in the park. 'It's not safe to get all sentimental so soon.' That was before she knew that Sal was pregnant too. That she wanted to get rid of that pregnancy, that baby. It just wasn't fair. She knew that only small children thought that life would ever be fair but, all the same, it *wasn't* fair. She had just lost her baby, a baby whom she had already fallen in love with, and Sal was just going to throw hers away.

The lunch tray containing something that she hadn't asked for but which carried the description 'pavlova' was sitting beside her untouched when Charlie arrived to collect her.

'Let's get you home, darling. You'll feel much better there. Churston has given you the all-clear.' Inside her leather bag he had packed a navy Margaret Howell skirt and pale-blue sweater. A matching set of white lace bra and pants lay on top. Looking at the insubstantial white made her think of all that blood. If only she had a pair of large, thick knickers to put on that would reach up to her waist and cover everything.

'It's a lovely day out there – I drove with the hood down. Oh yes . . . and your friend Lee called and said that he was thinking of you. I told him you'd be off for a bit.'

'Why did you say that?' Annie snapped. 'You never asked me.'

'You weren't there to ask and surely you agree that you don't feel up to going back to the office now?'

'I'll be as OK as I'm going to be, in the next day or so. It's not as if, the longer I wait, the more likely it is that my baby is going to be alive. Is it?' The tears started and she left them to trickle down, the soft movement on her face strangely soothing.

'Don't cry, love. As Churston told us, it happens all the time. I'm sure we'll be able to have another one soon.'

'You make it sound like we can have another holiday or another drink. But we won't have that baby, will we? We don't even know if it was a boy or a girl.'

'It's probably better that way, if you think about it. We have to look ahead. Come on, darling.' Charlie reached to help her out of the bed, where the sheets were tucked in so tight she could hardly move. 'I'll wait outside while you get yourself organized. I've picked up some videos for you to watch when you get back, so you can just relax. *Out of Africa* . . . I remembered that you really enjoyed that. And the girl in the store recommended *The Color Purple* . . . it sounded more your thing than mine.'

Annie looked out of the window at the cars below, the people walking on the pavements, the world happening, just as it always did. Except hers had stopped.

The phone rang as Kendra was standing on the top rung of a ladder daubing Polyfilla on a crack that was threatening to become a crevice in the back wall of the Chapel. It was a hassle to get down now she was up, but it might be Gioia. She never liked to miss her calls.

It was unusual for Sal to phone her at the Chapel but stranger still to hear the hesitancy in her tone. 'I know it's short notice. Completely last minute. But are you free this afternoon?' Sal paused. 'Thing is . . . well . . . I'd really like it if you could come with me.

You're going to think this is typical, but I'm having an abortion and I thought I'd be fine about it but, now it's come to it, I feel pathetic. I'd rather not go alone. Of course, you probably can't. And I'll be all right if I do have to . . . have to go alone.'

'Hang on. What do you mean? Why didn't you tell me before?' Kendra immediately corrected herself. 'No need to answer. We can catch up later. Where do you want me to be?' Although this was awful for Sal, she couldn't help acknowledging a sliver of pleasure that she was needed by her friend. Recently, she had felt she was unravelling from both Annie and Sal's lives.

The large Edwardian building on the outer edge of London had undoubtedly been impressive in previous times but now the red-brick shell housed a sad business where nobody wanted to be. Everyone wanted to leave as soon as they could. In the reception area, the waiting patients kept eye contact to the minimum, voices low, emotions disguised. There's a special kind of green reserved for dismal places, thought Kendra, looking at the colour of the empty chairs opposite. It was flat, toneless. If you bit into it, it would taste like stale milk.

Sal had been taken away almost immediately they arrived. She'd watched her disappear through the swing doors, shoulder bag dangling at her side. Neither of them had any idea how long they would be there. Kendra was pleased that she'd brought something to read. The sound of sobs made her look up.

'Ssh, ssh, Dee. Let's get you outside.' An overweight blonde woman was clinging on to a man who was ushering her towards the exit. Aside from that, there was quiet, punctuated by the receptionist calling out appointments. Everyone jumped up instantly. Nobody wanted to hear their name called twice.

Eventually, after Kendra had eaten several packets of biscuits lying in a basket on a side table and twice walked to the front door to go for a stroll before deciding that she couldn't leave in case Sal returned, Sal reappeared with a small plastic bag and a smile which didn't quite reach her eyes but did a moderately convincing job of conveying relief.

'Let's go.' She walked ahead, leaving Kendra following. 'Don't ask me. I'm OK. Really. I'm fine.' She put on a pair of dark glasses, the bright sunshine of early summer providing both an excuse for wearing them and a glaring contrast to the grimness of the clinic and its proceedings. 'I'm a bit sore. What time is it? I've lost track . . . What I really want is a drink.'

'Surely that's not a good idea. What did the doctor say?'

'Is it likely I asked?'

'Well, I don't think you should drink today. Nor should you be on your own. Is there anyone in your flat tonight?'

'Yeah. Bound to be.' Sal worked out that, by the time they got back to Earls Court, the pub on the corner would be open. 'I suppose I should call Annie. To thank her. She'd want to know, don't you think?'

Kendra grabbed Sal's arm. 'No. Don't do that. I forgot. I had meant to tell you, but then you rang and I thought I'd wait till later. She had a miscarriage a couple of days ago and she's really cut up. She was past twelve weeks, so she thought she was safe, and it's been a nightmare for her.'

Sal kept walking. 'That's awful. It's so unfair, isn't it? Poor Annie.' She didn't like to think about Annie's vision, as they were lying in the park, of the baby and the garden and the pram. She was so pleased to be free of her own pregnancy, the relief was physical. All the tight worry she had felt for the past weeks was gone. She wouldn't have to wake up one more morning knowing she was pregnant.

'I must call her and go and see her, though. It would be odd not to just because I've had the abortion. I'm sure she'll understand how different it was for me.'

On the hottest days, the *Herald* offices could be a nightmare. Even with the windows open, the area around Sal's desk in the middle of the room was stifling. Desks near the windows were prime real estate, a reward for long service and canny negotiating. Even Andrea hadn't managed to get one.

'I've mentioned your story idea to Patrick. He's keen on aspects of it. Scamp out a draft.' Andrea was indulging in her ritual of applying Nivea, rubbing it along each finger into the cuticles. A pot always sat on her desk, alongside a bottle of 4711 cologne.

Sal watched her. 'What do you mean when you say "aspects"?'

'He thinks there's a big story about the property scenario in London and he wants to look at making it one of our round-up stories – get different angles on it from different people. But it's not on the agenda for this Sunday.'

'I'm nearly finished with the butchers,' Marsha interrupted with her usual superiority. 'There's some impressive information on what a lamb shortage would mean.'

'Butchers? What's that then?' Sal enjoyed the idea of Marsha trawling through dull facts on meat cuts. 'Aren't we the lucky ones? All the big stories on this desk.'

'Actually, Sal, it's a breaking news story, although it's been buried. I find that's often the way. The skill is in digging it out. I've been tracking this one all week.'

'Have you now? Fascinating. But what is it? Sainsbury's out of lamb cutlets? Traditional Sunday roast an endangered species?' The opportunities were endless. 'Sounds like a silly-season special to me.'

'And you'll find that's a myth, the silly season. Some of the most important events have taken place in summer: Hiroshima, Pompeii, the outbreak of two world wars . . .' Sal realized Marsha could continue on this theme for some time.

'Well, as far as I'm aware, there's no immediate danger of the Third World War breaking out any time soon, so I hope we might be able to squeeze my idea in after the lamb catastrophe.'

Marsha ignored her. 'The current story is that they're banning the slaughter of lambs in Cumbria. It's after Chernobyl. There's a worry about the fallout and now there's talk that the ban might extend south. It's potentially a nationwide concern. Sometimes we get so bound up with what's going on in London.' Sal's eye-rolling at this was visible to all. 'At any rate, the butchers, since you asked, are understandably nervous. I've got on to the restaurants and hotels, but now I'm waiting for a quote from Prue Leith to finish off.'

'Patrick's keen because it's an English story,' Andrea added, deciding, on this occasion, to support Marsha. 'He always worries when Ireland is dominating the news agenda like it is this week. We often get a drop-off in sales.'

'I can't believe the Irish have voted no on the divorce referendum. That place is still in the Dark Ages. When I last checked, it was 1986 not 1886.' Sal tilted her chair back, noting the stain on the front of her navy skirt as she attempted to reclaim some of the journalistic higher ground. Bloody annoying, that stain. She'd bought the skirt in Whistles a few months ago and, too late, she'd realized that the synthetic fabric meant that it was difficult to get stains out. She was grateful that at least she'd escaped Lambsgate.

Sal's punctuality always surprised Kendra, who had a tendency to be late. She was waiting outside W. H. Smith as agreed when Kendra arrived on her bike. The nights were drawing in, even though it was still August.

'Have you told Annie about the piece yet?' Kendra asked, trying to wheel her bicycle with one hand so she could walk next to Sal.

'Not quite. But you know what I've discovered? Charlie's deep in it with his Charterhouse crowd. He's on their board. The business guys filled me in. So he can't not know what's happening. I don't know what to say to her.'

'Poor Annie. It's all going wrong right now, isn't it? I don't even think she's getting on that well with Charlie after the miscarriage. She says he just doesn't get it. He keeps on saying they need to move forward. She's told me she's on anti-depressants, but don't mention that to her.'

'If I was stuck with a bloke like Charlie I'd be on them too. I still don't know why she married him.'

'You do. You told me the other day, on the Heath, that we had to just accept it. She thought he would make her safe. She thought it was what she wanted.'

'I suppose so . . . 'course, the Stones got it right.' Sal started to sing. '"You can't always get what you wa-a-aant . . ."'

'He's not what she needs either.'

Kendra always insisted on reading the entire menu at Pizza Express, even though she never ordered anything other than a Margarita. Sal had a theory that, although Kendra was veggie, she got a buzz out of contemplating the possibility of an Americano with its pepperoni. Annie, though, hadn't even glanced at the menu. Her thick blonde hair was tied into a lank ponytail. The sparkle of her wedding ring contrasted with the dull look of her eyes, as if a fine gauze was creating a layer between her and the rest of the world.

'Everyone happy with red?' Sal ordered it without waiting for an answer.

'Next week we could go to this new place I'm going to review in Battersea. The restaurant critic's on holiday, so they've given some of us a go at covering for him. We can make the bill look like there's only two of us. Anyway, I've seen his expenses. They're massive. Are you on for it, Annie? Though it'd almost be like work for you, I suppose.'

Annie's tight smile was no answer. She didn't know what to say. Everything had become difficult since losing the baby, even making a decision like whether to go to a restaurant with Sal. It was probably easiest to say yes.

'Sure.'

Sal's leg was jigging up and down on the floor. It was one of the many signs of her having had a few drinks – that and the particular set of her face, which Kendra could spot across a room. It started with a kind of oozy softness, a grin that bore no relation to anything anyone was saying and which then, as the drinking continued, became sharper, mocking and eventually often cruel. She'd hoped that Sal could have held it together for this night. Annie was enough to deal with.

The pizzas arrived quickly. Usually, the threesome would have been so busy talking that they'd become cold before they even began to eat them, only Kendra eating bits of the crust as she chatted, but this evening was different. Every conversational possibility could veer into disastrous territory. Pete would make Annie think of the abortion, Gioia could only lead them into the cul-de-sac of Charlie's bid for the land around the Chapel, Charlie – well, Charlie was obviously, judging by Annie's behaviour, becoming part of the problem rather than the solution.

Even feeling as she did, Annie knew she was the main cause for the failure of the evening. It wasn't that she didn't want to see her friends, to laugh with them at the kind of stupid things they always laughed about together, their very repetition reinforcing every time just how funny they were to them, and probably only to them. It was just that she couldn't do it. She was in a bubble of her own dull misery. Each morning, there was a lovely brief moment when she felt all right, but within minutes the depression would invade. She could almost feel it moving through her body, making her so heavy she could scarcely lift her head.

Charlie was doing his best, she knew that, but he was a man perpetually moving ahead. It was what made him so effective, whether he was closing a deal, installing a sound system or ensuring that they always had the room with the best view in a hotel. He saw little point in reviewing the past and, in the unusual event of something not working out, he would change direction and keep his eyes firmly fastened on the new route. It was as if he were on the other side of a sheet of glass. Now, all she could think of was the loss of their baby.

The three struggled to make the evening stretch to ten o'clock; leaving before then would be too grisly an admission that they were not able to make the evening work.

'I'm knackered,' Kendra offered, not remotely tired but feeling that she should allow Annie to escape. She had never seen her look so flat.

'Yes. I'm tired too. I can give you a lift, Sal – it's on my way.'

'It's early, I'm just going to make a call.'

They watched her weave her way through the tables to the phone box in the hall outside. High heels didn't suit her.

'There's something I've got to tell you,' Kendra said, Annie's silence encouraging her to speak. 'She's interviewed Gioia as part of a piece she's writing to try to help save the Chapel. I know that Charlie's involved in what's going on, but I'm sure the Chapel is small fry in the overall scheme. I don't think it's going to be a problem for him. And it's so important to them. Sal was going to tell you but, what with everything, I guess she never found the right moment.' She looked at Annie, but saw no reaction other than her reaching out to take one of Sal's cigarettes. 'They're taking a picture of her tomorrow.'

'Yeah . . . well. Let's see. It probably won't make much difference either way. I kind of wish you hadn't told me. But . . .' She shrugged.

Kendra looked across to where Sal was joking with the waiter who had brought them the bill. Her arms were gesturing all over the place, in choppy moves.

'We'll be here all night at this rate. I'll go and get her. You've got some wine – just there.' Kendra gestured to the upper corner of her mouth where Annie had a stain of red. She leant over and wiped it for her. 'There you go. Oh, Annie. You look so sad. It will get better, you know. It will. You have to give it time.'

'So everyone keeps telling me. Time. Sure. How much of it do you think it takes?'

Sal's noisy return broke them up.

'So, are you sure you're not coming? It's Tuesday night. It will be fun, Annie. It might cheer you up, a bit of a bop.' Every other Tuesday, a small club near Portobello was taken over by Arturo, a Brazilian boy with green eyes and red trousers whose contact book included socialites, deejays, old roués and suppliers of the essential mix of drugs.

'Don't be stupid, Sal. It's not what she feels like.' Sometimes Sal could be so insensitive. It was unbelievable that she could be so clever and at the same time so stupid. Kendra sat back down next to Annie. 'You go, though. Tell us about it tomorrow.' They were relieved to see her leave.

★

The walk to Arturo's took Sal from the bright light of the main road into silent streets punctuated with impromptu tables outside restaurants and pubs where drinkers were making the most of the last hour, drifting in and out. Turning a corner, she could see the flags strung across the streets for the approaching Carnival weekend and hear through the windows an enthusiastic beat of drums. In the darkness, with music, she felt free, so much better than she had at the table stuck in a soupy fog of problems with the others. Sometimes it was easier just to be on your own. She bent over to retie the ankle strap on her shoes, then heard footsteps approach. A figure stood over her. She looked up to see a high hat, scraggly beard and white teeth.

'Hey Jimmy. How you doing? Coming to Arturo's?' Standing up to greet him, she knew she would smell the strong grass he could always provide. They walked to the tatty blue-painted door together, Jimmy's gruff voice gaining them entrance to the small, long room, which had tables at either side and a bar in the corner. There were only a few people in the room and the noise of any new entrant made everyone look up. If you were a stranger, it could be a hostile place.

Her friends were already there, and she squeezed herself on to the end of the bench. They weren't really friends, more like people she knew from round and about: the son of a famous artist with a smack problem, a girl whose photographs had started to appear in *Tatler* and *The Face*, Chris, a foreign correspondent who would always pitch up when he was in London, and Tiger, who everybody said was having a scene with her stepfather and, even though her mother knew, nothing was being said about it. Ten thirty was still early, the room an audition for the real thing. At the table, they'd started playing Perudo, but Sal wasn't in the mood for a dice game so she got up to get a whiskey. Downstairs, there were a couple of boys manning the decks, handling the vinyl albums with the skill of jugglers. Jimmy followed her down. She knew he was only a moment away from making a move on her, even though he was totally stoned. She briefly wondered what it would be like to have sex with him and if he'd be able to get it up anyway. It was a drag no one was dancing. For a few moments, she swayed to herself in the centre of the room, the drink and a few tokes making her not care that she was alone. It probably wouldn't be long till someone had some coke. That would wake everyone up a bit.

It was two hours later when she crashed. 'I tripped on my ankle strap. Crazy shoes. I should never have bought them. I'm hopeless with heels,' she would say when asked how she had managed a compound fracture of her wrist and a cut running across the apple of her cheek deep enough to need stitches. When she fell on the dance floor, a colourful spinning top in her bright-pink dress, nobody had paid much attention. They were used to seeing her fall then pick herself up, laughing, and dancing even more crazily. It was only when she sat there in a heap as the figures shifted around her that Tiger saw tears mixing with the blood streaking her cheek, a glass in shards beside her on the floor. Chris had taken her to the nearby hospital in a cab but, after checking her into the crowded A&E, he'd left, returning to Arturo's. He said A&E reminded him of Beirut.

'I'm not sure about that leather jacket.' Kendra lay on the bed as Gioia examined herself in the cracked mirror in the wardrobe door. 'Look. I don't know about these things. Jeez, nobody ever came to me for style advice, but I think you need to tone it down for this.'

'I need to not be fucking doing it at all,' Gioia grumbled at her reflection as she adjusted her hair into an enormous top knot like a baker's bun. Kendra had debated whether to tell her that it wasn't her most appealing style, but didn't want to add more stress to the business of dressing for the *Herald*'s photographer.

'Have you still got that jacket, the one you wore when you went to the council last year?'

Gioia fished around in a pile of clothes by the wall, holding up a creased pillar-box-red object. 'This? No way. Look at the state of it.'

'If we had a working iron it would help.'

'Not now, Ken. I'm not wearing that bleedin' Father Christmas number. How's this?' She placed a safari-style jacket with big patch pockets against her.

It was nearly time to go. 'Wear it with those trousers, the ones you don't like but look kind of normal.' The trousers in question had a conventional waistband and straight legs rather than Gioia's favoured skintight shapes or dhoti pants. 'I'm going to call Sal, just to check.'

'Check on what?'

'That everything's still on for the picture.' She hoped it wasn't going to take for ever for someone to answer Sal's line. Sometimes it could just ring and ring. By the time the phone was picked up she had almost forgotten to listen.

'She's not in today. Can I take a message?'

'Isn't she coming in at all?'

'She's called in sick.' No surprise there. Kendra pictured Sal tottering off the previous evening. Her absence from the office had a depressing inevitability about it. How was she going to hold her job down if she carried on like this? Briefly, she considered how the compelling sprite of university had morphed into this character. The balance had shifted so that, whereas before, the pleasure and exhilaration of Sal's company outweighed the problems, now it was too often the reverse. At what point had that happened? She got up and shook her hair to rid herself of the thought, aware that if she betrayed any anxiety right now Gioia would pull out. Her conviction that this article might help with the Chapel was the only reason Gioia was tugging up the recalcitrant trouser zip. It didn't help that it was baking hot again. Not the kind of day Gioia would choose to be trussed up in a safari jacket.

Kendra then tried Sal at home, after a few moments debating whether to just leave her. 'Hi . . .Yes, we're leaving in a few minutes' time. But what's with you? Why aren't you at work? Oh shit . . . a cast? No . . . she never said . . . yeah, yeah, of course you weren't . . . Is it painful? Yeah. I know . . . But watch those pills. I remember Dad having them. He said he was poleaxed by them . . .' She laughed, in response to Sal's predictable enthusiasm for the escapist properties of painkillers. 'So the photographer's a good guy? No, of course you can't . . . call you after.' She envisioned Sal's jaunty lack of balance as she left the restaurant. Maybe it was Kendra's fault. Another accident. If she'd stopped her going on after the pizza, it wouldn't have happened. But then, how many things could you feel responsible for?

She went over to Gioia. 'Surprise, surprise, she got totally smashed at Arturo's and tripped up on the dance floor. She says someone stood on her ankle strap and wham! Naturally, it's not about anything that she did. She's got stitches in her cheek and her wrist in a cast . . . ya . . . di . . . ya . . . di . . . ya. After this, we've got to try and get her to see someone. We have to do something.'

'She's one sick girl, that Sal. She needs to clean up, elsewise she's going to end up in one of those crazy farms.' Gioia made her eyes exaggeratedly wide so that her dark-chocolate irises were surrounded completely by the white, and waved her arms like some voodoo queen. 'Come on. Let's get this thing over with. I'm ready for my close-up.'

The sink was filled with the mess of breakfast. After looking at the sodden cornflakes floating in milk, Sal decided to leave it all in there. It was a depressing place, this flat, and worse during the day when it was empty, with the dirty plates, the stained carpet, the windows that were painted shut in the sitting room. She felt like shit. She would have liked to have been at work when the photographs arrived but, when she'd called in yesterday and explained about her wrist, they'd told her to stay at home.

Andrea had, it was true, sounded exasperated but, all the same, she'd let her know that they were getting one of the guys on Business to run the figures on the ratio of new developments to council spend on housing, which must mean they were working on her idea. Being the *Herald*, they'd be on the side of the developments, but it would be good background for the Chapel item. Entrepreneurism was well and good, but you had to take into account the human cost. That was her point. It was a measure of Sal's astounding lack of either self-knowledge or empathy that she failed, for even a moment, to consider Charlie's reaction to this idea – even though he was married to her best friend.

Her small bedroom looked on to the central well of the block, the frosted-glass window opposite offering a view only of shadowy shapes when they switched the lights on. With difficulty, she managed to pull her blue vest over the cast, adding a pair of pants, a toothbrush and a couple of paperbacks to a small nylon rucksack. Since she had fallen, a nasty bruise had come up on the bone above her ankle.

By the time she boarded the train it was really hurting. If she lucked out, Pete wouldn't have finished off all the Black Pak – that would help with the pain. The depots and housing estates of west London soon gave way to small rivers and hay bales stacked in fields. Sal sat looking out, discomfited by both the itch under her cast and recent events which, although she had no wish to examine them, inconveniently kept coming to mind.

She probably shouldn't have gone to Arturo's, but she couldn't be blamed for wanting to have a bit of fun after that dinner. She hated seeing Annie so low and, since Kendra had hooked up with Gioia, the part of her that had always been there, the critical and censorious part, appeared to Sal to have intensified. Of course, she'd been brilliant over the abortion, coming to that horrible clinic with her, but it was obvious that she was in a state about Sal having got into the situation in the first place. Didn't they realize she was fine? This was just a bit of bad luck.

It wasn't her fault that she'd fallen over. She was just dancing. It was all that idiot's fault for stepping on her strap. OK, she admitted, she probably had had a bit too much to drink, but what would you expect when Jimmy was making moves on her? Anybody would. When she'd looked in the mirror, her cheek didn't look as bad as it felt. It felt huge, and the stitches nagged tightly at her skin.

By the time she arrived at the flat it was mid-afternoon. Pete had given her a key, accompanied by a stern order not to arrive unannounced, otherwise he'd be taking it back, pronto. But, even so, she got a buzz out of seeing it dangling on her keychain. The note on the table said 'Back 7 x.'

It would have been lovely to go and hang out in the park, stripping down to a bra and feeling the sun on her skin and knowing that soon she would be making love with Pete and tasting the salt of him and feeling him move over her. But, with the cast, the sunshine held little appeal. She imagined her encased skin clammy like a blancmange. She pulled open the drawer under the two electric hobs. With only one hand, it was difficult to open the battered tin she found at the back, but what were teeth for? As she prised the lid open, she got the anticipated whiff of the Black Pak. It was frustrating, though, having to acknowledge that there was no way she could manage to roll a joint. Still, she could manage a drink. She took the miniature carton of orange juice and the small bottle of tequila she had wrapped in her knickers from her bag.

Her mum would have had something to say about the dust in this flat. Riffling through the cassettes on the floor, she debated the possibilities: 'Let It Grow' (definitely her favourite Clapton, even if guys thought it was a cop-out), Blue Öyster Cult – she and Pete used to listen to '(Don't Fear) The Reaper' years back. Funny to see he'd got it on cassette now. Now you're talking – Neil Young. She clicked a tape into the small ghetto blaster. 'You are like a hurricane . . .' It doesn't get much better. All the aches had disappeared. Just. Like. That.

The orange juice had run out, but she had just poured another tot of the golden tequila when Pete returned.

'Well. What have we here? My injured bird . . .' He gave Sal a long kiss. 'Got to get this kit off . . . I'm shagged out. Bleeding hot out there today.'

'Do you want some?' Sal offered the tumbler. 'I'll pour you one – we're out of orange, though. I'm on cocktails, you're on the smokes.'

Pete walked across to the tiny bathroom, removing his black T-shirt as he walked. Only a minute later he reappeared, rubbing a small dark purple towel across his chest. There was a reddening at his neck and across his arms from the day in the sun.

'That's better . . .' He stood at the counter by the electric hob, crumbling the dark lump in the tin and rolling a huge joint. Sal loved to watch him. He made it appear a real craft. He took a drag and then another before passing it to her. As she smoked, he unzipped the back of her skirt, kneeling to remove her sandals one at a time. Running a long finger around the bruise on her ankle, he moved slowly up towards her thigh, the silver ring he always wore rubbing on her skin.

'I think you could do with a bit of decoration.' Pete sat on the old wicker chair near the window, pulling Sal on to his knee and reaching for a black felt-tip pen. He started to inscribe the cast silently with a mixture of intricate patterns and symbols. When he had finished on the cast, he started on her breasts as she passed the joint between their mouths. By the time she was covered, nothing else mattered.

16

It was seven o'clock and Kendra woke to discover there was no milk. She loved her morning tea and always heated the brown pot before adding the leaves and covering it with the Rasta-striped cosy. Unlike her girlfriend, she enjoyed the early morning and had learnt to tolerate Gioia's endless fascination with her own sleeping pattern. Recounting its multiple failings could keep Gioia absorbed for ages. This was the crack of dawn for Gioia, thought Kendra as she reached the corner shop. Handing over the cash for the milk she picked up a *Herald* too, an act of loyalty to Sal, since Gioia thought it was nothing but a Conservative newsletter. In any case, now certainly wasn't the time to knock it. Drastic situations called for drastic action and Gioia couldn't be picky about which paper was going to help with her plight. After all, the future of the Chapel was hardly headline news.

Back at the flat, she sat at the table, pouring the tea, which, as usual, dripped down the pot. There was a slight chip in the spout. Kendra flicked through the *Herald* and was about to put it down when she saw the picture of Gioia, or somebody who looked like a version of her. The figure who stood there, hands on hips and staring straight at the reader from the page, was her lover at her most intimidating. The jacket Kendra had advised her to wear made her look the kind of Scout leader no one would choose to leave in charge of their kids. What had Sal done?

She looked for Sal's name and at first couldn't see it. Then she spotted it in small type at the bottom of the page among a long list of writers which included the poisonous Marsha. She scanned the page and saw Charlie's name and that of Charterhouse in an article in a sidebar. As she started to read the story that accompanied the picture she knew immediately she wasn't going to like it. And she didn't. The quotes from Gioia were inoffensive, even to the point of dullness, but the damage was elsewhere. It was vicious. It was implied, if not spelt out, that Gioia was gay, there was a damning accusation of neglect of the property, and some local busybody was shit-stirring about Gerassimos. The piece was a deft character assassination and completely killed off any chance of the Chapel surviving. She looked over at the mound under the blankets that was Gioia, blissfully unaware. Small popping sounds came from her lips. What was the point of waking her, to see this? She'd use the phone box down the road to call Sal. As she walked there, she imagined Sal's voice. It would take on an accusatory tone: she would invariably, furiously, blame somebody other than herself. But how could this be somebody else? It was Sal's story.

It took for ever before some bloke in Sal's flat picked up the phone, and he said he hadn't seen her in days. The air was muggy, the sky an oppressive grey that was exceptionally depressing for the end of summer.

When Gioia woke and read the piece, her silence was worse than any tirade, allowing no possibility of discussion or excuse. The barricades were up, her face set in a stony rage, everything about her body advised distance. Gioia would, Kendra knew, remain like that until Kendra could prove that she was worthy of redemption, which would only be when she had proven that she was united with Gioia against *them*. Gioia thought in terms of war. *Them* would be everybody else – Sal, Annie, the neighbours, the papers. Everybody would be declared the enemy. Not taking sides would not be an option.

What idiot would call so early on a Sunday? Charlie leant across Annie, who was curled at the edge of the bed, to reach the phone.

'She's asleep . . . if it's that important.' He rubbed his wife's bare shoulder. 'Annie. It's Kendra.' Under the sheet, Annie shifted but didn't wake. 'No go . . . she's too heavily asleep. I'll get her to ring when she wakes.'

He lay back on his large pile of pillows, stretching to see if it was true that sleeping on them was going to give him the stiff neck Annie predicted, before sliding out of bed to collect a pile of newspapers from outside the front door. He was going to miss the block porter if they moved out of this place, and bought a house, like Annie wanted. Back in bed, he started to browse through them. It was obvious it was August. Even the business pages read as if they had been written weeks ago. His eye was briefly caught by an article in the fashion section about those leotard things – bodies. Come to think of it, they were right. Nipples did stick out in them. He'd bought Annie a black one by this guy Azzedine something or other, just before she was pregnant, which he considered pretty generous since, personally, he didn't rate them in the sexy stakes, nipples or not. He found fiddling around with those poppers a real turn-off.

Annie shifted again. She looked happier in her sleep than at any other point in the day. Charlie stroked her hair and threw the *Sunday Times* on the floor in the vague hope she might wake. It worked.

'Kendra called. I said you'd ring later. It doesn't say much for their sex life that she's on the blower first thing Sunday.' He felt the smooth curve of Annie's bottom.

'That's not like her . . . oh, I'm still so tired,' she whispered, reaching out for a glass of water. The pills meant that she woke with a dry mouth. As she moved away from Charlie, he sighed, resigning himself to no sex and instead giving the *Herald* the once-over. Turning towards the back of the paper, he stopped, and nudged Annie.

'Hey, isn't that your friend? Kendra's mate?' Annie dragged herself out from the half-awake place that she was inhabiting, trying to stay there as long as she could. It was the best place to be, before the heaviness took over. Leaning over his shoulder, she wiped the sleep from the corners of her eyes, taking in a picture of somebody who did indeed look like a version of Gioia. The woman was wearing a belted safari jacket, her hair tied back from her face as tightly as a sumo wrestler's. 'Bull Dyke', that's what the picture screamed to the *Herald*'s readers.

Charlie was now all concentration, scratching his hair as he read. 'Christ. She's not gonna like that,' he said.

'Like what?'

'This headline . . . "Double life of youth worker". Hang on . . . I'm trying to work it out. They seem to have something about her having a "dubious sexual history" – that's Kendra they must be talking about – and the space being used illegally. What's that all about then?'

As Charlie read, Annie's eye was caught by an item running in a column down the side of the page: "The Charterhouse consortium is in the vanguard of this movement which is sweeping across London, destroying local communities with little regard for residents or history. Witness the march of the new Yuppie tribe, eyes focused only as far as their next deal.' Oh no. The idea that Sal must have orchestrated this filtered through to Annie's foggy mind.

Charlie gave out a snort, slapping the paper in amusement at the side of the bed. 'I don't think we're going to have many problems getting that site now. That girl's days are numbered, big time. They haven't quite spelt out that she's a lesbian, but they don't need to – look at the snap. She looks terrifying. And they've found locals to say they want her out, the building's all but falling down, and they think something dodgy's going on, with vans coming and going at night. Sounds like your Kendra's got herself in a right bag of tricks.'

'That must be what she was calling about.' Annie closed her eyes in the hope of shutting out the day. 'I don't want to know any more right now. Poor Kendra.'

'Kendra! Never mind fucking Kendra. That's not the half of it.' Charlie had now seen the sidebar. 'Look at this.' He sat up in a movement that shook the duvet off the bed. 'Have you read this?' he spluttered, and began to read out the column where Charterhouse was mentioned, becoming more enraged with every word. 'Total crap. What does she think she's doing here? "Destroying local communities . . . march of the new Yuppie tribe." It's not going to make a blind bit of difference to our game plan, but it's plain nasty, isn't it? Total bollocks. Our PR is going to have to sort this out.' He threw the paper on the floor. 'I thought she was meant to be your friend.'

Annie kept silent. She didn't understand what Sal had hoped to achieve but it was obvious that she had thought she was doing something that would help Kendra. It was equally obvious that she hadn't given a moment's thought to what it was going to mean to Annie.

Charlie had left the bed to use the telephone in the sitting room. She could hear him barking down it. 'Yeah . . . totally . . . soft in the head and not to mention a fucking drunk . . .' Annie stayed exactly where she was, wishing that she would never have to move again.

When Annie called Kendra back, she could sense the atmosphere in Gioia's flat.

'Yeah, I know,' she said. 'Terrible. Total catastrophe all round. We don't know where she is. Have you been able to track her down?' Kendra noted the 'we'. Hadn't Annie realized, even now, that Charlie was just as much the problem as Sal? She tried to keep her fury in check, arranging to meet in the Polish café on Annie's side of town. Anything to escape Gioia's cloud of anger.

It didn't take long and she was out the door and on her way. In contrast to the empty streets where she lived, Annie's neighbourhood was crowded, as families straggled along in the direction of the nearby museums and couples wandered, arms around each other after a loving Sunday morning lie-in. At the café, a boy and a girl sat at the table next to theirs, their legs entwined as they shared a breakfast.

'So . . . I called her parents, but they haven't heard from her. Of course, I didn't tell her mum anything. She wanted to know how Sal was, so she obviously hasn't seen them for ages. I decided not to mention the wrist and everything.' Annie was sipping from a tall glass which was filled with hot water and a slice of lemon.

'You know something, Annie? I don't give a shit about her broken wrist. It's a broken head she deserves. She's lost me this time. Totally lost me. You can't imagine what this has done to Gioia. It's not just the gay thing, we could deal with that, but there's all this stuff about Gerassimos, and she *adores* him, and then about her being irresponsible, an inappropriate person to be in charge of kids. There's no way she can fight this.'

'What can have happened though?'

'The idiot got drunk and smashed herself up, didn't she? Then, I suppose, she must have given her notes to someone, and because she wasn't there someone – and no prizes for guessing it was Marsha – wrote it up the way she wanted to, or the way she thought it would make a better story. It's all tied in with this other stuff about new developments.'

'Yeah, don't I know it? Charlie's furious. It's not just you and Gioia, you know. Anyway, it's true, isn't it? Some of it. Like the stuff about the place falling down.'

'We're not going to get anywhere if you start down that road. We could look at your husband's plans, for a start. He didn't care about us, did he? Where's the loyalty here?'

'This isn't about him, Ken. Look. As far as he's concerned, business is business. The Chapel was a tiny part of this deal, and I guess he didn't let it be a factor. I know I should have spoken more to him about it, and if I'd been feeling stronger I would have, but . . .' She shrugged.

The casual movement infuriated Kendra, who stood up, knocking into the breakfasting couple next to them. 'I can see where *your* loyalties lie. This is pretty fucking pointless, sitting here with you.' She grabbed her bag. 'When you find Sal, if you get to her before I do, tell her I've got to speak to her.'

Annie didn't have the energy or the desire even to try to stop her leaving. The mess in her head was a knot that had no apparent beginning or end. She couldn't start to unravel it. As she watched Kendra's cycling figure climb the hill towards the park she wondered what was going to happen next, but, if she was honest, she didn't much care.

Sal's personal party had come to an end. It had been fun, thought Sal, as once again she stood on the station platform, but coming down from this one was major, and the bright sunshine wasn't a help. The pair of sunglasses she had found at Pete's made her look ridiculously like Ant from her childhood Ant and Bee books. But anything to help with her head . . . She'd overdone it because of the pain, of course, especially the pain in her wrist. Everybody knew she wouldn't normally touch Southern Comfort.

She looked at the *Herald*'s front page, in the disappointing knowledge that she wouldn't have any copy in that edition. Even the oldest hacks still got a kick out of seeing their bylines printed – they counted the week's achievement in column inches. The train arrived and as she settled into her seat she folded the large paper professionally into a manageable shape – no wonder most people just bought tabloids: they were so much easier to handle – and looked through it. At first she wasn't sure it was Gioia in the picture. She took off the sunglasses to look more closely at the caption: 'Gioia Cavallieri, the controversial leader at London's Chapel youth centre'. But it wasn't possible. This was her story, and she hadn't been at the office last week. She had given Andrea the outline and notes on her interview with Gioia so she could see how Sal was getting on, but it had always been clear that the interview was going to be part of a bigger piece about the scandal of development. As she read, she saw it wasn't an interview, more of an assassination. Her eyes scanned the double-page spread, taking in the several interlinked stories and spotting not only hers but Marsha and Doug's names in a list at the bottom. It was news to her that they'd been working on this. And it wasn't just Gioia they'd done in: 'Kendra Rootstein, her well-connected companion in life and work'. Kendra was going to kill her.

By the time the train reached London Sal had reread the page at least eight times, on each reading coming up with a different interpretation of what was in front of her. For some reason, Patrick must have decided he wanted to run the story this week. It was bloody August, holiday season, and nothing was happening, she supposed, no matter what Marsha said. And instead of running a piece in support of Gioia, somebody had put out this dirt-digging rubbish as the 'human interest' angle. Stuart must have told them to beef it up, and she hadn't been there to fight her corner and make sure that the emphasis wasn't warped in this way. It was all because of this bloody wrist. She made her way down into the Tube, her backpack over her shoulder, her arm hanging limply in its cast, the stitches in her cheek aching and her hangover still worsening.

Stopping in the centre of a stinking underpass, surrounded by people all going somewhere with suitcases and children, friends and parents, she knew she was in a terrible way. But she didn't know how to get back to where she once was, before she'd become this mess.

When she came out of the Tube station, dusk had taken over and the Earls Court Road was noisy, the pubs full, as they were every night. She thought about stopping in one of the phone boxes she passed to call Kendra, but her headache was so bad she didn't think she'd manage to say anything that would help. Of course, a quick drink would help. She walked mechanically to the pub on the corner. God, Sundays were awful. The dregs of the week, and it was just her luck that it was now her day off. She ordered a double vodka and tonic, the thought of its arrival making her feel a little better as she waited at the bar, surrounded by groups of noisy Aussies.

It seemed that only moments had passed when she heard the words 'Cheer up, love.' A beefy boy with a rugby shirt rubbed up against her, grinning jovially and winking at his friend.

'Fuck off,' Sal replied, draining her third drink. The first two had been excellent medicine, taking the edge off both her headache and her examination of the day's catastrophe. This one didn't seem to be making much difference. Luckily, she had got some more at home, she was pretty sure. She didn't want to see any of the other occupants of the flat, but they wouldn't care. She'd never fitted in with them. Message to self: she had to get out of there. Yeah, she had to get out of there, and she had to call Kendra and Annie. But first, another drink.

That black suit she'd bought all those years back in Joseph had been worth every penny. Sal could only see her top half in the bathroom mirror, but it was enough to show that, all things considered, she appeared almost respectable. She couldn't get the jacket over her cast, but she draped it over her shoulders and she could roll up the sleeves of the pale-blue shirt. It was important that she looked the part today for the confrontation with Andrea. She'd decided that she needed to have that meeting before she spoke to the others. At least then she'd have an explanation.

Walking up the road to the office, she could see the ornate clock that hung from the building over the street. Nine o'clock. It was heaven knows how long since she'd been in this early, and on a Tuesday too. It wouldn't surprise her if she was the first one there. But once she reached the first floor where the newsroom spread out in all directions, it was clear that many people regarded nine as the start of the day. In the corner, Jackie was making a cup of tea: three sugars and just a drip of milk, the way she knew (after six years in the job) her boss liked it.

At least Marsha wasn't in yet. Sal didn't want to have to start the conversation with Andrea in front of an audience. She nervously kept an eye on the door to the newsroom, hoping that her boss would arrive soon. She had felt reasonably confident until now, but as the minutes passed she was becoming nervous – nervous of what Andrea would say about what had happened, and nervous of what she would discover her own role in it was thought to be.

The older woman arrived shortly, unbuttoned her raincoat and hung it up on the hook. She placed a plastic bag of groceries far under the desk where it couldn't be seen and began to unscrew the top from her pot of Nivea.

'Andrea' – Sal walked up to her – 'can we have a chat?'

Andrea considered Sal, taking in her unusually neat appearance, and the cast on her arm.

'How's the arm? Can you work this week?'

'Yeah. Well, I hope so. That's what I want to talk to you about. About last week, and what happened?'

'Indeed. It might be good to discuss what happened,' Andrea replied, rhythmically smoothing the cream in a motion down her hand and into her wrist. 'I take it you saw the story.'

'Yes. Of course. But that wasn't the story. You know that wasn't the story. I don't have any idea how it came to turn out like that, but what I do know is that it's completely fucked up – no, sorry . . . screwed up . . . no, caused terrible problems for my friends.'

Andrea stood up and took Sal by the arm, walking her in the direction of the hooks on which her coat hung.

'I think it's time you and I had a talk. Here's not the place.'

They walked in silence out of the building and down Fleet Street to a small café. A photograph of the owner was placed on the wall and the windows were damp with steam from the canisters of boiling water. Andrea placed her handbag on a table at the back and gestured to Sal to sit down as she went up to buy them both a tea. She returned with the cups balanced, hot liquid so close to the brim that it couldn't help but spill over on to the saucer.

'You want to know what happened? You were on sick leave and we had a sudden hole in the paper when some key information was still lacking. Stuart thought we should save it till next week, when it would be stronger. So he looked around to find a filler and remembered that we'd been putting together a package on your subject. But he didn't want a puff piece about your friends – remember: he'd got all the information about Charterhouse and their development plans in the bag – so he asked Marsha to do some digging to get some more colour on that woman.'

'You mean Gioia.'

'Yes, her. And the rest, of course, is history.'

'But it's not fair doing that. Taking my story and twisting it in that way.'

'Maybe if you were professional enough to have been in the office, it wouldn't have worked out like this. Have you considered that? No. I doubt it. You were too busy smashing yourself up, getting pissed. Sal, you've got to pull yourself together. I've seen too many hacks done in by alcohol, and it's not a pretty sight. They're often the brightest ones. You've got talent, but you've got a problem. Everybody's noticed.'

'They have? What have they noticed?' Sal's tone became defensive. 'I don't drink so much. I don't drink any more than anyone else at lunch.'

'Maybe. Maybe not. But I've had people come up and talk to me about it. They can smell it on your breath. And it's not only drink sometimes, is it?' She watched as Sal took this in, her hand shaking as she raised the cup to her mouth before reaching down to get a cigarette from her bag.

'But – I do my job well. At least, I thought that's what I did. You never told me there was a problem with my work before. This last thing. That wasn't my fault. You know that somebody made me trip over and that's how I fractured my wrist, and it was you who told me to stay at home, not to come into the office. I was completely on top of it all.'

'Sal, there are too many old soaks in this business, and too many of them never get the chance to do something about it soon enough. You sound just like them all. And you *have* got the chance to do something. It was never their fault. It's never your fault. I'm telling you. You need help. I've got the names of some places you could go to sort yourself out – it will be easier if you take some leave, and I can probably fix that for you. I'm going to write the names down for you now, and you should think about it. But think seriously. This is the first and last time I'm going to talk to you about it.'

She took out a shorthand pad and a small address book and, writing a couple of names and numbers down, she tore out a sheet of the paper and put it before Sal.

'I'm going back to the office. I expect you at the desk in quarter of an hour. And think about it. There are no more second chances.'

Since it was impossible to contemplate Sal coming to Charlie and Annie's flat or Gioia's place, Kendra had suggested the three of them meet down by the river. They had agreed they had to talk, and the location would be neutral, she pointed out, and, anyway, it might be good to be walking, rather than sitting over a drink. Sal had at first tried to wriggle out of the meeting, claiming work, but Kendra, driven by Gioia's distress, had shouted down the phone at her that they weren't idiots, and of course she didn't have to work all of Sunday. The low tide that morning exposed the rubbish at the edges of the river: shoes, a bicycle, plastic bags and several tyres sat mired in the mud just past the exquisite waterside houses.

'Look,' Sal had said immediately they set off from their gathering point at the pub under the bridge, 'I know I fucked up. You don't need to tell me, but I do want you to know it wasn't my fault. Not all of it, anyway.'

'It's not about fault.' Kendra stopped to look over the stone wall that bordered the river. 'It's about what we have to deal with. Gioia's already got the council and some other God-knows-what-committee on her back. There's next to no chance of the Chapel surviving now – with all that and this property deal.' She tried not to think about Annie's connection with Charlie just now. 'And on top of that there's this terrible idea that she's an improper person. It's ludicrous.' She and Sal had only been together for about ten minutes and the meeting was already starting to look like a bad idea. What had she thought it would achieve? Annie was right when she said that they had to find a way through all this if they wanted to stay friends. But the problems were such a tangle. After all, Kendra was not only having to deal with Sal's craziness but with Annie's disloyalty too.

Annie was silent. It was days like this, when the sky was a clear blue and there was still a warmth to the air, even though there was a wind blowing leaves along the towpath, that made how she was feeling worse. She could see that it was lovely here – the river curving widely, the landscape open – but she couldn't feel it. It was, she had agreed with Kendra, important for them to meet, but she simply had no interest in saying anything. Even the article in the newspaper, denigrating as it was to Charlie, didn't make her feel any emotion other than that it was one more grim aspect to deal with when she couldn't deal with anything. She could hear Kendra and Sal talking as they walked slightly ahead.

'So what are you going to do?' Kendra was saying. 'You know you can't go on like this. You're going to blow everything. It's not just us. What about your work? They must be getting fed up with you and the hangovers and the absences, and now this accident?' Sal's wrist had graduated from a sling to a bandage. She might have a drink problem but obviously her immune system was still OK, thought Kendra, observing how well her stitches had healed. 'Annie' – she glanced back – 'Annie and I haven't said this before, but here we go: you've got to think, really seriously, about getting help.'

'Christ, that's what everyone's saying. "Get help." I had Andrea on at me about it last week.'

'Good. What did she say?'

Sal was surprised by the snap in Kendra's tone. She had always been so gentle, even when she was annoyed. It was a new timbre to her voice, and not very attractive.

'She gave me the names of some places. Drying-out clinics, I suppose. She said she could get me leave. But I know I don't need it. I accept that I have to drink less, but I don't need to go to some bin. I just need to pace myself better and, if I could get out of that flat, which I do find very depressing, that would help a lot.'

Annie finally spoke. 'I think you're wrong there. You do need help. You need to go somewhere away from all of this.' She waved her arm. 'Us, your work, that crowd you hang out with, probably that guy Pete. That's the point of those places. They really get to the root of what your problem is. God knows, you need it.'

'You're a fine one to speak,' Sal flung back. 'I mean, look at you. Completely miserable, aren't you? Maybe you need to get something sorted out too.'

'Stop it. This isn't getting us anywhere,' Kendra butted in. 'Of course Annie's miserable.' She prevented herself from saying that anybody would be if they were married to Charlie. 'But that's not why we're here, is it? It's you. Gioia always says there's never a good day to give up sniffing glue. There's never going to be a better time for you to give up alcohol.'

Sal stopped and looked down at the water as her two friends watched her. 'Yeah, Gioia got that line from *Airplane*. Everyone knows it,' she barked. Above her a formation of Canada geese squawked noisily on their migration. She didn't know why but she was starting to cry. She felt the way she had when she had got on the Tube that day and had been overwhelmed by the mess she was in. It was *all* a mess. Maybe they were right. Maybe it was something she should do. Anything was better than feeling like this – trapped and, even with her two best friends beside her, utterly lonely.

Annie looked at the small suitcase Sal was carrying as she emerged from the Earls Court flat. It drew attention to her fragile appearance, her smallness. She was devoid of the energy that usually made her appear taller, more substantial.

'Well, it's not for long, is it?' Sal commented, seeing their looks. Neither Annie nor Kendra reminded her that it would be at least three weeks and quite possibly nearer six. Let her enjoy denial while she could.

Annie drove, with Sal in the front beside her, following the seating plan she and Kendra had decided on.

'It's important we don't infantilize her. She needs to feel that this is a decision she's made herself, like an adult, not because we're coming over all parental and telling her what to do,' Kendra had said as they drove to pick her up.

South London stretched on for ever but eventually they passed the areas that Kendra never even realized were still part of the city – New Cross, Eltham, Sidcup – and the landscape changed. Their route took them through fields with only a few houses dotted among them, then a last turning to the right, down a short wooded track and past metal gates.

'Christ, it's a bit *Hound of the Baskervilles*. It looks terrifying.' Sal masked her true terror with a riff that took them through the parking lot and into the front hall of a large house with ruddy Virginia creeper covering the stonework and part of the huge windows. The quiet added to the unnerving quality, as if whatever was happening there was disguised.

'Maybe we've got the wrong place. Let's leave,' Sal offered hopefully, lighting a cigarette.

'Is this Sal Turner?' A woman in a navy sailor's sweater with the naïve face of a nun came to meet them. Funny, wasn't it, thought Sal rebelliously, how religious nuts always looked like this. Christ, they weren't going to make her go all religious, were they? That would be the final straw. Locked up and coming out a Jesus freak, sandals and all. 'I'm Sarah' – the woman's handshake was soft and undemanding – 'one of your counsellors.'

Annie was standing by the door, her hands in the pockets of the navy cashmere coat she wore, even though the weather was still mild. She had offered to drive, as neither of the others could, and Sal had been adamant that she didn't want her parents with her. But now she was desperate to leave. The place was so gloomy.

'I'm going to hang around outside.' She came up to Sal and gave her a hug. 'See you soon. I'll call.'

'We don't allow phone calls here. Your friend will be able to telephone you, but external communication is tightly controlled while in treatment.' Sarah looked at Sal. 'I'll take you to your room. Your roommates are in group right now – that's a group session. You'll meet them soon. You did remember that no reading materials are allowed, didn't you?'

As she led Sal off towards a huge staircase that climbed darkly up the hallway, allowing in none of the autumn sunlight, Kendra stood watching from below. How could they be abandoning Sal to this? But then she remembered Gioia, who was at this precise moment in a difficult meeting with a team from the council, and the sadness, rage and frustration that she was having to deal with, daily. Something had had to be done, and this was that something.

1987

17

Annie listened to the waste disposal churning the skin of her orange and apple along with the crusts of Charlie's toast. Behind her, she knew he would be flicking through the *Daily Mail*, licking the third finger of his right hand before using it to turn the pages. His hair, wet from the shower, was slicked back, giving him the look of a polished thug. He'd just bought a new coat in the Harrods sale, camel wool with a wide astrakhan collar, commenting, as he regarded himself, that he rather liked the Rachman look. On the same shopping trip he'd bought her a new Donna Karan dress that fitted tightly to her shape, its boat neck carved to expose the line of her shoulder blades. He'd picked out one with a deep V neckline, but she liked the one with a shallow neck and long sleeves which she could wear to the office.

'I've got to run. I'm meeting Paddy at the old Elephants shop. Can't remember if I told you – they're turning it into a sandwich bar. It's the first of a chain they're planning.'

'Sounds good. I've got a lot of time for Paddy and Marcus. They've made the Bank a roaring success.' He dabbed his mouth, with a piece of paper towel. 'Don't work too hard, babe. Sometimes I think you should just give this PR lark up and we should have a real go on the baby front.' Even Annie's back view, as she wiped down the sink, managed to convey her displeasure. 'Anyway . . . remember we're having dinner with Mark and Soph tonight. I've booked San Lorenzo.'

By the time Annie arrived at the shop, Paddy was already there, running his hand over the finish of the empty cool cabinets where the sandwiches would be stacked.

'This idea is sure-fire. Haven't you had enough of those horrible tubs of junk waiting to be spread on plastic bread? The ready-packed, super-fresh sandwich is what the customer wants.' Paddy presented this thought with a flourish, taking in the whole room. 'So what do you think?'

Annie had been in the business long enough to know that the definition of an opinion altered when you were hired as PR. She did think the sandwich chain was a clever idea but, even were that not the case, she would have kept that thought to herself. Personally, she didn't like all the zinc he was using, but she could see it gave the place the patina of a professional kitchen. And it looked clean. Not like all those old sandwich places.

'It's a terrific concept, and this is the perfect location. There's tons of little fashion businesses starting up round about and people need somewhere easy to get their lunch, grab a coffee. With your and Marcus's track record and our campaign, I feel very confident. I've already had requests from the *Independent* for the exclusive. I think that's the right one to go with – they're new, different, attracting a younger readership. And we're working with the *Standard*, not just for a review but aiming for a vox pop on launch day – nab some people on the street and ask them how this kind of place will change their lunchtime. It's three weeks till opening, isn't it?'

Paddy was peering at a piece of joinery in the corner with the concentration of a cat waiting for the reappearance of a mouse. 'Mmm. That's the plan. Still some things to be resolved with the snagging.'

They both turned to the front door, through which Lee had come and was now pacing the room.

'Neat . . . love the zinc. Makes me think of those counters in Paris, gives it a bit of the *ooh la la* factor.' Annie couldn't see any resemblance to the historic Parisian café but Paddy seemed pleased by the allusion. Lee was good at that stuff.

'Yeah, you've got it in one.' Paddy slapped Lee on the back. 'It's that mix between old and new.'

'I thought I'd try and get Bananarama in here during the first week. An old mate of mine works with them and he says the girls owe him a favour. Then we get the paps snapping them walking out with their nosh.' Lee's broad smile showed that he was pleased with his idea but also that he acknowledged the humorous side of it. It was one of the things Annie loved about him. He was obsessed with his job, but he would always get the joke.

Annie pulled her coat around her. Lee had left the front door open and there was a piercing wind coming through.

'Lee, I'm heading back to the office. I've got a meeting with Tania. Catch you later.' She gave Paddy a formal kiss on the cheek. 'I'll send you the press outline over tomorrow so you can cast your eye over it. Let me know if you want anything else.' It was a drab day. Heavy overnight rain had pooled at the side of the road, and spat out from the wheels of buses. She looked down at the dirty pavement, remembering how, when she was a child, her parents had brought her up to London as a treat, and Letty had told her not to step on the cracks otherwise a bear might get her. Annie had spent all afternoon becoming increasingly anxious about this possibility before her father had reassured her that it wasn't true, the bears would never attack a good girl like her.

Over the past two years Torrington's had increased their staff, so Tania was always thinking about moving somewhere bigger, somewhere they could go open plan, but it hadn't happened and the townhouse rooms were packed with too many staff, filing cabinets lining the walls and almost no space for visitors. Annie had just begun to go through the post when her phone rang. She picked it up, cradling it in her neck while tearing open a Jiffy bag.

'Sal, how are you?'

'OK. I wondered if you were free for lunch? I've got to come down your way later.'

In those few words, Annie could hear the difference in her friend. She still wasn't used to the new Sal, the one that had emerged from the country-house rehab and flung herself into the safety net of the AA community. The uncertainty of 'I wondered' grated. Before, she would have said, 'Whatever you're doing, drop it now. We're having lunch.' Everybody talked of this being a phase. Once people levelled out after treatment, they got more of their old selves back.

She knew it was selfish wishing that the Sal she remembered would return – after all, look at the havoc the drunk Sal had created. But she knew lunch was going to be a lot less fun than it used to be.

She'd been looking forward to an apple and coffee at her desk but she didn't feel able to let Sal down and agreed to meet in the basement Italian down the road where, in the old days, Sal would order several glasses of the bitter house red (always commenting on how small they were) to go with bread rolls and sticky *carbonara*. The windows, as always, were steamed up, and the noise from the kitchen drowned out most of the conversation as the two over-worked waitresses in their black dresses and white aprons piled dirty plates on their arms around the squash of tables.

Annie couldn't put her finger on what had changed, but Sal was different. It was as if somebody had turned down the volume. Her hair had grown longer, now reaching to her collarbone, and she wore it with a soft fringe. The smoking hadn't changed though.

'How are you doing? It's been ages. We haven't seen each other since that time when you just came out. I can't believe it.' Annie supposed they hadn't met because of Charlie. He was still utterly unforgiving, which made seeing Sal a treachery. If she was honest with herself, that probably wasn't all. She just hadn't wanted to see Sal. Otherwise, she might have tried to go to that awful rehab place. But it had been so much easier all round not to. Now that they were sitting together in the stuffy, bustling Italian, she realized that she had missed Sal, a lot.

'Don't feel bad. I've been busy since I got sober. Sometimes it's easier to be with other people who have gone through the same thing. I've been hanging out with my sponsor, who's wonderful.'

As they ordered food, Annie wasn't sure whether she should just assume that Sal would be on water or Diet Coke. It seemed odd not to be asking for their same old, same old with the house red. She thought she'd better not have wine either, not if Sal wasn't drinking.

'How's work?' she asked. 'I bet they're pleased to have you back.'

'They've been really good, giving me the time off. 'Course I feel all the time I've got to prove that I'm "cured". It's different working

264

with Andrea now. She even looks like another person to me. You know how when you see a room for the first time it looks one way and then, when you get used to it, it looks different? Well, that's how I feel about her, but in reverse. All that time, she was such an authority figure to me, but not really a person, and now, I see the person.'

Annie was grateful for the arrival of their *tricolore* salads. She hadn't got used to Sal saying things like that, and wasn't completely sure she wanted to.

'Makes it easier that *The Times* poached Marsha,' Sal continued. 'I don't think I could have borne having to sit opposite her as she looked all understanding about "my problems" while digging the knife in at every opportunity. I'm working on the Andy Warhol story this week. It's a shame he's died. I remember Kendra's parents had a couple of Warhols. It would have been good to go and have a chat with them, but I don't suppose that's a possibility now.'

'Probably not,' Annie confirmed.

'I really want to see her soon, I need to make amends. It's important to me.'

'But it's still too soon for Gioia, Sal.' That was an odd thing to say: 'make amends'. It was probably more AA speak. 'They lost their jobs, remember. Let Ken get herself together out there. I miss her too. But if she wanted to hear from us she would have let us know. Sometimes I think that last year was at least a decade ago.'

'How are you, anyway? I know it's not as if you can ever get over something as awful as losing the baby, but are you feeling any better?' Sal looked around for a waitress. 'I've become totally addicted to coffee. Coffee with a mountain of sugar.'

'You don't look any fatter . . . I guess the sugar replaces the alcohol.' Annie watched Sal pour two paper packetfuls into the cup when it arrived. 'I've come out of that depression, thank God. I don't ever want to feel like that again, but everything's changed. I just don't know what I want. It all used to be clear, but now I wonder. Do I want a baby right now? Can I face the risk of losing another one?' She shrugged. 'Charlie's keen. He keeps saying that I should think of working part time, and really going for it. He's always half blamed work for the miscarriage. But I've got lots of time, and work's going well.'

She'd been hesitant about bringing up Charlie. Sal had known her long enough to see that her picket-fence dream had not turned out to be what she'd hoped, but she didn't want to start on that topic. It wasn't Charlie's fault that things weren't going well. It was hers. She just didn't love him at the moment. She wasn't even sure if she had ever loved him. But then, people change. It was only fairy tales where you loved someone for ever with no problems. Where once Charlie's capability and sense of control and order had made her feel comfortable and safe, now they grated. Where once she had loved the way that he was besotted with her sexually and had enjoyed playing up to that role, now she often felt as if she was playing a part that didn't fit.

Work, on the other hand, was the thing that made her feel most like the person she was now, and it was where she was most comfortable. That was something she had never expected.

18

The floor of the fish market was inches deep in water and it was soaking into Kendra's plimsolls. Even so, it was better than when she wore flip-flops and the smelly liquid seeped between her toes. She and Gioia had made the mutual decision to loosen their commitment to vegetables and to eat fish once they reached the Algarve, enjoying the sardines tasted straight from the roadside grills or tearing the shells off giant prawns and dipping them into the garlicky mayonnaise. Kendra's favourite was the *bacalhau* and chips at the shacks in the dunes where the wind from the sea whistled around and the sun was hot on your face.

She decided on red mullet. Gioia was the better cook, which wasn't surprising since, before they'd lived together, Kendra had rarely attempted anything other than her veggie stews. But the move abroad had inspired her to cultivate a new skill. After all, Gioia had learnt to swim. She smiled, remembering those early lessons in the municipal pool down the coast with Gioia's noisy shrieks.

'I'm going to bloody drown. I'm getting out of here right now!' she would scream, as she pushed herself to complete a width. Since her wailing was in English, the local children couldn't understand the words, but it would have been hard not to get the general impression that she wasn't enjoying learning breaststroke. Now, though, only five months later, she was much more confident and, as the weather had begun to warm, she had started to swim some distance into the ocean.

By the time she arrived back at the flat Gioia was crouched in the concrete yard, where they had placed pots of vivid geraniums and were hoping that the bougainvillea would eventually climb the white wall. They'd arrived in late autumn but, even then, the sharp light that came off the Atlantic had encouraged them to adorn the yard, and the mild winter had allowed much of their planting to flourish.

'I got mullet in the end. Are there still some tomatoes?' Kendra, addressing Gioia's bent figure, was met only by an acquiescent nod. As she wedged the fish into the small, unreliable fridge, she tried to decide what would be the best moment to bring up the suggestion which increasingly scurried around her thoughts.

She had loved the calm of these recent months. They had been such a contrast to the terrible weeks before they left. As she predicted, Gioia had retreated into an impenetrable shell of her own fury and condemnation and would brook no discussion of what had happened. Her bitterness at the world in general, a world in which Charlie and Annie encapsulated the status quo, was obsessive. Her rage at Sal was so entrenched that Kendra had given up explaining that Sal was now in a course of rehab as a direct result of that piece in the paper. It didn't make any difference whatever she said.

Losing the Chapel, although inevitable, was agonizing for both of them. At first, Gioia had attempted to fight, arguing that she should be given the opportunity to clear her name, but it soon became obvious that the combination of the local council's desire to remove her (a fact which she had managed to ignore for some time previously) and the Charterhouse move on the property was going to make it impossible for her to stay. She had stopped talking to Kendra almost entirely – only speaking when absolutely necessary and so relegating her girlfriend, in this time of crisis, to somebody on the other side of the battle. After several weeks of this treatment Kendra had reached the point of phoning Art to broach the subject of moving back home. It was utterly miserable to have Gioia so present but so far from her, when they had always been so close. But then, one morning as they lay waiting for the sky to lighten with even the slightest evidence that it was now day, Gioia moved up and stretched her arms out to draw Kendra towards her warm body and announced, 'Get packed, girl. We're moving. I've had it here, but I know I still want to be with you. It's been a process, but I've got there. If they don't want me, I don't want them. I feel sorry for the kids of course, but I've – we've – got a life to get on with, and I can't be doing with clinging on here till somebody chops my hands off and I just fall. Let's get out of this shit-hole and head for the sun. You've got some cash in that account of yours – I knew it would come in handy. Just us.' Kendra could only agree.

Once they had arrived, their life together started anew. It wasn't just their prowess in cooking and swimming, the balance of their relationship had shifted, allowing Kendra to become a more equal partner and Gioia to admit occasionally to uncertainty. In London, Kendra had drifted along in her wake but, here, she found herself taking the initiative just as often as Gioia.

After unpacking the shopping, Kendra sat on their bed and once again read Sal's letter, which she had collected the previous week from the nearby poste restante:

I realize that this may be impossible for you to understand, but I have learnt so much in treatment. I miss you a lot and I really, really want to make amends for what happened, to both you and Gioia. I'd love to come and see you there – it would be fun and you'll be amazed by how I'm managing without the booze. Annie says I'm still Calamity Jane, but at least I'm sober. I don't know if you've heard from her, but I think things are bad with her and Charlie and I know she'd love to come too. Please think about it. Write soon x

She returned the letter to the drawer and went to the yard to suggest a trip to the sea.

'It's warm today. I thought I'd head to the beach. Coming?'

In a few minutes, after Gioia had grabbed a few oranges and a bottle of water and flung them into their plastic string bag, they climbed on to the moped, stuttering out on to the wide road. Eventually they turned off, on to increasingly rough and small tracks, taking a left where the wooden sign directed *Playa*. At the edge of the beach there were other mopeds parked, alongside an old Lada which looked unlikely to make the journey home.

When they reached their favourite spot, Kendra was reminded of their evening on another sandy beach, in Suffolk. 'Do you remember?' she said. 'It was when you first mentioned the idea of leaving, the first time I ever heard you say it. And when I discovered you couldn't swim.'

Gioia was nestling into a comfortable position on her thin mat laid out in the sand, her head resting on a cushion. 'Thing is, people say we don't know what's going to happen, but I reckon there's a part of us that can predict things. You have to know how to tap into it, how to get the access.'

The notion seemed possible to Kendra. She'd once read a book about how you could find out what you'd do in your life if you just recognized the signs as you went along – intuitive pathways, they called it. She still had that book, somewhere at home. She wondered where home was now. Wasn't home meant to be here? Art had written that Marisa felt strange about having Christmas in London without Kendra and they would be going to the States. She hadn't really expected that. She'd always thought that Christmas was simply the way Marisa had decided it would be. It had never occurred to her that the shape of that day had anything to do with her. It made her feel bad about leaving, especially after her parents had been surprisingly helpful when Gioia was thrown out of the Chapel.

Even Marisa hadn't uttered a word of criticism, or a satisfied 'I told you no good would come of it.' Art had tentatively mentioned that he'd thought of someone Gioia could talk to about work – a concert promoter. Fat chance of that. Not the job, but Gioia meeting the guy. Too proud.

She looked over at Gioia sprawled on the sand only inches away, so comfortable in her body. She never adjusted herself, the way most women did on the beach, bending a knee in an attempt at making their legs look thinner, or forever fiddling with their costumes so that everything was covered.

'I know this is going to sound like a bad idea, but' – Kendra took a breath, pleased that Gioia's eyes were closed – 'I'm going to put it to you. I don't miss London. I love being here with you. But last week when I picked up the post I got this letter from Sal. It's the first time I've heard from her since the rehab, and she suggested that she and Annie come and visit us. I really miss them, you know. I didn't think I would. I've surprised myself. Maybe it's because I want to get to a place where we can all move away from the past and, to do that, I need to see them.' She watched Gioia to gauge her reaction, waiting for the objections, possibly the straight-out refusal. 'You know it's not to do with how I feel about you. It's how I feel about them.'

'What?' Gioia sprang up to a kneeling position. 'Am I hearing what I think I'm hearing?' She spat on the ground. 'You want to bring that headcase out here?'

'It wouldn't be for long. Sal's cleaned up, and she's totally AA. Annie's having a difficult time with Charlie, you'll be pleased to hear. You have to understand what they mean to me.' Gioia began to walk towards the sea. Kendra wondered whether to leave her to it and then decided against it, knowing that Gioia would want her to run after her.

'I know how you feel about Annie too. But, believe me, I think she was so fixated on the baby that she didn't register what was going on. Sounds like she's realized she's made a mistake now.'

'Yeah . . . yeah. You've told me all this before. Remember, I never wanted to go near that Sal and her . . . journalism.'

'You'd be the first person to say that everyone deserves a second chance . . .' Kendra put her arm around the taller woman. 'Leave it. We don't need to decide now.' Sensing she might have made a break-through with the second-chance suggestion, she knew it wasn't a good idea to push it. She'd learnt that it was always better if she let Gioia feel that she'd made a decision entirely on her own terms.

Later that afternoon, Gioia had taken the moped into town, leaving Kendra alone in the apartment. Bundles of photographs tied with string lay around her: faded colour snaps with dried-out photo corners still on them; larger, black and white pictures she had pains-takingly printed herself. They appeared so old – her history. Seated cross-legged on the floor, she looked at the one of the three of them that afternoon on the downs. She remembered Sal mocking the soppiness of John Lennon's 'Woman' as if it were only a few days back, but there was also the spread of time, filled with the things they hadn't known would happen to each of them, that made it seem very long ago. She opened another bundle, picking up even older pictures of Marisa and Art. There was one of them all on a holiday in Tuscany at a long table, Kendra with her childish arms around the two of them, Marisa's hair in rat's tails over her shoulder, looking a little the way Kendra's did when she came out of the sea.

She had resisted opening the box of photographs until now – it was part of her strategy to make Portugal about the future. But from time to time she felt unanchored. It was one thing escaping but, when you had nothing familiar to latch on to, it wasn't always easy to remember what you were running away from and what you wanted to find. She had caved in that afternoon and pulled the box out from under the bed. It wasn't so much that the pictures were the past, she realized, but that they were her life. How could she have a future if she couldn't handle what she already had?

'There she is.' Sal waved at Kendra, who was waiting among the crowd of travel reps and relatives clustered outside the door of Arrivals watching each new person emerge.

'Look, she's cut her hair.' Kendra was at the furthest end of the line, her thick curls in a new wavy cap. She had lost weight too, demonstrated by her white shorts and tight T-shirt. She would never have exposed her legs like that before, even though both Sal and Annie were forever telling her that if they'd got legs that long they would show them off.

Kendra didn't know which of the two to embrace first, which led to a clumsy tangle of greeting. Sal slid away, looked Kendra directly in the eye and spoke.

'I'm so pleased to be here. You look fantastic. Check out Annie's luggage. You'd think we were moving out here, rather than staying for just a week.' Sal gestured at her friend's large green leather case and then at her own small black one.

'I can't believe you're both here.' Kendra steered them towards the glass doors separating the new arrivals from the bright, clear light of the Algarve. 'Let's go. I'm on the moped, but I can show you where the bus is and it'll drop you only a minute from where I've booked you a room.'

'Actually, I've hired a car. It just seemed easier.' Annie wasn't sure why, but she felt uncomfortable announcing this extravagance. 'What with all of us needing to get around, I thought it would make sense. And it means that Sal and I can split and do some touristy stuff too.'

'Fine. You'd better follow me then. It's a pretty straight road out from here. What is it? Avis? Hertz?'

The black Fiat Uno easily followed Kendra's moped along the broad road that tracked the coastline and occasionally offered a glimpse of the sea. All along its length grey concrete skeletons sat waiting to become seaside apartments. It wasn't particularly beautiful, Annie thought, squinting slightly with the unfamiliar glare from the sun. She wondered why they'd chosen this place.

'Wish I could share the driving with you.' Sal rolled down her window and started to search for a cigarette. 'Now I'm getting the flat, I'll never be able to afford a car, so what's the point of learning? I suppose it must say something about me that I'm committing to a mortgage. Christ, it's baking . . .' The car had still not managed to cool down from having sat in the sun in the parking lot they had collected it from. 'It's good to be here, isn't it? Seeing Ken. She didn't mention Gioia, though. When do you think we'll meet?'

'Gioia's got this gig teaching English, so we've got the afternoon alone,' Kendra explained as Annie drove them all to the beach a couple of hours later. 'It was one of the reasons we chose this place – there's a bit of work around. And it's hot. Gioia really wanted to just melt.'

'I wouldn't put it quite as strongly as being terrified, but can I say I'm pretty nervous about seeing her?' Sal piped up from the back of the car.

'She'll be fine. Relax.' Kendra didn't sound particularly convincing, even to herself. She hoped that, when they finally did meet up, Gioia wouldn't be defensive. Equally, she couldn't rely on Sal not to blow it. Her coltish enthusiasm so easily annoyed Gioia. 'By the way, the sun's misleading, because we're on the Atlantic and you get this fresh wind. You don't realize its strength so you have to watch it.'

Annie had already bought a large straw hat from a roadside vendor which shaded her bare shoulders. They walked along the slatted path towards a hut that was perched above the water. Below it, large waves gathered momentum and then slowed as they reached the sand, like a toddler's tantrum running out of steam.

'Try the coffee,' Kendra suggested as she found them a table. 'It's very milky. Completely different to the London stuff.' It was strange not to hear Sal say that she was gagging for a beer. She had always been relied upon to say that. You didn't even have to put the coin into the machine. Her friend had definitely altered, as if a layer had been peeled from her.

'I bought this for you.' Sal pulled an object from her bag. 'It's meant to be an old Inca game – Perudo. I can teach you how to play it later.' She handed over the long box in its fabric bag.

'Thanks. Gioia loves games. We both do. We've been playing a lot of cards. There's not much to do here at night, but there's a poker game in a bar in the next village which Gioia's in on. She thinks she's better than she is, but what gambler doesn't? If she wins, she comes home and wakes me up waving wads of cash. If she loses, we just don't talk about it.' Kendra laughed. 'I'm no gambler.' Of course, they knew that. They'd known her for ever.

'I went to a Tarot reader a few weeks ago.' Annie produced this information in the knowledge that her friends would be surprised. If any one of the three of them would go to a Tarot reader, it would be Kendra. 'Lee told me about this woman in south London who would know about the weirdest things. So we went together one evening. Funny, really. The room didn't look at all like I'd imagined, though. I guess I'd pictured it would be a bit more Mystic Meg, all embroidered shawls and candles. This place was pretty minimal.'

'And? Enough about the interiors . . . what happened?' Sal interrupted.

'I suppose I went because of the baby. I didn't particularly want to hear whether I was going to get pregnant again or anything but . . .' Annie stroked the length of her neck, with fingernails, Kendra noticed, painted a professional pale pink '. . . she did know some things. She said I'd been through a trauma. That, and there was a card that indicated some kind of shift, though she couldn't tell me what. Then she waffled on about challenges and how a man close to me was telling me something. I was pleased that Lee was there because, to be honest, I found the whole thing creepy and wished we hadn't gone.'

'Gioia's done it, but I think it's pointless.' Kendra was moving the red- and blue-topped salt and pepper containers around the table in a jig. 'After all, the future is the future, isn't it? I don't get the point of seeing what's going to happen if you can't change it. And that's what fate is, really. Things happen that happen.'

'Hmm, sort of. But . . . well, you can think differently about it,' Sal intervened with confidence. 'Like acknowledging that something else is in control, that it's not all up to you and chance. It kind of makes sense.' Her friends looked at each other, waiting for more on this line of thought. They knew enough about AA to recognize its stamp on Sal's views. It wasn't the kind of thing she would ever have said, or thought, before.

As she spoke, Sal was remembering a night, in previous times, when Pete had dealt the Tarot cards, delivering a reading that was highly memorable in its dramatic announcements. She hadn't seen him in months. She missed him. And God knows she missed the sex, but she couldn't hang out with him now. It wouldn't work when she was clean. It would be too high risk, and she wasn't even sure that Pete would want to be with her with her new persona. They had never thought that they were going to stay together. It had been kind of one day at a time, which was ironic when that was the way they kept telling her to think at the clinic. One day at a time.

'Am I the only one longing for that sea?' Sal changed the subject and walked over to watch a group of boys playing volleyball on the beach below.

'It's never warm, this water, but you feel great when you get out,' Kendra yelled as they reached the waves, chasing Sal towards them. Annie only managed a minute or so before fleeing back to the warmth of the sand, then looking out at the two friends bobbing around. She closed her eyes, letting the heat soften her goosebumps and feeling the water dry on her skin. She was nearly asleep when she heard the chatter of them returning.

'Brilliant.' Sal towelled off the water from her hair. 'I'm just so . . . so pleased to be here. With you two.' Again, the others heard a new voice from Sal. She had never been the one for emotional stuff but, now, it was as if she wanted them to share everything she was thinking. And to agree with it.

'You know, Ken – I have to say it. I couldn't say so at the time because you were furious. And I was a total mess. I know it was all my fault. What happened. I know that now. I also know it's going to take time for Gioia to forgive me. If she ever does. But it's important to acknowledge our mistakes.'

'OK. Thanks. But let's lighten up here.' Kendra flung herself down on a towel and ran her fingers across her bare belly, which was already slightly tanned. She wasn't prepared for such self-exposure from Sal and, although she had always considered herself the most emotionally understanding of the three, even she didn't feel comfortable with this kind of talk.

The arrangement was to rendezvous at Santos, where, Kendra assured them, they would eat the best sardines in the Algarve. Ugly fluorescent lighting, only slightly mitigated by the candles stuck in

Mateus Rosé bottles on each table, dominated the restaurant, and the room was empty when they arrived. It did not inspire confidence, until a boy showed them into a courtyard at the back where Gioia and Kendra were seated in a far corner, away from two long noisy tables. A pergola covered the majority of the yard, already, even though it was only April, supporting large leaves and thick-stemmed climbers.

Annie had taken trouble to dress for the occasion. It was important to her that she looked like the kind of person she imagined Gioia would feel comfortable with, although she realized that such an idea exposed her as the shallow character she knew Gioia thought she was. But, even so, it mattered to her – she couldn't help it. She had been torn between a panelled black linen skirt that floated just above her ankles and a pair of loose white Nicole Farhi trousers which didn't appear particularly expensive but managed not to look ungainly. It was a pity she'd got rid of so many of her second-hand dresses. They would have been perfect with their colours and patterns. When she got back, she decided she was going to buy some more, even if Charlie didn't like them. She decided on the trousers and a pale sea-green Ghost shirt with small buttons that fitted into hoops of the fabric all the way down the front.

'It's a bit like walking into the saloon bar in a Western and not knowing if it's going to turn nasty,' Sal muttered as they walked towards the couple, who showed no awareness, until the last moment, of their arrival. Kendra jumped up and came round to kiss them, while Gioia remained seated, holding the palm of her hand up in more of a benediction than a greeting. Kendra suggested that Annie sit next to Gioia, with Sal opposite Annie, and, for the first minutes, her chatter gave away her own anxiety about the meeting.

'So. You have to have the sardines, like I said, and we'll get some *vinho verde*, which is the local white – a bit fizzy,' Kendra pronounced, taking control in a way neither Sal nor Annie remembered of her. 'Gioia was just saying that you should take a look at the

Mouth of Hell if you get time, which is the furthest point of the mainland before the ocean.' Both the others found themselves smiling at Gioia with exaggerated pleasure at this suggestion.

Initially, Gioia let the friends' chat flutter around her, not reacting at all, until Annie said something about how happy Kendra looked, and her mask broke into a smile.

From that point on, nobody could have suggested that the conversation rattled along, but each of them around the table did their best to place tentative conversational bandages over the areas where they considered another wounded, apart from Gioia, who, appearing to feel that she had made her peace offering, was now seated monumentally, receiving homage graciously but also as if it were her due.

A fly fizzed noisily on the electric fly killer above the table as Sal offered her apology, over the huge sardines, which dwarfed anything of that description in London.

'I don't know if you know, Gioia, but I'm on the programme now. It's made me understand how important it is – and not just for me but for other people – to make amends for the things I've done that have hurt people.' She started to pick at the dribbles of wax on the wine bottle. 'I know none of us want to go over everything, but I've got to say I'm so sorry for the pain I've caused you and, of course, Ken. And while I'm at it, I might as well say it to you too, Annie, because I know it was hurtful to Charlie too.'

Annie kicked Kendra under the table, mouthing 'AA', but she also wished that Sal hadn't brought up Charlie's name. He was an intruder at this table and, although it was behind them, it was of course partially his operation that had driven Kendra and Gioia out.

'I don't know much about that stuff, but let's say the past's the past,' Gioia declared, pausing to give her verdict the necessary weight. 'We have to move on. Me and Ken have. We're starting over, good and proper.' Annie looked at Kendra, who was seated opposite her. Was that what she wanted? She wasn't quite sure. Gioia reached out for the last piece of bread in the basket to wipe over the garlicky detritus of her plate. 'Now, let's get coffee down the road.'

It was a short distance to the local harbour once they had finished the meal. There, large boats were moored at the quay, alongside smaller ones which lay on the ground with their hulls in the air like babies positioned on their stomachs for the night. It was cooler by far than in daytime, and the masts rattled noisily in the dark as they strolled past before agreeing on an early turn-in.

'Tomorrow, though, I'm going to hammer you at poker,' Gioia offered as she and Kendra walked them home. 'No mercy.'

Sal took that as forgiveness.

The next few days slipped past. Annie was unable to resist buying three huge platters with small oranges painted on them and had wanted to spend hours in the roadside pottery, much to the boredom of Sal, who had confined herself to a single coffee cup and saucer.

'I know Charlie's going to hate these, but too bad,' Annie said as they drove away. 'He can't stand this kind of stuff, but I'm going to start getting my own things again.'

'Tomorrow, Gioia's free all day, so we decided we'd take you to this great beach we know further down the coast. We'll take a picnic – it's spectacular there.'

They pulled into the fish stall to buy that evening's barbecue. 'I can't bear it. We're halfway through our stay already. I really don't want to go back,' said Annie. Watching Kendra examine the catches of the previous night, she realized that what she had said was really true. It was becoming clearer that, by returning to Charlie, she would be going back to somewhere she didn't want to be.

'I'll tell you something,' Kendra replied once she had been handed the bag of fillets. 'Gioia's right. Up to a point. We've made a new start over here. But, when you do that, you bring yourselves with you. It's not really possible to get away from everything.'

'On the programme, we call it doing a geographical.' Sal bobbed up.

Kendra realized that Sal probably had to buy into the whole thing lock, stock and barrel, but surely it wasn't necessary to talk

AA jargon all the time? They all had lives to live, and not everything had to be put into a twelve-step context. It was irritating, all this 'One day at a time', 'Keep it simple' – it wasn't as if these were new ideas. 'I mean, don't get me wrong,' she continued, ignoring Sal's interruption, 'I love it here, but I'm finding – weird as this must sound – that I kind of miss my folks. I know . . . I know . . . I did everything I could to get as far away from them as possible. But now they're not in my face, I can see them more clearly. I don't want to live with them, but I'm not 100 per cent about being this cut off. It's not the distance I'm talking about – after all, the Algarve is hardly the Falkland Islands. No. It's more psychological. I think Gioia's enjoying the desperado thing more than me. It's like we're on the run, in some ways. Having you both here has made me realize that, I guess.'

They strolled to the little café where the chequered tablecloths were clipped against the wind and plates of buns sat under glass covered with grains of sugar large as sea salt.

'Will you come back?' Sal asked.

'Don't know. It's difficult. I'm not going to think about it right now. I will. But not today. Nor tomorrow. Probably.'

When Sal opened the dark wooden shutters the next morning, the sky revealed was not its usual blue. She had suspected as much as she lay on her bed looking at where the join in the warped wood had allowed a chink of light. On other days, it would be sharp, but not today. Since she'd stopped drinking, she'd been waking early. In the past, she didn't remember ever being awake before Annie, unless she'd set at least two alarms and, even then, when they lived together, her flatmate would often have to come in and shake her.

'What's the time?' A groggy voice emerged from the other bed.

'Nearly nine, but the weather looks like it's turned. It's not sunny. I wonder if that means we'll scrap the picnic.'

'The cloud will probably burn off.' Annie sat up. A pale-blue slip was rumpled around her and Sal could see a red patch near the crease of her underarm.

Everything looked different without the glaze of sun: the white-wash of the houses grubbier, the dusty yards revealed as the parched patches they were, saved only by the bright pots of flowers. Even the café down the road where they had made a habit of breakfasting on coffee and rolls with a slab of delicious rubbery cheese had lost a degree of its charm.

'It must be pretty gloomy here in the winter,' Annie said, looking over to where a cement mixer sat outside a half-built house. 'The Algarve is made for the sun. When you come down to it, there's not much else here. Apart from the sea.'

'I suppose, after how it was in London, this still felt good. And it's cheap. Anyway,' Sal added briskly, 'look over there – the cloud is breaking.'

There was enough brightness lurking behind the cloud for them all to agree that the picnic was still on. As they drove towards the west, the small car began to fill with the smell of cheese and an undefined fishiness.

'Bit of a pong in here.' Sal was the first to comment.

'That's Gioia's paste. It's delicious. Wait till you taste it – ancho-vies, garlic, parsley, all smashed up,' Kendra told them.

'Maybe . . .' Sal sounded unsure. 'But can you open the window, Gioia? These back ones won't budge, and I'm feeling sick.' Gioia sniffed the air as she wound down the glass.

'There's hardly any wind today. Last night there was a storm out to sea, and it's left this calm.' She stuck her nose out like a dog. 'It's muggy. Unusual.'

The beach was bordered by a dramatic cliff that rose to the left and a low promontory of rock that stretched into the sea, allowing small pools to form where it met the sand. They walked from the car in single file, following Kendra.

'Most families don't come this far down, as it's not near the huts,' she shouted back over her shoulder. 'And they don't like it with kids because of the rocks.'

Annie and Sal were grateful to have finally arrived where they were going to settle, laden as they were with food, blankets, baskets of towels. Despite the grey sky, the sand was already warm. Gioia walked towards the rocks, where she floated a bottle of wine and cans of beer in a natural pool.

'Can you see out there? How the water has those dark streaks in it today? Normally, you don't get those colours,' Kendra pointed out as she sat hugging her knees against her chin under a sweatshirt. 'And it's much flatter than usual. I don't think I've seen it like this before.' She watched Gioia, who had removed the cotton trousers she had been wearing, walk into the sea, her cuff of silver ankle bracelets clearly defined against her skin.

'It's fantastic the way she swims. It's meant to be harder to learn as you get older, but she's done really well.'

The others watched Gioia as she reached waist high in the water before launching herself in, swimming only a short distance before turning back towards them and then turning around again, in a childlike display.

'She looks pretty strong already.' Annie was rubbing suntan cream on to her shoulders, peering at the red under her arm. 'It's probably just as well for me it's not so hot today. I'm starting to peel.'

By the time they began to unpack the picnic, everybody had been in the water, returning with their own story of its chill. It was just like old times, thought Sal, Annie all in a dither about whether to leave the bread in one piece or slice it. She looked in a bag to find the hard-boiled eggs and a little twist of silver foil.

'Salt?' she asked Kendra. 'All mod cons today.' Sitting cross-legged, she cracked the egg, picking off the shell as Gioia spread her paste on chunks of bread and handed them out. Refusal was clearly not an option.

'Portugal joined the EC last year, didn't it?' Sal asked, munching enthusiastically on the offering. 'And Spain, I think, too? Has that changed things here?'

'Most of the guys I speak to seem to think it will. But it's a waiting game. They were told it would make them richer,' Gioia replied. 'I don't think they know a blind bit about what it means, but this is a piss-poor country. You just have to look. And they reckon they'll attract more cash if they're in with the others. 'Course we don't really know whether prices have changed, or what's happened with other things, do we, Ken?'

'It'll probably be easier to tell when the tourist season kicks in properly. It's still so cheap compared to London. That's how we can live here, at least for now.'

After the picnic was finished, Annie moved away from the others. She had brought her watercolours with her and was experimenting with the effect of using water from the rockpool to give her paintings an initial colour wash. The previous days she had worked with a pure blue but, today, with the different light, she was mixing in Payne's Grey and some Sap Green. This afternoon there was a completely different look to the sea. Those dark streaks in the water just off the rocks and close to the shore were quite dramatic. To the left she could see a tanker, the red of its hull obvious even at a great distance. It was a welcome addition to the picture. She decided not to include the beach at all, making this one just a study in sea and sky, its impact greatest where they joined.

It was peaceful. Since her depression, painting had been a help. The concentration demanded by looking at things intensely was a diversion from uncomfortable thoughts. Of course, when she was right in the middle of it, she hadn't been able to go anywhere near her paints. She hadn't seen the point. But now it was one of the things that had come back, a reminder of what she used to enjoy but had stopped doing and, although it wasn't Charlie's fault, somehow she blamed him. The shape of her life had changed and its new form didn't have the space for some things. When she got back to London, though, she would make sure it did.

Kendra came up to her, looking over her shoulder and commenting appreciatively. 'I'm going back to the car to get the bats,' she went on. 'I want a walk, and a game of beach tennis will wake us all up.' Her voice woke Gioia, who had fallen asleep near Annie. She rubbed her eyes and shook sand from the array of plaits and dread-locks that hung down her back.

'I'm going in again. That beer's done me in.'

'I'll come too,' Sal offered, walking ahead before waiting for her at the water's edge. They both stepped gingerly in, stopping after each cold step to splash the icy water on their bodies in order to acclimatize.

'At least it's sandy here. It makes getting in a bit easier, not having to balance on the stones. But Christ it's cold.' Sal considered return-ing to the beach, wishing that it was not a blue and white striped bikini she was wearing but a wetsuit. Had it got colder than before? After a few seconds, she saw Gioia fling herself in, her schoolgirl breaststroke taking her to the area of darker water on the left. She looked away, in the opposite direction, to where the beach was more populated. People were paddling on the edges, playing games on the sand. Now she was warming up, she thought she might try and swim out so that she could see what was on the other side of the rocks.

Annie had watched the two walk towards the sea, laughing to herself about the contrast between them – little and large. Little? Even though Sal was small, somehow 'little' was never a word any-one would use about her. She could see that Gioia was splitting off in one direction, while Sal had the determined movements of some-one embarking on a proper swim rather than a paddle. Now that the sun had broken through, it was hard to use watercolour, as the paint dried so quickly. She tipped the dirty water out of a plastic mug, fascinated by the ants that emerged from the sand and scur-ried from where it sank in. What was it they said about ants? How there were billions of them and they were going to take over the world one day? That must have been something Kendra had told her.

She saw Gioia wave and waved back automatically, even though the swimmer wouldn't be able to see her as she was facing out to sea. Then Gioia's arm rose up again. That was odd. Why did she keep waving? At the same time, she saw Sal – she was pretty sure it was Sal, although it was hard to be certain in this light – turning towards Gioia. But where was Gioia now? She wasn't where she had been only moments before. Annie stood up sharply, tugging at her bikini bottom as she walked quickly towards the water's edge. Now Sal was waving too. She started to run.

Sal could see Gioia was struggling as soon as she turned towards her to check out where she was going. The more Gioia tried to swim, the more she seemed to be stuck. She'd occasionally disappear under the swell only to emerge, but she clearly was not in control. Sal immediately struck out to help, but there was a different, stronger pull of the water the nearer she came to Gioia, and her powerful crawl became more futile as she started to feel the drag from underneath. She was being pulled in different directions and it was almost impossible to get anywhere. But she focused on the splash around Gioia – not that far from her now but, all the same, in these conditions, too far. She was desperate to reach her but she simply wasn't fast enough. It was like a dream where you can't move, no matter how hard you try. She remembered what she had heard about currents. Rip tides, that was it. She had to stop battling to swim towards the beach and start swimming parallel to the shore. That was the way you dealt with them. They'd never make it if they kept heading for the beach. She finally reached Gioia, hooked her arms around her and dragged her like a bag of coals, unwieldy, unhelpful. All her instincts made her want to turn towards the land. Gioia was an incredible weight, and she wasn't moving. Sal couldn't keep this up for much longer. It would be so lovely just to stop. So much easier. Her legs were being pulled by the strong undertow. She was going to have to let go of Gioia if she was to stand any chance herself. Then she was sunk under a large wave that washed over them, filling her mouth with water, and her nose. It was impossible to keep hanging on.

If the boat had arrived a minute later, Gioia would tell anybody who might be listening, 'It would have been curtains. Total curtains.

'Course I would have been a goner ages back, if it hadn't been for Sal.'

The boat – a tiny motorized dinghy – had been commandeered from further along the beach by Kendra. Returning from the car, she had been tempted to go for a short stroll but, without her flip-flops, the hot sand was hard work. Turning back to where they had picnicked, she looked towards the rocks to see if Sal and Gioia were still in the sea. She hadn't been sure, but she thought that a figure to the far left might be Gioia. It was almost impossible to tell, but whoever it was was waving. It would be strange if it was Gioia, as she never normally swam out that far. She wasn't that confident yet. Maybe Sal had encouraged her. It would be good if they were bonding in the water. But then she realized that that wasn't what was happening. She ran. 'Not waving but drowning' – it was a cliché, but the words were insistent, drumming through her as she bolted down the beach towards two boys who were pushing their boat from the shallows on to the sand.

'I need you!' she screamed. 'I need that boat. We have to go out. My friend's in trouble.' Although the boys could not understand English, they grasped the urgency of the message as she crashed into the water, grabbing the boat herself, and gestured crazily in the direction of the figure she thought was Gioia. The dinghy bounced out, Kendra urging them to go faster, faster, and as they got closer it was obvious that she had been right. On the surface the sea looked unusually flat compared to the usual crashing waves, but Kendra could tell from the boys' faces as they got nearer to where Sal was trying to drag Gioia towards the rocks that they were frightened too. It was taking for ever to get there. Jesus, now Annie was in the water as well, swimming out in the direction of Sal and Gioia. She shrieked, 'Go back! Go back! The tide. *Don't swim there!*'

Annie appeared to have got Kendra's screamed message and stopped where she stood, waist high in the sea.

This couldn't be happening, Kendra thought briefly. It couldn't be. It happened to other people, hapless people that you read about in the paper. Drowning wasn't what happened to people you knew. Her hair kept blowing in front of her eyes as she tried to focus on the figures in the water ahead. As they drew up beside them, the smallness of the dinghy made the business of leaning over to try to grab them both precarious and slow. Gioia first, eventually hauled over the sides like a porpoise by all three of them, then Sal. They were all piled on top of each other, Gioia motionless and Sal gasping and spluttering, as the boat headed back to the beach, where the shore was now lined with observers. The ball games ceased, parents hugged their children to them and the shallows were completely empty as everyone stood to watch the drama. Kendra leant over her girlfriend, her lips on Gioia's unresponsive mouth, in the most important kiss of her life.

'She would have died without you, Sal.' Kendra poured out small glasses of syrupy Portuguese sherry to compensate for the lack of warmth of the basic furnishings and plastic blinds of the flat. 'I suppose I'd better not offer you this, but nobody could say you don't deserve a drink. The doctor in the hospital said we got to her just in time.' If she started to cry now, she might not stop.

She craved somewhere comfortable, a deep bath even. She hadn't had a bath since the day they arrived. How good would it feel to soak and then emerge to a big soft towel instead of standing under the trickle from their shower next to the sticky shower curtain? It was trivial, after what had happened, but that was what she really wanted. Annie was hugging her knees under a huge sweater while Sal sat with Kendra at a fold-up table, the wooden slats more suited to a garden than inside.

'Well, she's all right now,' Sal replied. 'I don't think I've ever been so terrified as when I realized what was happening. Thank God I remembered about the tides. The Algarve's renowned for them, rip tides. They occur at different times of year. They should have warnings. It's ridiculous not to, on a public beach like that.'

'They probably do on the bigger beaches round the main tourist parts – nearer Albufeira maybe – but we were at more of a locals' hang-out. It's still unsupervised. Of course, thinking back, maybe everyone knew the water might be dangerous. Nobody was swimming out further down the beach – they were just paddling around in the shallows. Fucking lethal. Literally.' Kendra rubbed her eyes. 'That was one freaky experience. Gioia might have died. It's only just sinking in.'

'If we hadn't been here, you probably wouldn't have gone for that picnic, would you?' asked Annie, as she sipped the sherry, its treacly texture almost medicinal.

'Who knows?' Kendra asked. 'What does it matter? Maybe.'

'I'm just thinking about it. That's all. No reason. Gioia will be out of hospital tomorrow, won't she, Ken?'

'So they say. Imagine if it had happened without you two here. I'd be having to deal with tonight alone, and all the what-ifs that keep going around in my head. It makes me think how vulnerable I am with no one other than Gioia here.' Kendra considered her surroundings, the table more suited to the garden, the chairs tinny and uncomfortable. It wasn't really like a home, more like a campsite. Perhaps that's what she and Gioia were doing after all. Camping.

'Well, we *are* here, and Gioia's going to be fine. I know she is,' said Annie. 'Things like this make you think, don't they? About everything. Even before today I've been trying to work out Charlie and me. When you get away from the day to day, you see things differently. It's easy on holiday to think you want to change your life, but this is more than that. Charlie and me haven't been right for ages now. I don't need some spooky Tarot reader, I can see the future all by myself. Something's got to give. I hate to hear myself say this to you, before saying it to him. It feels so disloyal – he is my husband – but events like today . . . I know it's a cliché . . . but it makes you realize how precarious life is and how you have to get it right. Maybe I'll change my mind again tomorrow, but I think I have to leave him.'

Both Sal and Kendra were silenced by Annie's admission of the failure of her marriage. It was the first time she'd said it. Neither thought it would be helpful to agree. Experience had shown them all that, when it came to the question of friends' lovers, it was always a better idea to wait and see what happened before jumping in and saying that you'd never liked them anyway.

'And it's not like we've got kids or anything to keep us together.' Annie's laugh was more of a snort. 'I guess Tania was right when she said "Everybody's got to get a first marriage under their belt" when I told her I was getting married. It sounded horribly unromantic at the time.'

'Do you really think you'll leave him?' Sal probed. She'd been warned against making hasty decisions when she came out of rehab, but she supposed this was not exactly hasty and, of course, it wasn't Annie who had been in rehab. It had probably been a long time coming. 'Are you sure it's not just a holiday thing?'

'I've changed since I met Charlie. Before, I thought having a husband would make me happy. Now I've got one I realize it doesn't work like that. Or it hasn't in my case. They're not a solution, and I feel foolish having thought that way. You can't expect a husband to make things right for you, and poor Charlie is just making things wrong. I suppose that means I don't love him.' There didn't seem to be much to add.

'Christ, this is getting heavy. Gioia nearly drowns and now you're about to leave your husband.' Sal jumped up. 'Any chance of dinner? Some of us can't rely on the booze to lighten the mood.' Kendra didn't speak as she cleared the glasses and screwed the cork back into the bottle.

19

Kendra pulled cutlery from the drawer disguised in the marble counter in her parents' kitchen, laying knives and forks on a tray to carry into the dining room next door. She'd always craved a kitchen table as a child, somewhere she could sit and have tea and do homework, but Marisa and Art had favoured the counter, with its high stools and view into the garden.

'Can you let them in?' she shouted to Gioia at the sound of the doorbell. The rhythm of Gioia's tread, now so familiar, sounded on the stone floor of the house. Kendra knew exactly how long it would take her to walk from the snug to the door. First Sal and then Annie came into the kitchen, followed by the cold air that descended with the arrival of December.

'Wow,' Sal said, her boots scattering dirt from the pavement on to the clean kitchen floor. 'It's weird you being here, isn't it?'

'It's good timing. They went to Dad's brother for Thanksgiving, so we've got the place to ourselves.'

Sal flicked through a copy of the Bruno Bettelheim paperback Kendra had left on the counter, commenting on her obvious note-taking on the pages. 'So you've already started on the reading list.'

'Sort of. It's going to take ages to qualify, but I'll be able to do a bit of initial counselling work with children after a year.'

Sal flicked her cigarette ash into the steel sink. 'You could fit my whole flat into this room.' Nobody could dispute Sal's statement.

'But that flat's yours.' Annie had perched herself on one of the stools after removing her long coat. 'And that's what counts.'

'Who would have thought it – me, a fully signed-up member of the property-owning class? And even getting a thrill from buying a set of saucepans. Tragic really.' Taking on the mortgage was the first time Sal had committed to any form of long-term planning, but she had surprised herself with the discovery that, having spent her whole life trying to escape her Cheltenham childhood, she now wanted to create a home of her own. The oddest things gave her satisfaction. She had got a kick the first time she had seen a utility bill in her own name. And she liked the fact that, tiny as the basement flat was, it was new, streamlined, functional, a fresh canvas. It was easier for her to live somewhere without any resemblance to the flats she had hung out in before, in her nocturnal existence. No rooms permanently curtained against potential daylight, no strangers around coffee tables strewn with silver foil and whiskey bottles when dawn broke, no more front-door intercoms that buzzed through the night.

'Mum and Dad were so keen to have us when I told them we were coming back, and it made sense. Just for a while. And it's only till we get ourselves sorted out.' Kendra looked at Gioia, who was removing the lids from cartons of takeaway, vaguely wondering whether Marisa would be so enthusiastic if she could see the red colouring from the curry dripping on the counter. 'We've got the top floor, and there's another bedroom up there stuffed with the furniture that Gioia had in the old flat. It pleases Mum to think she's got a commune here. She's decided to ditch the Thursday-evening parties, but now she's saying it's all about soirées – "Smaller, darling. More of a cultural exchange. Your father and I are so privileged, we feel it's incumbent on us to provide a forum and, God knows, we rattle around in this place."' Kendra mimicked Marisa's deep drawl, but the bitterness she had felt towards her mother previously was now replaced by amusement.

After Portugal, everything had changed. Gioia's accident had been the lever that had switched their direction. In the aftermath of that day, Kendra had resolved that they should return to London. Theirs had been a long holiday, but holidays had to end. That was her view, but not Gioia's, whose immediate reaction after her recovery was to entrench herself further in their Portuguese life. The accident didn't mean anything, she argued. It could have happened to anyone. Why should they leave? But Kendra was insistent, driven by the isolation she had felt so clearly, saved by the presence of Sal and Annie. It was time to confront reality.

'I'm not playing this game any more, Gioia. I know I want to go home. This' – she gestured around the apartment – 'it's been great, but it's not for real. And we need to get real. We can't be on the run for ever. We'll stay for the summer, and then I'm going back. What to do, I don't know. But I know I'm returning.'

Kendra picked up the tray and gestured to the others to follow her into a room where the only furniture was a square table, twelve chairs placed at equal distance around it.

'Maybe I should move in here too,' Annie joked, looping her hair into a knot at the nape of her neck. 'Not that I don't love it with you, Sal. Me and that sofa bed.' Kendra thought how beautiful she was now. All the old bounty had returned to her face, which had, for the past year, looked a poor imitation of its previous self. She must find it odd dossing in Sal's small flat.

'Seriously,' Annie continued, 'I've got to decide what to do. Charlie's finally agreed to give me some cash. So I can buy somewhere.'

'That doesn't seem fair. After all, you left him,' Sal said, reaching over for a poppadum.

Gioia laughed. 'You still talking about fair? Surely you've learnt that nothing's fair. Annie's lucky she can get Charlie to pay up. He's got the dosh.'

'I know it's not fair,' Annie replied. 'But that's the way it works when you get divorced – the blokes pay up. And, anyway, firstly, he earns a ton more than me and, secondly, he'll be happier, rid of the old misery guts I'd become. I don't think the money bit's bothering him. He just wants to move on. You know that's how he is. Don't worry. I've learnt my lesson. I'm not getting married again for ages. Not for at least a year.' She laughed. 'Anyway, Tania's got me working so hard I'm not going to have much time for anything. She dumped all of Lee's accounts on me when he went to Milan. I miss him. It's not so much fun without him there, but I'm going visit him soon. He says he can't wait to take me to one of the Versace parties, and he's sent me a photo of himself in one of those silk shirts with his hair dyed black. He thinks it makes him look more "authentic",' she said, her fingers mimicking quote marks.

'I need some more fags.' Sal stood up. 'I'll just run round the corner.'

'Let me go. I want some air. You can pay me later.' Annie was in the hallway before Sal had time to argue. As they heard the thud of the heavy front door, Kendra spoke, picking at the remnants of the vegetable biryani on one of the square plates that Marisa had bought to reflect the lines of the table.

'She's looking wonderful again. Normally when people leave their husbands they're meant to be traumatized, not glowing.'

'She discovered she'd made a mistake with Charlie far quicker than we realized. She's as good as told me that.' Sal spoke. 'I think she knew even before she became pregnant, but she so wanted to have a baby that she wasn't going to allow herself to think that way. Now, she's just relieved to be out of it. She says it's like somebody removed the net curtains and she can see out. I almost feel sorry for Charlie. I don't think he knew what hit him when she said she was leaving.'

'Well, let's hope the next one is a better bet.'

'Don't you go interfering, Ken. That girl's life is her own business. You can't go telling everyone who they should and shouldn't be with,' said Gioia. 'Look at us. Here. It's got no logic, has it? You wanted to get away from your folks, and now we're playing happy families round this table. Annie wanted her marriage and kids, and she's dumped the guy. Sal's clean and got herself a flat. And me . . .' Gioia shrugged. 'I've always been a leader, and here I am trailing around after you. Not for long, mind you. Don't think it will always be like this. Stuff changes. You don't know what's round the corner. I don't think you ever get to join the dots up nice and neat.'

Sal tipped her chair back. 'You're probably right, Gioia. Who knows what's next? None of this is what we planned. Talking of which, guess what? Annie's seeing Jackson again – but don't say I said so. I saw him dropping her off the other day. I bet that's what she's doing now. Fresh air? Don't you believe it. She's nipped off to the phone box to call him.'

Kendra got up to open the door when the bell rang, returning with a knowing look as she followed Annie into the room.

'What's going on?' she asked, throwing Sal her cigarette packet. 'Why are you all staring at me like that?'

Nobody answered until Sal spoke. 'We were just talking about how all our lives have changed and how could we have known we'd be where we are now? Come to think of it' – she leant forward to take a cigarette from the pack, an unsatisfactory ten rather than the twenty she would have bought – 'you could say it's all part of this thing I'm working on. Chaos theory. There's this book – it's a best-seller in the States – all about how it works. It's not random, what happens to everything. Chaos is something different. Don't ask me to explain but, when you come down to it, chaos is good.'

Kendra smiled at Annie; it sounded like the old Sal. Gioia stood to pile the plates and food on to the tray and take them back to the kitchen as the three friends remained happily, in momentary silence, around the table.